Exceptional praise for *A D...*
and the Inspector Ian Rutledge Series

"Todd's astute character studies . . . offer a fascinating cross section of postwar life. . . . While delivering a satisfying puzzle-mystery, the story also tasks us to think about the women who lost their lives during the war, too." —*The New York Times Book Review*

"A superb series: an exquisite sense of time and place, a satisfying mystery with a breathless conclusion, and above all the complex, haunted, charismatic Inspector Ian Rutledge himself—truly one of crime fiction's most absorbing characters."
—Lee Child, #1 *New York Times* bestselling author

"You're going to love Todd. . . . [Rutledge is] far from the usual dauntless hero. Beset by memories of the World War I trenches and tottering on the edge of mental collapse, Rutledge stars in a decidedly uncozy series of British mysteries."
—Stephen King, *Entertainment Weekly*

"If there's ever been a more complex and compelling hero in crime fiction than Inspector Rutledge, I can't think of one."
—Jeffery Deaver, #1 internationally bestselling author

"Rutledge is one of the most complicated and finely drawn characters in contemporary crime fiction. . . . There's not a weak episode to be found in Todd's terrific series." —*BookPage* (starred review)

"Inspector Rutledge shares the pantheon with Morse, Rebus, and even Sherlock Holmes—a fascinating, complex, and heartbreaking hero we admire, respect, and cannot forget. Charles Todd's brilliantly evocative and historically revealing mysteries are top shelf, top drawer, and top of my list."
—Hank Phillippi Ryan, winner of the Anthony, Agatha, and Mary Higgins Clark Awards and author of *Say No More*

"This is a series, written by a mother-and-son team under the Charles Todd pseudonym, that shows no signs of slowing down. As always, this one combines crisp plotting with stylish prose. Ideal for historical-mystery devotees."   —*Booklist*

"Each person dealt with the war differently, as Todd so poignantly shows with each character. Ian's resilience and his complex persona continue to make him an endearing character. And Todd, the mother-and-son writing team of Caroline and Charles Todd, continue their superior storytelling with *A Divided Loyalty*."

—*Sun-Sentinel* (Florida)

"*A Divided Loyalty* finds Rutledge at his most vulnerable and persistent, and it is this dichotomy that gives the book its character and tense atmosphere. It is an intense ride to take with him, but one that is well worth it."   —Bookreporter.com

"The atmospheric and moody descriptions of the remote village [are] enthralling."   —Historical Novel Society

"Fans of historical fiction surrounding WWI should rely on these books. . . . A poignant and engrossing story."   —*Military Press*

"This long-running series shows no sign of losing steam."

—*Publishers Weekly*

A Divided Loyalty

Also by Charles Todd

A DIVIDED LOYALTY

An Inspector Ian Rutledge Mystery

Charles Todd

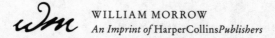

WILLIAM MORROW
An Imprint of HarperCollinsPublishers

P.S.™ is a trademark of HarperCollins Publishers.

A DIVIDED LOYALTY. Copyright © 2020 by Charles Todd. All rights reserved. Printed in the United States of America. No part of this book may be used or reproduced in any manner whatsoever without written permission except in the case of brief quotations embodied in critical articles and reviews. For information, address HarperCollins Publishers, 195 Broadway, New York, NY 10007.

HarperCollins books may be purchased for educational, business, or sales promotional use. For information, please email the Special Markets Department at SPsales@harper collins.com.

A hardcover edition of this book was published in 2020 by William Morrow, an imprint of HarperCollins Publishers.

FIRST WILLIAM MORROW PAPERBACK EDITION PUBLISHED 2021.

Library of Congress Cataloging-in-Publication Data has been applied for.

ISBN 978-0-06-290554-3

21 22 23 24 25 LSC 10 9 8 7 6 5 4 3 2 1

Mommy Kitty, so tiny, so pretty, so strong in spirit, who survived so much before finding a home and the love she so deserved. Love she gave back for seventeen wonderful years, and left her paw print on our hearts forever. God bless her!

Mark McLucas, whose heart failed him too soon, and yet it was his kind heart that endeared him to those who cared about him. He was an artist, a lover of all things Harley, a lover of dogs, especially his wonderful Jenny, who was with him to the very end. A father who loved his young children and fast cars and movies. Who left no great mark on this world and yet left it a kinder and better place for having been in it. May he find peace at last . . .

Jackson, so beautifully marked, a bashful giant, a veritable lapful, who offered love and loyalty and a wonderful spirit to the very end. Who found his forever home, alas without his brother, Jesse, and had his own special place in two big people's lives.

I

London and Wiltshire
February 1921

Ian Rutledge was walking down the stairs at Scotland Yard when he met Chief Inspector Leslie coming up them two at a time.

"Markham in?" Leslie asked, pausing on the landing.

"He was just stepping into his office as I came out of mine." Rutledge didn't add that he'd heard the man's voice in the passage and purposely waited for the Chief Superintendent to pass his door before opening it. Markham was back from leave, and in a foul mood. He'd already had much to say regarding Rutledge's last inquiry and Jameson's report.

They were not at present on the best of terms. Rutledge's unopened letter of resignation still lay in a side drawer of the Chief Superintendent's desk. The sword of Damocles held over Rutledge's head, and at the same time a bitter frustration on Markham's part as well as Jameson's that both were prevented from accepting it immediately. Not while praise was still being heaped on the Yard for closing the Barrington matter.

It had been made quite clear to Rutledge that any weakness on his part, any lapse in performance, any mistake in judgment, even any hint of insubordination, however unintended, might be a welcome opportunity to open the drawer and take out the envelope.

Leslie grimaced. "Inspector Bradley has come down with an appendix. I just got word. Are you working on an inquiry just now?"

"I'm giving evidence in the Trotter trial at half past eleven. What do you need?"

"Someone to go to Avebury. There's a body."

Rutledge knew Avebury: a great prehistoric stone circle with a small village almost in the center of it.

"Sorry, I can't help."

"Damn it, I was just away myself, and looking forward to a day or two off." Leslie grimaced. "I expect he'll insist that I go to Wiltshire, like it or not." With a nod he went on up the flight.

Rutledge had known Brian Leslie before the war and had encountered him in France a number of times, where they'd both served in the trenches. They had become friends in spite of the difference in rank at the Yard and the fact that Leslie was married. Brian Leslie was an intelligent and interesting man, at home in any situation. It was one of the qualities that had made him a successful interrogator during the war, dealing with German prisoners. But the war had changed him too, made him a little edgier, a little more aloof. God knew, they were all haunted by something.

Continuing down the stairs, Rutledge thought to himself that he would have preferred Avebury to the stuffy, overcrowded, overheated courtroom where his claustrophobia made him feel cornered.

But duty called.

B rian Leslie had taken the train to Wiltshire, where he'd been met by Constable Henderson and driven on to Avebury in a horse and carriage.

Henderson was apologetic.

"There's no other way of getting there from Marlborough railway station. As you'll see, sir, it's a good distance."

"No matter," his companion snapped.

Looking out across the winter landscape, Leslie rubbed his gloved hands together against the cold wind that had sprung up in late afternoon and brought heavy clouds with it. He mustn't blame Henderson, he told himself.

If anyone was at fault, *he* was. *And* the Chief Superintendent, for being so bloody stubborn. If he himself hadn't been in such a hurry to get back to London, if he'd had the sense to spend another night on the road, he wouldn't have been available when Markham was casting about for someone to take over the inquiry here. No one would have questioned another twenty-four hours. Even his wife had been surprised to see him walk through the door.

Rousing himself, he began the questions that were expected of him. "All right. The Yard was vague. Tell me what I'm going to find."

"Do you know Avebury, sir?"

"Yes." He added as an afterthought, "As a child."

"There are the stones, of course, sir. Weathered into various shapes, but some of them still quite tall. There are gaps—my granddad told me that over the centuries many of them have been knocked down or even broken up. They stood in a giant circle, and surrounding the lot was a deep ditch. The village was built later, inside the circle."

"Yes, I recall that," he said impatiently, immediately regretted it, and said mildly, "Go on."

"Two mornings ago, one of the lads on his way to school saw the butcher's dog sniffing at the base of one of the larger stones. Curious, he went over to see what it was Bouncer had discovered. The grass was beaten down and sticky with something dark, most of it already seeped into the earth below. Stephen scratched at it with his ruler, and saw the tip was a rusty color. He showed this to the other lads when he reached the schoolhouse, making out it was blood on the tip, and one of them was my son, Barry. When he came home to his lunch, he told me, and I went to investigate. I thought it must be a ewe, sir, that one of the dogs had got at. The sheep do graze there sometimes. But as I looked around for it, and got as far as the ditch behind this part of the ring, there *she* was."

Training took over. "Clothed?"

"Yes, sir. They were in some disarray, as if she'd been rolled down into the ditch. You couldn't see her until you were right on her."

"How was she lying?"

"On her face. I could tell from the way her arms and legs were spread out that she must be either unconscious or dead. That's to say, it wasn't natural. My first thought, sir, was that she might have been alive when young Stephen saw Bouncer, and we'd left it too late. I scrambled down the bank into the ditch—it's precarious just there—and managed to turn her over. There was blood all over her clothing and her eyes were open. I knew then that she was dead."

Henderson paused, busy guiding the horse into a long straight stretch of road.

Leslie waited.

"She was slim, black hair, dressed nicely. Clearly not down on her luck. But not dressed for walking about in a field, either. She's not local, sir, I saw that straightaway. I was in a dilemma about how to fetch the doctor when I heard Ben Wainwright just coming over the causeway. He delivers kegs to the inn, and it's a fairly heavy wagon. I got myself up to where he could see me and shouted to him to fetch Dr. Mason. He went on to where the road stopped, got down, and hurried toward the surgery. A few minutes later, he came back with the doctor, and in the end we got her out of there. There wasn't a stretcher, but she was light, and a blanket did well enough to transport her to the surgery."

"No chance that Wainwright had anything to do with putting her there?"

"No, sir. He's Chapel, married with three daughters. But I checked, and he was at home till it was time to take the team into Marlborough to load. Three in the morning. She was likely already dead by then, according to the doctor."

"You're sure she wasn't local? There are any number of small villages only a few miles in any direction."

"I asked around the village, in the event she was related to someone here or was expected to visit. And I'm fairly certain I got the truth, sir. Then while I was waiting for the Yard to send someone, I spoke to every Constable in a good ten-mile radius, and not only was there no missing woman fitting her description, nobody had seen her about. And she was the sort of woman you'd remember, sir, if you'd seen her. Not so much a beauty as—" He searched for the right word, then shrugged. "I don't know. Different, somehow. The doctor can tell you the rest."

It was a concise report, informative and to the point. Leslie glanced at Henderson. "In the war, were you?"

"Yes, sir." He grinned. "Lied about my age, said I was thirty-one when I was thirty-six. But they took me anyway."

Then that was where Henderson had learned to report properly, if his training as a Constable hadn't taught him.

Leslie nodded. "Regiment?"

"The Wiltshires, of course. Rose to the rank of Sergeant," he confided proudly. "But of course, that was easy to do, given how many we lost. The Germans, we heard, were in worse straits." Then he grinned. "I was happy to come home, sir, where no one was shooting at me."

Leslie asked, "Many murders in this part of the county?"

"No, sir. At least not like this one. The last one I recall was in 1913, when a farmer fell out of his hayloft onto a pitchfork. Only, the doctor told us that the angle of his wounds didn't fit the account given us. Seems the pitchfork had been in him before he fell."

Farm accidents were always difficult inquiries. Too easy to pass off murder as an accident when there were no witnesses to say otherwise.

He could see the first of the standing stones in the distance. They were nearly there. "Any idea who could have done this? No witnesses coming forward?"

"No, sir. And no other strangers to account for. We don't even know how she got here without anybody noticing. It's not the time of year when people on holiday come to stare at the stones."

True enough, Leslie thought. With the turn, the wind was playing around his shoulders, even in the carriage. He was grateful for the rug over his knees. He shoved his gloved hands into his pockets, to keep them still.

He could see some of the stones clearly now, as they followed the road that led toward the village. To his left was a double line of smaller stones, the ancient avenue leading to the circle, paralleling the present road. To his right, the land stretched out more, hummocked and rippled with ancient earthworks.

He had come to Avebury in childhood, free to play among the stones while his parents visited at the Rectory. Magical then. Now, in the gray afternoon light they were foreboding, unwelcoming. Looking away from them, Leslie made an effort to remember the Rector at that time. He'd been at school with his father, hadn't he? Tall, a deep laugh. Mrs. Townsend was a more shadowy figure, rather aloof. Surely they weren't still here? Turning to Henderson, he asked, "Who is Rector now?"

"Mr. Marshall."

"What became of Mr. Townsend?"

Henderson glanced at him. "Did you know him?"

"My parents did."

"He was offered a living in Shropshire, I believe, and he died there some ten years later. I don't remember him myself, but my mother does. She says he christened me."

That would account, Leslie thought, for the visits to have stopped before he was seven. Shropshire was too far from London to dine with a friend.

"But Mr. Marshall is a good man. Christened *my* son."

Leslie said nothing. They passed over the causeway, put there ages ago to bridge the ditch. To the right, beyond the bare tops of a few trees, smoke curled from a chimney, darker than the clouds. The inn, he remembered.

"That's the stone just there." Henderson had slowed the mare and was pointing toward a half a dozen stones standing in a field to his left. "You can't really pick out the ditch from here, unless you know to look. I can't quite see how the killer knew it was there. Not in the dark. You'll want to go there later, of course. I thought it best to carry you directly to the surgery, to see her."

Not *the body. Her.*

Leslie glanced at him, then turned in the direction Henderson was pointing. It was true, the ditch wasn't well defined at this distance. "No one reported cries in the night? Any disturbance at all? Dogs barking?"

"Not so far as I have been able to discover," Henderson said. "And I've asked those living closest. But if the attack was sudden, and she didn't know it was coming, I doubt she had time to cry out. Doctor says it was a stabbing. Quick." He turned slightly to point in the other direction. "Just there is the inn, sir. Where I've put you up. They were glad of the company. This time of year you'll mostly have it to yourself."

They moved on, not turning until they reached the end of the present road, then left on a rougher one that ran down toward the church, its tower just visible. The doctor's surgery was before it, across the road from the churchyard, and Leslie recognized the doctor's house if not the name on the brass plate by the gate. He'd once been taken there for a cut on his chin after tumbling out of one of the Rectory trees.

Dr. Mason was a thin man with graying hair. He wore spectacles, peering over them at Leslie as Constable Henderson introduced them.

"Chief Inspector." He held out his hand in acknowledgment, then ushered the two men through a door by the stairs, toward his surgery.

"Sorry to bring you all this way," he went on, "but there's no doubt the young woman was murdered, and as I told the Chief Constable, the circumstances worried me."

"How so?" Leslie asked, frowning as he took the chair offered him before Mason walked around to his own behind the desk. "What have you uncovered?"

"Not to say uncovered, but these stones attract a good number of visitors. The curious, of course, and those who enjoy touching a bit of history. Students from time to time, and even a schoolmaster or two. Holidaymakers often bring a picnic basket with them or stop over at the inn. We aren't all that far from Stonehenge, it's an easy journey between the two. But there are also a few with more sinister intentions. *This* death doesn't have the hallmarks of ritual, but on the other hand, she wasn't just killed in an empty field somewhere. There was blood at the base of one of the largest stones, and no attempt to conceal it. I grant you there wasn't a full moon, but it was clear and bright enough by midnight. That might have been tempting to someone."

"Have there been other incidents like this in the past?" Leslie asked him, surprised. There had been no mention of Mason's concerns in the thin file he'd been given. But it explained why the Yard had been called in almost at once. "In *Avebury*?"

"Not here that I'm aware of, not yet, but the worry is that once it starts, it draws others. I don't want Avebury to suffer the way other prehistoric sites have done—there are people who convince themselves that the stones have some magic powers left by their builders or that their religion has a force that can be tapped for personal gain. It's not too great a stretch from worship to a human sacrifice to the stones or the gods behind them. Sadly, we don't know enough about these ancient cultures to make those obsessed by them see reason."

Henderson cleared his throat, making his own point. "What concerns *me* is that in this part of Wiltshire, his chances of getting clear before he's seen are far better. If he had a motorcar, he could well have been anywhere by first light. The next county. London. Wales, even. The Chief Constable did warn neighboring counties to keep an eye out, but it may already be too late."

Leslie took out his notebook, making a note. Looking up again, he said in an attempt to keep them to the facts, "And she wasn't interfered with, in any way?"

"No. Not that sort of crime."

"Anything we might use to help us identify her?"

"No broken bones, no prominent moles or birthmarks, nothing unusual that I could find. She'd had a child, but not a recent birth. Her hair is dark enough that she might be Welsh. That's all." He let the man opposite him write something more, then rose. "Would you like to see her now?"

Leslie took his time putting away his notebook. Anything to put off the inevitable a little longer . . . They would think him odd if he refused. It was standard procedure.

Would they believe him, if he told them that the war had made examining the body of the dead nearly impossible for him? No, if that got back to the Yard, it could cause no end of problems.

Mason was waiting.

Steeling himself, he and Henderson followed Mason to a small, windowless, frigid back room. As the doctor lit a lamp and the dimness flared into brightness, he could see the shape on the table, draped in a white sheet. Mason led the way and pulled back the covering. It fell into place along the line of her white shoulders. No longer soft, too white for the living.

This was how the dead always looked, he warned himself. This was just one more. When all was said and done.

Mason was busy arranging the sheet, leaving the body some dignity. Henderson was looking down at the dead woman, his expression somber, and then Mason stepped back, and he could see her face, framed in that dark, dark hair.

And he stopped thinking altogether.

The next thing he remembered with any clarity was sitting in the carriage as the Constable drove up the road. Henderson was saying, "It's for your use while you're here, sir. The carriage. You'll need transport. I borrowed it from the inn where you're staying. The Green Man is probably not what you're accustomed to in London, sir, but the food is excellent. Sam Bryant's wife is the finest cook for miles around. You'll want to try Mary's apple tarts."

Leslie barely heard him. His mind was filled with images he couldn't stop thinking about. The sheet-covered body on a table in that wretched little room, her face still and cold in death. A rising tide of guilt so powerful he couldn't remember how he'd got out of there, much less out of that house.

Whisky. He remembered that. The doctor had offered them whisky afterward, and he'd wondered if Mason had suspected—guessed—he'd needed it. He'd managed some excuse. He dared not let either of them see just how badly he needed it. He was terrified that he'd already given himself away, and getting out of there was suddenly all that mattered.

Henderson was pulling up at the inn door. Leslie got down and reached for his valise before the Constable could hand it to him. To make amends, he let the man walk with him inside The Green Man and fetch his key from the innkeeper. Then blessedly, Henderson left him alone to find his room himself.

He got up the stairs somehow, stumbled through the door, and sat down heavily on the chair by the window without even removing his coat or hat. He could see nothing but the images in his head.

Her body. Those three ugly gashes while Mason was going on and on about the knife that had caused them. And later, the silk scarf that the doctor had neatly folded inside her coat. That had nearly undone him, because he remembered it so well, remembered buying it, and thinking how perfectly it would suit.

Why—why—why? But it was too late to ask himself that now. There was no way to escape what he'd done.

His fists were pounding against his knees, but he didn't feel it.

He hadn't told them who she was. He couldn't tell them what she'd meant to him. He couldn't even tell them why she'd come to England.

Welsh—they thought she might be Welsh because of her lovely black hair. He'd let them. It was bad enough that he'd had to hurt her in life. Now he was betraying her in death. But he'd had no choice, had he?

Guilt was crushing him. *Oh, God, how was he to go on?*

It wasn't until much later, rousing up enough to notice how cold he was, that he had the coherent thought that *he* was the investigating officer. *He* could make absolutely certain of the inquiry's outcome.

If he didn't, there was the hangman. Shuddering, he couldn't stop himself from reliving the hangings he'd had to witness. He'd have to get himself in hand, he'd have to finish this bloody inquiry somehow, without betraying himself. If he hadn't already . . .

As he got stiffly to his feet and went to light the fire laid ready on the narrow hearth, he told himself he had to find a way to take up the burden of what he'd done. And try to make it right.

But how do you make murder right? How *could* one live with such a thing on his conscience?

Leslie closed his eyes and begged her to forgive him—for what he'd done and for what he was about to do. Begged her to understand.

Then, drawing a ragged breath, he knelt and put the match to the tinder beneath the coal.

By the time the fire was drawing well, he'd got himself in hand.

He wasn't proud of it.

Rutledge didn't know the details of the inquiry that Chief Inspector Leslie had conducted in Wiltshire. He'd heard some talk that the inquest had brought in murder by person or persons unknown, which was surprising, since Leslie, like Rutledge himself, had a reputation for tenacity, working the evidence until he found the one clue that might lead to finding the guilty party.

But as he heard more about the crime itself, he could understand the lack of a solution. A single murder, with no witnesses, no weapon, and no real evidence to break open the investigation, was the hardest to solve. And dealing with someone obsessed with Druids and stone circles and possibly believing that human sacrifice had been practiced when the stones were new was especially difficult. If he'd got what he wanted from the god or gods he'd sacrificed to, whoever he was, he might never kill again.

It was early March when Rutledge went to The Strand Restaurant for a late supper, only noticing the time because he'd come to the last of the reports he'd been reading and realized that he was hungry. And he couldn't remember anything palatable in the pantry at the flat.

He had avoided The Strand after running into Kate Gordon and her mother there one evening. He hadn't seen Kate since the nightmare of what had happened on his own doorstep, and he didn't want to encounter her now and cause embarrassment for both of them.

Her mother had made it plain enough in December that a policeman was not an acceptable suitor for her daughter, who could aspire as high as she liked. After all, Kate's father was a high-ranking officer in the Army, and his distinguished record during the war had led to his being received by the King. Rumor had it that he was on a first-name basis with half the war department. True or not, it had given Mrs. Gordon a reason to conclude that Kate could marry very well indeed. In fact, the Prince of Wales had danced twice with Kate at a ball marking the end of the Paris peace talks in June 1919, although it was known that he generally favored married women.

Rutledge had barely recovered enough from his own war that June to care who had danced with whom. He'd known Kate then only as the sensible cousin of the woman he'd been engaged to marry in the summer of '14, and while he'd liked her then, he'd been too blinded by his love for Jean to see that Kate was worth two of her.

But he felt safe enough tonight, late as it was. The Gordons kept early hours.

As he followed the waiter to a quiet corner, Rutledge saw Leslie dining alone and stopped by his table.

"Working late, also?"

Leslie looked up and smiled. "My wife's in Suffolk, and my own cooking is not edible. Join me. I'm tired of my own thoughts for company."

Rutledge nodded to the waiter and took the chair opposite Leslie.

In the light of the chandeliers, Leslie looked very tired.

Noticing that, Rutledge asked as he took up his serviette, "Busy with an inquiry?"

"Not at the moment. No. Thank God. You?"

"I just got in from a village not far from Derby. I found my desk buried in files. I've dealt with them and taken the lot down to Gibson's desk, to bury it next."

Leslie laughed. "The Sergeant is a marvel. If he ever retires, the Yard will collapse. Did you get your man?"

"I expect it will." He shook his head, indicating that he would have no wine tonight, and the sommelier moved away. "As a matter of fact I did, or rather, my woman. A nasty one at that. The Vicar had lost his wife to influenza, and she was barely in the ground when the house-keeper's sister began accusing every woman in the parish under forty of setting her cap for him if not worse. That was bad enough. Then she poisoned one of them because she was convinced the Vicar favored her. The Constable whose lot it was to take her into custody had his hands full—she fought and kicked all the way to the police station. Browning suffered a cut on his chin and bruised shins."

"Good God."

Rutledge gave the waiter his order and handed him the menu. Turning back to the Chief Inspector, he said, "From what I've heard, you had a rather nasty inquiry yourself last month."

Leslie's eyes hardened. "I didn't catch the killer, if that's what you mean. I've put out word that if anyone discovers a similar case on his turf, I'm to be told of it at once."

Something in his expression brought a quiet "*'Ware*" from Hamish.

Rutledge heeded the warning. He couldn't have said why, except that he could sense something in the man opposite him. A sudden tension in his body, the unexpected glare. It wasn't like Leslie, but then he hadn't taken any time off for weeks. He could be found at the Yard early in the morning and late at night, whether there was a major case on or not.

Rutledge said easily, "Well, supper isn't the place to talk about murder. I hear that Sutton is getting married next month. He knew that my sister was wed in December, and he's been asking me about the groom's duties."

The stiffness faded, and the glare as well. "Poor Sutton. His future mother-in-law will keep him in line. I don't envy him."

The conversation moved on to the war. Leslie finished his wine, and set the glass down. "I shouldn't say this. It's been two years. But I can't seem to put France behind me." He appeared to be thinking aloud rather than speaking to Rutledge.

"That's not unusual." Rutledge pushed the remains of his meal across his plate, refusing to be drawn. They all knew—he could see it in their faces sometimes when he caught them looking at him. Shell shock. But he was damned if that knowledge was going to force him to resign. That would be what was expected of a coward.

"No, I expect it isn't," Leslie answered thoughtfully. "I can't talk to my wife about what happened out there. I couldn't do that to her." His gaze moved from the empty glass next to his plate to focus on Rutledge. "You aren't married. That must be easier. And at the same time, more difficult."

"I don't think there *is* a solution." He suddenly found himself remembering a friend. A suicide. He cleared his throat. He wanted to add, *We live with it until we can't any longer.* But suicide, given the recent past, was not a subject he wanted to bring up. Instead he commented, "For many of us, the war didn't end when the guns stopped firing. That's the problem. We saw too much. Things that can't be shared. Things we can't forget."

"You put it well." Leslie was silent for a moment, then he said, striving to push the darkness aside, "Cheese or pudding?"

"I'll finish with a second pot of tea."

"Yes, I think that's best." He turned to signal the waiter.

The next day, Chief Superintendent Markham sent for Rutledge and handed him a file as he walked in the door.

"A rather nasty murder in Shropshire. See what you make of it."

Rutledge opened the file and scanned it. There wasn't a great deal of information. There rarely was.

A parish sexton had dug a grave in late afternoon for the next morning's funeral service for a man in his fifties. As it was to be left overnight, the sexton had covered the opening with boards and sacking, to prevent any damage to it or to a person who might unwittingly fall in. The next day, an hour before the ten o'clock service, the tocsin already tolling the man's years, the sexton went out to remove the boards and sacking, and set the coiled ropes to one side, ready to hand when the coffin was brought from the church. As he drew back the second of the boards, he discovered that the grave was already occupied. A woman's body lay in the bottom, and even in his shock, he realized that she was dead and had surely been murdered. There was a great deal of dark, drying blood on her clothing and her face. Far more than a fall could have caused.

He sent the equally shocked Rector for the doctor and the Constable.

By the end of the day, the village Constable had asked for the Yard to be brought in.

"Can't say that I blame the local man," Markham commented as Rutledge finished reading and closed the file. "Apparently no one knows who the dead woman is. Much less who might have wanted her dead." He smiled, but it was cold. "Just your sort of inquiry, I should think."

Rutledge had angered Markham last month in the course of another case, and this was the Chief Superintendent's less-than-subtle way of reminding him of that.

"I'll do my best, sir," Rutledge answered mildly, refusing to rise to the bait. "I finished the reports on my desk last evening. I can leave for Shropshire straightaway."

"See that you do," Markham replied, and picked up another file from his desk.

Dismissal.

Rutledge closed the Chief Superintendent's door behind him, and in the passage, where no one else was about just then, he swore under his breath.

He reported to Sergeant Gibson that he was going to his flat to pack a valise for Shropshire, and left the Yard.

2

Rutledge spent the night in a small village halfway to his destination, and arrived in Tern Bridge just as dusk was falling the next evening.

He took a few minutes to explore. This was a flat part of the county, with a river that ran past the outskirts of the village. There was an ancient bridge across it, hardly as wide as his motorcar, and just beyond that was a fortified manor house, in ruins now, the empty windows black spaces in the brick walls and what had once been a garden, now wild with brambles and weeds, running down to the water.

The small village itself was a mixture of Tudor and Georgian buildings, some of the former still possessing their overhanging upper stories, diamond-paned windows, and tall chimney pots. The dying light was reflected in the old glass, and it faded as he watched.

Constable Leigh was mending a chair in the small police station when Rutledge opened the door and identified himself.

Rising from his knees, Leigh said, "Good evening, sir. Sorry about that." He set his tools and the chair to one side. "I wasn't expecting you this soon. You made good time. Have you found your room in The

Dun Cow?" He grinned. "It's far nicer than it sounds. Seems the original owner ran off with the money his father had been paid for a dun cow, and with it won enough at cards that he could afford to build the inn. That was in 1742, and no one's changed the name since."

"Sounds like the excuse a highwayman might have used to explain his sudden wealth."

Leigh's grin broadened. "You're the second person I've heard say that. The first was my own father. For all I know, you're both right."

"Where is the inn?"

"Across the street and down past the whitewashed house with the green shutters. You can't miss it."

"Is it too late to call on the doctor?"

"I expect he's dining just now."

Rutledge pulled off his hat and coat, and took the only other chair across from the Constable. "Then I'll speak to you first. Tell me what happened."

"You have the file, sir?" Leigh asked, frowning. "I spoke to a Sergeant Gibson and gave him the details."

"I'd rather hear your version."

"Indeed, sir." He cleared his throat and began his account of events.

"Sexton dug Mr. Simmons's grave late in the afternoon before the day of the funeral. We were expecting rain in the night, and he wanted to do it proper, not in mud. When he'd finished, he put boards across the opening, and laid a bit of sacking over them. But the rain never came, passing south of us, and the next morning Sexton came to remove the boards and make the grave ready for the service. He'd got the sacking off and was hauling back the second of the boards when he happened to glance down into the grave, and there was a young woman just lying there. It looked as if she'd just been rolled over the edge and let fall where she may. He ran for the church, yelling for Rector. Rector was that shocked, he hardly knew what to do. But neither of them had any doubt that the poor woman was dead. I brought Dr. Allen with me, and we lowered him into the grave. He shook his head, and we threw him the casket ropes to wrap around her, and the three of us pulled her up. There was a terrible lot of blood, most of it caked and dry, and when Doctor opened her coat, it was plain she'd been stabbed. Rigor was already setting in, and Doctor thought she'd been dead since last evening. He called it murder, and that was confirmed when he got her back to his surgery for a better look. Three wounds, he said. And bruising where a hand was clamped over her mouth to keep her from screaming as the knife went in. Neither Rector nor Sexton nor Doctor recognized her, and I went 'round the village to see if anyone there knew her. No one did. She was a pretty woman, young, fair hair, blue eyes. And dressed nicely, as if on her way to church or to dine out with friends."

"What have you done about identifying her?"

"I asked at The Dun Cow, but she hadn't taken a room there. There's an omnibus that comes through in the afternoon, near to four o'clock, sometimes as late as five, and I asked the driver on duty if he'd brought her here the day before. He said he'd had no passengers for the village. And there are others who remembered the omnibus passing through but not stopping. Meanwhile, I went door-to-door, up and down the streets, but no one had seen her. And everyone I spoke with claimed not to know who she was." He stopped, then added, "At least no one has admitted to knowing her."

"Do you think someone is lying?"

"That's the problem, sir. They all seemed to be telling the truth. I know these people, I can usually tell if they're hiding something."

"Much traffic through the village?"

"We're not the main road to anywhere. But we get the occasional lorry, some motorcars each day, and more than a few carts and goods vans. As you'll see, the churchyard is on the far side of the church, and there are a good many trees about. One ancient yew by the gate in the churchyard wall. How could a passerby know there was an open grave sitting there ready to hand for hiding a body? Of course everyone knew Mr. Simmons was to be buried there next day. Even those who weren't expecting to attend the funeral. But I've spoken to all of them. Everyone over the age of twelve. And made myself available here if anyone wanted to tell me something in private."

"Perhaps her killer didn't know the grave was there. Perhaps it was fortuitous, when he'd been planning to leave her body by, say, the apse, where she wouldn't be discovered straightaway."

Dubious, Constable Leigh shook his head. "That's rather cold-blooded of him, after killing her. And he was taking a chance, carrying her across the churchyard in the dark. Best way to trip over a stone."

"He may know the churchyard. Or possibly have scouted it."

"You're saying *he's* local, even if she isn't."

"You can't rule that out."

"I don't know, sir. But then I haven't spoken to everyone on the outlying farms."

"He could work for the undertaker. Or he drives the van that supplies the baker with flour or the butcher with meat."

Leigh sighed. "That's a large field, sir."

"It is." Rutledge looked at his watch. "After I've taken a room at The Dun Cow, we can call on Dr. Allen."

Constable Leigh got to his feet. "I'll go with you. I wouldn't mind having a ride in your motorcar," he said diffidently.

They drove down the street and found the inn just where Leigh had said it would be. A handsome Tudor structure, the black-and-white work well maintained, and the glass in the diamond-paned windows on the lower floor looked to be as old as the rest of the building.

The pub was full, although the dining room had only one or two couples in it. Leigh walked through the door and nodded to the man behind the bar, who picked up a cloth and dried his hands, then came out to greet the Constable.

"Inspector Rutledge, Mr. Grissom. He's come for a room."

Grissom nodded to him. "We're not too busy this time of year. Would you prefer a room on the back? It's quieter."

"I'd prefer the front."

"It's over the pub."

"No matter."

Grissom led him through a door, and he saw the staircase rising from the center of the hall, with a separate door to the outside. Grissom picked up the lamp on the table near the door and climbed the stairs, Rutledge at his heels.

There were two front rooms, and Rutledge chose the second. It was more spacious, with two windows instead of one. "This will do very well," he told Grissom.

"I'll have the key ready for you when you bring up your valise."

"Fair enough."

They went back down the stairs, and Rutledge collected the Constable, who gave him directions to the doctor's surgery. It was a fair-size house on the corner of Butter Lane and the High Street. There was a low stone wall around the shallow front garden, and two doors, each reached by a separate path.

"That's the surgery door," Leigh said, pointing to the left. They followed the walk there and Leigh knocked. A light was showing in the pretty fanlight above the door, but the window to their left was dark.

It was several minutes before the doctor answered the summons. There was a lamp on the table by the door, illuminating the entry and his face.

He was a middle-aged man with graying hair and an officer's mustache.

"Constable," he said, nodding.

"This is Inspector Rutledge, sir. Scotland Yard. He's come to view the body."

"Tonight?"

"If you don't mind," Rutledge said pleasantly.

"Very well." He led them down a passage lit only by the light of the lamp at the outer door. "I'm afraid I don't have much time—I've a lying-in to keep an eye on tonight." He opened a door at the far end. "She's in here," he was saying over his shoulder as he went into the room and stopped just inside to fumble with matches and a lamp. As light filled the darkness, Rutledge could see the table and the body, under a sheet.

Allen crossed to set the lamp down at the head of the table, and drew back the covering.

The face was pale and expressionless in death, but she had been an attractive woman with fair hair and a sweet face. The half-open eyes were a dark blue. Rutledge put her age at about twenty-eight, possibly even thirty.

"Pity," the doctor said quietly, and then showed them the three stab wounds in her chest. "First one was fatal, but whoever it was made sure of that, having two more goes at it." He lifted her hands, one after the other. "She didn't put up much of a fight. No cuts or bruising except around her mouth. That tells me she might have known her killer and didn't expect him or her to harm her until he or she drew the knife."

Rutledge looked at her fingers. Smooth, the nails almond shaped and well kept. Whoever this was, she hadn't worked with her hands.

The doctor was saying, "She wasn't killed in the grave. Not enough blood there. Whoever it was put her there to rid himself of the body."

He made to draw up the sheet again, but Rutledge put out a hand to stop him. Pointing to the three wounds, he said, "They're narrow. What sort of knife do you think was used?"

Dr. Allen sighed. "Anything at all. There are narrow-enough blades in my wife's kitchen. I've got scalpels. Any of a dozen trades might use something similar. The butcher, for one. For all I know, the baker or the draper's shop."

Rutledge stepped back and let him lower the sheet. "Her clothing?"

"She must come from a family that's comfortably off. Good-quality dark gray wool coat, a silk shirtwaist, and a walking dress of dark blue wool, with a matching jacket. Not the latest fashion, perhaps, but certainly last year's? You could see for yourself that her hands aren't those of a working-class woman, nails well kept, skin soft. Good sturdy leather boots, but with silk stockings. There's no hat. I just realized that. She must have been wearing a hat. And there's no purse, of course. No jewelry. She doesn't appear to have had a wedding ring—there is no trace of it on her finger. But she did wear a ring on her little finger. Gone, of course, but you could see that it had been there."

"We'll search for it tomorrow in the daylight." Rutledge turned to the Constable. "Was the man for whom the grave had been dug buried in it?"

"No, sir. He's at the undertaker's. His family was that upset, they wouldn't let the service be held." He glanced at the doctor and then looked back at Rutledge. "Rector insisted they be informed, and of course it was a crime scene."

"Good. We'll have a look tomorrow." To the doctor, he said, "Is there any more you can tell us?"

"It was a long knife. It penetrated deeply. My guess is that either a man or a woman might have struck those blows, if there was enough anger or determination behind them."

"Thank you."

The doctor picked up the lamp and walked out of the room with them, pausing only to set it aside and turn down the wick.

"I hope you find him. Or her," he said as he opened the house door and stood back to let them pass. "We don't have many murders here."

Rutledge and the Constable bade him a good night and walked in silence to the motorcar.

Remembering the mustache, Rutledge asked when they were back to the street again, "Was the doctor in the war?"

"Yes, sir, he was. Served on a ship. From what I gathered, he saw action any number of times. There's a scar above his right wrist. Nasty-looking. Shrapnel, he told me. But he's not one to talk about what he did or saw."

That spoke well of him.

"Go home, Constable. Meet me for breakfast at eight thirty, and we'll have a look at the churchyard."

"Then I'm walking this way. Good night, sir." He turned and went on in the opposite direction. Rutledge looked after him, then drove back to The Dun Cow. A wind had come up, and the sign above the inn was moving a little. The brown cow was shown in a field beside a river, and there was a coach and horses on the road behind it.

Hamish, speaking for the first time since Rutledge had arrived in the village, said, "Ye could be right about yon highwayman."

As he opened the door that led to the staircase, Rutledge replied quietly, "He had a steady nerve to put it on the sign. If that's the original."

Rutledge was used to the voice in his head. It had been there since the summer of 1916, at the height of the battle of the Somme. It had been the bloodiest of battles, and men died before his eyes, day and night, until the trenches reeked of rotting flesh and black mud and death. He wasn't the only one on the verge of breaking as the Germans had pressed harder and harder, hoping to end the stalemate of 1915.

And then orders had come down to take out a German machine-gun nest that was perfectly situated to halt the next British attack. But it was too well protected, and wave after wave of men had tried and failed to take it. Their wounded and their dead seemed to be piled high around them, and Corporal Hamish MacLeod had finally refused to lead another attack against the position. He pointed out what Rutledge had known from the start, that it was hopeless and a waste of good men. But the next attack was coming, and Rutledge was all too aware that the slaughter would be unimaginable if the first waves were caught in the open with that gun on their flank.

He'd reasoned with Hamish, he'd threatened, and it did no good. Hamish was as sick of the killing as he was, and weary of dragging their dying wounded back to the trench.

Hamish had looked at the men who were left, and he'd said, "It's murder, pure and simple. I willna' do it any longer. I canna' do it again. No man in his right mind can justify it."

And with the next assault only hours away, coming with the dawn, Rutledge had had no choice but to make an example of his Corporal before the rest of his men lost heart and refused to follow orders as well. *Military necessity.* The words still haunted him.

Bare seconds later, as Rutledge bent to deliver the coup de grâce, the shelling began, softening up the German trenches before the dawn advance. One of the first ranging shots fell short. And Rutledge, the firing squad, and his dead Corporal had been buried by the explosion. He had been the only survivor, and he'd only lived long enough to be dug out because his face had been pressed against the chest of the man he's just executed. *A tiny pocket of air . . .*

Shell shock, it was called. Breaking under fire. But Rutledge couldn't accept that he'd been the lone survivor—or that the shell had come too late to stop the execution. He'd sacrificed one to save the many. *For nothing.* And when the war was over Hamish came home with Rutledge in the only way possible. Not as a ghost, not as a living man, but as a voice that haunted Rutledge night and day. A reminder of that night. Survivor's guilt, Dr. Fleming had called it. Seeing in Hamish MacLeod all the many dead he'd sent into battle, while he himself, always at their forefront, had hardly a scar on him. A charmed life, his men had called it, only half joking.

Rutledge had been tormented by Hamish in the darkness and stench of the earth suffocating him, and the voice hadn't faded with the Armistice. Dr. Fleming, who had saved his sanity by breaking his will and forcing him to talk about Hamish MacLeod, had also warned him that it might never stop, that the voice might be there for the rest of his life. Enough to drive a man to suicide—and yet if he killed himself, he killed Hamish again. And he couldn't have that *too* on his soul.

Now as he stepped into the dimly lit entry and found a candle to light his way up the dark stairs, Rutledge heard Hamish say, "Ah, weel, he must ha' been a bonny highwayman, no' to get caught."

He climbed the stairs with Hamish's voice in the recesses of his own mind, and braced himself for what lay ahead—a long and sleepless night, with nightmares of the war raging in his memory.

Constable Leigh stepped into the small dining room on the far side of the pub just as Rutledge was about to order his breakfast, and when they had finished their meal, they walked on to the church-yard.

The church was old but plain, with very little decoration and a squat tower barely rising above the tops of the trees. Shropshire wasn't known for its churches, or its castles and great houses, although it had its share of Tudor and Georgian buildings.

They scoured the churchyard for three quarters of an hour, searching behind the gravestones and under the yew trees whose branches drooped almost to the ground, pushing aside the tall winter grass, probing it wherever something might have fallen. But there was no sign of either the woman's hat or her purse.

"I hadn't expected to find them," Rutledge admitted as he called a halt to the search. The cold wind was biting, and Constable Leigh was blowing on his hands and stamping his feet as they conferred. "But we couldn't overlook the possibility. The only reason she kept her shoes was the lacing."

First, he'd stopped by the open grave, helping Leigh remove the boards and the sacking the sexton had pulled over it again, and squatting on the bruised grass at the edge, looking down at where the body had been lying. "One person put those boards across—the sexton. One person could move them far enough to roll the body into the pit. It wouldn't require two people. And she didn't look as if she'd been too heavy to carry from the gate over there, to this place. Was there a moon that night, or was it cloudy?"

"It had been cloudy all day, and feeling like rain. But it cleared at sunset, and at about midnight, I woke to see moonlight coming through my window."

"Then that would have helped him find his way. In spite of the shadows." He glanced up at the Constable. "Why did you wake up at midnight?"

Leigh frowned. "I don't really know, sir. I hadn't thought about it."

"A dog barking? A heavy lorry passing through?"

"No, sir, I don't remember anything like that. And my cottage is the other end of town from here."

"A pity." Rutledge got to his feet. There was no use wasting time by the grave. Too many boots had trod any evidence into the grass and the earth after the digging and the recovery of the body. But it was natural to hope that some small clue might have been overlooked. The woman's ring, perhaps. Something to prove it wasn't theft. The missing ring and purse hinted at that, and yet Rutledge didn't think that she'd been robbed. The purse would have contained her identity, and perhaps the ring might have been traced to wherever she'd come from. Something a jeweler might recognize.

Walking back to the gate, he said, "Have you asked any of the other villages around here if they have a missing woman matching our body's description?"

"Yes, sir, I sent word around that afternoon, when I realized no one here knew her. Or said they didn't. But none of my queries brought back anything helpful."

"Good man. That saves time." Remembering what he'd been told about the quality of her clothing, Rutledge thought she might well have come from one of the larger towns. Shrewsbury, possibly. Or even London for that matter. "The question then becomes, who or what lured her here to her death?"

"Needle in a haystack," Leigh commented as they drove back to the police station. "I don't see how we're going to find out who she is."

"Too soon to give up, Constable."

"There's that, sir. But the question is, where do we even begin?"

"It's likely that no one has realized she's gone missing. Not yet. Her family could still believe she took the train, intending to stay with friends. They might not be expecting to hear from her this soon. Meanwhile, the friends are worried, but not yet worried enough to sound the alarm. Especially if she wasn't certain which train she would take. Or perhaps she asked a friend for a lift, and something went wrong."

Leigh's cold-chafed face brightened. "That's true, sir." He considered the possibilities. "She could even have run off with the wrong man. Someone her family disapproved of, and with good reason. Only she didn't see it that way."

"There's the other side of the coin as well. In her travels she could have seen something she shouldn't have. And someone was afraid she might talk." Rutledge paused to turn the crank. "That's assuming she was the victim, not part of the problem. But she might also have been involved in something she shouldn't have been, and there was a falling-out with someone."

"She didn't look like the sort who would be involved with anything criminal," Leigh said, getting in.

"No. But that's not proof that she wasn't."

"What now, sir?"

They had arrived at the police station, and Rutledge pulled up in front of it. "There are the outlying farms you spoke of. I want to interview the tenants and owners. The dead woman wasn't dressed for a farmyard. Still, if I'd killed someone on my property, it might occur to me to carry her body to the village churchyard and lay the blame elsewhere."

Frowning, Leigh said, "I can't see someone like Mr. Wilkins or Nate Harding doing murder. What's more, it might be easier if I went with you. I know them better, sir. I can convince them to talk to us. They'll not want to waste the winter light standing around answering questions."

Rutledge said thoughtfully, "I take your point, Constable. Still, whether she came to visit or to cause trouble, it would be relatively easy to keep news of her arrival from the rest of the village. Who would know?"

Leigh sighed. "You're right, of course." He made to get out.

"Can you drive, Constable?"

"Yes, sir."

"Then take the motorcar and call at the farms. Poke around. It might go faster that way."

"Sir?" Leigh stared at him.

"Farm dogs bark, Constable. Start with that. See where it leads. We also need to know how the killer got the body to the churchyard. Which direction he might have come from. If he didn't go through the village, how *did* he get here? Or leave here? He didn't fly. He drove. A carriage, a cart, a motorcar. Even a lorry. A country lane will do as well as a parish road, if you don't want to be seen in the middle of the night."

Rutledge watched him drive on down the street, then began to walk. It was time to draw a rough map in his head of the village, and that was best done on foot and alone. Villagers cast curious glances his way or nodded civilly as they passed him, well aware of who he was and why he was there. But no one came up to speak to him. No one crossed the road ahead to avoid him. By the time he turned his steps back toward The Dun Cow, he had a sense of Tern Bridge and its inhabitants. What that was telling him supported what he'd learned so far. If there was a killer in their midst, the villagers hadn't started to point fingers. Not yet. They still felt safe in the prevailing assumption that if the woman was a stranger, so was her murderer. When would that begin to change? When the Constable came back with his interviews of the farmers?

If the Constable found answers there, it would be a very good piece of luck indeed. Rutledge knew better than to count on it.

R eplies from neighboring villages began to arrive later. None of them reported having any information about a missing woman. And that supported Rutledge's budding theory that the dead woman had been left here precisely because she was far away from anyone who might know her.

Constable Leigh soon returned from speaking to the owners of the nearby farms and the men working for them, and he had come up empty-handed. "Not that I expected much help in that direction, sir. No visitors, not this time of year, and with the windows closed tight against the cold, they didn't hear anything that was useful. The dogs keep to the barn most nights. Still, you never know until you ask."

Rutledge remembered the difficulties Chief Inspector Leslie had had finding the killer of the woman in Avebury. He had a feeling his inquiry might turn out the same way, a murderer eluding him. Was there by any chance a connection? The same killer moving across England? He didn't know enough about the Avebury murder to be certain. The problem was, how had the killer known about the open grave at Tern Bridge? Unless he was one of the expected mourners?

Rutledge said to Constable Leigh, "You told me the grave was prepared for a Mr. Simmons?"

"That's right, sir. Fifty-three, a widower with a daughter in Shrewsbury. But she's been here for the past fortnight, ever since he took ill. If you're thinking she might be the woman in the grave."

"Any other relatives expected for the funeral?"

"Two cousins in their seventies, and a friend of Miss Simmons. She's staying over to help with the clearing out of the house. They're accounted for, sir."

"The undertaker. Where is he from?"

"The next village. Norham. It's twice the size of ours, and better situated for the firm to serve other villages. Quite reputable, they are, sir."

"The sexton. What's known about him?"

"He's lived here all his life. I've heard nothing against him. In his late thirties, I'd say. He's not much for the ladies. Lost his wife some eight years ago. She ran off with the man who came to dig a new well at the Rectory. Gossip claimed she'd ended up in London, and no better than she ought to be."

"Could she have come home? The prodigal wife?"

Leigh stared at him.

"If she did, and the sexton wanted no part of her, what better place to leave her body than the freshly dug grave."

Shaking his head, the Constable said, "I'd never have thought about her. But the dead woman is too young. Joan was younger than he was, there's that. But she left here eight years ago. And she didn't dress as modestly."

"Perhaps she reminded him of his wife, and he killed her for that."

Constable Leigh was skeptical, but he accompanied Rutledge to the church.

They found the sexton removing the dead greenery left there from the funeral that was never held. He looked up as he heard the south porch door scraping open across the stone flagging.

Courtney Miller was in his late thirties, a broad-shouldered man with fair hair so bleached by the sun that it was almost white. His eyes were a startling blue in a face roughened by weather. It was as if they stared out from behind a mask.

"Good afternoon," he said, straightening up, his arms full of dry greenery. "Looking for Rector? He's at the Taylor farm. Mrs. Taylor had a boy at four in the morning. Eight pound, according to the midwife."

"The doctor didn't attend her?" Rutledge asked.

"I've heard it said she didn't care too much for his modern ways. Old Sally, now, has been midwife for as long as I can remember, and there are women who swear by her."

"I understand you were married," Rutledge commented. "Any chance that the woman in the grave is your wife, returning to Shropshire because she's had enough of London?"

Miller had been looking directly at Rutledge, apparently untroubled until his wife was mentioned. His gaze went to Leigh, accusing.

"He had no right to draw her name into this business. But no, it's not Joan, and even if she did turn up here one day, I'm not likely to be taking a knife to her." He faced Rutledge now. "When she first left me, yes, I was boiling mad. I don't know what I might have done back then. But it's been seven—no, eight years, and I've got over her now. It was a mistake to marry her in the first place, and that's a fact."

Leigh said, "Sorry, Court. But the Inspector did ask."

Rutledge said easily, "Don't blame the Constable. He's right, I was asking questions about all the villagers, and that perforce included you. A man with the opportunity—you knew about the grave—and you found the body."

"Anyone could have told you it wasn't Joan."

"People change. If no one was expecting her to come back to Shropshire, it's possible no one recognized her."

"I would've," Miller replied curtly. "Don't you think that would have been the first thing I noticed?"

"Do you remember her birthdate?"

"'Course I do," he said. "She'd be thirty-five this May. The seventeenth."

Rutledge had put the dead woman's age at around twenty-eight or -nine.

"Does the dead woman look anything like your wife? Could she have been mistaken in the dark for Joan? Someone who might not want her to come back to Tern Bridge?"

Something in the sexton's face changed. "What do you mean? Not want her back? You're not saying my mother mistook her for Joan?" He shook his head. "No, I won't believe that. Mum hated her, that's true enough. But she wouldn't go killing a stranger she saw in the dark. What was that woman doing wandering about, anyway? It doesn't make sense. Where did she come from? How did she get here? That's the question you ought to be asking."

He had a very good point. But Rutledge quietly reserved judgment about Miller's mother.

He said, "Thank you, Mr. Miller. You do understand we had to ask?"

"If my mother had killed Joan," the sexton retorted harshly, "I'd have taken care of her myself."

So much for the man who claimed to have put aside his feelings for his straying wife.

They left him there, still holding the drying greenery, one branch spread across the flagstones at his feet.

"He's a deep one," Constable Leigh was saying, once they were out of earshot. "I sometimes wondered if he'd killed Joan rather than let her go. But there was never any proof. And London's a big town to be looking for one person."

"If she's there, the Yard will find her."

Rutledge was just bending down to turn the crank when he saw a man in a dark coat walking up the steps of the Rectory.

"Rector," Constable Leigh said quietly.

With the Constable at his heels, Rutledge cut across the churchyard in time to reach the side door of the tall, narrow brick house just beyond a second gate in the low wall. They followed the path around to the main door and knocked.

The Rector himself answered it, saying with a smile, "Mariah, is—oh, I'm sorry, I was expecting Mrs. Brooks. Constable. And this must be the man from Scotland Yard." He held out his hand. "Ralph Ellis."

"Ian Rutledge."

"Come in, come in." He opened the door wider, and stood aside to allow them to enter, then led them to the front room. A small man with an absent air, graying hair, and gray eyes, he had a barely perceptible limp.

It was like so many other Vicarage or Rectory parlors Rutledge had seen: dark furnishings, a hearth that was cold at this hour of the day, and an air of seldom being used. A flourishing aspidistra in a china pot sat on a table in the window, its luxuriant green leaves spreading across the table's top, nearly covering it. It was a plant that, along with ferns, had been popular in Victorian homes and solariums.

Ellis looked around, then said, "Hmmm. We'd be more comfortable in my study, I think. I hadn't realized how frigid it is in here. Scott would feel right at home, eh? No need to explore the South Pole." He ushered them toward the passage again, and walked on down to another door, opening it and crossing to the cluttered desk. A roaring fire had made the room stuffy, almost stifling. He gestured to the chairs in front of the desk.

Rutledge took off his coat and put it with his hat on a table by the door before sitting down. After a moment Constable Leigh followed suit as Ellis apologized.

"I've forgot my manners. I was up all night with the proud father of a newborn, who insisted on wetting his son's head until first light. I got him to bed at dawn, then fell asleep in a chair myself. The midwife found me there, snoring so loudly I was keeping the new mother awake." He grinned. "I doubt it was that bad, Sally has a tendency to overdramatize, but she was right, I ought to have been in my own bed. And I walked in to find a note from my wife. She's visiting the sick this morning. I haven't even had my tea."

Constable Leigh asked after the baby, and then Ellis said, "But you aren't here about the child. It's that poor soul in Simmons's grave." He leaned back in his own chair, and it creaked a little. "I wish I could help you there. But my bedroom is on the far side of the house, and I neither heard nor saw anything Tuesday night. The first I knew of anything wrong was the shout from the sexton. I'd just gone into the church, to be sure everything was as it should be for the funeral service. I came out the door, saw him pointing toward the grave, realized that he'd pulled some of the boards away, and wondered if someone's cat or dog had managed to fall in. You can't imagine my shock when I reached the grave and realized that it was a person—a woman." He shook his head. "I've seen some terrible things in my lifetime, Inspector. But nothing to compare with that poor woman's body, lying there. All I could think of was that she must be unbearably cold. And then of course, I realized that she was beyond feeling anything more on this earth. I knelt by the grave and prayed for the comfort of her soul."

"You've never seen her before?"

"No. At least, I can't remember ever having seen her. I've been in the church for twenty-three years. That's a good many faces, to recall all of them."

"Do you remember the sexton's wife, Joan Miller?"

"No, it couldn't have been her. I am confident that I would have recognized her. Surely you aren't saying that Miller had anything to do with that young woman?"

"I must consider everyone in Tern Bridge."

"I expect that's so, myself included, but I refuse to believe Miller could be guilty of murder."

"There were just the two of you, there by the grave?"

"Yes. I told Miller I'd stay with her while he went to find Constable Leigh, but he insisted that I go. He had to clear away the remaining boards, so that Allen—Dr. Allen—could reach her. I brought them back, and we'd just got her up out of the grave when Mrs. Branson walked by. Allen, thank heavens, had thought to bring a blanket to cover the body."

Rutledge looked from the Rector to Constable Leigh. "There was no mention of a Mrs. Branson in the reports."

"Well, no," Constable Leigh said apologetically. "She's at least eighty, and with time on her hands, she minds everyone's business but her own." He glanced at the Rector for confirmation.

"Yes, I did my best to stop her from coming too close to the grave, but she's a willful soul, Inspector, and it's hard to distract her when her mind's made up. She could just see the face, the blanket had fallen away from it, and Mrs. Branson asked if the woman was dead. The Constable stepped forward and told her this might be a crime scene, then the doctor stopped his examination and finally talked Mrs. Branson into leaving. He warned her to say nothing, and to the best of my knowledge, she kept her promise not to mention what she'd seen. When she'd well and truly gone away, we got on with it. As soon as the doctor told us he was finished, we wrapped the body in the doctor's blanket, and carried her to his motorcar, standing by the gate. Constable got in with him and they drove the short distance to his surgery."

"Did you look around you, or see anything unusual?"

"To be quite honest, I didn't think about that until the Constable and the doctor had left. But there was nothing out of place that I could see." He shook his head. "I am used to deathbeds, Inspector. But not murder in my own churchyard."

"Do you have any idea why someone would leave a body there?"

"Well, assuming she wasn't one of our flock, I'd guess that her killer wanted to be sure she couldn't be connected in any way with him. Or her. Although I'm not sure a woman could have carried her that far from the road. I did ask the doctor about the stab wounds. He told me that she hadn't suffered. That the first wound would have killed her quickly, and the others were delivered just to make certain she was dead. But the attack wasn't vicious—wild. Just deadly. That had been something that was worrying me, Inspector. I didn't want to think of her surviving the attack, to die alone in that grave, unable to call for help."

"I understand." Rutledge rose. "No one in your parish had mentioned earlier that he or she might be expecting a guest? A friend or a relative."

"They tell me most things, one way or another. But I've heard nothing about that. I am sorry there isn't more I could do to help. I've been as shocked as Leigh, here."

He saw them out, and watched them walk down the short path from the door to the street.

As they reached the motorcar and got in, Constable Leigh asked, "You're not really thinking it might be Joan Miller that's dead? I can't believe that she'd dare show her face around here, after walking off the way she did. And her reputation was not spotless before she went. The village women would shun her. Besides, that woman in the doctor's surgery is more respectable than Joan ever was."

"Her return would depend on just how desperate she was. But then you never take into account that women such as Joan might come to their senses, change their ways, and in the end come home like the prodigal daughter. It does happen."

"Leopards don't change their spots," Leigh said stubbornly.

Rutledge smiled grimly. "I might not believe that Joan Miller had come back, but I can't help but wonder if someone could have thought she had. The question is, how *did* the woman get here? She didn't fall out of the sky onto the High Street."

"Her clothes aren't those of a woman in dire straits."

"Which supports my theory that she had changed her ways."

"We don't know how she came by them. A church jumble sale? Someone who took pity on her?"

But Rutledge refused to argue any further. And Leigh finally took the hint.

Back on the High Street once more, the Constable said, "Mind, if I were to kill someone, I wouldn't leave the body where it might be found, and the finger pointed at me. I'd take her to another village, and let *them* wonder who she was."

"That's something to look into. I do wish Tern Bridge ran to a telephone."

"Sorry, sir. But I don't know who we'd call if we had one."

He left Leigh at the police station and drove on to the inn.

Getting out, Rutledge was just bending over to look at the right rear tire when someone behind him spoke. "Young man? Are you the policeman from London?"

Straightening up, he saw a woman in a stylish hat, a floral print scarf at the throat of her dark coat, and an anxious expression on her lined face.

"Inspector Rutledge, yes. How can I help you?"

"Helen Branson. I've been waiting for an opportunity to speak to you, Mr. Rutledge."

"Shall we go into The Dun Cow?" he asked. "Out of the wind?" This must be the woman from the churchyard, and he found it hard to believe that her sharp green eyes missed anything.

But she shook her head at the invitation. "I have a feeling I knew that young woman."

"Is she from Tern Bridge?" he asked. "Or possibly lived here at some point?"

"No, of course not. I know everyone in this village. After all, I've lived here seventy of my eighty-one years," she said tartly.

"Then do you know where she might have come from?"

"That's just it. I can't put my finger on where I saw her before. But her face is familiar."

"Can you give me a name?" he asked, holding on to his patience. "I would be very grateful."

"I don't know her name. I just feel I know her face."

"Have you told the Constable that you might know her?"

"I haven't. I was afraid it might be dangerous for me to tell anyone."

"And why should you be afraid?"

"She was murdered. I don't want her killer to come looking for me."

"You've told *me*."

"You're Scotland Yard. I expect you to protect me." She reached up a gloved hand and drew the scarf a little closer against the cold wind. "There are daffodils blooming in the southeast corner of my house. You'd think they had more sense than to come out this early."

"May I drive you home, Mrs. Branson?"

"Thank you, no. Walking is how I pass the time. Although I do wish it was a little warmer today. It was, on Saturday last, you know. Quite unexpectedly warm." She looked around. "I shouldn't even be seen talking to you, Inspector." And she turned quickly and walked on.

"Do ye believe her?" Hamish asked as Rutledge watched her move on down the street.

It's possible she's just confused. With the best of intentions, wanting to help, he silently answered.

As he turned toward the inn door, he saw the barman standing there in the pub doorway, smoking a cigarette and watching Mrs. Branson as well. He put out the cigarette and went back inside when he realized that Rutledge had seen him there.

3

Rutledge found a telephone in a larger village some ten miles from Tern Bridge, saving him the drive to Shrewsbury. He put through a call to the Yard, and asked for Sergeant Gibson.

"Good day, sir," Gibson said, in a dark voice that predicted a bad morning was about to get much worse.

Rutledge smiled, then said, "There's a woman in London I need to find—she's not a suspect, but she might be our victim. I need to know if she's alive."

"I don't know if we have the men to search at the moment, sir. But I'll try. Give me the name and tell me how to reach you."

"I'll have to call you again. There's no telephone in the village. The name is Joan Miller." He went on to describe the dead woman. "And no distinguishing—"

"Joan Miller, sir?" Gibson broke in. "Well, I can tell you she's alive. Two days ago, Inspector Kent was interviewing her about a break-in at the house where she's an upstairs maid."

"Is she a suspect in that inquiry?"

"No, sir. She was asleep on the servants' floor when someone came through a window in the pantry. Inspector Kent wanted to know more about one of the sons in the family. He's got gambling debts."

"And you're certain it's the same Joan Miller I'm looking for?"

"According to the Inspector's report, she came to London some six or seven years ago and went into service. References from a house in Shrewsbury where she was a kitchen maid for two years."

If this was the Joan Miller who had run away with the Rector's well-digger, she had landed on her feet. Moreover, she'd kept her husband's name. Still, it was common enough.

In Rutledge's experience, women who were looking to leave another life behind reverted to their maiden name, or even their mother's maiden name, to ensure a fresh beginning.

Had she used the other man to cover her escape from Miller? What did that have to say about the sexton?

And did it make him a suspect, even if the dead woman wasn't his wife?

Rutledge said, "Age?"

"Thirty-four, birthday coming up in May. The seventeenth, according to the report."

He thanked Gibson and put up the telephone.

There couldn't be any doubt about Joan Miller. The same name *and* the same birthday couldn't be wrong.

Which left him with no identification and possibly no suspect. But then it would have been almost too easy for the killer to find his victim.

Hamish reminded him, "You canna' be certain yon lass wasn't mistaken for her. If she had left the well-digger and turned respectable. And someone knew it."

But Rutledge had a feeling that his inquiry had just hit a dead end.

Driving back to the village, he found himself thinking ruefully that Chief Superintendent Markham would have been very pleased with such a swift and tidy solution: the sexton killing the straying wife who had returned hoping for forgiveness.

It was the sort of conclusion the man preferred: straightforward and uncomplicated by nuances.

Rutledge looked for Mrs. Branson as he came into the village, wondering if she might still be wandering the streets. *Was* her memory as trustworthy as she claimed, or was it a victim of lonely old age and imagination?

There was no sign of her. And the light was going.

It was just at the evening supper hour when he walked into The Dun Cow's crowded bar and asked for sandwiches and tea to be sent up to his room. It was Saturday night, he realized.

The middle-aged woman who took his order said, "There's a message from Constable, sir. I put it under your door."

Rutledge took the stairs two at a time, hoping for good news. But the folded square of paper slipped under his door said only, *Doctor wants to know what to do with the body if there's no one to claim it.*

It was premature to be thinking about a burial when there had been neither an inquest nor an arrest. But the surgery was small, and a dead body was a problem.

The question would have to wait. He slipped the square into his notebook, just as there was a knock at his door, and the woman from downstairs came into the room with his meal.

He sat by the window and ate it, grateful for the meager fire on his hearth, and thinking about the overheated study at the Rectory.

And there was the answer. Let the Rector decide what to do with the unclaimed body. Rutledge thought it was very likely that he would take on the charge as a matter of course. But surely there would be a name by the time such a decision had to be made.

That raised another thought: the Simmons funeral must still be waiting for the grieving family to decide whether they wanted to bury him in that grave after all.

The sandwiches—egg mayonnaise and a ham and cheese—were well made, and he finished them before taking out his notebook and putting down what he'd learned since his arrival.

Looking at what he'd written, he thought it seemed like very little progress had been made. He'd ruled out Joan Miller as the victim, but there was no one to put in her place.

He remembered the bruised, torn grass by the grave. Impossible to say now if there was blood around the site. If the woman hadn't been killed there in the churchyard just before she was put into the empty grave, where *had* she been killed? In the vehicle that had brought her to the churchyard? In someone's house? Her own? Wherever it had occurred, there would have been blood to clean up. The killer would have faced a dilemma—getting rid of the body or getting rid of the blood left behind somewhere . . .

He considered the empty ruin he'd seen by the river. But the woman didn't appear to be the sort who would let herself be lured into such a place, even by someone she knew. It must now be the realm of bats, foxes, and owls. Hardly a romantic rendezvous.

And where was the weapon? Back in someone's kitchen? Before it was noticed as missing? He remembered the man from the bar staring after Mrs. Branson. In the inn kitchen, perhaps.

Needles in a haystack, he thought wryly. But he closed his notebook and put on his coat again.

Driving out of the village, he came to the old bridge, stopped short of it, and then walked slowly across, casting about as he went. It would certainly be a far more romantic spot for two people to stand here in the middle of the bridge, watching the sun set, its winter brightness seeming to sink into the water below. Or as the moon rose, casting long shadows and lighting the water . . .

What if it wasn't romance that had brought the woman here but fear? Or anger. Why then would she let herself be lured to this isolated place, where she was vulnerable? Perhaps it was jealousy, and she had threatened to make a scene?

But how had she got here? From the description of her clothing, she wasn't dressed to walk far. In her killer's motorcar? Was this where he felt it was safe enough to finish what he had planned for her? But why kill her? What had she done or done to him, that required murder?

Halfway across, he stopped.

Were those dark stains in the road bed? Or his imagination?

It hadn't rained since the murder. Pulling off his gloves, he scratched at the dark spots. Then, taking out his handkerchief, he collected as much as he could before folding it and putting it into his pocket again.

He went twice over the bridge, but there was nothing more to be seen. He even walked along both banks some distance in both directions, letting the torch taken from the boot of his motorcar play along the water's edge, under tree roots, or where the grass and brambles had drooped into the water.

Rutledge was about to turn away when he saw it. There, where a drifting dead limb had caught in the roots of another tree, along the bank on the far side, was that something snagged on the limb? He moved closer to the water, hoping he could reach out and fish whatever it was free. But he had to go back to the motorcar and put on his Wellingtons before he could get near enough on the spongy earth to find out what it was he'd seen.

Even so, he could feel his boots sinking into the soft, wet ground along the river's edge, and he caught the heavy odor of rotting vegetation and stagnant water here by the roots. Reaching out as far as he dared, he just managed to touch whatever it was with the tips of his fingers. Getting a grip was impossible. He backed away, found a suitable length of branch farther up the bank, and with that in hand, tried again.

This time he was able to lift the object with his stick and slowly draw it toward him. Impatient, he forced himself to take his time, for the stream itself was flowing fast enough to carry his quarry off if he dropped it in the current.

And then it was finally where he could grasp it with his left hand as his right brought the object closer.

Dropping the branch, he stood there and examined his find.

It was a woman's blue glove. It had been made of a fine leather, possibly Italian, but it had stretched and was soggy now.

Had it been dropped over the rampart of the bridge as she struggled with her assailant? And where was the other glove? Had the killer kept it along with a hat and a purse because he realized that one glove might lead someone like Rutledge to look for the other?

There was no way to tell. He smoothed the soggy leather and tried to judge the size of the hand that had been in it. It was too stretched now even to guess. And once dry, it would very likely shrink. But there was a round pearl button that closed the glove at the wrist. And that could be matched if the size could not.

Pleased with his success, he started back to the motorcar.

Coming into the village, he drove straight to the doctor's surgery, and found Allen was just seeing a last patient out, a woman coughing heavily.

As Rutledge was stepping out of the motorcar, the young woman had reached the street. She ducked her head shyly as she passed him. He walked on toward the doorway where the doctor was still waiting.

"Rutledge."

"I've brought something. I need your knowledge as a medical man."

"Sounds intriguing. Come in."

Dr. Allen led him to his office, and turned up the lamp on his desk. "Now then. What do you need to ask me?"

Rutledge took out his handkerchief and carefully spread it open. "Can you tell me whether this is human blood? Look, just here, the rusty color on the cloth. Not the earth and pebbles around it."

"Let me see."

Allen took the handkerchief from him and put it under the light. "Are you sure this is blood?"

"I think it might be."

"Where did you find it?"

"That's not the issue. Is it animal or human?"

"Give me a few minutes." He left the office, carrying the handkerchief with him. Rutledge started to follow, but Allen said, "No, let me work on it."

He waited impatiently, pacing the floor. And then Allen came back.

"My guess is that this is indeed blood. Human or animal I can't be sure. Nor could I swear to it in a courtroom. Still, it might help you to know what I think. There's a strong possibility that it could be human."

"Yes, it does help. I won't keep you from your evening." He held out his hand for the handkerchief, and Allen gave it back to him. "Thank you."

"And you found this where?"

"It's best not to answer that. At least for the moment."

Allen smiled grimly. "I can't say that I blame you. The fewer people who know, the better." He followed Rutledge to the outer door. "Good evening, Inspector."

"Good evening." He walked down the path to the motorcar. He now had the specks of blood on his handkerchief, and the blue glove. And the bridge. It was a start. Finally.

H e sat there in his room, staring at the street below, working out what he'd found and what it told him about the inquiry.

The most likely explanation for the woman's body being found in the churchyard had been that she was murdered elsewhere and the killer had left her as far from the scene as possible—where, most likely, she wouldn't be easily identified. No weapon, no clues, nothing to put a name to her killer. It was clever, and it had worked.

But the glove in the water and the likelihood that he'd found blood on the bridge now pointed to the murder having occurred there. In the dark, and the lost glove had gone unnoticed. Or she might have set them with her handbag on the stone top of the bridge, and they'd fallen over during the struggle.

That brought the murder closer to home.

Which meant that her killer might already have known about the open grave.

Hamish said, "She was wearing a dark coat. It wasna' blue."

"But the walking dress was blue."

Could it have been a chance encounter, there on the bridge?

Rutledge thought not. For one thing, where had the woman walked from, and where was she going? Surely not very far on such a cold night. And not along an old, deserted road to nowhere.

Who, then, had she been meeting?

There was no train service to Tern Bridge. Nor omnibus except for the afternoon run. And that driver had claimed he hadn't seen the woman nor put her down in the village.

But had anyone asked the driver later, on his next run, if he'd seen her walking toward the river and the old bridge?

Where would she have gone from there? If not to the village, then to one of the outlying farms?

He got up, reached for his coat and hat, and ran down the stairs.

Constable Leigh hadn't left the police station. He'd finished his evening rounds, and was warming his hands over the dying fire in the hearth before going back out into the cold.

He looked up as Rutledge came in. "Any news, sir?"

Rutledge told him about the blood on the bridge but said nothing about the glove he'd found.

"Well, that sheds new light on where the victim was killed, sir. That could mean you might be right about the sexton's wife, after all. I still find it hard to believe he could have murdered her. He'd be more likely to look for the well-digger."

"He didn't kill his wife. Joan Miller is alive and well in London."

The Constable's eyebrows flew up in surprise. "It was true then? The gossip? I'll be damned—Court never believed it."

"I doubt he wanted to. I think he'd have told us when we were questioning him. It would have cleared him straightaway. All right, assuming for the moment that this murder has nothing to do with the Millers, who could our unknown woman have been meeting on that bridge?"

"It's a common enough place for lovers, sir. But generally not this time of year." Leigh frowned, going over his knowledge of likely village men. "Rector is happily married. Dr. Allen as well. Grissom, at the pub, is not married, but he's been courting the woman who works behind the bar for these three years. The ironmonger is married to the postmistress, and the greengrocer, Mr. Bishop, is a widower. We lost eleven of our young men in the war, and three more haven't recovered from their wounds. They're not likely to be meeting strange women at the bridge. The rest are over fifty."

Rutledge said, "The farms, then. Are any of them closer to the bridge than the village?"

"No, sir. But none of the farmers are likely to be out courting at that hour. Even in winter, there are chores that need doing, and most are up by first light." He shook his head. "Of course there's Mr. Ward, who fancies himself and is always chatting up the women when he comes in on market day. He's known to travel around to other villages too, on whatever excuse he can think of. I expect he's no better behaved then. His wife tolerates the flirting, but keeps him on a tight rein. If she ever caught him in a real dalliance, she'd take a pitchfork to him."

"Would she indeed? I think we ought to have a talk with Mr. Ward. There might have been a dalliance that got out of hand, and our victim appeared in Tern Bridge thinking he was free. He might be desperate enough to kill her before his wife found out."

"At this hour, sir?" Leigh took out his watch. "It's nearly half past eleven. He's bound to be in bed."

"Then he's less likely to lie to us, with his wife within hearing."

The farm was on the same side of the village as the old bridge. When they'd bounced and slid along the rutted lane and reached the house, there were still lamps lit, one of them showing through the dark windows of the front room.

"That's odd, at this hour," Leigh said, staring at it. Just then a large brown dog came racing out of the barn barking furiously at them. "What's the matter, Rusty? Why is everybody awake?"

The barking changed its tone to an announcement of visitors as the house door opened and a man's deep voice called, "Who's there?"

"Constable Leigh, Ward. With Inspector Rutledge." He was stepping out of the motorcar, bending over to scratch Rusty behind the ears. "We'd like to speak to you, if we could."

There was silence for a moment, then Ward looked over his shoulder before saying, "It won't take long, will it? I'm up at four."

"Not long at all," Rutledge said easily, and together he and Leigh walked toward the farmhouse door, Rusty sniffing at his heels.

Ward took them into the front room, turned up the wick in the lamp, and then closed the door before gesturing to the chairs by the hearth.

It was like many farmhouse parlors, rather old-fashioned, with a framed photograph on the wall of what must have been Ward's parents, staring at the camera with unsmiling faces. The man had the same hairline as Ward's, and the woman had the same chin. There was a rosewood chair with a brocade seat standing beneath the photograph, and it appeared to be the same one the woman had been sitting in.

Ward himself had thick dark hair already graying, dark eyes, and a face that had been handsome in his youth but was sagging along the jawline now. Rutledge could see why Constable Leigh had mentioned that he fancied himself. It was there in the way he stood and looked at them before sitting down.

"Right, then," he said. His boots were unlaced, and there was a button undone on his flannel shirt, as if he'd been preparing for bed. "Been up with a sick bull. I think he's going to be all right. Cost enough to buy him in the first place."

Rutledge spoke before the Constable could. "I think you were asked earlier about the woman found in the churchyard."

"I was."

"I'm sorry I don't have a photograph to show you. And the description we have is rather vague. We've been unable to identify her. I'm told that you travel from time to time to other villages on market days. I'd like to have you look at the body and tell me if you've seen her on those occasions. In a pub, perhaps, or at one of the market stalls. It would help with our inquiries."

"I don't have the time to come into the doctor's surgery."

He hadn't denied going to markets.

"I have a motorcar, as you've seen. It will take very little of your time." He'd begun pleasantly, as if asking a favor of the man. There was steel in his voice now, and Ward heard it.

"Even if I had seen her before, I'm not likely to remember where. Market is a busy time," he said stubbornly.

"That may well be. On the other hand, you might give us a name. If not hers, then that of the village."

Ward was about to object again, but Rutledge didn't give him the opportunity.

"Unless of course you know who she is, and why she came to Tern Bridge."

"Here, I've said no such thing."

"Then you'll come with us now?" Rutledge rose. They hadn't taken off their coats in the chill of the room, and he added, "You'll need your coat."

He got to the door before Ward could rise and opened it. And he was just in time to see the door down the passage close quietly, shutting off the lamplight in what must be the kitchen.

Ward, his face a thundercloud, walked out of the room and down the passage, to open the same door. He said something to his wife, and came back with his coat.

They moved in silence out to the motorcar, and Rutledge tried not to think of Hamish in his accustomed place as Ward climbed heavily into the rear seats. It was where the voice seemed to come from sometimes.

It took them a quarter of an hour to reach the doctor's surgery, and it was clear that Ward was unhappy about accompanying them. His answers were mere grunts, as if his mind wasn't on what was being said to him.

"It's late—" Allen began when he saw Rutledge and Leigh standing at his surgery door, but Rutledge spoke across him.

"Sorry to disturb you again, Doctor. I've brought Mr. Ward to help us with our inquiries. I'd like him to see the body."

Allen stared at them for a moment, then said, "Oh, very well." He stood aside, and Rutledge led the way down the passage to the room where the woman lay.

Allen stopped them at the door, moved ahead to light the lamp, and then went to draw back the sheet so that only the woman's face showed.

Ward hesitated on the threshold, then walked straight to the table and looked down at the body.

"No," he said decisively. "Never saw her before." There was a firmness in the words that had the ring of truth. He turned and left. Dr. Allen began pulling the sheet back in place, but Rutledge was already following Ward. By the time he reached the outer door, the farmer was already on his way to the motorcar standing in front of the house.

"Bloody waste of time," Ward was saying, loud enough to be heard.

Allen stopped Rutledge. "What was this all about? Is he a suspect?"

"No. He goes to market here and in other villages. He could have seen her somewhere. I'm told he has an eye for the ladies. And she's pretty. It was possible he knew who she was."

"And you believe him when he says he doesn't know her?"

"That remains to be seen." He thanked Allen and followed Leigh out to the motorcar, where the Constable was already turning the crank. The surgery door closed, and the lamp in the entry was put out, leaving the three men in darkness.

Ward grumbled all the way back to the farm, but Rutledge ignored him. As soon as they pulled up at the house, Ward had the door open and was already shouting at Rusty to stop his barking. He went straight to the house, went inside, and didn't look back.

"Do you believe him?" Constable Leigh asked, echoing the doctor's question.

"Yes. I think so. I watched his face as he looked down at her. There was neither recognition nor any sign that he was uncomfortable seeing his victim in the presence of others."

Rutledge reversed, and said as he started back down the twisting lane, "His wife was listening at the door. She may be more aware of his straying than he knows. I don't think I'd like to be in his shoes tonight."

"Nor I," Constable Leigh said fervently.

They drove in silence the rest of the way and Rutledge took the Constable to his cottage at the far end of the village.

Returning to The Dun Cow, Rutledge listened to Hamish pointing out that the inquiry was still going nowhere.

"Ye canna' even be certain yon blue glove belonged to her."

I t was a long night, and Rutledge had known it was going to be. He listened to Hamish until the hands of his watch pointed to two. And then he drifted into a troubled sleep.

At breakfast, Constable Leigh was morose. "I can't think what to do next, sir, and that's the truth. It appears our victim was killed here, but her murderer could be anywhere. What if he was arguing with her in his motorcar, saw the bridge, and decided it was as likely a place as any to rid himself of her? Then why not leave her there? Or in the water? Why risk taking her as far as the churchyard?"

"To keep us guessing?" Rutledge shook his head. "No, there's something we aren't seeing. Ward, for instance, could have met her in one of his forays to other villages. What if someone else had the same opportunity? If the dead woman wasn't from Tern Bridge, how *did* the killer know her? Was he related to her? If so, why hadn't she come here from time to time to visit?"

"A matter of an inheritance, then? If she was removed, he stood to gain?"

"Possible of course. Is there anyone in the village expecting to inherit? Simmons, for instance. Was there someone else coming to claim part of his inheritance?"

"That's not likely. He only had the one child, sir, a daughter. And she grew up in Tern Bridge. Besides, there's not that much to quarrel over. He was a careful man, saw her married well, but he's not rich by any stretch."

"Who else in the village leaves from time to time?"

"I—let me think, sir." He closed his eyes, mentally running through what he knew about his patch. "From time to time? Rector will fill in for another parish when there's the need. He went as far as the Welsh borders once or twice. But he always takes his wife with him. The ironmonger's daughter Nell lives in Shrewsbury. He and his wife go to visit her a few times a year. Dr. Allen has a sister in Bristol. The baker, Mr. Swindon, has a brother in Gloucester, although he's most likely to visit here than the reverse. Mr. Swindon doesn't care to leave the baking to his wife. The late Mr. Branson and his wife often went to Bath. He was fond of the concerts there. He's the nephew of Sir Alan Grant."

Grant had been a crony of the late King Edward, a wealthy landowner with some of the best shooting in Scotland.

"Still, we'll speak to Simmons's daughter first. And then—" Rutledge stopped in midsentence. Branson—*Mrs.* Branson. She'd spoken to him by the inn. And she'd said something—that the woman in the grave had seemed to be familiar, although she couldn't place her. At the time, he'd taken that to mean she wasn't really certain.

Rutledge put down his teacup and started for the door. "Carry on with Simmons's daughter, Constable. There's something I need to see to. Possibly in London."

"Joan Miller?" Leigh looked confused. "Again?"

"No, I think not."

He was gone before Leigh could ask another question. He had no idea where Mrs. Branson lived, but as she had walked away from their conversation, he'd registered the fact that she was going beyond The

Dun Cow. It only took him ten minutes to find the Branson house on his own. It was one of the best examples of Georgian brick in the village. And the gate to the walk had a large and ornate *B* in the center of the ironwork.

He was prepared to cover his tracks if he was mistaken.

A deep breath, and then he was walking up the path to the door, and lifting the knocker.

4

Mrs. Branson was reading in her sitting room when Rutledge was shown in. She marked her place, looked up at him, and frowned. With a nod she dismissed her maid, then said, "Come in, Inspector. I'm not sure I welcome your visit."

"I expect you're quite safe, Mrs. Branson. And you'll be even safer once we have a murderer in hand," he said reassuringly.

She was wearing lavender today and it complemented her white hair. An attractive woman still. One tended to miss the sharp eyes. Constable Leigh had all but said she was a meddler, a busybody. He himself had wondered if she might be more than a little confused. Looking at her now, in her own surroundings, not wandering about the streets, Rutledge was rapidly revising his earlier view of her.

She gestured to a chair and politely asked if he'd care for tea. "Or there's my late husband's whisky, if you'd prefer it."

"It's rather early for both," he said. "But thank you."

Mrs. Branson nodded approvingly. "Yes, so it is. Well, then, what has brought you to my door?"

"You told me you thought you might have recognized the woman taken from the late Mr. Simmons's grave."

"No, I believe I told you she seemed familiar."

"I stand corrected. Someone you feel you might have known or seen here in Tern Bridge?"

"The more I've thought about her, the more I've come to believe she wasn't someone who had lived or worked in the village. I no longer travel as widely as I did when my late husband was alive. But I still visit Bath from time to time. I have friends there."

"I see." He wanted to urge her on, but he was learning that it was best to let her tell her own story in her own way.

"My late husband enjoyed the concerts, and I began to wonder if I'd seen her there, at one of the musical evenings. I couldn't picture her in evening dress, try as I would. And so I wondered if she'd visited while we were staying with our friends. But I can't recall her in that setting, either."

"You've given this a great deal of thought," he commented.

"I know my civic duty, Inspector. But more than that, the poor young woman in Dr. Allen's surgery deserves a name and a history. She was deprived of both when she was killed."

Rutledge accepted the rebuke. "That's why I am here, Mrs. Branson," he responded quietly.

"Yes, so you are. But I have nothing to give you, try as I may. For that I must apologize. Even if I sent you to Bath, how would you go about finding her? She might have been a visitor, as I was." A note of anxiety crept into her voice. "It's frightening, not being able to remember. Yet I am sure I have seen her face before."

"Still, it could be worth my while. If she in fact lived there, someone must surely have reported her missing. Judging by her clothing, she was a respectable young woman. And I shan't have to search the city. I can begin by calling in at the Bath police station."

Her face brightened. "Yes, how clever of you. I hadn't thought of that. It gives me some comfort." She paused, then said, the anxiety creeping in again, "Will I be safe, do you think, while you are searching?"

"I believe you will. I've instructed Constable Leigh to question everyone who might have traveled out of Tern Bridge, either to local markets or farther afield. You will be only one of a number of people asked to give statements. If I were you, I would say that your age has clouded your memory, and you would like to have time to think about your answers."

A flash of fire from her eyes told him she had resented the suggestion, even as she recognized its wisdom.

"Yes, I expect I can bring myself to do that."

"If you are right, and I find this woman did come from Bath, we can rethink your failing memory," he said lightly, smiling.

"Of course. You are sure you won't take tea with me, Mr. Rutledge?"

"Later perhaps. I've informed Constable Leigh that I'm off to London at the moment. If I lose my way and find myself in Bath instead, I shan't be at all surprised."

She smiled then, and it changed her face. He had a brief glimpse of a younger and very attractive woman. Mr. Branson, he thought to himself, had been a very lucky man.

Thanking her, he rose and let himself out.

Bath was a beautiful city, one Rutledge had always liked. The cathedral, the Pump Room, the Roman baths—they were interesting, but most of all he'd enjoyed bright summer evening strolls along the Crescents, looking up at the differences in doors and windows and architectural decorations. His godfather, an architect, had taken him there with his own son, Ross, and made a game out of following threads of details. As Rutledge and Ross had competed, walking up and down the streets, pointing out variations, Trevor had rewarded them with sweets from his pockets. It had sealed Rutledge's affection for the Crescents, those semicircular rows of elegant white terraces that had once made Bath a famous Regency spa.

He went to the central police station and asked to see an Inspector.

A few minutes later, a tall, thin man in his fifties came out, looking like nothing so much as a scarecrow given a nicer suit of clothes.

"Scotland Yard," he said with a rueful grin as he held out his hand. "Now what have we done to deserve this honor?"

Rutledge smiled, shaking hands. "I hope I'm about to clear up one of your inquiries."

"God knows that would be helpful. Inspector Graves. Come back to my office." He led Rutledge to a room that was almost shockingly neat, except for the cluttered desk, and pointed to the files spread out there. "If you can find the answers to these, I'd be grateful."

Rutledge took the chair Graves offered. "A missing person case, recent, a young woman between late twenties and early thirties. Fair, blue eyes, nicely dressed in a dark coat, blue walking dress and jacket. One matching blue leather glove. Purse and hat still missing."

Graves stared at him. "Good God." Then he shook his head. "You've been talking to my Sergeant. I thought you were being glib with your promises of help."

"I'm describing a body discovered in Shropshire. Tern Bridge to be precise. She was killed outside the village, then left in an open grave prepared for a funeral on the next morning. We don't know who she is."

"Well, then, your search can also end here. She was reported missing three days ago. Serena Palmer. Schoolmistress at a small private girls' school in Bath. She went to see her doctor on Monday week for a stomach complaint, told the Head that he had ordered bed rest. She intended to stay with a cousin in the city, where she could be cared for properly. When the Head sent someone round to see how Miss Palmer was recovering, the cousin knew nothing about any illness. Or where Miss Palmer might be." He searched his desk for a folder, and found the one he was looking for. Opening it, he produced a photograph and passed it to Rutledge. "This was taken three years ago. But it should do."

Rutledge looked at it.

Two women standing together, dressed for an evening party, smiling at the camera. They looked very much alike, except that one was about ten years older. Sister? Cousin? The younger one was the woman in Dr. Allen's surgery. Rutledge had no doubt about it.

Graves, watching him, said unnecessarily, "Miss Serena Palmer is on the left, there."

"Yes, I recognize her." He passed the photograph back. "What was the diagnosis? Why did the doctor recommend bed rest?"

"He didn't. We sent someone round to ask." Graves shrugged. "She'd taken a valise with her. In case? A good many young women who go missing are pregnant. They sometimes intend to take their own lives. Others go to face down the father. A few find a doctor in the back streets of London. The brave ones try to find a way to raise the child somewhere they can pass as a widow."

"*Was* she pregnant?"

"That was the surprise. No. She was found to have a venereal disease. My guess was, she'd killed herself. Many do. The treatment is not pleasant."

"The doctor who examined the body didn't mention any disease. Could I borrow that photograph for a few days? The Yard will see that it's returned."

Graves hesitated, and then said, "Why not? If she's your body, we can call off our own search. But the cousin—the older woman in the photograph, Margaret Palmer—has asked us to return it." He gave it to Rutledge.

"Yes, I understand." He rose, shook hands again, and added, "I'm sorry this was the conclusion of your inquiry. I'm glad to have a name for mine. I expect the cousin will have to come to Tern Bridge to identify the body. After that, it can be released in her care."

"My Sergeant will give you her direction and send a Constable with you to her house. She's going to take this hard, Rutledge. She's been here every day asking for news. *Any* hope. They were close." He looked at the thin file. "I'll see you get copies of what little I have here, for the inquest. A pity, isn't it?"

"Sadly, yes. Does Margaret Palmer have any idea who the man is? Or where he could be?"

"She says she doesn't. Her cousin never mentioned him. Or any man. As a mistress at the school, she was particularly careful of her reputation. At the outset, when I thought pregnancy might be the cause of her disappearance, I asked. I was told that she'd lost her fiancé in the war and was still in mourning for him. I questioned the Head at the school and several of Serena Palmer's friends. No one had any idea she was seeing someone. This suggests to me that he must have been married."

"She came to Tern Bridge for a reason. It's hardly the place to drop out of sight—the village is too small, everyone knows everyone else's business. The nearest railway station is several miles away. Too far for her to walk, dressed as she was, and carrying a valise. Someone met her train, listened to her accusations, and killed her."

Had they stopped at the bridge, not for the romantic moonrise but to finish their quarrel? And had the man decided there and then that he couldn't reason with her? That the only way out for him was to kill her? She must have been terribly angry, refusing his help, determined to make him suffer as she was suffering. And he'd brought a weapon with him . . . *Had this happened before?*

"I hope you find the bastard."

"Oh, I shall," Rutledge told him grimly, and was gone.

It was never easy to bring the worst of news to a family still living in hope. As long as one didn't know, one could still wait for the footstep at the door, the voice calling one's name. *I'm home—*

Margaret Palmer looked at the two policemen on her doorstep in the shadows of the evening, and her face crumpled.

"Where is she? *What's happened?*"

Rutledge took her arm and gently led her back into the house, say-ing, "I'm sorry. So sorry. We have found Serena, but I regret to have to tell you she is dead."

The first door in the entry stood open. A parlor, bright with paint-ings of gardens on the wall and a fire on the hearth, a comfortable and pretty room that was welcoming.

Miss Palmer sat down heavily in the nearest chair. Seeing her clearly in the lamplight, he found himself thinking that if Serena had lived, she would look very much like this when she reached her cousin's age.

He took the chair across from her while the Constable stood be-hind him, and with care, he told her the truth. There was no way to make it pleasanter. But he let her absorb it slowly, his voice quiet and even, only leaving out the worst details. She would learn them soon enough.

She cried, as he knew she would, a wrenching grief, and he ges-tured for the Constable to wait in the entry. After a time, she sobbed softly, then asked what she must do.

An hour later, Miss Palmer's maid returned from her afternoon off and despite her own shock made tea for them. Rutledge had not wanted to leave Miss Palmer until there was someone else in the house.

She barely touched her tea, although the Constable drank his down.

"Must I see her?" she asked again.

"It must be official. The identification," he said. "I'm sorry."

"I have a cousin in Ireland. I'll send for him. He can bring me to this—Tern Bridge, was it?"

"I'll write it down for you. And there will be an inquest, as I said."

"And I've told you I won't attend. I don't want to see that man's face. Whoever he is, he destroyed Serena. And then he killed her. I only want to hear that he has hanged."

There was a ruthlessness in her last words that surprised him. She could have been a schoolmistress herself, sternly admonishing a way-ward student.

Rutledge stopped, late as it was, to speak to the doctor who had examined Serena Palmer. He confirmed the diagnosis.

"She took it well. Which disturbed me. I exacted a promise from her to come back the next week to begin treatment. I impressed upon her the need for haste, given the progression of the disease. And she agreed. But somehow I wasn't surprised when the police came calling. She had been on my mind."

"She understood the dangers of the treatment?"

"Yes. It would leave her barren. She would have no children. I think that was what distressed her most of all. I told her that the man would require treatment as well, but she smiled and said he would have to cure himself. An odd comment, but I thought it grew out of her disillusionment. I concluded that she had discovered he was married."

"Did she say that in so many words?"

"No. She didn't have to." He sighed. "Miss Palmer was not my first patient with venereal disease. I fear she won't be the last either."

Rutledge thanked him and left.

It was two o'clock in the morning of the next day before he reached Tern Bridge. He had made several stops on his way. Angry as he was, he went directly to the doctor's surgery and pounded on the door.

Several minutes later, Allen came to answer the door, his nightclothes stuffed into his trousers, and a shirt over them.

"What is—" He stopped short. "Rutledge? Has there been another death?"

"I need to see the body again. Now."

"Couldn't it wait until morning? I had a difficult deliver—"

"Now."

"Very well." He lit the lamp as Rutledge stepped into the entry, out of the wind. They walked down the passage, carrying the lamp with them, and Allen moved ahead to pull the covering back from her face.

Rutledge took the photograph from his coat pocket and looked from it to the woman on the table. He'd felt no doubts, sitting there in Inspector Graves's office. He had none now. But he made a show of making the comparison.

"You have a photograph of her?" Allen asked, watching him.

"I do. And a name. Serena Palmer."

"Well, that's a relief, I must say. Will her family be claiming the body?"

"Not before we have another doctor confirm your findings."

"Confirm—?" He shook his head. "I don't understand. The cause of death is straightforward."

"I expect you thought it would go to her grave with her. The venereal disease."

"I—" He moved slightly, away from the table. "I felt that her family would have enough sorrow without learning that."

"I'm not her family. I'm the investigating officer. How did you meet her?"

Allen didn't reply.

"It doesn't matter. I showed this photograph to the ticket agent at the railway station in Bath. He remembers selling her a ticket to Shrewsbury. And the ticket agent there remembers her as well. She'd been crying. He was worried about her, and kept an eye on her. He saw the man who finally arrived to collect her. He described you. You couldn't bring her back to the village. Instead you took her to the old bridge and there you killed her. You'd attended Mr. Simmons in his last hours. You knew he was to be buried the next morning. It was the perfect place to leave the body."

"No. None of this is true."

"I stopped at the ruined manor house. Miss Palmer had with her a purse and a hat and a valise. I found all of them where you'd stuffed them under the section of roof that had fallen in." He held up his driving gloves, filthy from shifting beams and years of windblown debris. "That didn't improve my mood."

"I was at a confinement that night. I could hardly have done what you're suggesting."

"In fact, you were late getting to Shrewsbury, because of the confinement. You kept Miss Palmer waiting, and the stationmaster can confirm that. How had she contacted you? A letter, telling you to meet her?" When Allen didn't answer, Rutledge said, "I have only to ask the postmistress what letters came in the post for you. What did you tell your wife about that night? That you were concerned about the mother? The baby you'd just delivered?"

There was the sound of the door opening behind them. A woman wearing a robe over her nightdress stepped in. She was small and dark-haired, not as pretty as Serena Palmer. "There's someone—oh. I didn't know—" She looked from one to the other, sensing the tension between the two men. "It's the Bailey child, my dear. He has croup."

Allen turned, quickly covering Serena Palmer with the sheet, then moving on to a cabinet against the far wall. He opened it and took out a powder, mixing that with water in a small vial. He shook the vial vigorously, capped it, and crossed the room to hand it to his wife. "Mrs. Bailey knows what to do. Give her husband this, and tell him I'll look in on Billy in the morning."

She took the vial, then looked closely at her husband. "Is everything all right?"

"Yes. Mr. Rutledge won't be long."

"I'll go back to bed then?" It was a question, not a statement.

"Do that. I'll be up soon."

She left, pulling the door shut after her.

Rutledge listened to her receding footsteps, her loose slippers tapping rhythmically as she walked down the passage.

"Is she infected?" he asked quietly, his gaze still on the door she'd closed.

"No. I've told her I've a pinched nerve in my back, and until it goes away, I must sleep in the guest room. Meanwhile I'm treating myself. It's not pleasant."

He would have to cure himself . . .

Allen moved quickly, with the speed of resolve. Hamish shouted something as Rutledge spun around to face him.

The doctor had picked up a scalpel from somewhere while his wife was distracting Rutledge, and now he was lunging forward, his right hand raised to strike, his eyes wide with determination.

Allen was aiming for the throat, but Rutledge leaped back. As he did, the sharp blade slashed downward with all the force of the doctor's shoulder behind it, and Rutledge felt it slice through his greatcoat and the clothes beneath, barely missing flesh. Ignoring everything but the flashing steel as Allen drew it back to slash again, Rutledge went on the attack, taking Allen off guard. He'd fought hand-to-hand in the trenches, and he waited until Allen's arm was fully extended, then caught it, and using the weight of his body, forced it up and back.

Rutledge shifted his grip, and before Allen could recover his balance, Rutledge twisted the arm in his grasp, ignoring Allen's empty left fist battering at his face and shoulder.

He thought the man was going to let the shoulder dislocate before he gave up, and then he cried out in pain and frustration. The scalpel clattered to the floor. Rutledge released the arm, and Allen bent double against the pain, his fingers wide and attempting to flex.

"Damn you, damn you!" he swore, his face taut with fury as he sank to his knees.

Rutledge said harshly, "Try that again, and it will be your neck I twist." Reaching down, he took the doctor under the other arm, pulled him unceremoniously to his feet, then pushed him toward the door.

"Don't touch me," Allen snapped, jerking away, massaging his right shoulder again.

With Rutledge behind him, he walked out of the surgery into the cold night air, and five minutes later he was locked in the cell at the rear of the police station.

"I'll be out of here tomorrow," he shouted as Rutledge turned away, ignoring him.

But he was not out by morning. Four days later, an inquest found sufficient evidence to charge Dr. Allen in the death of Serena Palmer.

Rutledge saw Mrs. Allen in the room where the inquest was held, the Rector beside her. She was struggling to keep her composure as she listened to the witnesses give their evidence.

But he noticed that not once did she look at her husband, even when he was being taken away.

I t was late when Rutledge reached London and drove on to his flat. His report could wait until the morning.

He'd made good time, and the rain had held off until he was in the outskirts of the city. Dashing from the motorcar to his door rather than look in the boot for his umbrella, he lit the lamp in the front room, then took off his damp hat and coat and carried them through to the kitchen, where he spread out the coat on the backs of two chairs. There had been no chance to have the torn wool mended, where the scalpel had cut through the cloth. That too could wait until morning. At least he didn't require mending as well, he told himself.

Standing there, he debated putting the kettle on to make a cup of tea, then decided he was too tired to wait for it.

He lit the lamp in his bedroom, and then went back to the sitting room to put out the one by the door.

The woman who came in twice a week to clean also brought in the post, and he saw that she'd left a telegram on the table by his chair, where he was sure to see it when he came home.

Frowning, he picked it up and after a moment's hesitation, opened it.

Unfolding the sheet inside, he saw that it began quite formally and was unusually long for a telegram.

Monsieur Rutledge, I am writing because your name was found
in the personal effects of Madame—

He stopped, standing there with the sheet in his hand while he
stared out the window at the rainy night.

He didn't want to know more. He couldn't bear to finish it.

Hamish said, "Ye must."

Personal effects . . .

"No."

He dropped the telegram on the table, went to the cabinet on the
far side of the room and opened it, taking out the decanter and pouring
himself a whisky. Standing there, he finished it.

Personal effects . . .

The words seemed to echo around the room, but he knew they were
only in his head.

"There's no turning back time. Ye opened it. Ye canna walk away
fra' it."

He was still standing there when the clock on the mantelpiece
struck one, the silvery chimes almost a benediction. How long had
it been? Five minutes? Fifteen? He had lost track of time, remembering.

Rousing himself, he crossed the room, took a deep breath, and
picked up the telegram once more.

—of Madame Channing. It is with great sadness that we inform
you that Madame died Friday last, and will be buried tomorrow
here in Belgium, next to her husband. There was a tragic
accident on the stairs. Her husband was unusually difficult that
afternoon and attacked the orderly. Another came to that one's
aid, but Monsieur had the strength of ten. Madame hurried
to calm him, but it was in vain. He lost his footing and they
fell together down the stairs. He was killed instantly, while she
lived three hours. There was nothing the doctor could do. Her

*last words were, My heart. If you wish her belongings to be sent
to England, please contact us. May God be with Madame and
Monsieur Channing. And with you.*

It was signed *Soeur Marie Andre,* and under that the name of the
convent that had taken in soldiers who were too damaged to be sent
home.

Among them had been an unidentified officer who lived in violent
darkness.

Meredith had been told her husband was missing, presumed dead,
but she had never given up hope of finding him. Even after she had
fallen in love with another man. And when her husband had finally
been identified, she had gone to him and chosen to stay with him and
help him recover. She had seen it as her duty. It was the sort of woman
she was.

And in the end, he'd died, and he'd taken her with him . . .

Rutledge read the telegram a second time, looking at the date.

It was too late to consider attending the funeral. It was already over.

He sat down in the nearest chair, staring at memory.

Jean had died, married to another man. And now Meredith.

It was much later when he remembered her last gift to him.

It was a small heart on a gold chain. A promise? He'd taken it as
that. He saw now that it was a farewell, that she had realized her husband would never recover. And she could never walk away and leave
him in the dark place where he spent most of his days. How much
of her strength came from love and how much from duty, he would
never know.

Till death do us part . . . She had promised that at the altar.

Had she also foreseen, somehow, that her husband's violence would
one day be turned against her?

There was no way of guessing.

She'd had a stillness about her. It was what had attracted him to
her in the beginning. It had been somehow comforting. A sign of the

peace he himself longed for. He had loved her for that. And for many other things as well. What he hadn't known, until too late, was that she also had infinite patience, waiting for news that might never come. She could not walk away.

Till death do us part . . .

He desperately wanted to curse her husband for taking her from him. And at the same time he knew he could not. The choice—and the courage—had been hers.

He would always love her for that too. Because she would have stood by *him* with the same courage.

It was almost dawn when he stood up and went out into the cold morning air, walking until the sun had risen and he was due at the Yard.

As so often since August of 1916, work would be his salvation. Whether it was being a competent officer to the men in his command or being a competent officer of the Yard.

However hard that might be.

5

He shaved and dressed with care, and drank a cup of tea to kill the whisky on his breath.

The telegram was still open on the table by his chair when he walked out the door and drove to Scotland Yard.

Chief Superintendent Markham was pleased with the conclusion of the inquiry into the death of Serena Palmer.

"A pity that she allowed herself to be taken in by him."

"We can't measure how persuasive he was," Rutledge replied, in her defense.

"Yes, I see that." He fiddled with a pen on the blotter. "How long will it take you to write your report?"

Rutledge took a deep breath. "This morning. I'd hope for a day or two of leave after that." He could visit her grave . . .

"Then I'll expect to see the report on my desk by noon."

Big Ben was just chiming the noon hour when Rutledge carried his report to the Chief Superintendent's office and handed it across the desk.

"Thank you, Rutledge." He opened the file and began to scan it.

He was turning to leave when Markham held up a hand. "There's another matter that needs your immediate attention."

"Sir?" He was about to add that he'd already asked permission to take a few days of leave. Still, if this matter didn't take very long, better to get it out of the way. Then go.

"Sit down, sit down," Markham said irritably, still scanning the report. Finally he said, "Yes, just as I thought," and closed the file. "Do you recall the inquiry that Chief Inspector Leslie was called upon to deal with in Avebury?"

"The body found near one of the standing stones? Yes." He braced himself. Markham, he thought, was about to draw parallels.

"It was never solved."

Rutledge waited.

"Leslie is busy with another inquiry, one in Yorkshire. Since you discovered who that unidentified woman in Shropshire was, the one found in a grave, I think you might be just the man to take over this business in Avebury."

"I don't believe they're in any way connected, sir," he began. "Dr. Allen had other liaisons, it's how he contracted syphilis. But there's the distance to consider. I don't think the victim in Avebury was one of those women."

"Nor do I, for that matter," Markham said sharply. "That's not the point I'm making. You showed some initiative in Shropshire. Got results. I want to see that again in Avebury. Gibson will bring the file to you. Study it, and then go there and bring back some answers. I'm counting on you."

It was hollow praise, the point of it being to bring pressure on Rutledge to finish what Leslie had begun, as well as leaving open all possible blame if he also failed.

"Surely it would be best for Leslie to finish his own inquiry. He saw the body, he saw the murder scene—he'll have the details memorized. And as you know," Rutledge went on with more enthusiasm than he actually felt, "not every detail makes it into a report. Intuition—"

But Markham wasn't listening. "I've made up my mind, Rutledge. There's nothing more to say. Except that I shall expect to hear of progress."

He set the Shropshire report aside, his mouth drawn in a tight line, and picked up another one.

Rutledge left.

So much, he thought grimly, for any possibility of leave. Belgium would have to wait.

Hamish said bluntly, "She wouldna' expect ye to come. She made her choice, ye ken. And it wasna' you."

He didn't want to accept it.

G ibson was busy, but a quarter of an hour later, he brought the Leslie file up to Rutledge's office.

"It's all here, sir. I don't quite know why Himself handed it on to you. Chief Inspector Leslie is a good man. If he couldn't solve it, with all respect, can you?"

"It seems I'm expected to," Rutledge replied grimly, and thanked Gibson before either of them said too much.

Markham be damned, he thought, waiting until Gibson had gone before collecting his hat and coat—and the file—and leaving the Yard.

No one seemed to take any notice.

R utledge read the file through twice.

Leslie had done his work well. The report was clear, concise, objective. Thorough.

Slowly turning the pages, Rutledge could follow the Chief Inspector's thinking. He himself would have done precisely what Leslie had done. Not always in the same order, possibly, reflecting the differences between the two men. But it was all there, every detail checked and rechecked. Nothing left undone.

A classic example of careful, conscientious police work.

He put the report aside. Resting his head against the back of the chair, he stared at the painting over the hearth. It was done by an artist he'd met in another inquiry, in fact his first after the war. It was a field of blood-red poppies blowing in a light wind, the sky a hazy summer blue. July . . . At first glance the painting was soothing, peaceful. Almost beautiful. Unless the viewer noticed the black soil in which they grew. The black, unspeakable earth of No Man's Land.

She had caught it perfectly.

Even though poppies didn't bloom in the summer.

Shutting it out of his mind, he thought back to the inquiry he himself had just finished. Brought to a successful conclusion, the killer in custody, the inquest held.

Still. If Dr. Allen had reported the syphilis when he conducted the autopsy, it would have been impossible to connect him to Serena Palmer's murder. Without Mrs. Branson's vague memory to guide him, he could have searched in vain for the man responsible.

So many times an inquiry rested on such a thin thread of fact. Did it apply here, in Avebury? According to Leslie, the manor house was closed for the winter. Why not leave the body in the walled garden? By the spring, it would have been little more than bones, even the time of death uncertain.

What was important about killing her at the standing stones?

Rutledge stood up, stretched, and went to pour himself a whisky.

Was there a Mrs. Branson somewhere in Avebury? Or a Mr. Branson, come to that?

Whoever had killed the woman there had covered his tracks very well, with every intention of getting away with murder. He had been clever, where Dr. Allen had been arrogant.

Sometimes the best way to find an elusive killer was to wait until he killed again or was careless. Certain he'd fooled the police once and could do it again. Yet he hadn't . . .

But what if this killer in Avebury didn't intend—didn't have a reason—to kill again?

That had been the conclusion at the end of Leslie's report.

I fear that whoever he is, he has done what he came here to do, and gone back to wherever he came from. And that will make him impossible to find.

Rutledge finished his whisky and put Leslie's report back in its folder.

There was nothing for it but to go to Avebury. Markham had made that clear enough. Whether he could find answers that Leslie had missed was debatable.

What he would have to do is put Leslie's careful work out of his head and approach the inquiry as if he were the first officer of the Yard sent to Avebury.

And keep an open mind.

As if reflecting his mood, the next day dawned gray and damp as Rutledge left London and its choking fog behind.

Ten miles beyond London, the fog shredded and vanished. Rain followed until he crossed into Wiltshire, but it was clearing by the time he'd reached Marlborough and decided not to continue. He preferred to arrive in daylight, as Leslie had done.

Avebury's great megalithic stone circle was old. In its day it must have been an impressive sight. And the people who had begun it hadn't lived to see what it would become, for it had taken centuries to complete. The sarsens, those great stone sentinels that had formed the avenues to the circle, and then the circle itself, had weathered with time, and the deep ditch that had been dug around the flat center on which the circle sat had filled in, its shape lost to vines and brambles and even saplings that had become trees. A village had even been built inside the circle, and fanatics had toppled the great stones to lessen their supposed power while avaricious men had thought nothing of splitting them into rubble to build barns and cottages. Less than a hundred still stood out of more than an estimated six hundred.

Excavations had tried to find answers to the questions of who had built the circle and what it had been used for. Work had been done as late as 1914, but the diggers had hardly learned any more about the men who had labored with deer antlers to create something beautiful on Marlborough Down than they had centuries before. But for anyone with imagination, it never failed to astonish.

This part of Wiltshire was cluttered with remains of a past so distant that it was lost in the shadows of time. There were even chalk horses cut into the hillsides—not like the graceful running horse at Uffington—but still impressive.

There were long barrows and round barrows and chambered tombs standing out in the flat land of the plain as Rutledge drove up along the Kennet Avenue. He recognized Silbury Hill and the Long Barrow, a man-made ridge. Once, he'd eaten his lunch on top of the Long Barrow and lost count of the sites he could see from there.

The causeway into Avebury over the ancient ditch was just ahead, and he slowed to pass between the two stones guarding the approach.

Hamish had not been happy from the moment they had begun to see the first Neolithic sites. His Covenanter soul had no time for these strange ancient places, and he had let Rutledge know how he felt.

Ignoring him as best he could, Rutledge slowed again to gaze at the stones still standing in the quadrant to his left. A sad few. He'd seen them before, once with his parents on an excursion and later on a walking tour that one summer. But they seemed fewer now, and in the gray of a winter morning, somehow desolate, as if they'd lost their way.

Sheep grazed among them, oblivious to their importance, and one ewe was scratching her back against the rough side of one megalith, moving rhythmically back and forth, some of her thick coat of wool catching there. Another ewe knelt by the edge of the ditch, craning her neck to feed on a patch of grass growing nearly out of reach below.

There had been cattle here, Rutledge remembered, when he'd walked through the village.

Which was the stone where the woman's body had been found? He couldn't be sure from Leslie's notes. And by now, any evidence had either been found straightaway or trampled into the grass. Any possibility of finding something that Leslie had missed was so remote he felt a wave of frustration. Rutledge had no illusions. Chief Superintendent Markham had sent him here expecting him to fail.

He drove on, and to his right could see the inn where Leslie had taken a room for the duration of the inquiry. It was just beyond where the road he was on ended at a junction, a T. Instead of going directly to the police station or to the inn to bespeak a room, Rutledge decided as early as it was that he would survey the village and familiarize himself with it again. He hadn't seen it with a policeman's eye when he'd passed through on his walking tour.

Taking the left-hand turn, he glimpsed the churchyard at the foot of the gentle slope ahead. The manor house, also in this direction, wouldn't be visible yet, for it was farther along the lane that passed by the church, its extensive gardens protected now from the winter. He could see how the ditch had been replaced along here by the building of the village.

On his left he was now parallel with the stones, and he could see them standing out against the murky sky, sentinels on a grassy, man-made plateau. Their size from this vantage point was deceptive.

Rutledge sat there for a moment, gazing at them, and then became aware of being watched.

Just past where the ditch ended prematurely was a house set back from the road. He could pick out the rooftop over a line of trees that concealed what was on the far side of the ditch. A man with white hair stood there, a hammer in his hand, staring toward Rutledge.

He'd been mending a section of the wooden fence that separated his property from the road. Waiting until Rutledge picked up speed a little and came abreast of him, he said, his expression speculative, "Looking for someone?"

Rutledge had hoped to arrive unnoticed in the village, to take his time and reconnoiter before announcing his presence. That, besides his weariness and a need for petrol, had decided him to stop the night in Marlborough and continue toward Avebury this morning.

So much for well-laid plans, he thought wryly.

He quickly revised his intentions. Reaching for the brake, he brought the motorcar to a halt by the man.

"Yes. The Constable."

"Constable Henderson has gone to visit his brother for a few days. He's been taken ill—the brother. I'm Dr. Mason. How can I help you?"

"Inspector Rutledge, Scotland Yard."

The doctor's expression was still wary. "The Chief Constable sent word that someone was coming to take over the inquiry. The inquest had left it at person or persons unknown."

Rutledge swore to himself. It was just like Chief Superintendent Markham to alert the Chief Constable that the Yard was sending another man to take Chief Inspector Leslie's place. It would have been better to let the new man follow his own instincts, and reopen the inquiry as he saw fit.

He said, nodding, "I've been sent to take a fresh look into the matter of the body found here recently. Yes."

"I'm not surprised Leslie couldn't find any answers. Whoever killed that poor woman left nothing behind." Dr. Mason took a packet of nails out of his pocket and dropped them into the pail at his feet. Dusting his hands, he said, "I can show you what there is to see. God knows I had enough opportunity to commit the lot to memory." Gesturing toward his fence, he added, "It's to keep the sheep out. My late wife didn't care for them eating her garden flowers. I've got into the habit of keeping up the good work."

He left the pail beside his gate, and without asking if this was agreeable with Rutledge or not, opened the door to the motorcar and stepped in.

"Do you know Leslie well?" he asked, turning to consider Rutledge again. As if weighing him up.

"Yes. We're friends." It was true enough, even though there was little social interaction outside Yard events. They'd dined together a time or two, but Leslie was married, and the married officers tended to club together. Rutledge began reversing, to drive back the way he'd come.

"Then I don't have to tell you he's thorough."

"I've seen his report. I agree with you." He stopped, waiting for Mason to tell him where to drive next. "I assume you saw the body. Do you think the woman was killed elsewhere or brought here to die?"

"Killed just there at the stone, I should think. That's where we found the bruised grass and the bloody ground. Then the body was dragged to the ditch, where it lay out of sight until we looked for it. Well, it makes sense, you know. We're some distance from the next village, and that's a long way to carry a dead body. They're heavier than most people expect. What's more, no one heard a cart or a motorcar that night. That would suggest the woman was still alive and either came here of her own free will or was under duress." He shook his head. "This is hardly the place for a romantic encounter. I can't really see how one could persuade a sweetheart to come all this way, just for a few stolen kisses. And the day and age when it was believed that the stones had some mystical properties is for the most part long past. Still, there are those who want to believe they have powers. I expect there will always be."

"Have you lived here long?" Rutledge asked, glancing at his passenger. Close to, he looked older than he had standing there by the fence. In his late sixties, perhaps?

"My wife was born in that house. Our house now. But I was in Bristol for most of my career. She persuaded me to retire and bring her back to Avebury. There's no other doctor here. He was killed in the war, and so people were happy enough for someone to take his place. Did you know, in the early days of the war, doctors stood in the trenches and fought like everyone else, doing what they could for the wounded meanwhile? The Army finally got clever enough to see what a waste that was, and stopped the practice. But of course you were in the war? I needn't tell you that."

"The Somme."

"Dear God, that was another waste of good men." He gestured up the road. "Drive on."

They passed the handful of shops on their right and a few houses on their left. One offered rooms for holidaymakers. When they reached the junction with the main road, Mason said, "Turn right here—back the way you must have come in. It's how most people arrive, unless they're calling at the manor house. That's closed just now." He paused as the bonnet of the motorcar pointed toward the causeway, then gestured to either side. "The land is flatter just along here, but it's actually like a stage, the level the builders designed for their stones, raised up to be seen from some distance. Must have been impressive too. My house, the church, the manor house—they were built centuries later, where part of the original circle and stage had been pulled down to make room for the village." Mason glanced toward Rutledge. "Do you know much about this circle? The stones themselves?"

"A little," he said.

"Well, it was quite vast, that original circle. Quite amazingly large, when you consider they had such primitive tools to create the surrounding ditch. No shovels or spades or picks. Just, we're told, deer antlers."

Intrigued, Rutledge let him chatter on. Mason was as different as night and day from Dr. Allen. And more intelligent as well. Was the man lonely, a widower with no one to talk to and eager to find a fresh audience? Or was he in his own way trying to manipulate the direction of the new inquiry?

Mason was pointing now. "The murder is confined to just one section—here, to our right, where the larger stones are still standing. Rather like a gap-tooth smile. Their size is even more impressive because the rest are missing. You get a better feel for the height and breadth of them. Right, we can stop just here."

They got down, and Dr. Mason tramped across the grass toward one of the larger stones. "Watch for sheep dung. Sometimes in summer, the cows also come here to graze."

Rutledge followed him to the stone he was pointing out. When they reached it, Mason put his hand on the rough, uneven surface, looking up to the top, well above his head and Rutledge's.

Like all the other remaining stones, this one was irregular in shape. And yes, larger up close than it and its brethren appeared to be at a distance.

He stepped back for a better look at this particular stone.

His first impression was of a tall, shrouded figure with head bowed, looming above him. It was so real, it took his breath away.

And startling, like something slipping out of the mists of time. Or something the French sculptor Rodin might have hacked out of a block of rough, dark granite and left unfinished. Yet all the more powerful because of that, the missing details supplied instead by the mind's eye.

And then as quickly as the resemblance had appeared, it faded. A stone, oddly shaped to be sure. But nothing more.

Mason, watching him, smiled, but said only, "You could dig them out of the surrounding chalk, these huge stones. They needn't be transported here like those blue monoliths at Stonehenge. The trick was in standing them upright. I'm told they packed rubble around them at the base, but whatever they did, these have stayed here until the 1700s. Men had to work at it to knock them down. And then they hammered them to bits, filling a line of ox carts, to be carried off to whatever new building site there was. A tragedy really. Someone's byre now holds the remnants of history."

Dropping down to one knee closer to the base, he added, "You can't see the blood now, of course. I should think she died with the first thrust of the knife. But whoever it was made certain of that, striking twice more before dragging her to the ditch." He gestured toward it, filled with the brown, dry debris of last summer and the bare trees growing there. "It must have been quite deep, when it was dug. And very wide. You'd hardly know it now." He walked on, stopping at the lip. "She was tumbled in, but didn't go far, caught up on that fallen tree just there. Pulled by the feet, her hair matted with earth and chalk and grass. Then rolled in." There was disgust in his voice.

"And she wasn't interfered with?"

"No. No attempt at rape. And no sign that she'd been bound, brought here against her will. Interestingly enough, I did discover she'd had a child some time ago. Years, that is, not months. I put her age at about twenty-eight."

That was surely what had appealed to Markham—three stab wounds, the body in the ditch, the closeness in age. The fact that neither woman could be identified.

"Any sign of venereal disease?"

"No, no, not at all." Mason sighed. "So why was she brought here, and who came with her, with murder on his mind? Yet she must have trusted him enough to travel this far in the dark with him. We have owls, and any sound she made might have sounded like one. No scream. Taken by surprise, very likely. My thought is a husband who wanted to be rid of her. But she was attractive, not plain."

Rutledge said, "And the child?"

"There you have me. Dead, perhaps? That might have been the problem, she was still mourning for it, and her husband tired of her tears and her unwillingness to sleep with him. And so he found comfort elsewhere."

"It's an interesting possibility. But surely if she lived in a village somewhere close by, she'd have been missed. He'd have to come up with a reason for her absence. She'd gone home to her parents. She'd run off with another man. Something believable that wouldn't arouse suspicion."

"Leslie considered that too, and he went to speak to the Constables in the nearer villages. But no one was missing, no one had left mysteriously without telling her friends or the Rector or the daily that she was planning to go away." Mason frowned. "Oddly enough, I didn't feel she was English."

Rutledge regarded him. "How so?"

"Her hair. It was silky, and very black. The old phrase *raven's wing* comes to mind. And her skin was slightly olive. Welsh? Mediterranean? There was a Greek fellow in medical school with me. Handsome man, the thickest head of hair I'd ever seen. But that's not quite it either." Mason shrugged. "I might be wrong. I've not traveled to Europe. And yet that was my view."

"What became of the body? It couldn't have been claimed."

"We couldn't identify her, however hard Constable Henderson and Leslie tried. We weren't even certain what her faith was." There was infinite sadness in his voice. "And so after the inquest we took up a subscription and buried her in the churchyard here. Chief Inspector Leslie contributed to it too. I think he took it badly that he couldn't name her or find her killer. A personal failure, as if he prided himself on his record. Well. I can show you her grave, if you like." He turned and walked back to the stone, putting his hand on it again. As if it were an old friend, and he was offering comfort. "We kept her silk scarf, in the event someone came looking for her and might recognize it. And we took her photograph, you know, when she was dressed by the undertaker. To show round the other villages and towns. All to no avail. Leslie took it with him. For the report, he said."

There was no photograph in Leslie's report. No mention of one.

"Where is the original negative now?"

"I thought Leslie kept that too. For that matter, no one has come to claim her so far. I expect no one ever will." Mason turned to look back at the ditch. "She was *discarded*, Rutledge. Like an old pair of shoes or a broken tool no one had any use for. That's abominable."

"What became of her clothing?"

"The Rector's wife cleaned and brushed them as best she could. And then the poor woman was buried in them. It was all she had."

"Anything of interest about them?"

"Not of the best quality, but not cheap either. I wouldn't classify her as a servant girl got into trouble by her employer. More like a young woman married to a man who was starting out in life. A clerk, perhaps. Or apprenticed to someone."

Rutledge said, "You've given this woman a great deal of thought." It was a statement, not a question. Mason had told him more than Leslie had put into the report.

Mason sighed. "She got under my skin. I'll be honest with you. I've dealt with a good many dead bodies in my time, and I'm not sentimental about them as a rule. A child still touches me. They seem so much smaller in death, frailer somehow. But this woman's fate was different from someone dying of illness or old age or the like. That's inevitable, Rutledge. *She* was killed before her time, and viciously. She must have known as she was forced back against the stone and the knife came out that she would die. I don't see how he could do it, to tell the truth. There was something about her. A fragility, if you like." He gestured to the sarsens and the circle they formed, taking in the ditch and the surroundings. "She's rather like this place. A mystery we can never hope to solve. An enigma. And so I can't get her out of my mind."

Rutledge's gaze sharpened. "How do you know she was forced up against that stone as she was stabbed?"

"We found some threads from the coat there. Just where they ought to be. Where she might have struggled briefly or was shoved back against the rough stone." He put his hand out to touch the place where he'd found the threads. "Her killer would have watched her face as she died. And still he finished the job. Two more wounds. You couldn't do that to someone you loved. Could you?"

"It would depend," Rutledge said, "on why she had to be killed."

After a moment, Dr. Mason turned away and began walking toward the motorcar.

Rutledge went back to the ditch, finally dropping down on his heels to look more closely at the fallen tree, some five feet below him. It was hardly larger than a sapling, but having brought down the undergrowth around it, forming a sort of matting, it had managed to catch the body. In time, the warming weather would cover the scene with new vines and brush, but now it looked much the same, except where the edge of the ditch had been scarred by the efforts to remove the victim. He could picture the woman lying there, crumpled, her clothing in disarray, a sleeve caught on one of the thinner limbs, her hair coming down and half covering her face.

It was easy to see why Dr. Mason had described her as "discarded."

Not far from where she'd lain, there was a battered pail, the bottom rusted through, and below that, he could see shards of glass from a bottle.

If the woman had had anything in her pockets, her killer had taken them, according to Leslie's report. But had there been anything over-looked in the darkness of the night, that might have fallen deeper into the ditch?

He studied the area carefully, inch by inch. But as far as he could tell, there was nothing to find. The killer must have seen to that.

He got to his feet, looking around him at the other stones and the gaps between them where their neighbors had once stood.

How had the killer and the victim got here?

Turning to his left, he could see how the land sloped to the road that passed the surgery, and several houses facing in this direction. They were some distance away from the stones, but closer than any other habitation, if one didn't count the doctor's house. Mason's roof was just visible over the trees on the far side of the ditch.

The report indicated that her boots, of soft leather, didn't show signs of walking great distances. In fact, they were well polished.

A motorcar, then? Not a horse and carriage, the wheels would have rattled over the ruts in the road. And according to Leslie, Constable Henderson had looked and found no tracks of horse or wheels on the quadrant of grass where these stones stood. On the road coming from the entrance there had been too many tracks to point to any one set. There was mention of the driver taking kegs to the inn. He and his horses would surely have covered over any sign that might have survived.

And if a carriage or motorcar had been left at the edge of the road—where his own motorcar was standing just now—anyone waking in the night and looking out a window might have spotted it. Surely the killer hadn't risked that? Motorcars weren't that prevalent here in the countryside. It would be remembered.

Giving it up for the moment, with a last glance at the ditch and then the great stone, he walked back to the motorcar, where Mason was leaning against a wing.

"It's rather late for lunch," the doctor said to him as he reached for the crank, "but I could do with a cup of tea. The inn over there does a fairly decent ale, if you'd rather have that."

Rutledge bent to turn the crank. "Yes, I'd as soon get out of this wind."

It was rising, dark clouds scudding across the already grim sky. There would be rain soon enough.

As he got into the motorcar and Mason swung his own door shut, Rutledge commented, "The question has always appeared to be, how did the woman get here. But what if she was already here? In someone's house. Or what if she'd appeared on someone's doorstep and had to be got rid of?"

"Leslie and Henderson and I talked about that. There's really no one in the village here who might have had such an unexpected caller in the middle of the night. What's more, in that event, who brought her here? She hadn't walked."

"Yes, I agree. If she'd hired someone to bring her here, the inquiries in the neighboring villages would have turned up her driver. If only to be sure he himself wasn't considered as a suspect."

"You're beginning to see why Leslie didn't get anywhere with the inquiry."

They went into the inn, sat down at a table near the window, and ordered tea.

"You seem to know a great deal about what Leslie was doing as he went about looking for evidence," Rutledge observed after they'd given their order.

Mason grinned. "I'm too old to have a paramour or even a daughter her age." The smile faded. "Leslie was rather shocked by what he saw. I could tell that. Well, so was I for that matter when first I saw her lying in the ditch like a broken doll. We got her out and took her to my surgery, where I could have a proper look at her. I didn't cut her open, I knew what had killed her. But I examined the body carefully for anything that might help us. No real defensive wounds, only a cut on one hand, possibly throwing it up at the last second. Or to fend off the pain. I don't think she was prepared for what happened. Leslie said something about that at the inquest. He was also telling me that since the war, he'd found it harder to view the dead. But as I reported what my examination had shown, he seemed to collect himself and was quite professional after that."

Rutledge had seen too many dead as well. This was an unusual inquiry, with the dead already buried. He realized he was grateful.

Mason was looking out the window at the smaller stones in the quadrant nearest the inn. "The fact is, I don't have much to occupy my time here in the village, my neighbors are a healthy lot for the most part, and quite frankly I was curious about the poor woman. Leslie interviewed every man in the village, but got nowhere. And he was frustrated, to say the least. No one saw or heard anything—no one recognized her—no one appeared to have a reason for bringing her here, much less murdering her." He turned back to Rutledge. "I know the people here rather well. God knows I've treated most of them for everything from broken bones to last breath. We don't see many murders here. And as far as I know this site never went in for human sacrifices, willing or unwilling. There isn't a history here that would attract the mad. No wild tales of orgies or mass murder. Still, someone might not know that, and believe such things. I was worried about that at the start, but there's been no other sign of ritual."

Their tea arrived.

"It's not like Leslie to give up. I don't think he was very happy about it," Rutledge said.

"Why did the Yard send you here? No disrespect, but if an experienced Chief Inspector hadn't got very far, a younger Inspector probably won't either."

"For my sins," Rutledge said. "Such as they are."

Mason nodded. "Well, then. Do you want to go over the same ground? Meanwhile I'll try to find out about that film negative I mentioned. We can speak to Rector about it. And I can see that you talk to anyone Leslie spoke to."

"That would be helpful. When is Henderson coming back?"

"That will depend on his brother's situation. Frankly, I don't hold out much hope, but that's not for anyone's ears other than yours. Renal failure."

"Forgive me, but I must ask. Henderson himself is above suspicion?"

"I'd trust him with my life. A good man. He's been Constable here for a good many years, and no breath of scandal touching him."

Thirty minutes later, they left the inn and began to make a circuit of the buildings closest to the quadrant of the circle where the woman's body had been found. They began with those on the far side of the road that crossed the causeway, then worked their way down the street past Mason's house.

By seven o'clock that evening, they'd found everyone Leslie had spoken to, or as Mason put it, the butcher, the baker, the candlestick maker. And the results were the same: no one had heard anything that night and no one had seen either a motorcar or carriage on the road coming in. Rutledge, well aware of the statements each man and woman had given at the time, listened carefully to each response. And he heard nothing that would make him doubt the speaker or sense that he or she was hiding something. People were naturally curious about the new man from London, but no one appeared to be particularly worried by his arrival. A good few wanted answers.

Dr. Mason was tiring from the walking and the introductions he'd made, a task that Constable Henderson would have carried out if he'd been available.

"We can dine at the inn. But where are you staying tonight?"

Rutledge had already given that some thought. "The inn, I expect. It's where Leslie stayed. Meanwhile, there's the house with the bay window. I'd like to speak to that woman again. Mrs. Parrish? She had the clearest view of the stones where the murder occurred."

Mason sighed. "Very well. I'll not tell you how to do your work. But Mary Parrish is nearsighted and couldn't have seen anything out there if it had been broad daylight. My old legs aren't eager to walk back that far. I'll find us a table, and tell Bryant that you'd like a room. It's not like they're full up with summer visitors."

Rutledge left the doctor and the motorcar at the inn and walked on to his destination.

Mrs. Parrish opened the door only a crack, peering out into the darkness to see who had knocked. When she realized it was the man from London, she smiled and opened it wider to allow him to step inside. "I didn't expect you again this evening," she said, gesturing to the front room, where he and the doctor had interviewed her earlier. She looked past him, as if expecting Dr. Mason to follow him.

"I've left the doctor at the inn. It's been a long day for him," Rutledge told her as he stepped inside.

"Yes, he's feeling his age this winter," she agreed, shutting the door and leading the way to the parlor. "There's a fire on the hearth. We can be comfortable in here."

The lamp was already lit, picking out the darker greens of the carpet and lighter shades in the curtains. He could see that Mary Parrish had set aside her knitting to answer the door.

She was sixty, he thought, her hair that soft white that blondes often have when the color had faded, and worried hazel eyes behind rimless spectacles watched him take the chair she'd offered.

"I've some biscuits left from my tea," she said, "if you'd care for some?"

"Thank you, no," Rutledge said, smiling. "It won't do to spoil my appetite. Dr. Mason is counting on dining at the inn."

"He does like their roast chicken," she agreed, "but mainly it's the company, I expect." She sighed. "I wouldn't mind going to the inn occasionally, but I don't care to be out after nightfall. Especially after what happened to that poor woman."

"And are you sure you neither heard nor saw anything that night?" he asked. He'd posed the same question at three o'clock that afternoon. He couldn't have said, really, why he'd come back here. Except for the view he had seen from the window as he'd sat there. The stones had been framed by the glass, enigmatic shapes in the distance. It was, as he'd discovered, the best view in the village.

"No," she said firmly, picking up her knitting and winding the gray yarn around the needles before setting it in the bag by her chair. Blue forget-me-nots were embroidered around the opening, and below them he could just see the initials *M F E P* embroidered in a matching blue thread.

"I don't think that's quite true," he replied gently, rapidly considering how best to approach her. "I think you did."

"Young man, I don't lie," she retorted, her gaze holding his, a slight flush on her face.

"I'm not sure that you lied. But I have a feeling you *are* afraid to admit that you did see something. You aren't sure who killed that woman, and you don't want him coming after you next."

She started to deny it vehemently, then stopped. "Guilty as charged," she went on tartly.

"Did you tell Chief Inspector Leslie the truth?"

"No. And it wouldn't have made any difference to his investigation."

"He should have been the one who decided that. Not you."

"No. I am the one at risk. It was my decision to make."

"Then tell *me*."

Mrs. Parrish glanced past him at the pretty green curtains, drawn now across the window. Leaning forward, she lowered her voice, as if fearful that someone might be listening.

"I daren't."

"If you don't, he will always be out there. Watching."

She glared at him. "That's a cruel thing to say to a woman living alone."

"I don't think he's within a hundred miles of Avebury now. He got away with murder, Mrs. Parrish. He's not coming back. It would be the height of foolishness to take such a risk, when he's completely clear. Unless you can put a name to him, he had nothing to fear from you."

"Of course I can't put a name to him. I'd have told Chief Inspector Leslie straightaway if I'd known who it was. It would have sent him to prison. I'd have been safe then."

He hadn't meant his remark literally, but she had taken it in that sense.

"We'll have no chance of stopping him if everyone keeps a small piece of the puzzle to himself, thinking that it won't matter all that much if the police aren't told. Hoping that somehow they'll find it out without his help. A very comforting way of avoiding doing one's duty in something as nasty as murder."

Her lips tightened. After a moment she snapped, "It's *not* a piece of the puzzle, as you put it."

"But how can you be the judge?" he asked quietly.

He thought he'd lost her, but then she started to speak again.

"I don't sleep very well, I haven't since my husband died. Sometimes I read at night, sometimes I knit until I'm ready to sleep. That night I came down to the kitchen to heat a little milk, to see if that would make me drowsy. I didn't bring a lamp down with me, I can find my way even in the dark. When I'd finished the milk, I went back up to my room and paused to look out my window. I often do, even when I don't wish to. Those stones have always made me a little uneasy, although my husband loved them. He was born here, you see, they had always been out there. He was used to them. For me they're—I don't quite know. But sometimes I've wondered if the builders who put them up all those centuries ago are ever drawn back to them. Or the dead from the barrows out on the plain. Not ghosts, you know. I don't believe in ghosts. But I found it hard to believe that they could bear to see what they'd built changed so much."

He listened patiently now, letting her get around in her own fashion to what had disturbed her.

Taking a deep breath, she continued. "I've never seen anything, not in all these years of looking. It was reassuring, in a way. My husband would have laughed at me, if he'd known."

Picking at the wool of her skirt, she said, "That night it began as a pinprick of light. I saw it coming from out there where the barrows are. Silbury Hill and the others. Just a pinprick." She looked away from him. "You'll call me a silly old woman. But I couldn't turn away, I felt as if I'd been turned to stone myself. And it grew larger. Ever larger, and it moved from the road to the grass, and across the grass to the stones. And then it went out. I dropped the curtain I'd been holding open, and went quickly back to my bed. And I stayed there until the sun was well up." She paused. "Later I heard the news. About the murder. I didn't know what to make of that when they told me where she was found."

"Did you know—afterward—what that light actually was?"

"No. I didn't want to know. I'd let that superstitious nonsense rule my thinking, and all the while a woman was being killed. Could I have stopped it? I don't see how. But the thought that I hadn't tried was horrifying to me." She shook her head, looking inward, not at Rutledge. "Still. At the same time, in the back of my mind, I couldn't rid myself of the possibility that she was a sacrifice against any further desecration of the stones. More nonsense, but I see the stones differently from anyone who was born here. They're strange, unsettling. They don't have such things in Kent, where I was born. How could I confess to feeling that? With Constable Henderson sitting there, big as life, hearing every word?" She shuddered. "The whole village would have learned about it, and they'd think I was out of my mind. Mad. A mad old woman. But I'm not."

"You have told me now."

"Yes, but you'd already guessed something. And my conscience wouldn't let me lie again." She smiled uneasily. "You think me a fool, don't you?"

"Was the pace of the light slow, as if someone was walking—leading a procession or the like?"

"No, it grew larger rather quickly. Faster than a man can walk. That's why I was so—so confused."

"And you didn't hear anything? The trotting of a horse? A motorcar?"

"In the first place there was only a single light. Hardly a motorcar. And as for a carriage, there was no sound. Not hoofbeats, nor the rumble of the wheels over the ruts. It was a quiet night, and sound carries. That's why I was so—so certain." She hesitated, then added, as if asking for forgiveness, "It wouldn't have changed anything. It wouldn't have told Chief Inspector Leslie who had done such a terrible thing."

"It could have told him how the killer had come here. And from which direction."

"I don't see how it possibly could do that," she countered, frowning. "You're just trying to make me feel guilty."

"The killer came from the direction of the Down. Not up from the church—nor down from the inn. Not even along the ancient avenue. And he was probably riding a bicycle. With a torch to help him find his way."

"But where was *she*, then? Was she already here? Waiting by the stone? I didn't see her bicycle. And he didn't leave it behind. How could he have taken both bicycles away with him? After—after what he'd done? That would be awkward, impossible. No, I don't see how." Her voice rose a little with her anxiety.

"It wouldn't have been awkward at all," Rutledge answered, thinking through it. "If they'd come together on the same one. Not if it was a tandem bicycle."

6

I haven't seen one of those since I was a girl in Kent. My uncle bought one, but my aunt refused to get on it. And so he took me up instead." Mrs. Parrish shook her head. "Where would such a thing have come from? Besides, the ground is so uneven here, no one rides for pleasure. What must it be like at night?"

"*Is* there one in Avebury?" he asked, struck by how adamant she was.

"I've lived here for forty-two years, and no one in the village has ever owned a tandem bicycle. I mean to say, where would you ride it, even if you bought one? Up and down the causeway road perhaps, but anywhere else the ground isn't smooth enough for a pleasant outing. Besides, they don't manage very well with only one person pedaling."

Hamish, speaking for the first time since Rutledge had come through Mrs. Parrish's door, said, "She doesna' want to believe it wasna' spirits."

Rutledge thought that Hamish might well be right. Frightened as she was of them, even though she'd called them nonsense, the light somehow justified all her fears, gave the spirits validity.

"That's just it, they didn't come from the village, did they? The two people on the bicycle. They would have to come from wherever it was kept."

She still wasn't convinced by the time he'd left. But he thought some of that was lingering guilt. If he was wrong about the bicycle, she needn't feel she had kept important information from the police. And oddly enough her defense of her fears had deepened them. If there had been a bicycle, then there had been interlopers. The body had proven that. And she had gone to bed, done nothing to prevent the killing. Because she was afraid.

"What will happen to me?" she asked as she followed him to the door. She was anxious again. "I'm still in danger. I shouldn't have told—but you made me feel so very awful."

"Did Chief Inspector Leslie interview you a second time?" That hadn't been in any of the notes. He'd have remembered. "Asking you anything more about that night?"

"He seemed satisfied with my statement," she said. "And I made rather a point of staying out of his way, since I couldn't help him."

Rutledge prepared to leave. "Thank you, Mrs. Parrish. I'll keep what you've told me in confidence. For the time being. That should keep you safe enough."

"Yes—yes, that's very kind of you." She nodded, eager now to shut the door behind him. Certain that the sooner he was gone, the safer she would be. "Good night, Inspector." He had barely crossed the threshold before she was closing the door and shoving the bolt home. Locking out the night.

Rutledge turned and looked across the field. There was hardly any light from the village houses, or even from the inn. The stones were ominous, undefined shapes. He could see why Mrs. Parrish feared them, having had to look out at them all her married life. No streetlamps like those in London to bring familiarity to the dark. And out of that darkness had come that single beam of light.

She wouldn't have seen it from her parlor. Or here by her door. Upstairs, at her bedroom window, however, it would be clearly visible, growing larger as it approached. And her husband hadn't been there to tell her it was nothing. She had had to cope with the sight on her own.

Satisfied, he walked down the path to the street and turned toward the inn.

When he got there, Dr. Mason was impatient to order, only asking if Mrs. Parrish had been helpful.

"Yes, she cleared up a question or two," Rutledge answered easily, reaching for the other menu. "She closes her curtains at night."

His room looked out on the back of the inn, and in the first light of morning when he got up and was dressing, he could see more stones. It pointed up how vast the circle was, just as Dr. Mason had said. He wondered as he shaved how many people in this village felt as Mrs. Parrish did about the megaliths. And told no one.

After his breakfast, he went out to the motorcar and drove through the village, looking toward the church and the manor house gardens before retracing his route and leaving by the causeway where he'd come in.

He spent the better part of the day exploring the nearest villages, the ones that Chief Inspector Leslie himself had called on. And then he went farther afield, from Winterbourne Monkton to Chiswell to East Kennett and nearly as far as Marlborough, stopping at the local police stations to inquire about a missing woman and to ask if anyone in the parish owned a tandem bicycle.

There were no fresh reports of missing women of any age. There was no new information at all. Conscientious men, village constables assured him that they would have passed it on to Henderson, if they had learned anything useful.

As for tandem bicycles, he was told about seven of them. Rutledge spent several hours tracking down each owner.

Two of them belonged to older couples who had used them in the early days of their courtship, but had relegated them to a shed after the first of their children was born. In each case he walked with the man of the house out to the shed. And in each case, they were still there, the seats a haven for mice and the chains rusted. A bicycle shop had another two on display inside, but not in the shop's windows.

"Not much call for them," the owner told Rutledge. "Not since the war. I've had this pair since 1915. Always had it in the back of my mind to give one of them a try, but my wife isn't enthusiastic."

In Winterbourne, the greengrocer's twin daughters owned a fifth, and Rutledge was shown it in the back passage of the shop, where it was kept.

"The girls are in Derby, visiting their grandmother."

"Has anyone, a friend perhaps, borrowed it recently?"

"No, they don't care to lend it out. The seats are adjusted for their height."

"Here, in this back passage, anyone might have access to it."

"I lock the rear door every evening when I close up the shop. I'd have known if it went missing."

"Do you know of any others?" He was nearly out of names.

"Can't say that I do. Long before the war there was a man and his wife who owned one. You'd see them come down the road now and again. Sometimes they'd stop at the tea shop before pedaling back home. In fact, that's where my twins got the notion of having a tandem. They used to run out to watch them when they were passing by. And once the couple stopped and let my girls have a ride. They were six, and wanted their own tandem straightaway. My wife put her foot down. Not till they were twelve, she said."

"Any idea where they lived? Was it nearby?"

"No, if I remember aright, they came from the neighborhood of Marlborough. I did hear that they'd died. We hadn't seen them for a while, and so I asked around. Miss Mott, at the tea shop, said she thought the house was left to cousins."

"Did you ever see the cousins ride this way?"

"No, never did."

"You don't recall the couple's name?"

"Blakely? No, that's not it. You might ask at the tea shop. Miss Mott's sister is still there."

Rutledge did, walking down to the small shop. The owner, calling from the kitchen, said, "Oh, you must mean the Nelsons. Such lovely people. Yes, they lived in Stokesbury. We went to her funeral, we felt we needed to go, you see, to support Mr. Nelson. And I'm glad we did, he died soon after her. Sad, really."

"Who owns the house now?"

"Um—it's been some time. I don't think I remember their names. Or perhaps it's Nelson as well. They were related. We met them at the funeral, and I'm glad they've kept the house. Mrs. Nelson was so fond on it. Of course I haven't been there since. Nor seen that charming bicycle."

Drying her hands on a towel, she came around from the back. She was older than her voice had sounded, perhaps mid-fifties.

"Could you tell me how to find the house? I'll be driving that way. Perhaps the owners kept the bicycle as well."

"It's been years—such a pretty house, the way the drive curves in by the steps, and of course the two urns. There were petunias in them that summer. You can't miss it. Down Courtney Street, I think it's called."

He thanked her and left. But her directions had been quite good, and he found the house on his own, without having to speak to the local Constable about it.

It was not as large as he'd expected. Still, it was a three-story Victorian, brick with stone trim, set behind a tall hedge. And a clutch of tall brick pseudo-Elizabethan chimney pots with decorative rims adorned the roof. The drive made a circle in front of the house, just as the tea shop owner had described, and there was a pair of stone urns on either side of the three shallow steps up to the door. There was nothing in them at this time of year, but they were deep enough to hold a handsome display.

He found himself thinking that the house must be quite attractive in summer.

He knocked at the door, but there was no answer. As he was leaving, the woman in the house across the street was standing in the walk to her own door, arms tightly crossed over her chest as she tried to ignore the cold wind.

"Looking for the family, are you?" she called to Rutledge. "They're in London at the moment."

"Are they indeed?" he answered. "Do they come down often? Recently?"

"I expect he did. I noticed a light one evening, but when I walked over the next morning, to ask if they were staying and needed anything, no one was at home. I haven't seen them since."

"When was this visit? Do you recall?"

But his questions were making her uneasy. "I can't say." She looked away, down the street.

"They own a tandem bicycle, I've been told. I was looking to buy it."

"I don't remember it. But then we've lived here only since the war. It could be out in one of the sheds, but I'd not go in search of it if I were you. Not if they're not at home. No one said anything about selling it."

"I wouldn't think of it," he said, smiling as he thanked her. But she waited there in the cold wind until he had driven away. She was still there as he turned the corner, as if she didn't trust him not to trespass.

The seventh and last tandem belonged to the Rector in the next village. When Rutledge stopped to ask about the bicycle, he found Mr. Steadman standing on the steps of the Rectory, admiring a patch of early daffodils that had a single bloom. He looked up as Rutledge drew up before the door, and smiled.

"Good afternoon. Are you looking for me, perhaps?" He gestured toward the gold trumpet of the small bloom nodding in the corner of the porch. "Spring is coming, whatever the calendar may say. I find it gives me hope to remember that." A slender man with white hair, he had an unexpectedly deep voice that must have rolled through the church when he spoke.

"I understand you own a tandem bicycle. I was looking to buy one."

"The chain is hopelessly broken, I'm afraid. It wouldn't do you much good. But there's a shop in Marlborough that might have one for sale. I'm so sorry you've come all this way for nothing."

"I just stopped in Stokesbury. They also have one, I'm told, but no one is at home. Use it often, do they? If not, perhaps he'd be willing to sell."

"I'm not that well acquainted with the present owners, but I did know their cousins. They often rode that bicycle, even into their fifties. On pleasant afternoons we'd play chess, Mr. Nelson and I, while our wives did a little marketing. And I'd often see them out and about on a fine day. She died first, and he followed soon after. They were that close. No children of course. I don't know when the present owners might be coming down. I'd offer to take a message, but I'm sure you'll have found what you're looking for elsewhere, long before they open the house again in the spring." It was a very courteous way of washing his hands of any duty.

"No, no message. But thank you for volunteering to pass it on." Something the Rector said caught Rutledge's attention. "They don't live here year-round?"

"I've heard they expect to retire there one day. It's a fine house, we've dined there many times when the Nelsons were alive."

"What is the present owner's name?"

"I must apologize there. I only met them at the funerals. Lovely couple, much younger than my wife and I." There was an undercurrent in his voice.

In other words, the new owners hadn't kept up the acquaintance. And the Rector—or his wife—had been disappointed about that.

He nodded his thanks and walked back to the motorcar.

All the known tandems had been tracked down. Some were in such a state of disrepair that they couldn't have been borrowed, and others were well accounted for, with the exception of the Nelsons'. And no one had said anything about a policeman inquiring about tandems recently. Rutledge had to assume that Leslie hadn't stumbled on the possibility of one having been used.

Hamish, who had been quiet most of the day, said, "Ye canna be certain of anything. There's only yon light to account for a tandem." He didn't add that Mrs. Parrish might after all be an untrustworthy witness, believing after she learned of the murder that she'd seen something in the circle.

As he turned back toward Avebury, Rutledge had to admit it did seem odd that the killer had risked such a bright light, when he'd been so very careful about every other detail. Still, it had been necessary to look into available tandems.

"And how far is it from here to yon stones? Four miles as the crow flies? Five? It's a great distance in the dark."

Late at night, on a bicycle . . . Familiar or unfamiliar territory? That made a huge difference.

Rutledge had walked some of that countryside. He wasn't sure he'd chance doing it again on a bicycle late at night.

But until he found evidence to support a different means of getting to Avebury, he intended to go on looking at tandems. There could be others no one remembered, rusting away in an old barn or shed, even a cellar. Somehow the killer could have known it was there.

It was the first hint that the killer might be familiar with the villages around Avebury. Not a stranger but a neighbor. Even a former neighbor with a long memory.

Mrs. Parrish had seen what she most dreaded to see. And so she had described it in the context of her fear. It was he who had leaped to the conclusion there was a tandem bicycle. Or—that the light was not as bright as she claimed it was.

Maybe—perhaps—possibly—could—might. Hopeful words, a far cry from any real evidence.

As he turned back toward Avebury, he swore.

Chief Superintendent Markham had known what he was doing

when he sent Rutledge to the stones. There was nothing here to find. Except for failure.

Rutledge pulled to the verge, angry enough to salvage what he could from this day's apparent defeat.

But *how*? Ten minutes later, he'd decided on the best way to do just that.

Reversing, he went back the way he'd come. The farthest away from Avebury was the tandem owned by a Mr. and Mrs. Blake.

They were in their sixties, a small, spry, good-natured pair with graying hair and, he thought, a little lonely with both their children away in London. They had been particularly helpful with his inquiry into the tandem bicycle, and he'd liked both of them.

Their cottage was on the outskirts of a village not far from Marlborough, and it was well kept inside and out. There were the dry sticks of hydrangeas by the steps and empty flower boxes at the windows, and the short path to the door was lined with round river stones that had been whitewashed, so that they could be clearly seen after dark.

When he tapped at their door for the second time, Mr. Blake opened it and smiled up at him. "Back again?"

Mrs. Blake's voice came from the passage behind him. "Bring him back, dear, I've just put the kettle on."

Rutledge followed her husband down the passage to the kitchen, where Mrs. Blake was setting out cups and saucers, before disappearing into the pantry for the milk jug.

"More questions about the tandem, Inspector?"

"Not precisely. I'd like to borrow it, if I may. Just for a few hours. Before I make any decisions."

"It's nearly dark. And I don't know that mine is in the best condition," Blake replied, frowning. "But we'll have a look all the same."

Rutledge drank his tea, talked to them about London—Mrs. Blake was surprised to learn he wasn't married—and the war.

"But you've got a sweetheart, haven't you?" she asked after a bit.

He had a sudden memory of Meredith Channing, sitting across from him in a hotel dining room, asking him to help her find her missing husband.

"Not at the moment," he said, managing a smile.

"Well, our daughter is married, but I'm sure she has any number of friends."

"Sadie, the poor man wants to choose his own wife," Blake said.

"Yes, but—" she began, turning to her husband.

"It's very kind of you, Mrs. Blake, but my sister is adept at introducing me to any number of her own friends."

Only partly mollified, she subsided, and her husband said, smothering a smile, "We'll have a look at that bicycle, then."

Rutledge thanked her for the tea and followed Blake out to the shed. The tandem was in better condition than had first appeared. Blake dug around in a box until he found a tin of oil and worked on the chains for a few minutes until he was satisfied that they were moving smoothly.

"There," he said, standing up and wiping his hands on a rag. "That should do well enough. Now let's have a look at the seats." He inspected them carefully. "The leather is a bit brittle, but it should do."

Rutledge hadn't told them why he was interested in tandems. He'd left the impression that he was possibly looking to buy one.

"There's one other thing," Rutledge said. "I need a large sack. Something that would be the weight of the second person. Otherwise, I'm not testing it properly."

"A sack won't do. It can't help with the pedaling. To test it properly, you need a person." He put the rag back where he'd found it. "You'll need clips to protect your trousers and something other than that heavy coat flapping about your ankles. I'll be back."

Rutledge was on the point of arguing when he realized that Blake was right. It would be impossible to manage an unconscious or drugged woman on a tandem bicycle. If nothing else, the erratic shifting of her weight would have made the machine unwieldy. So much for testing the viability of one.

Still, it was against his better judgment to use a civilian, and he wasn't sure Blake could stand up to the ride he was planning.

Blake had caught the sudden frown and grinned. "My heart is as sound as yours, if that's what's worrying you. And I've been retired for three years. I'd like to do something besides cutting wood for the hearth and planting flowers for my wife and writing letters of a Sunday afternoon to my son and daughter."

He came back a few minutes later with heavy jackets, knit caps, and the clips. "My son's jacket ought to fit you. And you'll need a cap as well. Blue or green?"

Laughing, Rutledge chose the blue.

"And where might we be going? I know this countryside. I ought to, I was born and brought up on a farm just north of here."

"I want to pedal to—let's say, Avebury," he said, after hesitating for a split second in which he thought that if Leslie had intended to test such a theory as this, he'd have run up against the same set of problems. Small wonder there was no mention of tandems in the report. It was a mad idea.

Still, looking at Blake, he saw that he was as wiry as a jockey, and must weigh hardly more than the dead woman.

The excited twinkle faded from Blake's eye. "It's that body found by the stone you're investigating. Scotland Yard, are you?"

"What?"

Blake tilted his head, watching the surprise that Rutledge couldn't stop from showing on his face. "When you came the first time, I guessed you must be a policeman. There was something in the way you observed things, and listened to what I had to say. And you didn't look or sound like someone from this part of Wiltshire. I thought then it might be about a stolen bicycle. But it's not, is it?"

"Would it matter if I'm looking into her death?" he asked defensively.

"Not matter, no. But I'd have a better understanding of what you're after. And why. Give me the lead here, and I'll take you to Avebury my way. I used to play there as a lad, when I should have been in school. I'll lash a torch below my handlebars. We'll need it on the Down."

Even if they had to turn around, midjourney, it would prove something, wouldn't it?

Rutledge reluctantly agreed, and they guided the bicycle out of the shed, shutting the door behind them. He looked at his watch before mounting. They set out, pedaling smoothly after they'd adjusted to each other's pace.

Blake chose back roads and farm lanes, rough terrain sometimes, but well within their ability on the tandem. They nearly came to grief once splashing through a muddy puddle, but sheer power got them through.

Before very long, they were on the Kennet approach to the stones, and Blake, hardly out of breath, said, "I used to try to imagine who had built this circle. There's the old legend that Merlin helped to build Stonehenge, but we never had wizards here."

"Let's stop at this point," Rutledge said. "I'd rather not be seen in the village."

They came to a halt, and Blake said, "That woman. The one killed here. What sort of tale was *she* told, to come this far on a tandem? It must have been urgent enough for her to agree."

And in the dark of night, where they wouldn't be seen. But he didn't add that aloud. Taking out his watch, he said, "An hour and twenty-five minutes. Twenty-six or -seven as far as the stone."

"Which stone was it?"

"The large one on the left quadrant as you cross the causeway. The one like a hooded figure."

"That one? A pity. I always et my lunch there, at the foot of that one. Funny you should have seen the likeness as well. I found it comforting. I wonder if she did." He shook his head. "What sort of man would choose this place to kill a woman?"

"That's what I hope to find out. All right, are you up to pedaling back?"

"I would be, after a pint at the pub."

"Not this one. I'd prefer to go where neither of us is known."

"I know just the place."

It was quite late when they reached the Blake cottage again. The stop at the pub had taken longer than expected, both men choosing to add a sandwich to their pint.

An anxious Mrs. Blake had put a lamp in the window and was watching for them. They took the bicycle around to the shed before going in the house proper, thoroughly wiping it down.

As they stepped into the kitchen, she said, "What took so long? It was only a trial run, you told me."

Blake didn't glance at Rutledge. "We got lost once, and stopped to chat with a farmer who was unhappy with us for crossing his land and scaring his cows. And Mr. Rutledge here couldn't make it back straightaway, so we stopped at Langley's pub for a quick pint. There was no way to let you know, love."

She took a deep breath. "It was you needed the pint, I'll be bound. I expect it wasn't only Langley's you stopped in. Don't scare me like that, Larry. It's not right. I thought you'd taken a bad fall, at your age."

Rutledge retrieved his hat and coat and thanked them again. Mrs. Blake didn't ask him to stay for supper, even though it had been cooking earlier as they had been preparing to set out.

It was a measure of her worry, he thought.

But he had a feeling that both he and Larry would feel the soreness in their calf muscles tomorrow after the unaccustomed use.

Driving back toward Avebury, Rutledge went back over his conversation with Larry Blake. The man had come to the conclusion that he himself had reached—what was so important that the victim had agreed to take a bicycle that distance in the dark? What was it in Ave-

bury that she wanted to reach so badly that it couldn't wait until morning? Or *who*?

Over a late supper at the inn, he gave the matter some serious
thought.

Interviewing the villagers earlier, he had put the usual questions
in such cases—questions much like those Chief Inspector Leslie had
asked before him.

Did you know this woman?

Have you seen or met her before, here in the village or elsewhere?

Do you know of anyone she might have come here to find or to meet?

*Did you see or hear anything unusual among the stones or on the
road over the causeway the night of the murder?*

*Can you account for your whereabouts the night the woman was
killed? Between ten in the evening and dawn? Can someone vouch for
you during that period?*

Did you leave Avebury at any time the day before the murder?

The responses that he'd been given echoed what Leslie had reported in the file.

Except of course for Mrs. Parrish, who had witnessed the light
moving toward the stones, and told no one.

Who else had failed to come forward when Leslie questioned them?
Or for that matter, when he himself covered the same ground?

Hamish said, "If ye go back wi' these same questions, ye ken ye'll
hear the same answers."

Rutledge quickly turned his head to see if anyone else had heard
the deep Scottish voice. But the four or five people still dining were
busy with their food and hadn't noticed anything amiss.

Very well, then, he asked himself, what questions ought I to be
asking?

By the time he'd risen from the table, he'd worked out a possible
solution.

The next morning Rutledge went to find Dr. Mason, who was
scrubbing potatoes for the pot.

He shrugged wryly. "I've learned to do many things that my wife once did for us," he said, leading Rutledge to the kitchen at the back of the house. "I'll put the kettle on, if you like."

"Actually I've just come for some advice. Who is the finest gossip in the village?"

Mason had picked up the brush again, and he turned to stare at Rutledge. "Are you interested in hearing rumors—or starting them?"

"I don't know. Both, possibly."

"That would be Mrs. Dunlop. Her husband was the shoemaker. She does for me and for the Rectory and for Mrs. Parrish. Several others. But not at the manor house. There's no one in residence just now, and they have their own staff. I daresay she knows one or two of *them*."

"Where can I find her?"

"She'll beat the carpets at Mrs. Parrish's this morning. Sure you won't stay for a cup?" he added wistfully, a lonely man with time on his hands.

"Later perhaps." He buttoned his coat. "Do I need an introduction?"

"I doubt it. She's probably already talked about you to everyone who will listen."

Rutledge smiled and went down the passage to the outer door.

He walked back up the road to the Parrish house. A woman with a kerchief over her hair and a floral-patterned apron over her dress was just sweeping the front steps, and she looked up as he started up the path to the door.

"Mrs. Dunlop?"

She nodded.

"I'd like to speak to you if I may?"

"I'm doing for Mrs. Parrish. She won't care for it if I spend my time speaking to you. I'll be off at four."

"I won't keep you very long."

She turned back to the door. "Come in, then. There's no one in the kitchen."

He followed her down the passage, thinking that he'd seen more kitchens in Avebury than front parlors. But this was her domain, and it was spotless. There was a large pot on the cooker, and it smelled like a stew.

"That's for Mrs. Parrish's dinner. She's fond of my cooking." She indicated a chair, but she herself remained standing.

"You know most of the people here in Avebury, I think?"

"I'm no gossip," she said, bristling.

"So I'm told," Rutledge said pleasantly. "But there are questions I must put to you, if I'm to find who killed the woman found by the stones. Helping the police in the course of their inquiries is not gossip."

But she continued to regard him warily.

"There are several possible reasons why the victim came to Avebury. She knew someone here. She was meeting someone here. Or she thought someone she wanted to meet might be here."

"Or she was lost," Mrs. Dunlop added.

"Or she was lost," Rutledge agreed, although he didn't believe that was what had brought her to this rather out-of-the-way village. "Did she know someone here? Or had she come to meet someone here?"

"That's not likely, not to my way of thinking. Most everyone seemed to be shocked by violent death on our doorstep. We've lived with these stones, we're used to them. But there are others who think the stones have powers."

"What sort of powers?"

"How am I to know?" she demanded tartly. "I'm a good Christian woman and go regular to services at St. James's."

"Something sinister—even evil?"

"There was a man found dead on one of the stones at Stonehenge. Not that long ago. It worried us, that killing. What if people like that came *here*?"

But he himself had been given that inquiry, and the death at Stonehenge had had nothing to do with the powers of the stones.

"A man with a secret might use that as a blind for ridding himself of a woman he no longer cared for. Or believed she could tell his wife what he'd been up to."

"He'd be stupid to kill her on his doorstep."

"Not if she'd surprised him by appearing without warning."

"He'd be better off taking her to one of the barrows and leaving her there. Besides, where did he meet her in the first place? It's not as if this is on the main road with people coming and going."

It was an interesting point.

"He could have met her in London. During the war."

Mrs. Dunlop shook her head. "We lost more men than we got back."

"She might not know that."

"It's two years since the war was over. Where has she been all this time?"

She was as good at questioning as any Constable at the Yard, he thought wryly, listening to her.

"Ill, perhaps? Uncertain where he was now? Not enough money to travel and search?"

Watching him in her turn, she said, "I saw the photograph. She wasn't a woman a man would forget easily."

Interested, Rutledge said, "How do you mean?"

"She wasn't a woman of the streets. She was respectable. And if she came all this way to find him, she wanted something. Needed something from him."

"And he killed her because he couldn't do as she asked?"

Mrs. Dunlop looked at him almost with pity, as if he knew nothing about women. "It could be his wife saw her first."

And that was a view of the murder no one else had considered. Both he and Leslie had questioned every man in Avebury, but they'd spoken to the wives of these men only to verify their husbands' statements.

"Who in this village is jealous enough that she'd kill to keep her husband away from the woman searching for him?"

"I could name you three or four who wouldn't like it. Only I don't see them doing murder, however much they might want to. My grandmother, now, she could have done it. She was a farmer's wife and could dress a pig or kill a chicken. Blood didn't bother her. I was afraid of her as a child." She stopped and looked at the ceiling above her head. "Mrs. Parrish is moving about upstairs. You'd best go."

"If not a wife, could there have been a widow, trying to protect her husband's good name from scandal? A soldier's wife who didn't want his memory tainted?"

"A widow would be more likely to laugh and send her packing. What could her man do for that woman, if he was in his grave?"

A woman living in Avebury wouldn't have needed a tandem bicycle.

"Is there a woman in Avebury whom either Chief Inspector Leslie or I have failed to speak to?" he insisted. "Someone like your grandmother?"

She was ushering him out of the kitchen as she replied, her attention on the movements upstairs. "Not since the war. The war changed everything."

He was about to thank her, but she shook her head to silence him, then shut the door quietly as soon as he was clear of the threshold.

R utledge went on to the inn, mulling over what Mrs. Dunlop had told him. Was she a great reader of the more sensational novels? Or was her imagination that lively?

All the same, her views on the women of Avebury made sense. He'd need to keep an open mind in spite of her denials.

Walking through the door to the inn, he found the barmaid polishing glasses. Smiling, asking for a cup of tea, he added, "Did you have any guests staying here the night the woman was murdered by the stone?"

He knew what the answer would be—Leslie had been there before him.

"Guests? Not that night, no. We're often empty in winter." Disappearing into the kitchen, she was back soon with a tray.

That made Avebury an attractive place to do murder. There would be no strangers wandering about, and on a cold night, the local people would likely be in their beds, asleep.

As he drank his tea sitting at the bar, he considered what that offered as a possibility.

What if the woman had been *told* that a person she was looking for—hoping to meet—was already here in Avebury and waiting for her? And then he'd arranged to meet her somewhere and bring her the rest of the way?

That opened up an entirely different line of questions.

A plausible excuse to get the victim to a place where neither of them were known, and she could be killed with impunity.

"It's not the best weather for coming here to see the stones, is it?" the young woman behind the bar was saying, putting the towel aside and leaning on her elbows, glad of someone to talk to. "We had three people here in early January, and they were caught out in bad weather. After that, only Chief Inspector Leslie before you. It's a good thing the people here like the food we serve, or the Bryants would have to shut down much of the winter."

He let her chatter, all the while his mind explored the new direction. Then the door opened, someone else came into the pub, and she moved on to greet him.

Hamish said, "She's no fra' this place, ye ken. Yon dead woman. No' fra' the villages close by. It would be easy to lie to her."

Rutledge stood and walked to the window, looking out across the road, beyond the grassy stretch to the standing stones. They appeared to be smaller at this distance. Less threatening. Or perhaps that was because so many had been pulled down. Most of them were misshapen, irregular now, worn by the wind and rain for several thousand years. Had they always been that way? Or had they been shaped alike at the start so that the circle appeared to be regular, perfect? Had that mattered to those ancient builders? He tried to imagine it that way.

It would have been impressive. Taller than any man-made stone structures those builders had ever seen. Powerful.

Given that this woman hadn't been local, she could be persuaded to see the stones up close, before moving on to the inn where—supposedly—her killer was staying.

It's an amazing stone circle. Wait until you see it. Best at night too, and we'll have to pass them on our way. After that, we'll rouse the Bryants and have something warm to drink, a fire in the room . . .

He paid for his tea, collected his hat and coat, and left the inn. After a moment's hesitation, he walked on as far as the stone where the woman had died.

In the gray light, it was surreal, a great figure whose shrouded head was bowed almost as if in sorrow, its arms about to reach out and offer shelter. The face veiled, unclear.

Rutledge shook himself. It was only a megalith.

But was that how the woman had been persuaded to cross the grass to reach the stone?

It's something you won't see anywhere else. My favorite stone. We'll walk the bicycle the rest of the way . . .

He could hear the man's voice in his ear. Cajoling, gently urging. A whisper.

A woman was more likely to trust someone she knew. More likely to pedal out into a dark, unfamiliar landscape filled with ancient tombs and monuments looming out of whatever ambient light was there.

And while she was looking up, trying to see what the voice was telling her about the stone rising above her head, the knife had come out. Had something warned her? A slight movement? Or had her killer softly spoken her name so that she turned, only to be shoved back against the rough stone as the knife went in?

It was fanciful, a reflection of his need to find answers, to take them back to London and throw them in Chief Superintendent Markham's face.

Sorry about the bicycle. The horse was out all day, they said I couldn't

borrow the carriage after all. So I brought this. Do you think you can
manage? Well, it will be an adventure of sorts. And it's not far. And who
will think to look for us here, in this godforsaken place?

That brought Rutledge up short. Was this an assignation, a
Miss Palmer tricked into thinking she was loved and would be safe?

This woman must have had a valise too. Toothbrush, brush and
comb, a change of clothes. She'd insist on it, to look her best. Not like a
Gypsy, windblown, her boots muddy. She'd have dressed well to meet
him, expecting a motorcar—a carriage at the very least. She hadn't
seemed to be the kind of woman used to rough living.

Everything she needed or might want would be in that valise. So
where was it now? What had her killer done with it?

Just the opposite, in fact, from the murder of Miss Palmer, who
had angrily come to confront Dr. Allen, forcing him to act. Whose
doorstep—metaphorically—had this unidentified victim turned up on?

And where, if not in Avebury?

Leslie hadn't had any better luck finding where the woman had
come from. Wales? The doctor had said she could have been Welsh.

Hamish said, "Ye found Miss Palmer."

But there was no Mrs. Branson in Avebury to point the way to Bath.

Rutledge turned and walked on, down the grassy slope to the road
in front of Mrs. Parrish's house.

He was nearly to Dr. Mason's surgery when the doctor came out the
door, waving his hand, his coat clutched in the other.

"Rutledge? I've found out. A photograph was left in the Rector's
charge, in the event anyone came later on to search for her."

"Was it, indeed? Thank you, Doctor." And he walked on, not waiting for Mason to catch him up. After a moment he heard the surgery
door close.

He hadn't intended to be rude, but this was something he himself
needed to do, alone.

He wanted to see the dead woman's photograph. She had been
different things to different people. Mason, more than a little fasci-

nated by her, had lived in a wider world than Avebury. And the daily, Mrs. Dunlop, who did for the upstanding women in the village, had called her *respectable*. A subscription had been taken up to bury her. It was a weathervane for which way public opinion was pointing. What would he read in her face? Something in between?

Using Leslie's final report to the Yard as his guide, he'd walked in Leslie's footsteps so far. It had had to be done, of course. He had had to eliminate the people or possible bits of evidence Leslie had eliminated. Or else make the same mistake Leslie might have made in overlooking a possible suspect. But the bicycle sighting was the one piece of the puzzle Leslie had never had, and in questioning local Constables about the tandems, there had been no indication that Leslie had even considered such a means of transport across the distance between Avebury and—where?

It widened the scope of the inquiry.

The bicycle hadn't materialized out of thin air. The killer must have known where to find one. He wouldn't have wasted precious time scouring the countryside for one while his intended victim waited impatiently.

One could travel long distances by motorcar. It could have been left on the approach to Avebury, well out of sight, and then killer and victim could have walked the rest of the way. Why hadn't they? Why use a bicycle at all?

He left it. It was more important to have a look at that photograph, now.

7

He found Mr. Marshall, the Rector, in the church. It was impressive, of Saxon origin with Norman changes. A wooden beam ceiling. And a rood screen that had been plastered over at the Reformation and only discovered in the last century. It gleamed in the dimness, the gold leaf catching the pale light as the apostles stared back at him. He had the fleeting thought that his godfather, the architect, should come and see it.

The Rector, a stout balding man, was just coming up the aisle and greeted him with a smile. "What do you think of our church?"

"It's quite interesting, isn't it? I'm glad I came inside."

"We're very proud of it," he said, looking around him. Then he turned back to Rutledge. "Looking for me, are you? More questions?"

Both Leslie and Rutledge had taken his statement along with those of the other men of the village. He had claimed he was in Chiswell at a meeting with other Rectors about fund-raising in the spring to pay for church repairs. Three churchwardens had been there as well. Constable Henderson had confirmed it in the course of the first inquiry.

Rutledge said, "When I spoke to you earlier, nothing was said about a photograph of the dead woman."

Surprised, the Rector said, "I'm sorry. It never occurred to me. This one was not for Yard use. Leslie had one for his report, and as you were taking over, I assumed you must have seen it. No, we kept one for the church records. If someone had ever come here looking for the poor woman, we had nothing but a description to give them. She was buried in her own clothing. My wife saw to it that these were properly cleaned and pressed. We did keep her pretty scarf in the hope someone might recognize it. My wife, who knows a bit about fashion, believed it was silk, possibly a gift." He shook his head. "So little, you see, to mark a life, and even silk doesn't last. The photograph was my wife's idea—she's in the habit of taking photographs of the floral arrangements for services and weddings. It helps the flower committee to have a record of what's been done, and it provides suggestions for the future. I must say, it's proven amazingly useful."

What had Mrs. Dunlop said? That the police had questioned the men, but not the women?

What was the dead woman to the Rector's wife, to have done so much for a stranger?

"Had she done this before? Made a photograph of a corpse?"

"Well, no. No, of course not. Several times during the war she's taken one of a bridal couple who asked her." He sighed. "For a few brides, it was all they had to remember their soldier husband by. The Army photograph had gone to the man's mother, you see. They were so young, all of them. I have kept them in my prayers."

Bringing him back to the present, Rutledge said, "I wasn't here when the body was discovered. Chief Inspector Leslie saw it, I didn't. It would have been helpful."

The sharpness in Rutledge's voice galvanized the Rector. "Um, well, yes, of course. I hadn't considered—I'll be happy to show it to you. Yes," he replied. "It's in my study at the Rectory. It was my impression that you were merely covering the same ground as the Chief Inspector . . ." His voice trailed off, his embarrassment evident.

Rutledge swallowed his impatience. Marshall wasn't to know there had been no photograph in the report. "Did you think your wife might have recognized the dead woman?" Rutledge asked.

"Recog—of course she didn't recognize her, Inspector. Dorothea is a caring woman who takes her role as my wife quite seriously." He was suddenly angry. "Are you possibly suggesting that *she* could do such a heinous thing and still calmly take a *photograph* of her handiwork?"

"I believe she was at home alone the night of the murder."

"Come with me and meet her. Ask her yourself."

Rutledge followed him out of the church and across the churchyard to the Rectory. They went in the side door, and it led to a passage. They could hear the clatter of dishes being washed and set out to dry as they followed it down to a door at the far end.

The woman pouring hot water from the kettle into the tin wash pan looked up.

"I know, I said I'd wait until you came—" She broke off, staring at the man behind her husband. "I wasn't expecting guests—"

She was as thin as her husband was stout, with a lined face and kind eyes. Looking at her, Rutledge couldn't imagine her using a knife on anyone. He thought she might be ill, and trying quietly to live with it.

"Inspector Rutledge, Dorothea. He's here about the photograph we took of that poor woman."

"Indeed?" She looked from one to the other, sensing the stiffness between her husband and the man from London. "Is anything wrong, my dear?"

"Not at all," Rutledge said pleasantly, stepping in before her husband could frame an answer. "I should like to borrow it. It would have been very helpful when I was asking the other villages if they'd seen her."

She picked up a cloth and began to dry her hands. "It wasn't taken for the police. It's for her family or whoever comes to ask about her."

"Yes, I do understand that. But the copy intended for the Yard appears to have gone missing. I've never seen it. And so I should like to borrow the other copy for a time. You must have the negative."

He could see that she was about to refuse.

"I don't think it's proper to show it to everyone and his cat. Anyone who might simply be curious about her. The dead are so—vulnerable. I can't help but feel she wouldn't like it."

"It's more important, I think, to find her killer than to worry about her dignity." He kept his voice calm, gentle.

She looked to her husband, silently asking him his opinion.

The Rector said, "I'm not happy about it either, my dear. But if he promises faithfully to take care of it and return it to us as soon as his business here is finished, then I feel we must give it to him."

"You can't put a name to her?" Rutledge asked her. "It would save so much time if you could."

She faced him, drawing herself up. "If I could name that poor young woman, I would have done so, the minute I saw her. I was taking her clothing back to Dr. Mason, so that she could be suitably dressed for the undertaker's. She wasn't my size, and no one else had anything that would fit. Nor did the doctor's late wife. I saw her then, and I thought it such a pity. She must have a mother somewhere—a father—someone to whom she was precious."

"It's to your credit that you thought about a photograph. I'll take very good care of it, I promise you. And see that it's returned."

She hesitated, and then nodded.

Her husband left to fetch it. His wife looked at Rutledge for a moment and then said, "I hope you find whoever killed her. I thought Chief Inspector Leslie might, because he seemed to feel much as I did, that she was a tragic victim. I think it troubled him that he'd failed. I had a feeling that he wasn't a man used to failure."

She was a perceptive woman, and he asked, "If you saw her, if you worked with her clothing, even photographed her, what could you tell me about her?"

She smiled wryly. "If he's to be successful in the living he's sent to take up, a Rector's wife has to understand people. Not judge them, mind you, but take them as they are and still know what they are. I noticed her shoes. She'd walked a great deal, and although she kept them polished, the soles told their own story. Her clothing was good. Neither cheap nor overly expensive. The sort of things I might buy for myself, and so there must have been money, but not a great deal of it. Still, they were proud, and careful with what they did have. One of her undergarments had been beautifully mended along one side." She shrugged slightly, as if a little self-conscious. "Perhaps that in itself doesn't tell you much. We all did without during the war. We had no choice. But it says something about her too. Her clothes were made for her by an excellent seamstress, and I wondered if perhaps they were French. Like the little scarf. The stitching was exquisite. I wondered perhaps if she was a refugee? We had a few of those staying with us during the war. Does that sound far-fetched?"

Not Welsh, then? It was a new bit of evidence, and Rutledge felt certain that the Rector's wife was not lying to him.

"Not at all. In fact, I find it very helpful. Did you tell Chief Inspector Leslie these things?"

"No. He saw her body, you see. And he didn't ask."

The Rector returned just then with an envelope in his hand, and after the briefest hesitation, he held it out to Rutledge. He accepted the envelope but didn't open it.

He thanked both of them, and the Rector saw him out. He said only, "Good day, Inspector."

Rutledge turned. "Has no one come to look for her grave? Even if he didn't speak to you about her?" It was necessary to be sure.

"How could anyone come here to look? Only her killer knows where she died."

The door swung closed, and Rutledge found himself alone on the path from the side door to the church. As he walked back to the churchyard gate, he had the feeling that he was being watched. But he didn't turn around. He was sure it was the Rector, already having second thoughts.

There was nowhere private where he could look at the photograph, except for the church, and he rather thought that the Rector wouldn't follow him there.

He stepped inside, out of the wind, and walked to where enough light was coming through one of the windows that he could see properly. After the briefest hesitation, he took out the photograph.

Rutledge couldn't have said afterward what he'd expected to see. But the woman had been described briefly in Leslie's report, and he'd heard Mason's comments on her appearance.

The photograph was quite clear. The Rector's wife had taken an excellent likeness. Even in death, there was something about her. Around her throat, the pretty scarf the Vicar's wife had kept aside was beautifully tucked into the collar of her walking dress. He could see the fleur-de-lis pattern.

The dark hair had been properly dressed in a becoming style, and against the white lining of the coffin, he could see how unusually black it was. Her face was oval, the dark lashes pointing up the paleness of her skin.

Listening to Dr. Mason and Mrs. Dunlop, he'd expected a great beauty.

Instead what he saw was something else, even in the repose of death.

She was attractive. Pretty, even. But it wasn't that.

He moved slightly, and as he did, the clouds opened and for a moment the sun broke through, casting the rich colors of the window above his head across his hand and the photograph he held. Dark blues and greens and blood-red. And it was there now in the shifting light and shadow that he saw it.

Mrs. Dunlop was right. This woman was a threat, but not in the usual sense. Not beauty that stirred a man's blood, turned his head, and made him do foolish things that he'd regret in the clear light of day.

Nor temptation of a different sort, raw and earthy and available. Not even the sort a man coveted because with her on his arm, other men envied him.

He could feel it himself. An urge to protect her—to stand between her and whatever it was that had hurt her. To take away the sadness that was there even now.

What had happened to this woman, long before she died in a stone circle at a murderer's hand?

A refugee? As the Rector's wife suggested?

He remembered something that Dr. Mason had said to him while describing what he'd learned while examining the body. *She'd had a child. Not recently. Some time ago.*

Why had he felt there was sadness in the still features? The loss of that child?

Whose child was it, come to that? Where was the father? Had he deserted her? Died? Or was he in England, and she had come to find him?

The sun faded behind the clouds again, and it was just a photograph in his hand, in the usual tones of black and white and gray. A dead face, the eyes closed, and eyes told so much.

After a while, he put the photograph safely away, and with a last glance at the rood screen, left the church.

A little girl was quietly playing outside one of the shops as he walked back up the slight incline to where he'd left his motorcar by the inn.

She was squatting by the shop door, with a small spoon and a chipped bowl, and she was earnestly scraping at the dust with the spoon and scooping up pebbles to put into the bowl.

She was three, perhaps four, with a knit cap and a coat a little too large for her. But what attracted his eye was what she was wearing around her neck, the string of beads drooping almost to the ground as she worked.

He stared at them. They were lapis, a particular shade of blue, and he had seen them somewhere before. Or something that reminded him of these.

Glancing in the shop window, he could see a young woman chatting with the shopkeeper.

It was safe enough in this village to leave the child alone outside.

He went down on one knee beside her and said after a moment, "You have a lot of pebbles in your bowl."

"Peas," she said firmly, correcting him.

"For your dinner?"

She nodded, continuing her scraping at the ground outside the shop.

"That's a rather pretty necklace you're wearing."

"My brother give it me." She looked up for the first time, and he could see that she was a pretty child with long-lashed blue eyes.

"Where is your brother?"

"In school."

"Did he buy the necklace for you?"

She shook her head vigorously. "It was in a tree."

"A tree?"

"He climbed down to get it."

Down. Not up.

"Did he indeed?" Rutledge said softly. "How long have you had it?"

She dropped the spoon and held up four little fingers. "I was that many old."

"Ah, your birthday?"

Nodding, she went back to digging.

The shop door opened, and the young woman stepped out. He put her age at thirty. "Hallo," she said, frowning to see the man from London talking with her daughter.

Rutledge stood up. "Peas for your dinner," he said, indicating the half-filled bowl.

She smiled. "I shall have to cook them."

He returned the smile. "She tells me she recently had a birthday."

"Yes, she turned four. And nearly made herself sick eating too much cake, poor love."

"The necklace was a birthday gift from her brother?"

"Well, he's only seven. He found it somewhere, and she took an instant liking to it. I persuaded him it was a perfect gift for her. It's a cheap string of beads, no harm done if she loses it."

As casually as he could, he asked, "I wonder where he found it?"

"He told me it was near the causeway. I expect a summer visitor lost it." She seemed to be certain the beads were worthless. "Last summer it was an earbob. Pretty little thing someone had lost. I asked around, but nobody claimed it. A piece of broken pottery before that, and a rusted horseshoe." She sighed. "He's always bringing something home. The clasp on the beads was broken, but I tied the ends together with a bit of string. Peggy doesn't seem to care."

"Peggy seems to think he found it in a tree."

Smiling, she said, "Yes, that's her brother for you. He'll make up a better story, if he can. But he always tells me the truth." In spite of the smile, he could see that she was becoming impatient. "You're the man from London? The Inspector?"

"That's right. May I look more closely at the strand? Will she mind?"

"Here, love," she said, putting down the sack she was carrying. "Can Mum see your beads?"

It took some persuading because Peggy had found a pebble she liked, and she wanted to show that to her mother instead. Finally, the woman got the strand off, pulling the child's hair a little and getting an angry pout in return.

"I don't know why you should be interested in them," the woman said, handing the beads to him.

They were graduated in size, the largest bead in the center of the string, the smallest at either side of the broken clasp. And they were undoubtedly lapis. What was left of the clasp was surely gold. The softness of the color couldn't be anything else.

"How long ago did he find these?" Rutledge asked.

"I don't know. Just before her birthday. Last Tuesday week?"

After the body had been found. After the inquest, when Leslie had left.

"I had to wash them. They were that muddy."

If they were found by the causeway, it was well away from the area nearest the stone that had been searched so thoroughly. A good forty or fifty yards?

There was nothing to connect these beads to the murder. He found himself asking, "May I keep these for the time being? I'll give you a receipt for them, of course. But I'd like to find out more about them."

"I don't see why. It can't have anything to do with the dead woman, can it? It wouldn't have matched anything she was wearing. I helped the Rector's wife clean her clothes."

"That was kind of you. But I must be thorough, you see. I need to show them to someone in London."

The woman was annoyed. "Peggy's not going to like it. It was a birthday gift."

Rutledge tried to think of a substitute that might please the child. "I'll send her another strand from London, if for some reason I can't return them. She prefers blue?"

"Lavender is her favorite color."

He didn't know where he was going to find lavender beads, but he agreed. "I'll do my best."

"Then go on, while she's busy. I'll have to tell her she lost them. She won't be happy." There was resignation in her face and voice. He thought that she wouldn't have given the beads up to anyone but a policeman.

"Thank you. Your name?"

"Mrs. Alastair Johnson. *Her* name is Peggy."

"Thank you, Mrs. Johnson." He walked on briskly, listening to the mother trying to persuade her daughter to give up on hunting for peas.

He had nearly reached the road that crossed the causeway and ended just before the inn when he heard a child's wail behind him.

With a grimace, he continued walking. He rather thought the Johnsons' dinner was not going to be a pleasant one.

But when he'd left the inn and was traveling back the way he'd come in the motorcar, he stopped and searched the area by the causeway for over an hour.

There was nothing left to find.

W hen he reached London, the first person he happened to meet, as he was starting down Oxford Street in search of a shop where he could buy lavender beads, was Kate Gordon.

"Hallo, Ian," she said, smiling up at him.

She was alone. And she was—Kate. Her usual self. The rumors that had spread about him just weeks ago hadn't reached her ears, or if they had, she hadn't taken them seriously.

This was a meeting he'd dreaded, for fear she'd turn away in disgust. But she hadn't. If anything, she appeared to be glad to see him.

He returned the smile. And then, taking a deep breath, he plunged into what had brought him to this part of the city. It would do no harm, surely? "Well met. I'm on an errand of mercy. I had to take a strand of beads away from a small child. They were evidence in an inquiry. I promised the mother I'd find something simple to replace them. Peggy likes the color lavender, it seems."

Kate frowned. "Unless you want something like amethyst, I can't offhand think of a lavender stone."

"She's four. Something bright and shiny will do."

Looking around her, Kate said, "I don't believe we'll find them here. A children's shop. That's the place to begin."

They walked on, searching for a children's shop, and eventually they discovered what they were looking for.

Rutledge was aware again how comfortable they were together.

Kate was describing an exhibit of paintings that she'd attended the day before, and he found himself talking about Avebury and the stones. But not about the dead woman.

In the children's shop, they discovered a string of small pearls, designed for a young child, but Kate shook her head. "I don't think that's suitable. They are real." Her eye was caught by the dolls, and she said, "Over there." But the prettiest doll was nearly as big as the child. "This one?" she asked, moving on to a small doll wearing a walking dress and a fashionable hat over blonde curls.

But Rutledge had noticed a boxed set of a tea service for four, with painted tin plates and cups and saucers, a teapot, sugar bowl, and cream pitcher. When he looked more closely, he saw that the set included small silverware in a shiny metal. The design was pretty, a blue background with white and blue flowers held together by a lacey ribbon.

"I think this would appeal to her more," he said, remembering the peas and the bowl.

"It's rather expensive for a toy," Kate said doubtfully. "Although I must say, I'd have adored it as a child. My set was china, and I expect it's still somewhere in the nursery with my own dolls."

Rutledge reached out and lifted the box from the shelf. "Peggy will be delighted."

"They do lovely wrapping paper in this shop," Kate said. "I saw the rolls of tissue on the counter over there."

He had the box wrapped in lavender paper and gave the woman the address in Avebury. "Can this be sent?" He'd seen a post office in the village.

"Yes, of course. That charge is extra," the clerk assured him.

After the arrangements had been made and he'd paid for the postage as well as the tea service, Rutledge realized that with this errand completed, he'd have no reason to take up more of Kate's time.

As they stepped out into the street again, he said, "I owe you for services rendered. Would you care for a real cup of tea?"

"Yes, I would. Shopping is thirsty business."

He offered her his arm, and she took it lightly. "I think there's a shop just around the corner. Or is it the next one after that?"

They found the tea shop, with lovely confections in the window and a display of teapots and cozies that were as colorful as they were elegant.

They were offered a table by the window, but Rutledge prudently took another by a display of lacey cloths and napkins. This was a part of town where someone who recognized Kate might mention seeing her there with him. The last thing he wanted was to cause trouble for her with her parents.

When their tea came, they were well into a discussion of books, although he had much less time for reading, and Kate appeared to be enjoying the exchange as much as he was.

And then the shop door opened, a pair of young women came in, and Kate stopped in midsentence. But while they kept looking her way, they didn't come over to the table to speak to Kate or to him.

The spell was broken, although Kate tried valiantly to keep it alive. When they finished their tea and left the shop, she thanked him for the afternoon, and went her way.

He didn't know who the two young women were, but it was clear that Kate did. He had offered to see her home, but she thanked him and refused, saying she had several more errands to attend to. Still, her smile was warm, and he took heart at that.

Rutledge watched her cross the street and walk on. He wanted to go after her and apologize, but he had nothing to apologize for. But the brightness had gone out of the day, clouds moving in, promising rain. He found a cab to take him to where he'd left his motorcar, and drove back to the chill of the empty flat.

That evening, after supper, he sat by the lamp in the front room, and looked first at the photograph and then at the lapis beads.

According to the doctor she hadn't been wearing any jewelry except for a ring. Or if she had, her killer had taken it.

Frances had enjoyed wearing jewelry and so had his mother. He had dealt with any number of cases where jewelry had been stolen or had been cataloged in the autopsy or looked into as a motive for murder. He was accustomed to dealing with various gemstones. And he had no doubt the beads were lapis. Real and fairly expensive because of the intense color, without impurities.

What's more, as he sat there looking at them, he realized that they were oddly familiar, these beads.

He got up, poured himself a whisky, and scoured his memory for any past connection with lapis. Not a case, he finally decided—his sister's strand was double—someone else, then. A dinner party? No. A retirement party.

He closed his eyes, trying to recapture the memory. November? One of the senior officers in the Home Office was retiring. There had been a dinner in his honor. A woman guest was dressed in a cream top with dark blue sleeves that matched her skirt—

His eyes flew open. He'd been seated just down the table from Brian Leslie and his wife, Sara. And she had been wearing a single strand, graduated, like these in his hand.

The woman next to him at the table said something about how becoming the beads were with her gown, and Sara had been pleased, smiling as she lifted her fingers to touch them. Her reply had been lost in the general conversation. But the comment had drawn attention to her, and she had blushed a little.

Those couldn't be the only strand of lapis beads in London.

But the image stayed with him, making him uncomfortable.

This was Leslie's inquiry before his . . .

He picked up the strand again, examining it carefully. He'd come to London to make the rounds of better-known jewelers, hoping that one of them might recognize the beads. Instead he'd spent the afternoon with Kate Gordon.

Hamish was saying in the back of his mind, "There are jewelers in every town in Britain. No' only in London."

And that was true.

Rutledge walked to the window and looked out at the street. A light rain was falling, the night cloudy and dark. Then he turned back to his chair, and there was the photograph, the face of a nameless woman staring back at him. Only, her eyes were closed in death. Would *she* have owned lapis beads?

Finishing the whisky, Rutledge turned out the lamp and went on to his bedroom, leaving the beads and photograph on the table beside his chair.

But his mind wouldn't let the matter go. Where had Leslie looked to uncover the identity of the woman? There was nothing in the report to indicate he'd gone to Wales or even to London to search for her. It was possible that he'd had so little luck he hadn't felt it worthwhile to include his efforts in that direction. For that matter, what had he himself done so far?

He undressed and got into bed. And the question nagged at him for several hours, keeping him from sleep.

B y morning, Rutledge had made his decision. Kate Gordon was the only person who knew he'd returned to London.

The Yard would assume he was still in Wiltshire.

He spent the day calling on jewelers, going first to those his mother or sister had done business with, and then to others as well known in the City.

On Oxford Street he found what he was after.

The older man behind the counter looked at the beads as Rutledge took them out of his pocket and smiled with pleasure, then frowned. "If I may?" he said, taking them from Rutledge and examining them more carefully.

"Are you here to offer these for sale?" he asked after a moment.

"No. I found them and am trying to locate their owner."

"Ah. An honest man. A pity the clasp is broken, but perhaps that's why they were lost. I know the owner. I shall be happy to return them to him. If there is a reward, who shall I say found them and brought them in?"

Rutledge said, "Could you tell me his name? I'd prefer to return them myself."

"I'm sorry. I don't give out the names of my clients."

"A pity," Rutledge replied. "But I haven't done business with you, and I would rather not leave them. They are safe with me. My name is Douglas. If you speak to the owner, you can tell him he will find me at Scotland Yard."

The jeweler opened his mouth to say something, thought better of it, and nodded. "I shall be happy to pass your message on to him."

Rutledge turned and left the shop. He couldn't blame the man. But by the same token, he hadn't wished to give his own name. There was no one called Douglas at the Yard. But he was nearly sure that the jeweler had been about to tell him that the owner of the necklace could also be found at the Yard.

Unsettled, Rutledge went back to his flat for his valise, then left the city, intending to drive back to Avebury. Instead, he found himself traveling north, toward Yorkshire, where Leslie had been sent to look into a murder in a village not far from York itself.

Stopping one night on the road, he reached Denby by two o'clock the next day.

The village market, he discovered, was already in full swing, the streets crowded with people and stalls, and nowhere to leave his motorcar. He threaded his way past a group of men watching a farmer examine a bay mare for sale, then stopped to let a crocodile of schoolchildren cross in front of him. He finally found a spot near the ironmonger's shop where he could safely stop.

The stalls and tents were busy, and a magician in black evening dress was entertaining a group of admiring young women next to a stall selling hot pork pies.

Rutledge watched the ebb and flow of people for several minutes.

And then a middle-aged Constable strolled past, speaking to a stall owner here and nodding to another there.

Moving on, Rutledge looked into the Denby Arms, stopped at a tea shop called The Cozy Corner, and a pub, whose sign, The Golden Boar, had recently been repainted. It was the badge of Richard III, who had been quite popular in Yorkshire.

But there was no sign of Leslie.

"Ye passed him on his way to London," Hamish said.

That was possible, of course. But Rutledge didn't think it was likely.

He made another circuit of the stalls, and turned to look when a flurry of movement marked a motorcar making its slow way through the throng of people. Leslie was driving, another man beside him, while a third sat in the rear seat.

He pulled over next to the police station, and the two men got the third out of the rear and led him toward the door. As they paused to open it, Rutledge got a brief glimpse of the third man's bloody face. Someone had given him a severe beating.

Rutledge stepped quickly out of sight, went back to The Golden Boar, and sat down at a table by the window.

"We're closed," the man behind the bar told him.

"I'm waiting for a friend," Rutledge said.

The barman looked him over and decided not to press him to leave. It was only a quarter of an hour before opening.

But it was another two hours before Rutledge saw a grim-faced Leslie pass his window. He got up, caught up his hat and coat, pushed his way through the now busy pub, and went out to follow him.

Leslie kept up a brisk pace, passing through the crowded street without paying attention to the market-goers. He didn't stop until he had reached the quiet of the churchyard, put a hand on the gate, shoving it open, and going through to stand out of the wind in the protection of a large yew.

Rutledge had dropped back, giving him a few minutes before passing through the gate himself. It creaked loudly, and Leslie turned quickly, defensively.

His expression changed to surprise when he saw Rutledge.

"What, did Markham send you to press me to make an arrest?"

"No. I haven't seen him. What happened to your prisoner?"

"It's a nasty business here. Two young women have disappeared, and feelings are running high. That was an ex-soldier, looking for work. A stranger. He was set upon and beaten because he roughly fit the description of the man we're looking for. But he's what he says he is, and he can prove it."

"Lucky for him."

"Yes." Leslie reached up and with both hands pressed against his eyes said in a muffled voice, "I wish to God he *had* been my man." Dropping his hands to his sides again, he added, "It's going to get worse before it gets better."

"I'd have a look at that magician next to the pie seller. He attracts young women."

"I've had my eye on him. He travels from market day to market day. But there's not a shred of evidence that would allow me to bring him in. Not yet. Interesting that you saw something there as well." He frowned. "What *are* you doing here?"

"Passing through, as a matter of fact. Gibson said you were here." He reached into his pocket and pulled out the strand of blue beads. They dangled, dark blue and very pretty, from the fingers of his gloved hand.

Leslie's eye widened. "Good God. What—are those my wife's beads? No, they can't be. Do they belong to one of my victims here? Where did you find them?"

"In Wiltshire. Avebury."

"What the hell were you doing there?" he asked blankly. "No, don't tell me there's been another murder at the stones. The doctor was worried about that."

"Markham sent me there to take another look into your inquiry. To see if new eyes could find what you hadn't."

Leslie stiffened. "I knew he wasn't happy with the inquest. Neither was I. But he accepted the results." He regarded Rutledge, as if too much of a gentleman to mention the obvious: how could an Inspector succeed where a Chief Inspector had not.

Rutledge looked up at the church tower where rooks were squabbling. "I rather think he was expecting me to come to the same conclusions. Only in my case there were personal reasons for his wanting that." His gaze came back to Leslie. "Still, it's a hopeless inquiry to start with. I don't think the Chief Superintendent himself could have solved it."

Leslie's eyes dropped to the beads. "You say you found these there? I don't understand."

"A little girl of four was wearing them. Her brother had discovered them in mud by the causeway. No one knew what they were. Just—beads. I remembered seeing your wife wear something very like these."

Leslie reached out and took them from Rutledge's gloved hand, looking at the strand, examining it carefully.

"Yes, these could be hers. I don't quite know what this is." He fiddled with the string where Mrs. Johnson had tied the broken ends together. "I was leaving for Avebury, and my wife asked me to take her lapis beads to the jeweler's shop on my way to the railway station. The clasp needed mending, and I could pick them up when I got back to town. Only when I walked into the shop, I didn't have them. There was no time to go back to the house, the train was due in twenty minutes. I put them out of my mind, went on to Avebury. To be honest, I hadn't got around to telling her I couldn't find them. They must have been in my other clothes, in my valise. I kept hoping they would turn up at home." He looked up, smiling ruefully at Rutledge. "If these are hers, you've probably saved my marriage. They're her favorite beads." The smile faded. "I've looked in my motorcar, all over the house—it never

occurred to me they might have fallen out in Wiltshire of all places."
His voice trailed off, then he shook his head again. "I'm grateful."

A silence fell.

Rutledge said, "I've read your report on Avebury. So far I can't put
a name to the dead woman. How did you fare, searching for her? No
use going over the same ground. Not that I've got any better ideas." He
kept his voice light, not pressing.

"I never got very far." He sighed. "There was nothing to point me
toward her past. The Chief Constable put out a description to his
counterparts in neighboring counties, asking for help, and that didn't
bring in any leads either. No one recalled her, she hadn't gone missing,
no one was searching for her. A blank, Rutledge. As if she didn't exist.
Meanwhile, Markham was pressing for results, as usual. I called for an
inquest, but there was only one verdict it could bring in. I didn't like
it, but I had the feeling that if I stayed in Avebury for another fortnight,
and another after that, the verdict wouldn't change. I was angry about
that, but as I was leaving, Dr. Mason told me that if he'd killed once,
he'd kill again, and we'd have him then. Cold comfort for his next
victim!" He considered Rutledge for a moment, his eyes shadowed
by his hat. He was still holding the string of beads in his right hand.
"You mentioned something about a personal reason for Markham
sending you to Avebury?"

Rutledge said only, "It was because of another inquiry entirely. An
unidentified woman was killed and left in an open grave—not hers, it
was dug for a man who had just died in that village. I found her killer.
For some reason Markham felt that there was a similarity in the deaths
and the way the bodies were discovered. He thought I could find
answers in Avebury too. If I didn't, nothing lost."

Except, of course, Markham's confidence in him.

"But there's no connection?"

"Dr. Allen might have killed before, but he couldn't have been responsible for Avebury. He was in Bath at the time of that murder. Having an affair with a young schoolmistress. We examined his appointment

book after we took him into custody. He was supposed to be conferring with a colleague, but the dates coincided with what her cousin could tell us about the victim's evenings with a new friend she'd met at a concert. The cousin thought it was a woman."

"Well. I can only wish you better luck than I had. I hope Dr. Mason is wrong about his killing again, but our murderer brought a knife with him to Avebury. He knew he might use it." He dropped the beads into his greatcoat pocket. "Do you mind if I keep these?"

Rutledge was on the point of objecting. *Were* they evidence? But he'd seen Mrs. Leslie wearing just such a strand. If he turned them in with his report, Leslie would have to apply for their return. It could take years—and if he, Rutledge, also failed to bring someone to trial, they might never be released.

Hamish was saying, "Yon jeweler recognized them."

Leslie was adding ruefully, "I'll give them back, of course, if I'm wrong about them. The jeweler will know. And he can mend the clasp while he's about it."

"I'll hold you to that."

There was another silence.

Then Rutledge thanked him, adding, "I must be on my way. I hope you find your man." He turned to walk back to his motorcar, leaving Leslie there in the shadows of the yew.

Hamish said, "It was no' a verra guid idea to come here. Ye accomplished nothing."

It was too late to second-guess his decision now. And he was beginning to think that Avebury had never held the answer to the victim's murder. It had been the place, nothing more.

He closed the churchyard gate and turned toward the hum of people in the market square.

Passing a pair of men already the worse for drink, Rutledge threaded his way through the cluster of market-goers waiting for tables in the pub. One of the stall owners was loudly hawking his wares, while several others were taking advantage of the lull to eat boxed lunches they'd brought with them.

"He didna' ask you how long you'd be staying here," Hamish commented.

No, Rutledge answered silently. Usually he would have done.

They would have adjourned to The Golden Boar, and talked or dined together.

Giving Leslie the benefit of the doubt, Rutledge added, "It's a measure of his worry about what's happening here."

The magician was still there, talking to a pretty young woman wearing a dark blue coat. She was looking up at him with a shy smile. He was dark, attractive, and far more sophisticated than his audience. Rutledge crossed the street, walked up to the man and woman, and asked where he could find the post office. The magician looked blank, but the woman politely pointed in the direction he should go. Rutledge thanked her and went on his way.

But when he looked back before stepping into the post office, she had also walked on, the spell the man had cast broken. The magician was standing there, staring after her as he blew on his hands. Then he walked off, disappearing behind a line of makeshift stalls.

Satisfied, Rutledge went on to where he'd left his motorcar. He wasn't convinced that the magician was the killer Leslie was hunting, but the man was Trouble. There was something decidedly off about him, and the way young women looked at him was what also made Leslie's killer successful, that Pied Piper charm.

Not his inquiry, of course.

He drove out of Denby and turned south. He kept seeing Leslie drop the lapis beads into his pocket.

It could have happened the way Leslie had said. He told himself that several times.

The necklace falling out of his pocket as he was bent over, scanning for evidence. Or perhaps he reached for his gloves, having forgotten the beads were there, and the broken clasp caught somehow and they were pulled out.

Leslie was a Chief Inspector at Scotland Yard.

Then why had he, Rutledge, driven this long way to Yorkshire?

He concentrated on the road ahead, ignoring Hamish in the back of his mind.

Once he found the dead woman's name, he would ask her family if she had owned lapis beads. But on the whole he still believed they weren't hers. The killer would have made a point to take any distinctive jewelry she might have been wearing. It could have led to identifying her, and while struggling to manage the bicycle alone, he could well have lost them. And yet the man in the London shop had recognized them, after all.

"Ye ken," Hamish said, "it doesna' matter. You've just given evidence away. Ye had better hope it was Mrs. Leslie's beads."

8

Driving south from York with every intention of going on to Wiltshire, Rutledge changed his mind again. He had put off what he had known for some time he would eventually have to do. But he had no other choice now.

It went against the grain to ask this particular man for his help.

He could of course go on to Wiltshire and drive around the county showing the photograph of the dead woman to every Constable he could find. Make work, not progress. Before very long, Markham would be asking for a report, and there would be nothing to give him.

He reached London very early in the morning and stopped at his flat long enough to shave and change. And then at nine o'clock he drove the short distance to Chelsea.

Haldane lived in a house not far from the one Meredith Channing had occupied when Rutledge had first met her. Several streets over, but close enough to evoke memories.

Rutledge had met Haldane while interviewing residents of the street after a motorcar crash that had ended in a death. The initial investigation had rapidly expanded into a full-scale murder inquiry.

Haldane was an enigma. Then and now.

His credentials claimed he was in the Foot Police, the division that was in charge of Army discipline and crimes. But that was surely nothing more than a cover. For what, Rutledge hadn't discovered, but he'd have wagered his life it was Military Intelligence. The man's quiet manner and quick mind would have been wasted on finding other ranks away without leave or wanted for starting a fight in a pub. What's more, his contacts went beyond anything the Yard could draw on.

He disliked being beholden to this man, but sometimes his resources were the only certain way of gaining information that Sergeant Gibson couldn't uncover.

The man who acted as servant to Haldane—and kept the door—informed Rutledge that he was in. Ten minutes later, Haldane walked into the study where Rutledge had been waiting.

Haldane nodded. "Good morning."

"Good morning. I have a photograph I should like to have you look at for me."

Rutledge handed him the envelope. Haldane considered Rutledge for a moment, then he took out what it held.

He looked at the photograph intently. "She's dead."

"Yes. She was when she was discovered. No identification, nothing to tell us who she was or where she'd come from."

"May I keep this?"

"I promised the Rector it would be returned to him. In the event her family comes looking for her. A final identification of the dead woman."

Haldane looked up. "They won't be coming."

"What? Do you know her?" Even Haldane couldn't be that good.

He shook his head. "She's European, I think. Possibly Armenian. How she got to England I don't know. Or why she should wish to come here. Still. Who in Europe would know to look for her here? Perhaps that's what made her choose this country. Or perhaps she knew someone who could protect her. The Continent is awash with displaced persons. Refugees from the war, from political upheavals. People looking to settle old scores. Some of them are in danger, others are looking for peace. Some are even dangerous." Haldane hesitated. "A long way to travel to meet Death. Where was she found? London?"

"Avebury."

For the first time since Rutledge had known him, Haldane registered surprise.

"*Avebury?*" he repeated, looking again at the photograph.

"She was found in the ditch surrounding the megaliths. But she'd been killed by one of the stones. The one that resembles a hooded figure."

"Yes," Haldane said slowly. "I know which one. Of all the standing stones I've ever seen, it is the most—puzzling. One doesn't easily forget it." After a moment, he added almost to himself, "I wonder if that's why she was killed there."

"I don't follow?" Rutledge replied.

"As I said, one doesn't easily forget that stone. Don't you see? If you were looking to kill someone, casting about for a way to do it without being caught, the best plan would be to confuse the issue, so that the police are chasing shadows, not the truth. No offense, but there you are."

Dr. Allen had done just that. He'd put his victim into a grave dug for someone else, confusing the issue of who she was and where she'd come from, shock and mystery surrounding her death. He'd counted on that, to allow him to take charge of the body, and manipulate any evidence he didn't wish to come out. But who in Avebury fit the role of Dr. Allen?

Or was not there now to be questioned?

Constable Henderson?

"Is there any way to identify this woman? Or discover who it is she might have come to England to find?"

Haldane considered him. "If one's papers appear to be in order, he or she is admitted to the country. Even if by a stroke of extraordinary luck you find her papers, the name on them may or may not be

hers. Something you must take into account is that there are millions
dead. No one bothered to keep records of all of them. Their identity
shrouded in secrecy. She could claim to be one of them. Who in this
country would know if a woman purporting to be Italian was actually
speaking Italian or some other language? The average Englishman seldom knows any other tongue but his own." His voice was bleak. "It's
the proverbial needle in a haystack, only in searching through the hay,
one knows one is looking for a *needle*."

"I didn't think it was possible. I'd hoped it might be."

Returning the photograph to the envelope, Haldane said, "What is
it that's written above the gates to Hell? *Abandon hope, all ye who enter
here*." He passed it back to Rutledge. "I would count it a kindness, if
you would tell me what you discover, once the inquiry is finished."

"I don't know," Rutledge told him, "if it will ever be finished."

"I'm afraid I shall have to agree with you."

R utledge went on to Avebury and ran down Dr. Mason enjoying
a late breakfast at the inn.

"Hallo," Mason said as Rutledge came through the door, spotted the doctor, and turned toward his table. "Surprised—but quite
pleased—to see you again. Sit down. A farm accident. Nothing serious
as long as infection doesn't set in. But it pulled me from my bed before
the sun rose. You look as tired as I feel."

"A good deal of driving," Rutledge admitted.

"Found the answers you were seeking?"

"I'm not sure." He went to the bar and asked for toast and tea, then
came back to the doctor's table. They were alone at this hour, save for
the man behind the bar, who had stepped into the kitchen to give Rutledge's order to the cook.

Sitting down again, he said quietly, "You were there when Chief
Inspector Leslie saw the body for the first time."

Frowning, the doctor said slowly, "I was. Where is this going?"

Rutledge avoided a direct answer. "Do you think he recognized the woman?"

Dr. Mason opened his mouth to reply, then snapped it shut. Glancing around to be sure he couldn't be overheard, he said, "He responded to seeing her. Just as I did. I never considered that it might be *recognition*. On the contrary. He didn't give us a name, that much you know. But looking back at that moment from a quite different perspective . . ." His voice trailed off. "He must be quite good at concealing his emotions, if it *was* recognition."

Rutledge recalled Leslie's reaction to the lapis necklace. He'd admitted quite freely that it must be his wife's. And he had a plausible reason for it having been lost in Avebury. Nor had he made excuses.

The guilty usually looked for excuses.

The clasp *had* been broken. Mrs. Johnson had tied the ends together for Peggy to wear the beads.

"Sorry," Rutledge said, smiling as his toast arrived with a pot of jam. "I'm clutching at straws."

But Mason was still considering the suggestion. "It's odd, isn't it? How you think others are seeing what you're seeing? I've looked into many dead faces in the course of my medical life, but hers wasn't—there was that little smile, almost imperceptible. I doubt she died smiling. Those stab wounds were vicious. She must have felt horror, shock, and of course pain in her last moments. It was almost as if she welcomed the peace of death, once it came." He shook his head. "I'm growing maudlin in my old age. She was young, she had a long life ahead of her. I'm sure it's the *waste* I was feeling."

But it was there in the photograph. Not just in Dr. Mason's imagination. Rutledge had seen it, Haldane had seen it.

What had Leslie felt as he saw her body the first time? And if he knew her—why had he said nothing?

In ordinary circumstances, Rutledge would have gone to him and asked him. But now there were the beads, causing an unexpected chasm to open up between them.

But beads aside, there had to be a motive for murder. Why would a strange woman have sought out Leslie in the first place?

"What is it?" Dr. Mason leaned forward. "What are you thinking about?"

"About how difficult to interpret some evidence can be."

Mason leaned back, a fleeting expression of disappointment crossing his face.

As Rutledge's pot of tea arrived, the doctor replied, "Rather like medicine, I expect. People want answers I can't give them. I find it sad that she had to be buried under 'Unknown but to God.' I asked to have that last added. It seemed right, somehow. And as I'd helped pay for the burial, no one could argue." He smiled briefly at the memory. "I'm a sentimental old fool. She could have been my granddaughter."

Rutledge pushed his toast away. "She was someone's daughter. Someone's mother. Possibly someone's wife. What brought her here to die?"

9

He should have returned the photograph to the Rector, as he'd promised. But Rutledge wasn't ready to relinquish it. As well, he had a feeling that no one would ever come knocking at the Rectory asking about her. Haldane had been right about that. And so keeping that promise to the Rector and his wife could wait.

Before leaving the doctor at his door, Rutledge asked where Mrs. Johnson lived.

The Johnsons had a cottage farther down the road that ran past the inn and the doctor's house. Her husband had been the village farrier before the war and now made his living as a carpenter.

She was not happy to see Rutledge standing on her doorstep.

"It was wrong of you to send that tea service to Peggy. I don't have the money to repay you for it. Alastair said, send it straight back. But she'd seen it. I didn't have the heart. All the same, it goes against my principles."

"Why? I took Peggy's beads, and I couldn't find any to replace them that might please her. The tea service was a poor substitute."

He smiled deprecatingly. "I'm not married. I don't know much about children. I had to ask a friend for help."

It worked.

Mollified, she said, "Still, you shouldn't have."

"It's about the beads that I've come. You told me that Peggy's brother had found them by the causeway. I'd like to ask him about that."

"Here, he didn't steal them."

Rutledge took a deep breath. "I never thought he had. It's just that it's an odd place for someone to lose a necklace. While it's not likely to be related to the woman found dead by the stone, I'd be derelict in my duty if I didn't make certain of that."

"You're in luck," she said sourly. "Tommy has measles. He's come out all over in spots."

Rutledge stopped himself in time, but the words were running through his mind.

Tommy wouldn't have considered the measles a bit of luck.

"Perhaps if I just stood in the doorway?"

"Oh very well."

She let him in and led him to the stairs. Tommy was in the larger of the two small bedrooms at the top of the flight.

"Tommy, this is the policeman from London. He's curious about that string of beads you gave your sister for her birthday."

The room was dim, curtains drawn over the windows to keep out the light. The boy lay on his cot, looking wretched, but perked up when his mother stepped aside and he saw the man from London. His gaze went directly to Rutledge's hands, as if expecting a gift of his own. The disappointment in his eyes was evident.

Rutledge cursed himself for not thinking of that.

"Hallo, Tommy. How are you feeling?"

"I was sick this morning. All over my sheets."

"Bad luck, that. I'm sorry. I've come to say that it was generous of you, to give those beads to your sister for her birthday."

Tommy ducked his head, partly shyness, partly regret. "They was in the dust. As if stepped on."

"Were they indeed?" Rutledge asked. "Hard to see, then?"

"It was the brightness of the clasp I saw, not the beads. I thought it was a shilling."

"Were you disappointed when you retrieved it, to see beads attached to the bright bit?"

"What's a body to do with beads?" he asked. But Rutledge had a feeling that he had been rather proud of his discovery, useful to a boy or not.

When Rutledge didn't immediately respond, Tommy went on. "They're always finding bits and bobs here. Antlers. Broken pots you'd think was more important than a whole one. I'd never found anything. Not even that body left beside the stone."

"You weren't one of the boys who discovered her?"

"No, worse luck." He caught his mother's look of disapproval, and said stoutly, "Nothing ever happens to me here. 'Cept the measles."

"I'm confused. You discovered the beads after the body was found? Not before?"

"After. The day after the Chief Inspector left. Nobody was allowed to play there once the body was found. Or even drive along the road over the causeway, until he'd finished searching it."

Hamish said, his voice quiet in Rutledge's ear, "It's possible he was telling the truth. Yon Chief Inspector."

"Did you see the body in place, before it was moved to Dr. Mason's surgery?"

"Half the village did," Tommy claimed. "They came crowding round before Constable could push them back."

"Here, you didn't tell me that," his mother said, angry.

"I didn't want to worry you," her son replied, looking from her to Rutledge and back again.

"Did you think the beads were as old as the circle?" Rutledge asked.

"Had to be, didn't they? Only Mum says not, that you needed them for the inquiry."

"If it's any consolation, Tommy, they are much younger than the circle. And I found the proper owner. It was lost property."

He looked at Rutledge, saying in some disgust, "Just my luck."

"But there was a reward for finding them, you know." He reached into his pocket and took out a pound, setting it on the tall chest by the door. "I'll leave it here until you're well enough to take care of it."

The boy's face brightened. "I never got a reward before."

When Rutledge looked in on Constable Henderson, he found the man was still absent.

A neighbor informed him that Henderson's brother had died, and he was staying with the brother's family, helping with the services.

"That's kind of him," Rutledge commented.

"Not so much kindness as necessity. My cousin lives down the road from the widow, and she says Mrs. Henderson is prostrate. But she always was one to settle her burdens on the shoulders of others."

He had read Henderson's report. He'd told himself that under the circumstances he needn't interview the man. And yet the brother's illness had been timely, giving Henderson a convenient explanation for his absence just as a new man was assigned to the case. Rutledge asked Henderson's neighbor for directions to the brother's house.

He found it was a small tenant farm on the outskirts of Winterbourne and identified it easily from the black crepe on the door.

When he knocked, a block of a man answered.

"I'm here for Constable Henderson."

"You've found him," he said, stepping outside and walking halfway down the path from the farm lane to the door. "Trouble in Avebury, is it?" He wasn't as tall as Rutledge, but he was twice as wide, with reddish-brown hair and hazel eyes.

"No trouble. But I've come from there. Inspector Rutledge, Scotland Yard. I was sent to review Chief Inspector Leslie's findings."

Henderson nodded. "So I'd heard. Neither the Chief Inspector nor I could trace the woman or her killer. To be fair, there was precious little to go on. The body, the blood by the stone, the clothes she was wearing. Not even a murder weapon. As I told the Chief Inspector, it looked as if we were dealing with someone who knew what he was about. Most criminals now, they give themselves away fairly soon. But there she was, and nothing to tell us who she might be or who had killed her. He meant to kill her too. Why else did he bring a knife with him? And she didn't expect that. She never had a chance to defend herself."

As if by this cowardly act, the murderer had put himself beyond the pale. At least in Henderson's mind. But the words had been clipped, feeling tamped down.

"Did you find any tracks?"

"We searched, but there wasn't anything. By the time I called to the man delivering the kegs, half the village was hurrying after me to gawk. I didn't know there was a body, not at first. Not till I looked in the ditch. I was still thinking sheep. It's a mystery how she got there. Of course, Winterbourne Monkton is barely a mile away, not all that far to walk, but it's north of the circle. Kennet is just to the south. I'd put my money on the killer coming from that direction. Fewer windows to pass by, late as it must have been. But when I went to Kennet to ask around, nobody knew anything about her."

"What did you see when you found her?"

"I saw the bloody ground by the stone first. Too much for a hawk killing a bird. Bruised grass, bent over, as if trodden a bit. I came up by way of the shops, wanting to have a look at what it was the lad had been talking about. Then I looked around to see what had been bleeding that much. When I didn't find anything, I went to look in the ditch. I reckoned the body had been dragged there, after it was done. When

I got to the edge, I could see it. That was when I heard the heavy wagon coming. It wasn't easy getting her up out of the ditch. But after she was taken away to Dr. Mason's surgery, I searched the length of the ditch. No sign of any of her belongings. She struck me as the sort of woman who'd carry a purse, and I even took my torch and shone it in and around the brambles." He shook his head. "A nasty business. Have you made any inroads into finding out who she is?"

"Not yet. Nor have I discovered who was with her or who she might have come to see in Avebury." It annoyed Rutledge to have to admit to it.

"I went with Chief Inspector Leslie to conduct most interviews. But I could have told him before he began that it wasn't likely that anyone on my patch could have done anything like that." He glanced back at the house. "I'm not boasting, mind you, but sometimes you just *know*."

"How did she get to the stones in the first place, do you think?"

"The Chief Inspector and I talked about that. A motorcar, but it very likely stopped just short of the causeway. Too many ruts to be sure, but closer and someone might have seen it. We considered horses, but she wasn't dressed for riding, and besides Dr. Mason didn't find any hairs on her dress that looked like horse. There was a little mud along her hem in one place, but that could have been from walking."

No one had mentioned mud. It would fit with riding a bicycle, her skirts drooping down toward the chain. It was a hazard for women riding. And it was the first small corroboration of a tandem.

"You went down to bring her up?"

"I did. Took three men to anchor my weight on the rope, but I could lift her."

"Anything about the way she was lying, anything that might have fallen deeper into the trench?"

"Not that I could see. And the sun was shining. That helped."

So far his answers matched the statement he'd given to Leslie. Except for the mud.

"The formal report aside. What were your impressions about her?"

Henderson glanced back toward the house and moved on down the path, nearer the lane, where Rutledge's motorcar was waiting.

"A pity, that was my first thought. And then, why on my patch? I know Avebury, there's not that sort of meanness, if you know what I'm saying." He hesitated, then he said, not looking directly at Rutledge but across the fields on the far side of the lane, "Odd thing was, her hair. It must have come down when she was dragged, and it fell across my hands as I began to lift her. Black as night, but soft, silky. Fine. And I smelled a little of her perfume, over the blood. Like some roses, the dark ones. As if she was going out of an evening, to meet someone." He appeared to be more than a little embarrassed. None of this was in his statement. He'd kept to the facts. "I'm sorry, sir. You did ask."

"It helps, Constable. Were you present when Chief Inspector Leslie viewed the body in the doctor's surgery?"

"I was. I watched Dr. Mason settle the sheet. I expect he felt much the same as I did. Wondering what she'd done to be tossed into a ditch like an old coat or worn-out shoe. He did say that he found it harder to view the dead, since the war. France, was he?"

"Yes."

"One of my cousins won't look at the dead now. Not even my brother's body. He says he still sees them, all around him. I was there, I know what he means. But he was often the stretcher party. Makes a difference, I expect. I'd like to think you might find this bastard. If he was one of my people, I'd bring him in if I had to knock him down first." His voice was harsh as he said it.

Rutledge, watching Henderson's face, saw the same protectiveness Dr. Mason had mentioned. He'd felt it himself.

Remembering the photograph, he said, "Was there anything in her face when you brought Leslie to see her?"

"I didn't notice. I was too busy looking at the way her hair spilled across the table and caught the light." He shook his head. "I've never seen anything quite like it."

Rutledge left soon afterward, thanking Henderson for his help and offering sympathy for the death of his brother.

"We weren't prepared," the Constable said quietly. "But then you never are, are you?"

He wasn't sure whether Henderson was referring to his brother's death or what he'd felt about the murder on his patch.

Soon afterward, on a whim—needing to do more than search ground he'd covered, Leslie had covered, and hear the same answers from those who had been interviewed twice over—Rutledge set out for Dover. The Rector's wife had said the scarf the dead woman was wearing might be French silk, and Haldane had mentioned refugees. It would do no harm to try.

Southampton was nearer, but it was Dover or even Folkestone where travelers most often arrived from France and the rest of Europe. He wasn't certain what he could find this long after the fact, but he had the photograph. If Henderson and Mason and even Leslie had been moved by the dead woman, then someone in the port towns might remember her as well. Surely there was a man or even a woman who had seen her alive and given her more than a passing glance.

The sun was just coming up, burnishing the water, and turning what he could see of the chalk cliffs a delicate apricot. He found a room at one of the hotels overlooking the water, where he shaved and changed, ate a hasty breakfast, and walked down to the port to catch the night officials before they went off duty.

They stared at the photograph, asked a few questions, then shook their heads.

One of the younger officials said, "I'd remember *her*. Pity she's dead."

It gave him hope.

He spent the better part of the day speaking to anyone who handled the ferries coming in from France, then as soon as there was a lull in the traffic coming and going to Calais, he sought out the officials who dealt with passengers and their papers.

In late evening, he found one man on duty who looked at the photograph and said, "Familiar. Is she dead, then? I'm sorry. Who is she?"

He was tall, thin, possibly mid-thirties. Young enough to remember a pretty face. Rutledge refused to let himself hope.

"That's the problem. No one seems to know who she is."

"That's a shame. If you had a name, now, I might be able to check our records." He looked again at the photograph, then handed it back to Rutledge. "A pity."

"She came through recently. Say, after the first of the year? Mid-January? Later? Surely there aren't that many travelers making the crossing in winter."

"It's never quiet. But women alone, that's not as usual. Was she alone?"

"I expect she was. I can't be certain."

"Perhaps that's why I remember her, then." He smiled guiltily. "It does no harm, chatting them up. After the stiff-faced officers, Swiss bankers, and those without any English, it's pleasant to talk to a pretty face. Sets them at ease, as well."

"What language did she speak?"

The official had picked up his glasses to scan the roads outside Dover harbor, watching the craft coming in. "Good enough English," he said absently. "She must have done. She asked for the train to Lon—" He broke off, lowering the glasses to stare at Rutledge. "Now why should I remember that?" He shook his head. "Do you have any idea how many people pass through here, now the war's over? I'm lucky to remember my own name by the end of the day."

"What about the London train?"

"I didn't—it just came to me out of nowhere." He looked down at the glasses in his hand, thinking. "It must have been the late ferry she'd taken across. She seemed—I don't know—lost."

"What do you mean? Lost? Tired?"

"I don't—not in the sense—uncertain?" He lifted a shoulder, looking for the word. "Uncertain of her welcome, perhaps? Didn't appear that there was anyone meeting her, no one to show her where to find the train."

It was an interesting insight.

The man was saying apologetically, "I can't be sure, now, it might not have been the same woman." He gestured to the photograph in Rutledge's hand. "I'm sorry. It's the best I can do."

Rutledge thanked him and said, "I'll be at The Cliffs. If you remember anything else."

"What's she done?" the man asked. "To bring in the Yard?"

"Nothing. It was what was done to her," Rutledge answered somberly.

The man retorted grimly, "I wish I'd known. I'd have seen her to the train."

Rutledge didn't tell him she had died in Wiltshire, not Dover.

"There was nothing you could do." With a nod, he walked away.

"No' much help," Hamish said. He'd been there, silently watching, hour after hour. A presence that Rutledge could feel. It had been wearying after a while, that presence. Sometimes dividing his attention.

"It could have been Folkestone. Southampton." Rutledge walked back to his motorcar. "I'll try Folkestone tomorrow."

It was too late to drive far, and he'd already told the port official that he was staying at The Cliffs. Without waiting to dine, he went up to his room and dropped down across the bed. And slept deeply for six hours.

He woke to someone pounding on his door, and it took several seconds to remember where he was. The windows were still dark—he had no idea what the time was. Throwing off the last dregs of sleep, he went to the door and found one of the hotel clerks standing there.

"Sorry to disturb you, Mr. Rutledge. But there's a man at the desk asking to see you. He's from the port, he says."

"I'll be down in five minutes."

"I'll ask him to wait in the lounge, shall I?"

"Yes, thank you."

Rutledge washed his face, combed his dark hair, and straightened his shirt and tie. Putting on his suit coat, he went quickly down the stairs.

The dining room was closed, the lounge almost empty. He recognized the man who rose and came forward as Rutledge stepped into the room.

"Rutledge? James Westin. From the port? I was curious enough to do some digging."

Rutledge chose a table far enough away from the only other inhabitant so that they could speak privately. "What have you found?"

"Not much, I'm afraid. But I kept thinking about the photograph, and her face stayed with me. I wasn't sure in the beginning that I *did* remember her, to tell truth. It wasn't until I was about to go off duty that something else came back to me. Her eyes. That's what attracted me to her, that's why I looked for an excuse to talk to her. To watch a smile light them."

In the photograph her eyes were closed in death.

"I think she had French papers. They were in order, I didn't pay much attention to them. I had a feeling that France might not be her country, but there was nothing unusual about that. I made her laugh once, just a quiet laugh, but it was nice. She had a valise—I reached out to help her, asking if she needed a porter. It wasn't very heavy, as if she hadn't brought much with her, and she said she could manage it. Most can barely lift theirs, bulging out the sides. I looked to see, after she'd asked, and she was walking toward the London train. Still by herself."

Rutledge had listened patiently, waiting for the most important information—the woman's name. He said now, "It's a beginning, yes. I'm grateful."

Westin said, "I did ask where she'd come from, and I believe she said Paris. Or was it Rouen? France, anyway." He glanced behind him toward the man sleeping in the chair by the window, his newspaper slipped to the floor in a heap. Lowering his voice, he went on, "A good many refugees find their way to Paris. Russians, Armenians, all sorts. Still, I don't believe she was Russian. I wish I could recall her name. I tried all the way to the hotel, but I can't bring it back. Or the ship— anything that would help me search the records."

Making the best of it, Rutledge hid his disappointment, and asked instead, "Her given name. Was it a common French name? Marie. Françoise. Hélène." He suddenly recalled another French woman, one he'd met in the course of an inquiry. Aurore. She too had been someone to remember. "Lily? Violette? Catherine?"

"By God, I believe it *was* Catherine, but with a *K*. No, that's not quite it. But close enough. That's what made me think of the Russians. Catherine the Great, and all that. Her lashes matched that dark, dark hair. But not Gypsy black, mind you. Her dark gray coat and hat were nice enough, but they struck me as drab on her."

"Dark gray?" Rutledge asked, trying to keep the man's flood of memory moving forward.

"Still, there was a nice pin in the hat. Now what was it?" He closed his eyes, concentrating. "A crescent moon, I think. I remember wondering how she would look in moonlight." He flushed a little at the admission.

What had become of that hat?

"A last name?"

He shook his head. "Hopeless. Probably unpronounceable anyway. Most of those foreign names are." It was a very English attitude. "Not as if I'd be in London and had any hope of looking her up." Then he considered Rutledge. "You're very good, you know. I can't decide whether it's how you listen or the questions you ask. I couldn't have told you I knew all of this, when I sat down. In the war, were you? Intelligence?"

"Infantry."

"Artillery, myself. It's a wonder I have any hearing left." He stood up. "I must get some rest. I'm on the day watch tomorrow. Today. If I remember anything else, will you be here?" He gestured around him. "This hotel?"

"I might not be. But Sergeant Gibson at the Yard will see that I get any messages that come in for me."

They shook hands, then Westin said, almost against his will, as if he didn't want to hear the truth, "She is dead, then? You said, but I didn't want to believe what I was seeing in the photograph."

"Murdered."

Westin swore. "That's even worse."

With a nod, he was gone. Rutledge watched him walk through the lounge doors and disappear into the lobby.

Rutledge told himself he should be grateful. He knew more now than he had when he drove into Dover. And yet it was still so little.

If he'd learned nothing else about police work since he'd joined The Met in London, it was that answers never came smoothly, easily. If they had, the crime rate would have fallen off dramatically.

Standing there, Rutledge could smell coffee wafting from somewhere. He realized all at once that he was hungry. He went to the desk and asked that sandwiches and a pot of tea be sent to the lounge. Then he went back to sit down at the table where he'd spoken to Westin and reached for his notebook.

Hamish was asking how much credence Rutledge could put in the burst of memories.

"I have to begin somewhere. Until proved false, I'll see where it could lead."

A hat. A purse. A valise. What had become of them?

The sandwiches arrived with his tea, and he found himself considering that gray hat.

His sister Frances had a taste for fetching hats, and wore them astonishingly well. Like their mother.

If a port officer, looking at papers, remembered a hat, it must have been very becoming, gray or not. What had she done with it when she pedaled to Avebury with her killer? Even if she'd used her scarf to keep her hair tidy, surely she would have wanted to put the hat on again at the end of the journey.

He himself had borrowed a cap from Mr. Blake, and left his hat at the man's house because he knew he was coming back there.

Had she expected to return as well? There was her valise—she couldn't carry it with her on the tandem.

He went back over what he'd seen when he'd looked down into the ditch where the body had been found. Winter-dead fronds, briars and vines and the dried stalks of wildflowers, forming a thick, dark mat. A gray hat would have stood out—Henderson and Mason would have seen it. And they had both reported finding only her body in the ditch. That left the killer, carrying away with him anything that might be used to identify his victim.

A hat. A purse. A valise. The lapis beads?

But Leslie claimed they'd fallen out of his pocket.

A hat could be tossed in a dustbin miles away. An empty purse might find its way into another. A valise was harder to dispose of.

Where could you hide luggage?

With other luggage, where it would attract no attention for days, weeks . . .

He finished his sandwiches and went directly to his room, where he packed his valise except for what he would need for an early departure.

At first light, a boxed breakfast beside him, he set out for London.

His first stop when he reached the city was Victoria Station. She would have come in there, on the train from Dover. Had she been met? It was a busy public place, he'd not have been noticed coming up to her. Or had she herself decided not to take her valise with her but to collect it afterward, when she had found lodging or met someone? It could be here, an off chance but at least a chance.

He spoke to the man behind the window where lost and unclaimed luggage could be retrieved.

The man shook his head, staring down at the photograph Rutledge was holding up.

"Never saw her before. But I'm only on duty during the day. There's someone else at night."

"Scotland Yard," Rutledge said, replacing the photograph with his identification. "I'd like to have a look."

"Help yourself," the man said, gesturing to the door just beyond the window. "A good bit of it is left from the war."

Rutledge stepped into a room where luggage was piled in every direction. Resigned, he took off his greatcoat and coat, rolled up his shirtsleeves, and set to work. He had no idea what he was looking for. The woman could have borrowed her valise from a friend, male or female. Bought it at Worth's in Paris or a secondhand shop in the port of Calais.

It took him four hours to sort through each piece of luggage stacked in the room, setting aside trunks and heavy cases. Then he went through the smaller valises one at a time, opening those that were unlocked, briefly examining the contents. The locked cases he fiddled with until he could spring the latches. There was nothing remotely resembling the missing woman's belongings, although he was surprised at how many women had their initials embroidered on their shifts. He found he could ignore garments that were clearly too large, out of fashion, for older women, or English made.

As he searched he wondered about the women who had left their luggage here. Had they died in the influenza epidemic? Been killed in the early Zeppelin raids? He'd counted forty-seven valises.

The stationmaster, stepping in to watch him, was not happy about his opening cases, but Rutledge told him curtly that it was a matter of murder, and the man went away. Just after that, he found, back in a corner, the kits of three soldiers from a Yorkshire regiment. He was wondering what had become of them when the stationmaster looked in again to ask if Rutledge wanted a cup of tea from the canteen.

"Their last leave before going overseas. Killed in a Zeppelin raid, they were," he said. "Wall of a house collapsed on them when they were trying to dig people out of the rubble. Still, I call them heroes. No one claimed their kit. I thought their families might come and ask one day. I expect it's not likely to happen now."

An hour later, Rutledge had finished and restored some order to the room before he went to thank the stationmaster. Photograph in hand, he went on to Paddington, from which the dead woman might have taken a train to Wiltshire. There people gave the photograph a cursory glance, shook their heads, and told him too much time had passed.

One of the porters asked, "Are you certain she took a train?"

The truth was, he couldn't be certain. It had been a possibility, nothing more. For that matter, he couldn't even be certain that the woman who looked for the London train in Dover was the one who had died in Avebury. Despite what he'd learned at the port. And yet, his instincts told him she must be the same. That James Westin wasn't wrong. The problem was, had she come to London for a matter of a few hours? A few days? Longer? Or had she never reached London at all?

Giving it up, he went on to his flat.

What he needed was men to do his searching for him. But this wasn't a full-scale inquiry where time was short and the Yard put every available man at the disposal of the officer in charge.

There were the hotels, for one thing. If the victim had actually arrived in London, where had she stayed the first night? A stranger who knew no one in the city might choose a small but respectable hotel that catered to women who had no choice but to travel alone. Governesses, widows, spinsters. The stationmaster—a cabbie—someone could give her a direction. And if she had traveled on to Wiltshire or somewhere close by, she might have left her valise in one of them, most particularly if she expected to be away only for one night. A small satchel would have done. Or the missing purse.

Gibson wasn't likely to agree to putting men on that.

What's more, Rutledge wasn't eager to have the gossips at the Yard hear that he was succeeding where Leslie had failed. He'd learned long ago to keep his own counsel. If what he'd learned led nowhere, there would be no one any the wiser.

He made a list of four hotels that were well-enough known that one of them might have been recommended to a stranger. But the photograph and a brief conversation with the clerks behind the desk in each of the establishments proved hopeless. If she *had* stayed at one of them, which was doubtful, she hadn't left any luggage behind. That was frowned on in two of the hotels and discouraged in the others.

Rutledge was on his way back to where he'd left his motorcar when he turned a corner and nearly collided with Inspector Gaines.

"Watch what you're about—oh. Hallo, Ian. What are you doing in this part of London? I thought you were in the West Country."

"I was," Rutledge agreed. "Following a few leads."

"I've got the evening off. My sister is here, staying in Blackmon's Hotel. I'm to take her out to a play."

Rutledge had just left Blackmon's. "I hope you enjoy it."

"I doubt it. But she will. If you're heading to the Yard, a word of caution. Gibson isn't in the best of moods."

"I'll bear that in mind."

Gaines hurried on, but he had placed Rutledge in the position of having to call in at the Yard.

He found Gibson with a cluttered desk, a long list of requests from various officers, and a short temper.

Looking up as Rutledge appeared in front of him, he frowned and said, "I thought you were in Wiltshire, sir."

"I was. I'm on my way back there now. I needed something from my desk."

"I don't expect it will have anything to do with your inquiry. Still.

Have you heard? There's been a report of a break-in at Chief Inspector Leslie's country house near Marlborough. A local matter so far. Yard hasn't been called in, but he's gone down to have a look."

"*Where* near Marlborough?" Rutledge asked, trying to tamp down his shock. "Have they caught the intruder?"

"I haven't heard. But according to a neighbor, there was someone asking about the house only recently. Roused her suspicions. She also claims she'd seen lights in there one evening a few weeks ago. But neither Leslie nor his wife have been to Stokesbury since Boxing Day."

Stokesbury.

"That's closer to Avebury than I'd like. How did Leslie learn about this? I thought he was in Yorkshire."

"The neighbor spoke to the local Constable, and he sent word to me. I passed it on to Denby. In Yorkshire. According to Leslie, it's a quiet village, no troubles as a rule."

"Any idea what was taken?"

"Not yet. Leslie told the Constable not to go in until he gets there."

Rutledge's mind was already racing. Was *he* the suspicious person asking questions? He'd had no way of knowing that the Stokesbury house was Leslie's! His only interest had been the tandem belonging to the Nelsons.

He said, "I didn't know they had a country house in Wiltshire. The Leslies."

"Before your time, I should think. As I recall, a cousin died and left it to them. He thought they might wish to retire there someday. There's the Marlborough railway station, not far away. It wouldn't be too bad a journey if they chose to come into London from time to time. Not as close as Surrey, mind you."

Gibson's gaze was already straying back to the file in front of him. But Rutledge needed to keep him talking.

"Mrs. Leslie must be terribly upset," he said, infusing concern into his voice.

"I hear the Chief Inspector doesn't want her told until he's had a look around. No sense in upsetting her before he knows what's missing."

"I can't say that I blame him."

With a nod, he went along to his own office, stayed there five minutes, and then left the Yard as quickly as he could. The only person he met on the stairs was Chief Inspector Murray, who nodded and kept on going, a sheaf of papers in his hand.

Rutledge was nearly out the door when he had second thoughts. Turning, he avoided Gibson's office and went to Sergeant Richards's desk.

The man smiled as Rutledge approached. "Evening, sir. I was just preparing to leave for the day."

"I won't keep you. I'm told that Chief Inspector Leslie is still assigned to that inquiry in Yorkshire?"

"I expect so, sir. There's no final report come across my desk."

"No matter. It can wait." He made as if to turn away, then said, "Remind me. Where was he before the inquiry in Avebury? Was it Kent, by any chance?"

"That would have been Inspector Hayes, sir. He was in Maidstone. Chief Inspector Leslie was in Dartmouth. A pair of suspicious drownings upriver from the town. There was a possibility that they were connected to the Naval College there, which is why he was sent down. Turned out to be a matter of an inheritance that someone didn't want to share. The guilty party was taken into custody and bound over for trial."

"Difficult place to reach by train," he observed.

"He drove, I believe." Richards frowned. "He does, sometimes. Rumor had it he tried to find someone else willing to take on Avebury in his stead. He was that weary, from the long journey back to London."

"Yes, he asked if I'd go in his place, but I had to appear in court. Thank you, Sergeant."

"And you got Avebury after all. I call that a bit of bad luck," Richards commiserated. "Shall I give him a message, if I see him? That you're looking for him?"

"No. It will keep."

Standing by his motorcar, his hand on the wing before turning the crank, Rutledge reviewed a map of England in his head. Coming back from Dartmouth down on the coast in Devon, Chief Inspector Leslie would have had several choices of route. He could have driven to Bristol and then across to London. Taken the coastal road to Southampton and turned north to London there. Or come cross-country to London, taking the back roads. If he'd come across from Bristol, it wasn't all that far out of his way to go to Avebury.

Rutledge's mouth tightened into a thin line. The beads he'd claimed as his wife's. The house in Stokesbury with the Nelsons' tandem. Leslie's attempt to find someone to take his place in Avebury. In themselves they weren't important enough to notice. But put them all together—

What if those beads weren't Leslie's wife's after all? The jeweler had thought he recognized them, but he hadn't given the name of the client, had he? Rutledge had only assumed they belonged to Mrs. Leslie— and Leslie himself had confirmed that. Or appeared to. The beads couldn't be the only fine, graduated string in London.

Then why would Leslie lie?

Unless he'd taken them without his wife's knowledge. Why would he do that? Unless he could be sure he put them back before she missed them . . .

He didn't like what he was thinking. If it had been anyone but Leslie, he—Rutledge—would have had no hesitation in looking into the possibility that the man was somehow involved.

Hamish said, "There's yon break-in. He wouldna' break into his ain house."

"No. But he might have been there. I need to find out what night that neighbor saw the lights."

"Ye shouldna' have given him yon necklace."

"I didn't know then what I know now."

"Still. Ye could be wrong."

Rutledge's first inclination was to drive to Wiltshire at once. But if Leslie was there, determining what was missing from the house, this was not the time to run into him. Better to wait and find out what he reported to the local Constable. Have an early supper, he told himself, then leave.

There was a restaurant close by, within easy reach by motorcar. He found a place to leave it, just before The Wilton, and was about to step out of it into the street when a cabbie pulled in by the restaurant's door, to set two people down.

A man got out, turned to give his hand to the young woman inside, and she joined him. Rutledge stayed where he was. The young woman was Kate Gordon, dressed for an evening event, and the man with her was an officer in the Household Cavalry, his uniform catching the eyes of passersby. He said something to Kate, and she smiled. And then he was holding the restaurant door for her, and they disappeared inside.

Rutledge was fairly certain neither the officer nor Kate had seen him. Driving away, he found he'd lost his appetite.

IO

He was still thinking about Kate Gordon when he found himself not on the road to the western counties but in Kensington, two streets over from where Chief Inspector Leslie and his wife lived in a Victorian semidetached house. He'd been driving aimlessly.

Or had he? It would do no harm to find out if Leslie was back in London. The chances were, he kept his vehicle in a mews, but it would clear the way if he knew Leslie's whereabouts.

He had just driven up the street and had turned to drive down it again when he saw the house door begin to open. Pulling quickly to the edge of the street, he waited, considering what he would say if Leslie spotted him.

But it wasn't Leslie who was leaving. Two women stepped out of the door at number 30.

The taller of the two he recognized as Mrs. Leslie. She was dressed for the theater in a fashionable dark green velvet cloak, the hood perched carefully on her fair hair, the pin set in it reflecting in the glow of the streetlamps. Her companion, in a dark blue cloak, laughed with her over some comment, and the sound traveled to him. She was younger, and he thought she must be a relative, for she had the same fair hair and round face. There was something in the way they walked on, arm in arm, their heads together, that spoke of closeness, an accustomed intimacy.

He suddenly realized that they were coming in his direction. Mrs. Leslie would have no reason to recognize his motorcar, but she could very likely remember him. And then they paused in front of a house next but one to the corner where he was sitting.

As they did, another pair of women, accompanied by a man in evening dress, came out to join them. There were merry greetings, and Rutledge caught a glimpse of Mrs. Leslie's face, wreathed in smiles and pink with excitement. The third woman turned toward her, and he thought she might be Inspector Hadley's wife.

A motorcar, driven by a chauffeur, appeared at the corner, went down the street to reverse, returned, and stopped next to the party. The man began to help the four women inside. When the doors were finally shut, the motorcar began to move off.

If Leslie had been in London, surely he'd have joined his wife. Still, they could be meeting him at the theater.

As soon as they were out of sight, Rutledge got down, turned the crank, and slowly started after them.

He had met a number of the wives of the men he worked with. He didn't know any of them well—as a single man he was usually talking to the other men while the women tended to sit together in another part of the room. He'd exchanged greetings, polite courtesies, but seldom more than that. One or two he knew by sight, like Mrs. Leslie, because he'd worked closely with their husbands.

Keeping his distance, he followed the motorcar through the increasingly crowded streets, and found himself, as he'd expected, in the theater district.

The motorcar stopped before one of the theaters, its passengers alighted and moved toward the entrance. Glancing up, he saw that a revival of a Shaw play was opening that night, and the street was jammed with carriages and cabs and vehicles.

Hamish was saying, "She's no' meeting her husband." And it appeared to be true, he hadn't come forward to join the party.

Rutledge extricated himself from the throng of theater-goers, got himself back out of the city, picked up the main road west.

Mrs. Leslie had appeared to be relaxed, happy. Almost lighthearted as she greeted her friends. No shadows on her world. He realized that Leslie still had not mentioned the break-in to her. Not yet, until he was sure what had been taken.

What else hadn't he told his wife?

It was rather Edwardian, he thought, to protect women from the less savory world around them. The war had changed that—death and destruction had crept into everyone's life. But then Leslie worked daily with the sordid business of crime and murder. Perhaps he hadn't wanted to bring it home with him at night—perhaps he'd wanted something else, this raven-haired other woman who didn't remind him of a darker world.

How had he kept it from everyone, if there was another woman in his life?

Hamish said, "Ye canna' know fra' seeing his wife on the street what happens in yon house when they're alone."

It was true.

Of course, if she were suspicious, had felt the change in him without being aware of *why* he had changed, she might not be ready to confide in her friends, keeping up a good front.

The next question was, how had Leslie met the dead woman? In France, during the war? If it *was* she the port official Westin had remembered.

Rutledge still didn't like what he was considering. Brian Leslie was an excellent police officer, intelligent, experienced, and absolutely trustworthy. Surely there was another answer.

He drove all night, finding himself on the outskirts of Marlborough and then searching out a back road to his destination.

It was pitch-black on the lanes he was traveling, but his headlamps picked out the landscape around him, the one or two scattered farmhouses, and empty fields waiting for spring.

He came finally to the end of the road on which the Nelson house sat, and leaving his motorcar there, he quietly moved forward until he could see it clearly.

It was dark, there was no motorcar in front of it.

Leslie wasn't in residence.

He returned just as silently to his own motor, and reversing, drove back the way he'd come, finding an inn on the outskirts of Marlborough. He woke up the landlord, took a room, damp and with a bed like sacks of corn. Tired as he was, he slept until late afternoon.

In all the interviews he'd conducted in the immediate circle of villages surrounding Avebury, he hadn't gone as far afield as Stokesbury, and when he was searching out tandem bicycles, he'd done his best to avoid the local Constables to avoid broadcasting his interest.

Now he arrived at four o'clock, sought out the local man, and found him just finishing his tea. If news of his appearance got back to Leslie, it was something he could understand: Rutledge hoping the new information might in some way help him in Avebury.

The Constable was a portly man with brown eyes and a receding hairline, but his straight gaze as Rutledge came through the door belied his friendly greeting. Rutledge understood. Late callers at a police station usually meant a problem to be dealt with.

"Evening, sir. Constable Benning. How may I help you?"

"Inspector Rutledge, Scotland Yard. I was told by my Sergeant in London that there was a breaking and entering here, one that was only discovered recently. Apparently it happened close to the night that the murder I'm investigating in Avebury occurred. I'm hoping that there might be a connection between the two." He gave the date but kept his expression bland when Benning nodded.

"Aye, I remember that murder." Benning gestured to the other chair, across the desk, and asked if Rutledge cared for a cup of tea. "The kettle's still hot," he added.

"Thank you, no, I must return to Avebury."

"The first I knew about the break-in was Mrs. Shelby coming by to tell me she'd had some misgivings when a man stopped by and offered a poor excuse to ask questions about the house. She keeps an eye on it for the Leslies and remembered seeing lights in the house one night not long before. It wasn't until later, mind you, that we narrowed down that date. But neither of them had been down since the new year, and I went to have a look. I couldn't see anything wrong, but I sent word to London, and they passed it on to the Chief Inspector. He came down to have a look inside. A pity he never went to the house while he was in Avebury about the inquiry there. We'd have had a better shot at catching whoever it was. But of course he couldn't know that at the time."

"He didn't stay in Stokesbury on his way from London to Avebury?"

"I believe he was met in Marlborough when he came in by train."

That agreed with Leslie's report.

"What did he find, when he went to the house?"

"A back window had been forced. I couldn't see that from where I'd been standing when I went round there. But he showed me afterward where the window's lock had been broken. It's in the pantry, just above the sloping cellar door. Easy enough to clamber up there—no one could see him, and he could take his time about it. Still, the Chief Inspector told me he saw nothing amiss until he walked into the kitchen and found biscuit crumbs on the table, and a wrapper beside them. That's when he began searching from room to room and discovered the window. Whoever it was had also knocked over a pitcher kept there, as he climbed in. It was on the floor, smashed."

"He?"

"The thinking is, an ex-soldier down on his luck might have been looking for food. Then he took what he thought he could sell without getting caught, and left before first light."

"Have you had many ex-soldiers coming through?"

"Well, no. Not since the autumn." Benning picked up his cup and saucer, and carried it back to the shelf above the little stove. Resuming his seat, he went on. "I do what I can for them, a meal, a few coins, and they move on. There's no work here, no reason to stay. I had quite a time of it, assuring Mrs. Shelby she was safe enough, that he wouldn't be coming back."

"What did he look like? If she saw him?" Rutledge asked.

"She couldn't describe him, not in any useful way. She kept saying he was menacing. He wanted to know if the Leslies had anything to sell."

"And that's the only sighting of this man?"

Benning took a deep breath. "As to that, we can't be sure. The dogs on one of the farms west of here barked for about ten minutes on the night in question. A Tuesday night, that was. But they were shut up in the shed, to keep them from wandering. Their owner, Mr. Haskell, believes it was only another dog sniffing around. It could have been the vagrant, of course. There's an old road by the farm, not much used these days."

Had the Haskell dogs heard a tandem bicycle passing by?

"Where does that road lead?"

"Out to a farm that was sold off twenty years ago. House is gone, of course, but Haskell's neighbor owns the land and grows mostly corn and beans."

"You haven't told me what was taken?"

"That was odd. The Chief Inspector looked in his wardrobe, thinking the man might be after warmer clothes. Instead, he seems to have taken another packet of biscuits, some bits and bobs of jewelry, a man's gloves. Odd choice, but Leslie told me they'd bring in enough to have a decent meal, perhaps a night somewhere."

"No silver candlesticks? That sort of thing?"

Benning shook his head. "Questions might be asked, if he had anything too valuable."

"Clever man. Did Leslie believe this break-in had any bearing on the Avebury murder?"

"If he thought so, he never said. In my opinion, if whoever broke in that night was here in Stokesbury, he couldn't have been doing murder in Avebury. Besides, where did he meet the woman who was killed there?"

"What if she was there, in the Leslie house, with him, and they had a falling-out? That would account for the bits of jewelry." The dead woman—Katherine—had been too well dressed for a common thief, but he wanted to hear Benning's answer.

The Constable considered that for a moment, then shook his head. "There's still the distance to Avebury. And Leslie was of the opinion only one person had been in the house."

"Well, then," Rutledge said, rising. "If it has nothing to do with my inquiry, I'll be on my way." He had asked enough questions, he didn't want to rouse Benning's suspicions. And then, as if an afterthought, he said, "You mentioned that Leslie came by train to Marlborough. If he isn't met, how would he travel the rest of the way to Stokesbury?"

"At the Marlborough railway station, there's generally someone for hire." He rose as well, preparing to see Rutledge off.

Rutledge showed Benning the photograph of the dead woman, but he shook his head. "So that's what she looked like. I'd heard she was young. She was never here in Stokesbury. I'd have noticed her."

Walking on to the door of the small police station, Rutledge thanked the Constable and went out to his motorcar. But once he was completely away from the village, he pulled to the side of the road and considered the next step.

He had to stay well clear of Mrs. Shelby. She had convinced herself she had seen the housebreaker. Would she actually recognize him? He couldn't take the risk. But he also needed to get inside the Leslie house, without the Constable finding out. If an ex-soldier could manage it, so could he. Benning had said the window where the alleged thief had got in was well out of sight.

He looked at his watch in the reflected light of the headlamps. He had a little time before moonrise. Putting out the headlamps, he switched off the motor, and listened to the silence around him. In the far distance a dog barked, then was quiet again. He leaned his head against the back of his seat and closed his eyes. He'd learned to sleep standing up in the trenches—men on the line snatched whatever rest they could, depending on the sentries to keep them safe from sudden attack.

There were no sentries here, but he let himself drift for a time, then straightened in his seat and looked again at his watch, this time with the torch from under his seat.

It should be safe enough now. Benning would have finished his rounds and gone to his bed. And he could leave the motorcar here, away from anyone walking a dog or restless in the night.

Stokesbury was small, with the main road cutting through it from east to west, and spokes, hardly more than narrow lanes, radiating out from the center of the village. Meadow Street, where the Leslie house stood, was the only one that didn't end in fields, instead looping around to come back to the main road as Primrose Lane. Hardly a place to leave his motorcar for all to see.

It would mean a walk, from here, and he would have to wear his Wellingtons to keep his boots dry when he was in the house. Setting out, he could see just how dark the village was, no lights showing in any direction. Soon he could pick out the church tower, silhouetted against a cloudy sky, and a scattering of trees. A cat followed him part of the distance, striding beside him until it found its home, disappearing around to the back of the last house on Courtney Street.

He kept to the shadows, taking his time, making certain that all the houses were dark before he passed them. And there ahead was the Leslie house. He slipped around to the rear, staying close to the walls. In what little light there was, he could see the cellar doors, slanted from the rear wall to the ground, a patch of white against the blackness.

He felt the doors, found they would take his weight, and climbed up toward the window above them. The latch hadn't been repaired. Leslie must not have had time to attend to it. But Rutledge ran his fingertips over the cellar doors and discovered a small patch of splinters.

The window latch had been broken from the outside.

He got the window open with a minimum of fuss, changed from his Wellingtons to his dry boots, and found it was easy enough to raise the window and fling a leg over the sill. A few seconds later he was standing in the pantry, remembering the smashed pitcher. But there was nothing on the shelf beneath the window—it was completely bare.

The house was cold, dark, and silent around him as he made his way out of the pantry into the kitchen. If there had been biscuit crumbs on the table in there, they were gone now.

His torch, masked by a handkerchief, offered just enough light to move from room to room. White sheets, ghostly in the darkness, marked furnishings covered over for the winter months, but he could see the paintings hanging on the wall in the dining room, books on shelves in the sitting room, and a pretty chandelier in the parlor.

He found his way up the stairs. The Leslies shared a bedroom, but smaller rooms on either side had been converted into dressing rooms. He saw the jewelry box on the dressing table in Mrs. Leslie's room, and carefully opened it. But there was no half-moon pin there, just a few pieces of inexpensive jewelry, the kind that a woman might leave here to wear if an occasion arose. And he'd seen her wear the lapis beads in London.

Satisfied, he looked in her wardrobe for a gray hat or a purse that might have belonged to the dead woman. What better place to conceal it? Yet not expecting to find it or the valise. He even opened the drawers in the tall chest across from the window, making sure his torch couldn't be seen by Mrs. Shelby.

To be thorough, he looked as well in Leslie's dressing room, but there was nothing out of place. Nothing that shouldn't be there.

He moved on to the guest rooms, then found the stairs to the attic. There was nothing here but pieces of heavy Victorian furnishings that must have belonged to the Nelsons and a few trunks of linens that appeared to be nearly as old.

Finally satisfied, he came back to the kitchen, and the light of his torch swept past the cooker against the wall.

He paused. If anything had been burned here, it would surely be in the cooker.

He crossed to it, opened the box where the fire was set, and shone his torch inside. Ashes, gray and moving slightly as he leaned forward to look more carefully. The light, flickering over the ashes, found something dark in the far corner.

Careful of his cuffs and the sleeves of his greatcoat, he reached for it. His fingers just barely closed over it, and then, moving slowly, he drew it out of the box.

The torch light was too faint to examine what he'd found, but he dropped it into another handkerchief, put it into his pocket, and closed the cooker door.

Swearing, he realized his fingers were covered in ash, and he tried to clean them off on the handkerchief over the torch. He dared not track that about. Then he looked carefully at the floor, to see if any ash had floated down there.

It was clean. Rising, he made his way back to the pantry, stepped out into the night, and pulled the window down from the outside. That took skill and time, but he managed it. Then at the last second, it slipped from his fingers and closed with a *thump!* Rutledge froze.

A dog began barking, and he could hear its claws scraping at the garden wall. He couldn't see it, but he judged it was in the next house but one. He slipped to the far side of the cellar doors, crouching there, head down, letting his hat shield his face.

After several minutes, a door opened, a man shouted at the dog, but it didn't stop barking.

"What is it, then? What do you see?" the man demanded. And after a moment, he yelled, "Who's there? Come out, I see you."

But he couldn't, if Rutledge couldn't see him. He stayed where he was.

"All right, come inside, Sandy. That'll be enough," the annoyed male voice said finally. "You're after shadows, that's all."

The dog stopped, a door slammed, and the night was silent once more.

Still, Rutledge waited. A good ten minutes, by his estimation. In the event the owner, remembering a recent breaking in at the Leslie house, decided to dress and investigate.

Finally he managed to replace his dry boots with his Wellingtons, and then listened again for any sounds.

Satisfied, he edged his way through patchy shadows to the black rectangle near the bottom of the garden that must be a shed.

When he tried the door, he was surprised to find that it was unlocked. But he had to open it by inches, for the hinges were rusty. Once it was wide enough, he covered the torch with a handkerchief again and shone it around the interior.

And there was a tandem bicycle against the far wall.

Crossing a floor cluttered with an assortment of farm implements, watering pails, and even a small iron summer bench, he could see that a narrow path had been made to the bicycle. And it appeared to be in excellent condition. He pushed the pedals, watching their quiet, smooth movement. Then he knelt on the dry earthen floor beside it and pointed his torch toward the tires.

They were caked with earth and bits of dried weeds. But when had it last been used?

Hamish spoke, startling him. "Yon murderer would ha' been a fool to bring it back."

Which begged the question that it had been used to travel to Avebury. Surely it would simply have been abandoned as soon as the killer was safely away from the scene. A tandem would have attracted attention late at night, with only one person pedaling it.

And he dared not be caught with it. Better to have it discovered and traced back to the rightful owner, casting suspicion on *him*.

Rutledge rose to his feet.

Even in his early days as a London Constable, Rutledge had never encountered a thief who returned what he'd taken.

He didn't want to believe that Leslie himself might have slipped into the house, borrowed his own bicycle, and returned it to the shed after he'd finished with it.

But where was his victim all this while? Where had she been waiting? And how had he explained himself when he collected her?

How could he convince a respectable woman to ride a tandem bicycle cross-country to a prehistoric site in the middle of the night? If he'd brought her from London there were any number of desolate stretches along that road where she could be killed and left for anyone to find. Surely that would have been more sensible.

What if he was completely wrong about the tandem? What if the killer and his victim had come only as far as the ancient avenue by motorcar, leaving it there to walk together between the double rows of stone until they reached the circle, as the builders themselves must have done? He had only to walk back there, drive off, and disappear.

That would clear Leslie and even an ex-soldier looking for an empty house where he might find a little food.

Nights were still long this time of year.

But how had the victim reached here? Had her killer brought her all the way from London? Or for that matter, from Bristol or Bath or Swansea in Wales?

"Aye," Hamish said. "Ye canna ask yon victim to creep in and oot of a house ye own. It doesna' stand up."

Then how was it done? Rutledge wanted to ask him, even as he knew Hamish was right.

Making certain there was no one in the garden waiting to surprise him, he left the shed and took great care to shut the doors, stamping down any grass he might have displaced opening them. Then with a last look around, he started back the way he'd come.

He had just reached the corner of the house when something touched his face, and his heart leaped. But it was only a spider's web, invisible in the darkness. Brushing it away, he got himself down Meadow Street, to the field, and finally to his motorcar.

Using his torch now without covering it, he took out his other handkerchief and looked at what it contained.

The small charred remnant of stiff black ribbon lay in his palm.

And at the very edge of it was a bit of gray cloth.

He stared at it.

Someone had tried to burn what might well have been a woman's dark gray hat.

II

Rutledge drove directly to Marlborough, found the railway station, and went in search of the stationmaster.

"Good evening," he said as the man looked up from the newspaper he was reading. "Scotland Yard, Inspector Rutledge."

The stationmaster hastily put his newspaper aside and asked, "Is there some sort of trouble?" His hair was nearly white, his hands gnarled. Rutledge thought he had stayed at his post during the war, and had been kept on afterward because there was no one to take his place.

"The Yard is tracking a killer, and it's possible he—or she—got down from the London train when it stopped in Marlborough." Taking out the photograph, he showed it to the man. "Have you seen this woman? Alone or with another person, perhaps? We can't be certain of that." He gave the date. "Time has passed, I realize that, but perhaps you have a good memory for faces."

"Murder?" He took off his glasses and leaned forward to peer at the photograph Rutledge was holding. Shaking his head, he said, "I can't say that I remember her." He looked again. "Is she dead?"

"She was the victim."

The stationmaster stared at Rutledge. "Was she, now?"

He tried a different approach. "Who is usually waiting for the London train in the hope of a fare? Someone with a motorcar—or a carriage? He might be able to help me."

The man's face brightened. He knew the answer now. "That would be Mr. Barlow. An elderly gentleman. He died of pneumonia two weeks ago. Caught a chill in a heavy rain, and it went to his chest. A pity. I could count on him being there, if anyone asked."

A pity indeed.

"I've a friend who comes to Marlborough by train and sometimes hires a driver. Chief Inspector Leslie, who has a house in Stokesbury. Do you know if he's been here recently?"

"Mr. Leslie. I think he came through some time back. There was a Constable waiting to collect him."

"Several days before that."

The stationmaster shook his head. "I can't say that I remember seeing him." He peered once more at the photograph. "There was a fire on the train just as the passengers were disembarking. Might have been then. Some fool dropped a cigarette on a newspaper under his seat. No harm done, but there was smoke in the carriage and a passenger fainted, thinking she was about to be burned to death. Took me the better part of half an hour to bring her round. There was several people who got down, but I was too occupied to notice them. Three women, and a man? I expect that's right."

"Can you be sure about the date?" Rutledge persisted.

"It was a clear night—no one had umbrellas up." He picked up his glasses. "I did count the tickets, and there was the correct number. Four. They'd left them on the bench by the gate."

"Did you report the fire? Would there be a record of it?"

The man looked away, more than a little sheepish. "I didn't report it. I should have, yes, but no harm done, and there would be mountains of paperwork to see to."

As a witness in a murder trial, this man would be useless when questioned by the defense. Rutledge counted to ten, then asked, "Was one of the women alone?"

"I expect one was. But then I was hurrying into the carriage, you see." He set his glasses down, picked them up again, uncomfortable with so many questions.

"And the Chief Inspector didn't come to collect her?"

"No, he wasn't on the train. I'd remember him."

"The woman who had hysterics. Who was she?"

"I'd never seen her before. She kept telling me she mustn't get down in Marlborough, because her daughter would be waiting for her at her destination, and she mustn't keep her waiting."

"Did any of the people who got down that night have a return ticket?"

"I'm fairly sure no one did."

He thought of another way to get at an answer. "Did Mr. Barlow have a fare the night of the fire in the carriage?"

"I expect he did." He closed his eyes as he pinched the bridge of his nose. "It was a rare night when he didn't."

"Do you know any of the passengers that night by name?"

"No, sir. Not that night."

"Did Chief Inspector Leslie ever question you about the train from London?"

"No, sir. I can't think why he should have done."

Rutledge gave up. The man's memory was like a sieve. And so he put away the photograph, thanked the man, and left the station.

He swore as he turned the crank. Even if he could show that the dead woman had been on the train, there was no way to prove it without Mr. Barlow's testimony. Speculation was not proof.

Before he got behind the wheel, he scanned the street in front of the station. There were no waiting cabbies nor a driver hoping for a fare. Not surprising. The board had told him that the next London train wasn't due until late tomorrow afternoon.

The fire in the carriage. An accident, as the stationmaster had said, or intended as a distraction? But he couldn't quite see Katherine, as he was coming to think of her, covering her departure from the train.

He was back to the ex-soldier.

The church clock reminded him that it was late. But he still had one more call to make.

The only person he really hadn't interviewed as a potential suspect was Dr. Mason, and that was because he wasn't sure the man could physically have committed the crime. Someone his age would have been at a distinct disadvantage trying to stab a healthy young woman. Surely she'd have fought, screamed. He couldn't have smothered her cries and still wielded the knife so efficiently. The chances were, he'd have been scratched and bloody by the time anyone came running. Could he physically have dragged her body the distance to the ditch?

But as they left Marlborough behind them, Hamish disagreed. "If he were angry enough, he'd find the strength."

"His house is closest to the scene. She could have come to Avebury looking for him. She wouldn't have been a former patient. He didn't serve in the war. But it's possible she knew someone who had been his patient."

"If she hadna' come by bicycle, it was a verra' long walk from Marlborough station."

"Perhaps he met her at the station. Transport generally waited outside. Who would have noticed them together? An older man, welcoming his daughter home again? It's not likely. But it's possible. I need to be sure."

"Aye, but who was she? And why should he ha' wanted to kill her?"

None of his conversations with Mason had led him to believe the man had killed her. But there was the doctor in Shropshire—Allen—and Rutledge had had no doubts there, either, until he learned that there had been no mention of venereal disease in the report on that victim's death. Knowing that would have alerted the police to a past that might have led to murder.

It didn't appear that Leslie had treated Mason as a suspect. He was barely mentioned in the Yard report, and only then in his capacity as a doctor. If only for his own peace of mind, he had to question the man.

That done, he could face what that bit of stiffened ribbon and gray wool meant.

Hamish wasn't finished. "Ye've got nothing to be going on with. Ye said so yoursel'."

"I know," Rutledge said as his headlamps picked out the dark road ahead. "But then how do I explain what I found in the cooker?"

"They will say it was the man who broke into the house."

"That's true. He won't be here to defend himself but he'll take the blame for murder. The inquest will conclude it was murder by person or persons unknown. Just as it had before."

"Ye canna' be sure he didna' kill her. Ye canna' be certain he didna' come back to yon house afterward, and burn her hat because he'd no' remembered it."

"There's still the valise. The crescent moon pin. Her purse. Where are they? And why Leslie's house?"

Hamish said, "It's no' where anyone would look for a dead woman's belongings. It was empty, he couldna' ha' known it belonged to a Chief Inspector."

But Rutledge wasn't keen on coincidences.

He was making good time in spite of the ruts in the road, and he was halfway to Avebury when another thought struck him.

If he went back to Scotland Yard and reported that it was very likely that Leslie was somehow involved, and he needed to question him, who would Markham believe if Leslie called Rutledge a fool and refused?

When Rutledge knocked at the door of the surgery, Dr. Mason squinted in the bright lamplight.

"Hallo," he said with a smile. "Have you found her killer? Is that why you're so late? Come in and I'll offer you a sherry."

Rutledge said, "I'm here to review the facts of that young woman's murder. If I may?" And he made to enter the passage. He hadn't intended to be abrupt. But seeing the doctor unshaven, his hair tousled from sleep, his nightshirt tucked unevenly into his trousers, he was rapidly having second thoughts. Still, murderers didn't wear marks on their foreheads, like Caine, to identify their deeds.

Frowning, Mason stepped aside and took him into the chill front room, that looked as if nothing had been changed in it since his wife's death. It even smelled stale and musty, having been shut off from the rest of the house for so long a time.

Mason didn't bother to light the fire, but he did light the lamp by the window.

"Now then, what's this about?" he said, and waited.

Feeling like a fool, Rutledge said, "Had you ever seen that woman before you were called to the ditch where she was found?"

"Never. I'm not so pressed for trade that I go about making my own corpses."

"I'm serious, Dr. Mason."

"And so am I, Inspector. Yes, I know, you must do your duty. So must I. I've taken an oath to do no harm."

"And you haven't heard from any of your patients anything that would lead you to believe she was coming here, to see you or anyone else in Avebury? A doctor, like a priest, hears what a man can't tell his own family. Could she have been sent by a former patient, someone you knew, and Henderson didn't?"

"My patients appear to be as bewildered as I am. I would have spoken to Chief Inspector Leslie if I was worried that one of them might be involved in her death. As for former patients, my wife and I kept up acquaintance with some of them for a few years. They were busy with their lives, some have died. In good time, we made new friends here.

You know how it is. I think the last time I heard from the past, it was at my wife's death. A note of condolence."

"Did your late wife have among her jewelry a pin shaped like a crescent moon? One that might be worn on a coat? Even a hat?"

Surprised, Mason said, "I really don't know. I never gave her such a thing, but that's not to say she didn't own one or inherit one from her family. I can tell you quite truthfully that I never saw her wear it." He started toward the door. "I'll take you to her room, if you like, and you can see for yourself."

It was a genuine offer, and Rutledge, still standing, not having been invited to sit, shook his head. "That won't be necessary."

Mason stayed where he was. "I don't mind being questioned, Rutledge, but I do mind being suspected of murdering that poor woman. I'd have helped her in any way I could have done, even if she'd escaped from prison and needed sanctuary. That's part of my oath as well. It's never been tested, but I think I would have the courage to lie to the authorities, if I believed it was for the best."

Rutledge said quietly, "Forgive me. But I would have been remiss in my duty if I hadn't asked you the same questions I've asked your neighbors, just because I've enjoyed our conversations."

That mollified the doctor to a degree, but he still said, "I insist that you look at my late wife's jewelry. I shouldn't care to be treated differently."

And so Rutledge followed him, carrying the lamp, up the steep, narrow staircase, counting fourteen steps without a landing.

Mason turned to his left, and came to a door just down the passage. He took a deep breath, then opened it, standing aside to allow Rutledge to enter. "Her jewelry has always been kept in the top drawer of her dressing table."

Rutledge crossed the room, set the lamp down on the dressing table, and opened the drawer. There were three boxes inside. He opened them one after the other, and saw a string of lovely pearls, pearl earrings to match, and a pearl ring in the first one. Gifts, he thought, from her parents when she came of age.

In the second were several rings, a long gold necklace that might be worn with an evening gown, another of jet beads, and three bracelets. The last box held only Mrs. Mason's engagement ring and wedding ring, set in the satin bed made for them by the jeweler who had sold them to a young doctor who was about to propose.

"We have no children. I let her wear them in her coffin, but I couldn't bear to bury them with her. I wanted to look at them sometimes, and remember the evening I proposed to her."

Rutledge closed the box and put it back in the drawer, then quietly shut the drawer. "You've made your point," he said without emphasis. "Honor satisfied."

He took up the lamp again, and walked to the door, then down the stairs to the front room, without looking to see if Mason followed.

But Mason shut the door behind him as he came after Rutledge and said, "Now you owe me the courtesy of telling me what this was about."

"She was very likely wearing a hat that matched her coat. I found someone who remembered a woman with black hair and a hat with a crescent pin. You are the nearest house to the scene of that murder. You could have killed her and no one the wiser. You would know how to use a knife to best advantage, and you could have burned the clothes splattered with her blood. There's no one in the house who would notice if you never wore your red jumper or your blue shirt after that night. You might have discovered afterward that she'd left her hat behind, and burned it too. But decided not to burn the pin. It might have value, it might even have been a gift from you. And in Henderson's absence you made a point of helping the police."

"Remind me never to play chess with you. You have a devious mind."

"No. A policeman's mind, always suspicious."

Mason crossed the room to a tray with a decanter and several glasses. He inspected them for dust, then sniffed the sherry. "It seems all right." He poured two glasses, and handed one to Rutledge. "I saw in the beginning that you were different from the Chief Inspector. He did his duty. Fully and carefully, mind you. But his heart wasn't in it. I thought it might be something personal. An illness in the family, or the like. I'm a doctor, I've seen many men and women struggle to keep their feelings from showing when given the worst possible news. But there were no answers here in Avebury. He knew that, and still he didn't stint. He left here with that murder unsolved."

"That's a very good description of the Chief Inspector. What did you see in me?"

Mason sipped his sherry and nodded. "It's still good. You have a fine mind, and you are tenacious. It's more than duty with you, isn't it? A passion, I expect. Or perhaps there's something driving you. You see in the victim someone who must be spoken for. Whatever the cost. I wonder why."

"I don't know *why*," Rutledge said. It was the truth. He didn't. But he'd taken up police work because someone had to speak for the dead. "My father was a solicitor," he said after a moment. "He did what he could for people who came to him."

"Yes, well. The answer may come to you one day."

"Did you kill her?" he bluntly asked the doctor.

"Of course not."

Rutledge finished his sherry. "Then go back to your bed. I need to find mine."

Mason took their empty glasses and put them back on the tray. "I'll see they're washed later. We might want them again."

At the door, he stopped before opening it and letting in the cold night air. "You've found something, haven't you? Best to sleep on it."

He didn't seem to notice that Rutledge hadn't answered him.

Instead Rutledge said, "Know anyone in Avebury who owns a fine set of lapis beads?"

"Lapis?" Mason shook his head. "I don't believe I do. Now my wife could have answered that. She could tell you who wore what to, say, evensong or a wedding, describing the gown and the jewelry that set it off. She had an eye for that sort of thing."

But there were no beads . . . He'd given them back to Leslie.

He drove to the inn but stood there for a moment, listening to the silence of the night.

Once when he and Mason had dined at the inn, the woman who was serving them had asked if he was making any progress finding out who had killed the strange woman. He'd smiled and told her it was early days yet. But that hadn't satisfied her.

"It makes me anxious, walking home at night. The dark comes down early this time of year, and I'd never been afraid of it before. Now I'm torn between asking someone to walk with me and wondering if I do, whether I'm inviting a murderer to protect me."

When she'd walked away, Mason had said, "I agree. It's an odd place, especially at night. I'm not afraid of the dark—God knows, in my profession, I'm out at all hours, and a pretty thing it would be to fear shadows. Nor am I afraid of the circle. But they *loom*, those great monoliths. You can't escape them. And if you've any imagination at all, you wonder at the skill that put them here. The mystery is *why*."

"It's the same mystery with the dead woman. Why *here*?" Rutledge had finished his meal and shook his head when the woman waiting tables offered him more tea.

"That's no mystery at all. The design was to throw you—the police-man, whoever was sent to investigate—off the scent. As it has done, very well indeed."

But looking out into the darkness, Rutledge thought, There's more to it than that. He needed a place to bring her. And the stone circle wasn't new to him, he must have been here before. He must have known that hooded stone was there, and somehow it felt like the right place. Even at the risk of being found out.

What in God's name had this place meant to a killer?

A village this small couldn't go on hiding a secret so shameful. Not after *two* Scotland Yard Inspectors had come here and looked for answers. These people weren't hardened criminals. Someone would have broken down finally and confessed whatever it was he or she knew.

Hamish said, "Chief Inspector Leslie has a house not many miles from here."

And Rutledge answered silently, Yes. Then why had he taken the train from London to Marlborough, when he came down for the inquiry, rather than drive? He always drove. Even to Dartmouth, down on the coast. Unless of course he met her train in Marlborough, on his way back from Dartmouth, and feared that someone might remember the motorcar—and his passenger? That has to be considered.

It was very late, and he was bone tired. Anything began to seem logical when the mind was hungry for sleep.

With a last look at the stones, like ghosts in the distance, he turned and walked quietly into the inn, regretting that he'd treated Mason so shabbily when he couldn't even entertain the possibility that Leslie had been a killer.

"Because," Hamish said, his deep voice seeming to follow Rutledge up the stairs, "he's a Scotland Yard Chief Inspector. He's trained to look for proof. Who better to conceal it?"

Rutledge stopped, his hand on the handle to his room, Hamish's words seeming to echo in his mind.

Why hadn't there been a photograph of the victim in the Yard file? What had become of it?

He found it hard to believe that it had simply got lost.

Drifting in and out of sleep, Rutledge thought about France.

So many things still came back to the war.

There were women available to men given leave in Paris and Calais and Rouen. Women of the streets, women who plied their trade wherever they could. And there had been refugees desperate to survive, who were willing to sell their bodies for food and shelter.

Many of the officers avoided them because disease was often

rampant among those women. Others preferred the women of good family who became "aunties" and looked after their British soldiers as carefully as the women at home in England. Sending them packages, writing to them, waiting for their next leave. Far from home and loved ones, lonely, often frightened by what they must return to, men found respite wherever they could. And a good many wounded were sent to Rouen and then to Paris to recover.

Could Leslie have met her that way? And now that the war was over, had she somehow decided to find him again? Had that been her mistake?

She'd had a child.

Had she come here, hoping to find the father? It would explain a good deal.

And yet Rutledge found it hard to believe that Leslie would have walked away from her at war's end, without making some provision for the mother of his child. He wasn't that sort of man.

The blankets and coverlet were sliding off the bed, and he reached for them, pulling them back over his shoulders as he tried to shut off the thoughts tumbling over each other.

Mrs. Leslie hadn't borne any children. He might have loved that child more than the mother. What had become of it? Why had she left it behind? Affairs that might be forgiven in time of war would be viewed differently now, two years later. Especially if the child had died, the bond between a man and his mistress broken.

It was going on four before at last he fell asleep, but even his dreams were tangled, and he woke up at first light feeling as if he'd had no rest at all.

The next morning he made the rounds of villages close by Avebury, but no one had seen any indigent soldiers asking for work.

As one Constable put it, "This weather, they tend to stay close to the cities. No farm work to be had, and very little hiring at all."

Another told him, "If he took anything worth selling at that break-in in Stokesbury, he'd be looking for somewhere to sell it. He wouldn't be hanging about here, for fear a Constable might take it into his head to clap him in gaol and then find what he'd taken on him."

Both made very good sense, and by the time he returned to Avebury, Rutledge was of the opinion that the vagrant didn't exist.

He encountered Mrs. Marshall, the Rector's wife, as he walked down toward the doctor's surgery, and she paused to ask if he'd been coming to return the photograph.

"I'm sorry, not yet. But I assure you, I've taken very good care of it."

She wasn't best pleased with his answer, saying only, "Kindly see that you do." She was about to walk on when Rutledge remembered something.

"I'm told the victim was wearing a very pretty scarf when she was found. And you kept it, for further identification. Can you describe it for me?"

She bristled a little, as if half expecting that he intended to take that as well.

"It's a rather fine scarf. French silk, I think. Cream, with dark blue fleurs-de-lis embroidered on it. I'm hoping that it will mean something to someone."

"Thank you." He touched his hat as she nodded and then walked on.

He watched her go on her way.

Had the man Katherine sought in England given it to her?

Or was he, Rutledge, grasping at straws?

Experience told him he was not.

He changed his mind about stopping at the surgery, not ready to lose the train of thought that seemed to haunt him. At the next turning by the corner of the church, he felt as if he could put a name to every house in Avebury. Walking on, he passed the church, remembering how he'd stood beneath the windows and examined Katherine's photograph. Ahead were the walls of the manor house gardens, and beyond that the front of the house. Looking at them, he made a decision, crossing the road to the church, finding the sexton trimming a tree limb that was brushing against the walls.

Rutledge told him what he was after, and together they carried a tall ladder from the shed at the back of the Rectory and propped it against the manor house garden walls.

Rutledge climbed while the sexton, a short, wiry man by the name of White, steadied the ladder.

When he could see over the wall into the winter-dead garden, he realized how attractive it must be in summer. He wished he'd thought to bring his field glasses from the boot, but from his position on the ladder, he began to scan every foot of it, every shadow and wind drift of leaves.

White called to him, "All right, is it?"

"So far." And then, finished scanning, still unsatisfied, he went over it again.

A valise would be easy to pick out, its shape too regular. A woman's handbag another matter. But where better, after the deed was done, to toss both over the wall and out of sight?

Yet there was nothing in the garden's paths and borders and squares that remotely resembled what he was hoping to find.

"All right, coming down," he said, and descended the ladder. White grinned.

"Thought you might be taking root up there."

Rutledge shook his head. "Did Chief Inspector Leslie ask for a ladder to search the gardens?" He took up his end of the ladder and followed the sexton across the road.

"To my knowledge he didn't."

"Wiser man than I," Rutledge responded.

"There's some who'd argue that. He spoke to people, asked questions, but to my mind he knew from the start that it was hopeless. I ask you—what progress have you made?"

He couldn't use the standard reply—*early days*. Instead he was honest and answered, "Some. Not enough."

White nodded. "Aye. Poor lass. I keep the grass away from her headstone, if someone should show up looking. In the spring, I'll plant a few pansies there."

Pansies. For remembrance.

He thanked the sexton as they hung the ladder on its hooks in the shed, then walked on, pausing to look at the front of the manor house. There was a scattering of smaller stones across the well-kept lawns spread out before him. Still restless, he continued, completing the circle, finally back at the inn. Not stopping, he followed on down the road.

If there was any other hiding place for purse or valise, he hadn't found it.

They were most likely in a tip along a road well away from Avebury. He was wasting his time, looking.

Rutledge knocked at the door of the surgery.

Dr. Mason answered it. "Well, well," he said dryly, "coming back for more of my excellent sherry?"

"Later, perhaps. I do have some questions for you."

"How could I not have guessed? Not about my late wife's jewelry, I hope. Come in. The kitchen is warmer, and I've got the kettle on."

He led the way back to the kitchen. "I've been cleaning some of my instruments. No one is in need of my services today, it seems. Except for Scotland Yard. I ought to charge a consultation fee."

Rutledge didn't answer, well aware that the doctor was still smarting from their conversation of the night before.

He sat down in one of the kitchen chairs as Mason busied himself with teacups and the bowl of sugar, then went to the pantry to fetch the milk jug.

Ready to talk finally, Mason said, "Questions? Am I still a suspect, then?"

"Actually they're about Chief Inspector Leslie. I had the feeling, reading his report on the inquiry, that he'd been to Avebury before." It wasn't true, but it was a safer opening.

"I believe his parents were acquainted with Mr. Marshall's predecessor. Mr. Townsend had the living then. I got the impression they'd visited a time or two."

"Did you know Townsend?"

"He'd moved on to another living by the time I retired here. I've heard from some of my older patients that Townsend and his wife often had houseguests, and I recall Leslie mentioning that he'd played among the stones as a child." The kettle boiled, and Mason turned to deal with it.

"But not as an adult? I believe he knew the Nelsons, from Stokesbury."

"Did he? I don't think he ever mentioned them."

As Mason set his teacup in front of him, Rutledge said, "I encountered Mrs. Marshall earlier this morning. She was telling me about the scarf the victim was wearing. She said it was quite attractive."

"Yes, it was, although it was stained with blood when I first saw it. She managed to clean it, good woman that she is."

"Any idea where it might have come from? A London shop, perhaps?"

"She thought it was French. Silk, she said. My wife could have told you, of course. To me it was simply a pretty scarf."

Changing the subject once again, Rutledge asked, "Have you ever treated anyone from Stokesbury?"

"None of my patients come from as far away as that. They'd have gone into Marlborough, if there wasn't a closer doctor." He frowned. "Although, come to think of it, a woman by the name of Nelson was hanged at Devizes. For murder. Last century."

Rutledge stopped, his cup poised in midair. "Was she indeed?"

"I don't know the story. There was a song the older children sang in the schoolyard when I was a lad. Something about Mary Nelson broke her neck, falling on the hangman's knot. I don't recall the rest of it, but I asked my mother about the woman, because I couldn't quite understand falling on the hangman's knot. Seems Mary didn't wait for the drop, she tried to leap off the scaffold."

"Good God."

"The children thought it was quite diverting, leaping up in the air and falling down."

"Must have been appalling to watch."

"I'm sure it was, for the adults who knew who Mary was." He pushed a plate with slices of cake toward Rutledge.

But he shook his head, his appetite gone. Finishing his tea, he added, "I've a murderer to catch."

"I don't think there's a chance in hell that you'll do any such thing."

"I wonder . . ." He took out his handkerchief, unfolded it, and held it out to Mason.

"What's this?"

"I thought, having been a married man, you might tell me."

Mason leaned closer, poked the fragment with his finger, and said, "This has been burned. There's ash on it."

"Yes."

"I'm not sure—" He studied the fragment for a while, then said, "You know, in the practice of medicine, you must often guess about what you're seeing. If it's a rash, you consider all the rashes you know. If it's a fever, or vomiting, you do the same. And you treat what seems to be the most likely possibility. If I didn't know better—" He broke off again and rose. "I'll be back."

With some satisfaction, Rutledge listened as Mason hurried down the passage and then took the steps to the first floor.

Once he'd have asked his sister Frances about hats.

Mason was gone for several minutes, and then he came down the stairs again and strode back into the kitchen with a woman's hat in his hand. It was dark blue wool, of a style that had gone out of fashion in King Edward's day. There was a tiny veil attached at the front.

The doctor turned the hat over. "See this stiffening around the bottom? No idea what a milliner calls it. Helps the hat keep its shape, I expect. Or stay on the head. And then the fabric is sewn onto that. Now if you take that bit you have, and hold it—here, take the hat, and hold it just so—yes, and I'll put your bit beside it."

Rutledge held the hat open so that the back of it was clearly visible. And Mason took the fragment from the handkerchief and placed it carefully against the blue wool.

"What do you see?" Mason asked.

"It's a match. Well, enough of a match that it explains what I have here."

Mason grinned. "You don't have a wife. Else you'd know these things." He set the blue hat carefully to one side, and then returned the fragment to the handkerchief.

Rutledge suddenly remembered something. As a child, he'd put one of his sister's bonnets on the family dog, reducing her to tears when she saw Rover in the back garden wearing it.

"How did you come by that?" Mason asked, washing the ash from his fingers.

"In an unexpected place. Look at the gray, that little edging of gray. Do you think it might have matched the dead woman's coat? You told me it was a dark gray wool."

Mason peered at the scrap again. "I couldn't swear to it. But yes, I would say that to my eyes, it would. Rather a nice dark gray, you know."

James Westin had called it drab. "What became of the coat?"

"We buried it with her. Well, we didn't quite know what else to do with it."

Rutledge wrapped the fragment in his handkerchief again, and put it in his coat pocket. "A pity."

"In hindsight, yes."

Rutledge rose. "That's been the trouble with this inquiry. It's like a puzzle where many of the pieces are missing. It's difficult to be certain just what is important and what isn't."

Mason said slowly, "What else have you found?" When Rutledge didn't answer, he went on, "I've heard about those lapis beads. I am treating the boy with the measles, you know. His little sister is the proud owner of a new child's tea service. Your doing, the mother says. And you'd asked me about the family as well. Did the beads belong to the dead woman, do you think?"

"I found the owner. He told me he'd misplaced them."

Surprised, Mason said, "Here in Avebury?"

"That's a mystery I've yet to solve. Thank you for the tea. And I'd appreciate it if you didn't speak of that scrap from the fire. Or the lapis beads." Collecting his hat and heavy coat, he walked down the passage, with Mason just behind him.

"Have a care, Rutledge," the doctor said at the door. "I've got a feeling that there's something going on here that might be ugly."

12

It was an odd warning from Dr. Mason.

Hamish said, "Ye ken, whoever killed yon woman has covered his tracks verra' well."

And most murderers were not that clever. They were driven, and they made mistakes.

"Aye. But consider, if yon killer is sae clever, he could be just as clever putting the blame elsewhere."

"The vagrant."

"Or the Chief Inspector."

Rutledge had arrived at the inn. Taking the stairs to his room two at a time, he shut the door and gave that possibility some thought.

At the Yard, it was easy to make enemies. Advancement was slow in coming, but Leslie had risen quickly in his career, in spite of four years in France during the war. Who resented that? Who might be behind what was happening?

He could think of several names. Inspector Martin seemed to have Markham's ear, but he hadn't been promoted. Rutledge himself had

had a few problems with the man. And there was Chief Inspector Stanley. Leslie seemed to rub him the wrong way.

But were they killers?

Rutledge couldn't believe that they were. In his opinion, they weren't clever enough. But Leslie was. Why did so many small bits of fact seem to have the Leslie name on them?

He took out his notebook and scanned what he'd written there, and he found nothing he had overlooked, nothing he had misread, nothing he had not done.

If the killer *was* Leslie, he'd be a formidable opponent.

He was still wrestling with that problem when he left Avebury, heading for London.

P assing empty stretches, Rutledge wondered again why the killer hadn't simply left her body in a ditch at the side of the road. How was that different from leaving her in the ditch at Avebury?

There was some message here that he couldn't seem to decipher. There had been anger in the method of killing. Was there contempt in leaving her body in the ditch?

Or had that been necessary to give the killer time to get far away?

He went directly to Haldane's house. There was no one else to ask without endangering Leslie's career and his own.

The man was in his study when Rutledge was announced. He looked up and said, "Found the woman, have you?"

"Only that she might have arrived in England through Dover."

Haldane's eyebrows rose at that. "Well, well." He gestured to the chair across the desk from him.

Rutledge said, "The question is, why did she come to England? To visit a friend, to begin a new life, to look for someone she'd known in France or wherever she'd come from before that?"

"Which brings us back to the war."

"I expect it does."

Haldane considered Rutledge, his expression hard to read. "A great many Englishmen went to France during the war. Not all of them came home. It's possible she came to find someone who didn't survive—who didn't send for her when he came home, as he'd promised to do."

"If she hadn't found him—if he was dead—she wouldn't have been killed."

"I think you have a particular soldier in mind. An officer? Or a man in the ranks?"

"An officer. I can't really link him to this woman." But Leslie, who had a reputation for thoroughness, had failed to bring in her killer. "This is more an effort to eliminate than to confirm."

"To put your mind at ease? Or to spare him the embarrassment of bringing him in for questioning?"

"He was an officer in the war. He's presently an officer at the Yard."

Haldane sighed. "A complication indeed. May I ask why you wish to eliminate him from consideration?"

"I'm not sure. I've known him for some time. That's the problem."

"Then you are concerned about the repercussions if in the end, you must bring him in."

It was blunt. And astute.

"I have not wished to go that far." Rutledge was silent for a moment. Then he said, "He was assigned to the inquiry, and he failed to find the guilty party. I can see why, I've had the devil of a time as well. But there's something else that troubles me. Who better to shape the outcome of the inquiry than the man responsible for finding himself?"

"Then you want to know more about his war. If there is an enemy of this man. Or something that the Army never discovered. If he knew this woman."

With some reluctance he gave Haldane Leslie's name, regiment, and rank. But he knew there was no other way of learning what he needed to know.

Haldane said, "Thank you. It may take some time, you understand. But I will be in touch."

It was a dismissal, but Rutledge said, "I want to be wrong. I've always liked and respected the man."

"Perhaps you are wrong. But we shall soon know."

Too restless to go back to his flat, Rutledge drove through the busy streets of London until he reached the Tower, and found a place to leave his motorcar on a side street just above it. Getting out, he walked down to the entrance and stood there for a time, staring down into the moat. Clouds had moved in while he was speaking to Haldane, and now a spitting rain was beginning to fall. He ignored it.

His godfather, David Trevor, had told him once that he often went to the Tower to clear his mind when he encountered a problem with plans he was drawing up. An architect, he would stare at the White Tower, put up by the Normans to show a defeated country who had the power now. As a political statement, it had been very successful, but as a building, it had survived the men who had erected it through nine centuries of changing monarchies, intrigue, and even warfare. For Trevor, the Tower's very existence was satisfying, visible proof of what an architect's skill could achieve.

When it began to rain in earnest, Rutledge turned away, his thoughts no more settled than they had been when he arrived.

He walked back up the slight rise to where he'd left his motorcar. He was about to turn the crank when he noticed the pub just beyond where he was standing. He still wasn't in the mood to return to his flat, and on impulse, he walked on, opening the door and stepping into the dimly lit interior.

There was a young woman behind the bar, her blonde hair piled on top of her head like a coronet. She smiled, showing dimples, and said, "What will you have, love?"

"Tea," he said, realizing it was too early for anything stronger. She smiled, and disappeared into the kitchen, then came back with a towel, offering it to him. He wiped his wet face, grateful that the towel was clean and didn't smell of stale beer.

Chief Superintendent Markham would be demanding a report soon enough, and the question that had been on his mind standing by the Tower was how to forestall that demand until Haldane had had time to find the information he wanted.

And still inspiration failed him.

The tea came, and Rutledge handed the young woman the towel in exchange before adding milk and a little sugar, stirring absently. The cup was warm in his hand when he put down the spoon and drank a little.

Over the rim of the cup, he realized the young woman was watching him.

"You aren't a regular," she said. "Touring the Tower, were you, and caught in the rain?"

"No." He looked around and saw that he had the pub to himself. "You aren't very busy today."

"Wait another half hour. Then I'm run off my feet. Where are you from, if you don't mind my asking."

"London." He smiled.

Taking in his clothes and his manners, she said, "Barrister, then, are you?"

He wasn't in the mood to tell her the truth. And so he nodded.

"Is it a trial that's worrying you?"

Surprised, he said, "How did you know?"

"To be that wet, you must have been standing there in the rain. Thinking, most likely. And you finally come in here because it's dry and you don't want to return to your firm just now. You'd rather have a whisky, but it's too early. You don't chat me up."

After a moment, he said, "You're very good at reading people."

She smiled again. "I've nothing better to do, standing back here except to wash the glasses and give the customer what he wants. And see I make the correct change. So I study the faces of the people I see, and I've got good at guessing what brought them through the door." Shrugging, as if to make light of her skills, she said, "The tips are better when I know who I'm serving."

Intrigued, he said, "Do they usually try to lead you on?"

She considered the question. "Depends, doesn't it? If they've had enough to drink, they ask personal questions. If they're lonely, they just want someone to talk to, never mind how I answer back. If they've had a fight with the Missus, they're sullen, not much to say, and often no tip into the bargain." She nodded toward his cup. "Care for something with that tea? There are fresh scones today."

Rutledge shook his head. "Thanks, no. If someone has a problem he needs to work through, what does he do?"

"He sits over there, at the corner table, and broods. Sometimes if it's a woman he's thinking about, he might ask for advice."

He said idly, "And what if he's worried that a—a client of his might be guilty of a serious crime?"

She stared at him. "Is that why you were standing in the rain outside the Tower? I hear they shot traitors in there, during the war. Did you know? Is he likely to be hanged, your client? If he's guilty?"

"He might well be. Depends on the jury, doesn't it?"

The young woman nodded again. "Murder, then. Ask him. Face-to-face. It's the only way. Or hand him off to another barrister, and let *him* worry about the right and wrong of it."

He wasn't sure that Markham would hand over the inquiry to a third man. More than likely he would let it drop. For that matter, he might well decide that he'd got what he wanted, Rutledge's admission of failure.

"It's not quite that simple." He finished his tea.

"I don't see why not."

"I could be wrong."

"If you are thinking he's guilty, he probably is. But your choice," she said. "That's what it comes down to, anyway. Your choice."

He paid for the tea and asked her to join him in a drink later. She thanked him and pocketed the coin.

As he walked back to the motorcar her words echoed in his mind. *Your choice.*

Better to know your enemy . . .

And if he was wrong, there might still be time to find a killer.

The rain had dwindled to a heavy mist by the time Rutledge had driven back through the city. The top of Big Ben had disappeared, and the bridge over the Thames ended midriver in a thick wall of gray. London took on another character in such weather. Almost sinister, brooding. A place of secrets, where sound was muffled and voices preceded people before they appeared.

He avoided the Yard, taking a less direct way to his flat. He was just turning into the street that ran past his door when the fog stirred a little and he glimpsed another motorcar ahead of him.

Rutledge realized that it was very like the one he'd seen Leslie occasionally drive away from the Yard. He couldn't quite see it clearly enough to be sure who was driving. This was London, after all, motorcars were plentiful, and there were only so many variations in them.

Hamish said, "Is he back fra' Yorkshire? This is no' verra' close to his street."

Rutledge didn't answer, listening to the faint sounds the other motorcar made as it passed between the houses on either side of the street. His own echoed the whispering noise of passage only a few seconds afterward. When the sounds stopped at the next corner, he realized that the other driver must have turned left. He made the turn himself, just as a lorry materialized out of the murk, blotting out the slight whispers he'd followed. He found them again, made a second turn, and recognized where he was—these were the streets he would normally take to the Yard in the morning.

Had Leslie just returned to London—and decided to see if Rutledge was still in Wiltshire or back at the Yard?

Hamish said, "It's what ye would do, in his shoes."

Know your foe's whereabouts . . .

They had been taught that in the Army. Never lose sight of your enemy.

Rutledge took the next turning, picked up speed once he was beyond the other driver's hearing, and drove to the Yard in a roundabout fashion. Traffic was with him. But closer to the river, the fog was heavy, tickling the back of his throat as he left his motorcar near the Abbey, and set out on foot the rest of the way. He was just stepping off the pavement by Big Ben when a motorcar came out of the gray wall toward him, and he had to leap back out of its way.

He had only the briefest glimpse of the driver, not enough to be sure whether it was Leslie behind the wheel—or not. The dark shape disappeared in the direction of Downing Street and Horse Guards.

Had Leslie seen him? Rutledge started after him. The fog muffled sounds, blinded him to what was happening, but he could just see well enough to keep up a steady pace.

Footsteps were coming toward him, hollow in the fog. He stopped and listened to the rhythm of the steps. A man's pace, walking briskly. Had Leslie left his motorcar out of sight, and come back? Looking for Rutledge—or on his way to the Yard?

He decided to step out into the road and let Leslie pass him, then follow him down to the river where they could talk in private.

In the distance he could hear the muffled sound of horses stamping where the Household Cavalry stood guard.

The footsteps hurried past him. Then stopped.

Rutledge stayed where he was, his eyes on the wall of fog, all the while watching for any glimmer of the headlamps of an approaching vehicle.

There was silence all around him.

He smothered another cough as the fog caught the back of his throat again.

"*'Ware,*" Hamish exclaimed.

And the sixth sense that had saved him time and again in the trenches urged him to move.

He was nearly out of the road when a motorcar, its headlamps off, came up from Westminster behind him. He saw the brightness of chrome as the headlamps flared, pinning him where he was. Blinded, he couldn't see the driver—but the driver must have had a perfect view of his startled expression staring toward the invisible windscreen.

A spurt of speed, and the motorcar swerved toward him. Rutledge dove for the far side of the street. The wing brushed the edges of his coat and hip so hard, it spun him in a quarter circle, and he had to fight to keep from sprawling backward on the ground.

Almost as quickly as it had come, the motorcar disappeared, a swirl of gray fog in its wake.

Rutledge stood there, fighting for breath.

He could hear the motorcar moving faster still, and in the same instant there was a heavy *thud!* A woman screamed, high-pitched and then abruptly cut off.

Stiffly at first, he raced toward the cry, passing the horses, nearly stumbling over a purse lying in his path, unable to see the owner until he was almost on her.

She lay awkwardly, one leg twisted under her, her face a bloody mask.

He knelt down beside her, felt for a pulse. It was faint, irregular.

"Someone summon an ambulance," he shouted. "*Hurry!*"

In the distance a voice answered, "Where are you?"

"Send for an ambulance. I'll hear the bell." He got to his feet long enough to take off his coat and spread it over her, realizing as he did how tiny she was. Then he was back beside her.

He could hear footsteps running, but his attention was centered on the woman. The blood on her face was dripping into her fair hair, tumbled out of its pins. He took out a handkerchief to wipe the blood out of her eyes, and as he did, she opened them, looking up at him with pain and terror in her gaze.

"It's all right, help is coming," he said gently, fumbling for her gloved hand and holding it firmly in his. "I'm here, I won't leave you."

She clutched his fingers, a lifeline.

"Where does it hurt?" he asked, but she couldn't manage to speak. All he could see was the twisted limb and a wound on her scalp, by her hairline. Her dark green hat was just under her other hand, and he was reminded of the gray hat belonging to the dead woman. Shaking off the memory, he went on speaking to her, afraid to move her lest she have internal injuries. Telling her that she would be fine, that he wouldn't leave her. Asking her name.

Someone materialized out of the shrouding fog. He caught the gleam of the helmet badge first. A Constable. "There you are, sir. I've asked for an ambulance." He looked down at the woman, then knelt next to her, across her body from Rutledge. "Should we try to move her? She's still perilously in the road."

Rutledge shook his head slightly, and said to the woman, "Here's a policeman. You're in good hands."

But the light was fading from her eyes, and as the two men watched, she died.

The Constable crossed himself. "Who did this, sir?" he asked grimly. "Was it your motorcar?"

"I'm on foot. It was coming at speed, barely missed me, and then I heard it strike her. It was running without its headlamps. Then suddenly they were in my eyes. Almost impossible to see the vehicle or the driver. They might have blinded her as well."

"I take it that it didn't stop?"

"No." This close he could read the Constable's name. It was Fuller. "Who is she?"

"I don't know. She couldn't tell me. Her purse is over there somewhere."

The Constable rose and went to search for it. Rutledge closed her eyes, spread the bloody handkerchief across the dead face, and sat back on his heels.

He hadn't seen the motorcar. He couldn't describe it, and he most certainly couldn't claim he knew the owner. It could have been anyone.

The Constable was back, a black leather purse in his hands. He knelt again, opened it gingerly, and, taking off his gloves, he poked around with one finger.

"Handkerchief," he listed, taking it out. "Lace. Initials in the corner. *JRRF*. A small looking glass, same initials in silver on the back, a comb, a smaller purse containing money—ah. A case of calling cards." He lifted out the silver monogrammed case and opened it.

"Mrs. Gerald FitzPatrick. It has her direction as well." He was interrupted by the ambulance bell, and handed the contents of the purse to Rutledge as he stood up and prepared to stop it.

Rutledge set the contents back inside after abstracting one of the engraved calling cards, slipping it into his pocket. He could hear the Constable telling the attendants that the lady was sadly deceased. He went on, quietly giving information for the morgue.

When the attendants came to collect the body, Rutledge retrieved his coat and watched as she was placed on a stretcher and carried to the ambulance. Small as she was, she hadn't had a chance against the speeding vehicle. He felt a sudden surge of anger.

Looking down at the puddle of blood, already mixing with the dirty rainwater, he saw her hat, picked it up, and strode to the ambulance before the doors were closed. "This is hers."

The attendant thanked him and laid the dark green hat at her feet, next to her purse. Rutledge stepped back.

This was a case for the Metropolitan police, not the Yard. But he would make it his business to find out what he could.

He'd seen Leslie. He was certain of it. But where was he now?

As the ambulance pulled away, silent now, the Constable turned to Rutledge. "Your name, sir, in the event we can find the blackguard who did this."

He gave his name and direction, adding, "I'd like to know what you discover."

The Constable was about to tell him that he would find out in due course, if he was called on to testify to the speed of the motorcar. But when he looked up, what he saw in Rutledge's face stopped him in midsentence. "I'll see that you are, sir." His gaze moved on to the wall of white. "A pity, this. They'll send someone to speak to her family. I'm always grateful that's not my duty." He moved out into the street, searching for any evidence that might identify the motorcar. "It'll be dented. Must have been."

The two men searched for several minutes, but there was nothing. In the end he thanked Rutledge for his help, touched his helmet in a brief salute, and went back to his rounds.

Rutledge watched him disappear into the fog, then turned and walked back the way he'd come. He could hear the bell of Big Ben striking the hour, but almost missed his own motorcar, having to circle back twice before he saw it looming ahead of him.

Changing his mind, he walked on to the Yard. The Duty Sergeant looked up, greeted him, and was about to resume checking a list when Rutledge said, "I thought I saw Leslie on his way here."

"He was, sir. Just stopped long enough to drop off a file for Sergeant Gibson. Then he left."

"Heading home, was he?"

"He didn't say, sir."

Rutledge left, found his motorcar a second time, and drove with great care, watching for the shapes of pedestrians at every crossing.

In the aftermath of shock at the woman's death, he tried to bring back the image of Leslie driving past where he'd been standing at the corner. But it was hazy, almost unreal. Still—Leslie had stopped in at the Yard. He'd been close by.

Had that been Leslie's motorcar coming at him out of the fog? Try as he would, the only thing he could remember was the flash of chrome as the huge round headlamps flared in his eyes. Leslie's motorcar possessed those. As did his own. In the almost white brightness, he couldn't see past to the windscreen behind them, the radiator between them—not even the wings on either side. They had been blotted out.

Rutledge gave up trying.

Hamish said, "The police arena' likely to find him. Whoever he is."

Tempted, he took the next turning and made his way toward Carlton Square, where the FitzPatricks lived. It was not as fashionable a street as some, but the houses were handsomely kept up and spoke of old money. He drove past number 7, with its black trim and railing, leading down the pair of steps to the street. The lamps were lit in the front rooms, and he glimpsed a tall green-and-white vase with silk flowers in one of the windows, framed by what appeared to be matching dark green drapes.

Rounding the square, he drove on to the house where the Leslies lived. But there was no motorcar standing in front of it. Nor in front of any of the other houses. Which meant there was a mews in which they could be kept.

He looked for it, found the old horse stabling that had been converted behind some squares to house motorcars, but when he searched it, the Leslie vehicle wasn't among the half dozen kept there, although there was one with a black body that was very close to his.

There was no point in driving on to the silent, empty flat. The unseen driver of the motorcar must surely have felt the wing strike Rutledge a glancing blow. He had most certainly felt the weight of Mrs. FitzPatrick's slight body colliding with his headlamp and wing as he lost control of his forward speed. Let him wonder, then, just how much damage he had done.

He turned the motorcar toward the western road, but it was a good forty miles before he ran out of the fog into patches of light rain.

Tired and concerned about his own driving, late as it was, he found an inn in a small village well east of Marlborough and took a room. It was already ten o'clock, and he'd been on the road for some time. But he asked for warm water from the kitchen and sponged all traces of Mrs. FitzPatrick's blood from his coat, then brushed out the wet areas. He'd learned in the trenches how to keep his uniform tidy, how to sew on buttons, and even how to mend small tears. Necessity, he thought as he worked, was often the best teacher. They'd been given small sewing kits. His batman had been all thumbs when it came to a needle—but one of the best shots Rutledge had ever seen. It had been, he'd thought at the time, worth the aggravation of doing such tasks himself. Grant had very quickly taught German snipers to keep their heads down or risk a bullet between the eyes.

Spreading his coat over the back of the only chair, he paused. Private Archie Grant had died on the Somme of gangrene from a wound in the calf. There had been no time in the heat of that first battle for seemingly lighter wounds to be treated. Even the severest cases had been ignored while the doctors tried to save those who would live. There had been too many casualties to tend half of them . . . And in his dreams Rutledge still heard the moans and cries of the dying.

Hamish said, "He was a guid soldier. It wasna' an easy way to die."

His leg black and swollen three times its size, Grant had stood at his post until fever and exhaustion took its toll. He'd died of blood loss in a forward aid tent as they tried to take the limb.

Shaking off the memory, Rutledge washed his face and hands in what was left in the pitcher of warm water, then undressed.

There was a darkening bruise at his hip. It could have been worse.

He was too tired to dream.

He got a very early start the next morning. It had been raining steadily since sometime after midnight, and by sunrise a heavy mist had settled over the countryside. Once more he drove with care, having no wish to run off the road and lose an axle, for he could see barely five feet in front of the bonnet. Finally reaching the avenue into Avebury shortly after nine, he paused briefly between the two stones at the entrance. Here the mists had thinned slightly, the great stones on his left looming out of it like gray, ghostly sentinels, appearing and disappearing. Even accustomed as he was to this place, he felt a slight shiver.

He moved on down the avenue, and at the junction with the street that ran down by the church or right toward the inn, he was about to turn when a woman's figure materialized seemingly out of nowhere, directly in his path.

With images of Mrs. FitzPatrick lying bleeding in the rain, he reached for the brake.

It was the Rector's wife coming up from the direction of the church.

She stopped, a little startled, and then looked up at him, clearly expecting him to slow and speak to her.

His first thought as he turned toward her was that she was about to demand the photograph.

"Good morning," he said, offering her a smile. "Not that it is," he added.

She didn't return his greeting. "You are wanted," she said, as if he'd been delinquent on purpose and failed in his duty.

"What happened?" he asked quickly, braced for the worst.

"Constable Henderson and Dr. Mason have gone out to the Long Barrow. Do you know it? The doctor left a message for you. Apparently, he wasn't certain when you'd return."

"Yes, I know it. How long ago did they leave?" Rutledge asked.

"I've no idea. I went to the surgery just now for more of the Rector's headache powders. The doctor wasn't there, of course. I couldn't help but see the message. It's on his desk, prominently placed."

"Then I'll go directly to the surgery myself." Touching his hat to her, he moved on.

Drawing up in front of the gate he got down and walked up to the door. It was not latched, and he stepped into the silent house. Turning to his right, he went through the door by the stairs and into the part of the house where Mason saw his patients—where the body of the dead woman had been brought.

He walked through the tiny reception area just inside the separate surgery entrance, and into the doctor's office. On Mason's tidy desk a sheet of paper lay on the green blotter. As he reached for it, Rutledge heard Hamish saying, "Ye ken, this isna' a verra' guid sign."

Ignoring the voice in his head, Rutledge lifted the sheet from the blotter and scanned it before reading it a second time.

Rutledge. If you see this, we're just going, Henderson and I, to the Long Barrow on the plain beyond Silbury Hill. The far end. You'll see my carriage. There's my other horse in the stable behind the house. Your motorcar won't make it after all the rain we've had.

As an afterthought, Mason had left the date and time.

An hour ago . . .

But he had neglected to say *why* he was on his way there with the Constable. To prevent anyone who stopped in the surgery from spreading word before whatever it was could be confirmed?

That must mean another body.

He turned and went back into the house proper, walked into the kitchen, and saw that Mason must have just finished his breakfast. Dishes had been left on the table, nothing cleared away. The ends of toast, a smear of yellow yolk, congealing. The teapot was cold.

Going out into the yard, he crossed the puddled garden on the narrow path that separated vegetables and the house flower beds. He could hear the horse in the small stable, stirring as if eager for his breakfast as well.

Opening the door, he saw there were two stalls and an open space for feed and for the doctor's carriage. In the nearest stall was a tall chestnut gelding with a lopsided white blaze on his nose. It gave him a slightly tipsy appearance, but as Rutledge approached the stall's door and spoke to him, he reached out and sniffed Rutledge's clothing. He nodded his head, blowing a little, and waited.

Rutledge found bridle, blanket, and saddle on the wall beside where the carriage was kept. Carrying them back to the stall, he talked to the horse as he worked, and found it more eager to get out into the brisk air than objecting to what Rutledge was doing. Finishing the straps, he led the animal out into the small stable yard, and mounted.

It had been some time since he'd ridden, but once in the saddle, he felt at home and urged the horse forward. It set off at a steady trot, almost as if it knew where it was heading. But when they had passed through the two stones at the far end of the avenue and he turned the animal toward his left, it hesitated, as if more used to going in the opposite direction. There wouldn't be much call for a doctor on the broad and empty plain.

"Not this time, old son," he said, and the horse obediently followed the touch of his heel.

It was impossible to see any marker that would lead him to the Long Barrow. But he started forward, counting on his sense of direction to guide him. Or failing that, he thought wryly, the horse knowing where his stable mate might be. The ground beneath his mount's hooves was soggy with moisture, the chalk unable to absorb any more rain.

And then fifteen minutes later, the perfectly conical shape of Silbury Hill appeared out of the mist, to his right. He kept going, thinking that he might well collide with the Long Barrow before he could see it. He recalled the opening was at the east end of the long earthen, almost loaf-shaped mound. But that wasn't necessarily where Dr. Mason and Henderson would be. For all he knew, they'd already passed him, going back to the village. Sound traveled peculiarly in this heavy a mist.

Hamish said, "Ye should ha' left a message of ye're ain."

"He'll see my motorcar by the house." Rutledge was beginning to think he'd overshot his goal, traveling onward across the plain. Just then he heard a horse calling, his own mount responding.

Rising slightly in his stirrups, Rutledge shouted, "Mason? It's Rutledge."

"Damn it, man, I can't see a thing."

Following the direction of the voice, he trotted on. He'd walked through this green, quiet plain as a student on holiday, stopping here to eat his lunch before moving on. It had been an impressive trek, through prehistoric mounds and barrows. He'd had a compass then, and a good survey map. But he hadn't gone inside the barrow.

Mason called again, and Rutledge adjusted his direction. Then without warning, he was almost on the mound. Turning the horse to the right, he saw the back of a carriage appearing out of the mist, and then a horse, tail swishing in a steady rhythm.

Mason said, "Over here."

Rutledge dismounted, looped his reins over the high rear wheel of the carriage, and walked past the horse in the shafts to the line of misshapen stones that guarded the entrance to the barrow. Mason was waiting for him by one of them.

"Good, I'm glad you made it. This way." He rested a hand on a stone, guiding Rutledge back to where rough steps led through a narrow opening.

Hamish, busy in the back of Rutledge's mind, was not eager to go farther.

Ignoring the voice, Rutledge followed the doctor. He was in a sort of forecourt, now, the chamber to his left, a square stone blocking the exit from the forecourt to his right. Rainwater had darkened the rubble underfoot.

Henderson appeared out of the mist. He looked wary, as though he was not as pleased to see the Yard as Mason was.

"Just there. Behind the Constable," Mason was saying, and Henderson moved out of the way.

13

For the first time Rutledge saw what had brought them all here. A worn pair of boots, then trouser-clad legs, a greatcoat, and finally a head.

Thin dark hair framed a ravaged face.

Rutledge's first thought was, *It's a man.* Somehow, in the back of his mind, he'd feared they'd found another female victim. And then, *We'll have the devil's own time identifying him.*

For the man had been dead some days, he could see that clearly. Scavengers had been at the soft tissues, and worms as well. Along the chin, the bridge of the nose, and the ridge above the eyes, white bone showed through the torn flesh in places. The teeth were bared in a macabre grimace, lips and part of the cheeks missing.

His gaze moved down the body again. The greatcoat the man was wearing was an officer's, threadbare in places and dark with rainwater.

"Great God—" he began, and stopped. They didn't know, Mason or Henderson, about the break-in at the Leslie house, did they? Unless gossip from Stokesbury had already reached their ears.

"He won't be pleasant to take up," Henderson said sourly, as if agreeing with what Rutledge had been about to say.

The mists moved again, hiding the poor face.

"Does he come from Avebury? One of the other villages?" Rutledge asked. "Can you recognize him?"

Henderson shook his head. "There's not enough left to know. But from the look of him, he's a vagrant."

"How did he die? Doctor?"

Mason took a deep breath. "I can't be sure. There's a gin bottle over there, by the chamber entrance. Do you see?"

Rutledge leaned forward. He could just see the mouth of it.

"Drank himself into oblivion and died of the cold, most likely," Henderson added.

But why out here in the open, when he could have sheltered inside the narrow chamber, well out of the weather?

"Anything in his pockets? Have you checked?" Rutledge looked from one man to the other.

"Best to wait until I have him in the surgery."

"How long has he been dead? Can you tell?" he asked Mason.

"Hard to say until I've examined the remains. Less than a week, I'd guess, but he's lain out here in the elements. That changes a body. There were crows at him when we got here this morning. And not the first time, either. It took some doing to scatter them."

Crows, the traditional scavengers on battlefields.

"Who found him?"

"That was Mr. Downing," Mason said. "He lives on the far side of the church. He has two young retrievers he's training. Brings them out to run. One of them disappeared over the steps, and Downing feared it had cornered a polecat. He went after the dog, and damn near fell over the body. He came for me, and I collected Henderson. I asked Downing if he'd touched anything, he or the dog, but he told me he hadn't."

"How did the body come here? Any signs that he's been moved?"

"We'd scouted about the entrance when we got here," Henderson said. "Best we could in the circumstances. If there were any tracks, we couldn't find them. Not even Downing's. From the state of the corpse's boots, my guess is that he was caught out in the open when the rain started, and he took shelter here. There's a hole in one of them."

"How did he know there was a chamber here? A dry place? Unless he was local?"

Henderson shook his head. "There's no other shelter out here." He gestured toward the shrouded plain beyond—isolated, empty. Very wet. "Hard to say just where he might've come from, or even where he might be going. For all we know, he didn't want to show his face in Avebury or West Kennet."

"Have you gone into the chamber?"

It was Mason who answered him. "Only into the entrance. We hadn't thought to bring a torch. Not with this mist. From what we could see, he hadn't been living there."

The dead man wasn't tall. Five foot eight, perhaps? He himself had carried men of that size over his shoulder, across No Man's Land, or to the connecting trench, the dead sometimes left unceremoniously where no one could see them. Bad for morale if they were underfoot or propped against the trench wall to wait for the stretcher bearers.

"Is there a road nearby? I can't remember."

"A track of sorts. If you knew where to find it. If you're thinking he might have come that way, it makes sense."

"A motorcar might come that far?"

Mason said, "You needn't worry about that. We can get him into the carriage, I think." He pulled his coat tighter around him. "If you're finished, I'll fetch the sheet."

Rutledge glanced at Henderson, who said, "I'm satisfied."

Mason disappeared in the mist. Henderson was looking over his shoulder, as if half expecting someone to come out of the inner chamber.

When he saw that Rutledge had noticed his unease, he said, "I came here once as a lad. On a dare. It was at the September equinox. I was never so frightened as I was that night. There's something odd about what's inside there. I could feel it in my bones, and I slipped out, slept rough, rather than stay there. Just before sunup, I went a step or two back inside, before the others came to see if I'd spent the night in the chamber. I was shivering, wishing they'd hurry, when a spear of light came in through a crack over there, with the rising sun."

He gestured over his shoulder. "It started here, just inside. And it moved slowly around the wall until it reached the chamber at the rear. Then it moved down the other side, so bright I had to look away. When I opened my eyes, it was just about to vanish. As if it had never been. I couldn't have sworn what I saw was real. And I couldn't tell anyone, for fear they'd laugh at me. I'd never been afraid of the stones or the hills or the barrows before, but then I was. Took me years to get over it."

"I daresay the builders planned the opening that way."

"I didn't know that at ten, did I? It was a wonder I didn't lose my wits. The other lads thought I was brave. I never told them."

Mason came back into the forecourt, a bundle of canvas under his arm. He handed one end to Henderson, and they set about rolling the body onto it. That took some doing. Rigor had long since passed off, and they finally had to grip the shoulders of the greatcoat and ankles of his boots in order to shift him. The head lolled to one side and one arm dragged until Rutledge caught the sleeve and lifted it across the body.

Working the body out of the forecourt through the narrow, uneven opening was the next problem, but they finally managed to get clear of the stones and carry the dead man to the carriage. The final hurdle was setting it on the floorboards. While Mason was catching his breath, Rutledge went back to the chamber and retrieved the empty gin bottle. He scanned the ground where the body had lain, but it was as if the dead man had left no trace in the place where he'd died.

When he got back to the carriage, Henderson had already taken his place and Mason was just climbing in. Rutledge handed them the bottle, then took up his own reins and mounted.

The rest of the way to the doctor's surgery, Rutledge considered the dead man.

Was he the ex-soldier whom Leslie claimed had broken into his house on the night that the unknown woman had died? Rutledge had almost been convinced he hadn't existed.

But why was he still in the area now? If he was a thief, why had he lingered, in constant danger of being seen and taken up by a local Constable?

Hamish said, breaking the silence, "Unless he wasna' here at all, and it took his killer time to find a likely ex-soldier?"

Henderson and Rutledge stood to one side of the table as Dr. Mason began to cut away the dead man's clothes. The room was cold, but the smell of rotting flesh rose from the sodden clothing, with a strong odor of gin and wet wool. There was also a pervasive smell of chalky soil, where the back of his clothing had rested so long against the ground.

Mason worked at the seams, so as to destroy nothing that might prove useful, slowly removing the greatcoat, then the uniform beneath. It bore Corporal's stripes, and the insignia of the Royal Engineers. Mason, looking up, said, "The outer coat might have been given him when the weather changed. Or come from a charity?"

After a while, the thin white body lay on the table, exposed, oddly vulnerable.

"Poorly nourished," he went on. "He's been out of work for some time, I think. I'd put his age at early thirties. A young man. No recent wounds on the body to indicate foul play. But those scars—" He pointed to a long, badly healed one on the man's right leg, then to more across his shoulders, puckered and ugly. "War wounds. Shrapnel, on the shoulders." They helped him turn the remains over, and then he scanned the back. "Nothing new here, either. And there's not enough left of his fingers to judge whether he was in a fight, but the lack of bruising tells me there are no internal injuries that might have killed him. He didn't sustain a beating." He nodded, and they restored the body to its original position, faceup, damaged eyes staring at nothing. "I'll have to look inside later. So far I can't find anything that would call for more than the briefest of inquests."

"We still don't know who he is," Rutledge commented.

"There'll be something here." Mason moved on to the pile of clothing on a nearby table. The uniform yielded only his rank, the insignia of the Royal Engineers, two shillings, tuppence, and a farthing.

Rutledge, impatient now, said, "Try the coat pockets."

Mason picked up the greatcoat, reaching into the right-hand pocket first. "Something here . . ."

He pulled out the crumpled wrappings of a packet of biscuits. Rutledge stared at it but said nothing. It was a popular enough name.

Setting that half of the greatcoat aside, Mason took up the other half, reaching into the pocket. "You'd think he'd carry some identification. If he fell ill—no, this pocket is empty as well. Wait—" He withdrew his hand, opened the palm, and in it lay a pair of earrings.

Frowning, he looked down at them. "Earbobs," he said. "My wife has a similar pair—a rather nice pearl set in gold. Rather expensive for a down-on-his-luck ex-soldier. He could have sold them for enough food to see him through what's left of the winter."

Earrings had been taken from the Leslie house.

Rutledge said, "The tunic. Look at the pocket lining."

"I have already searched that pocket. It was empty."

"No, the lining itself."

The doctor retrieved the front of the dead man's tunic.

"Turn it over, please."

Mason glanced at him, but did as he was asked. There on the cloth of the pocket was a patch of faded ink that had run, and the rain hadn't helped it. He held it up, close to his eyes. "Something's written there. You're right."

"Men in the trenches sometimes wrote their names inside their pockets. To be sure they were identified." He gestured to the body on the table. "Still, we're assuming that that's his own uniform, that it wasn't given to him, like the officer's greatcoat."

"Look in that drawer. There's a glass there. It magnifies."

But try as they would, they couldn't make out the letters.

"Reilly," Henderson said at length, peering at the blue smudges on the cloth. Then he passed the glass to Mason again.

The doctor shook his head. "It looks more like Raleigh, I think."

Rutledge, taking his turn, finally said, "Radleigh." He brought the glass closer to the fabric, frowning. "*A*. And either *J* or *L*."

"If you say so," Mason replied. "Your eyes are the younger. All the same, I'd keep Raleigh in mind if I were you. Meanwhile, I'll see what's inside of him that might shed some light on the cause of death." He looked at the pale, thin body. "Made it through the war, didn't he, only to die alone with a bottle. Where is his family, I wonder?"

All the way to Marlborough, Hamish argued with Rutledge over the telephone call he was about to put through.

"You'll know the sooner if ye ask Haldane."

"No."

"If ye speak to yon Sergeant, word will get back to the Chief Inspector that a body has been found."

"It will reach him soon enough, once Constable Benning is told. And he'll have to be informed. He'll see that Leslie knows, as the householder."

"It will close the inquiry. In Avebury and in Stokesbury."

"Not if I can help it," Rutledge said grimly.

"Then speak to Haldane."

In the end, Rutledge compromised and spoke to a friend in the War Office.

"Corporal A. J. or L. Radleigh? Possibly the Royal Engineers? Good God, Rutledge, it's an impossible task."

"The war is over. You aren't all that busy, are you?" Rutledge countered.

Edwards laughed. "We're preparing for the next one. It will take Parliament that long to agree to fund it. No, seriously. Do you at least have a village or even a county to narrow the search?"

"Sorry. No. I've just found his body."

The voice on the other end of the line changed. "Pity. Murder, then? Or you wouldn't be asking me."

"We aren't sure. He's been out in the elements, you see. He could be from any part of England, wandering about looking for work. He's been at it for some time, and he must have gone hungry more often than not. The doctor who examined him has given his age as early thirties. Wounded twice, in the leg and across the shoulders. Light brown hair. Possibly brown eyes. Five eight at a guess. Thin build."

"Well. Let me see what I can do." There was resignation in the voice now. "Where are you?"

Rutledge told him. "I'll be back in two days' time. Will that work?"

"God knows. But I'll try." He rang off.

Rutledge put up the receiver, but he stood there for several minutes staring into space, mulling over the discovery of the soldier's body, and what it might mean. It wasn't until someone tapped impatiently on the glass doors that he stirred, and left the little room to the red-faced man in the passage.

When he got back to Avebury, he borrowed Mason's horse again, and set out for the Long Barrow.

Mason, questioning him, had said, "But what do you expect to find? The man died of acute alcohol poisoning. A pity," he added, echoing Edwards at the War Office. "But it's Henderson's inquiry, now, not yours. Hardly a Yard matter, drinking oneself to death."

"It's a matter of being thorough," Rutledge said, and he left it at that.

It was already late afternoon. The wind had risen, dispatching the mist and sending scudding dark clouds across the sky. What light there was came and went, and the stones in Avebury seemed to change shape with the changing shadows. He felt the full force of the wind out on the plain. A brief patch of sunlight threw Silbury Hill's long shadow across the land, and then he watched it shrink as the clouds closed.

Beyond lay the Long Barrow, and soon he could see the line of stones guarding the chamber at its eastern end, a stark cluster, misshapen and sinister in this light. It was odd, he thought, that only these monuments to the dead or whatever gods their builders worshipped were all that remained of such a distant past. No houses or huts or marketplaces, no graveyard or drawings or testaments to what they believed and why.

Shrugging off his mood, he guided the horse to circle the outside of the barrow, moving at a walk down one length and up the other, looking for anything that might tell him why a man had died here. But whoever he was, he'd left nothing behind.

And then Rutledge was back once more at the makeshift steps that led into the forecourt. He'd remembered to bring his torch, to look inside the chamber itself.

The horse was skittish in the wind, and Rutledge was careful to loop the reins around a stone. He had no desire to walk back to Avebury in the dark, even with a torch. The plain was littered with barely visible stones, a certain way to sprain an ankle or break one's neck.

He climbed into the forecourt. There was nothing to show now where the body had been found. Taking his time, he examined his surroundings, and then turned toward the chamber.

Recalling what Mason had said, that the dog's owner had been afraid he'd cornered a polecat, Rutledge flicked on the torch and shone it around the entrance to be sure. But nothing stirred, no eyes reflected the beam, and he walked inside.

It was noticeably chillier in here, and his footsteps crunched on the grit under his boots, echoing eerily. How had men five thousand years ago brought these heavy stones here and matched them well enough to build the outer passage, much less this chamber? Some of the stones were smooth, some rough, whether by design or not he couldn't judge. With no tools except for horn and human muscle, they had created two sides, a roof projecting a little beyond the opening to keep the entrance dry, and, as he could see ahead, a rounded alcove at the far end. All of it balanced perfectly, then the barrow had been mounded over with earth and chalk. It was still, he thought, just as they had left it, whoever they were.

As he proceeded, the dim light from the forecourt faded to darkness, and the torch beam grew brighter. Yet the roof was higher than his head, giving a sense of space around him.

Huge boulders stood on either side of him, a seemingly solid wall of them, and the skill with which they had been matched and set in place was impressive.

He could find no indication that the dead man had spent any time here, no blankets or bedding, no cache of food. No signs of a fire.

He'd been in caves before, and in the tunnels under the trenches that had been dug to blow up the enemy line. But he hadn't been claustrophobic then—not until the night on the Somme when the whole of the sector had all but vanished as a shell fell short and buried him, his men, and the man he'd just shot.

But he was beginning to feel a rising panic, the deeper he went, as if there was something about the nature of this passage into the earth that was tangible, as if the walls were closing in on him—something that seemed to move up from the balls of his feet thought his entire body, shaking his resolve. Even Hamish was silent.

It was as if a presence was there in the darkness behind him, and he whirled, casting the light from side to side almost in the same instant that he realized the presence might be Hamish, visible at last. His heart pounding now, he sent the torch light spiraling upward before turning it off.

He was looking back the way he'd come, toward the dwindling daylight in the forecourt. He could swear that he wasn't alone. And yet there was nothing to see.

He *was* alone . . .

Taking a deep breath, he turned his back on the passage, then flicked on the torch again.

He had reached the rounded end, like the end of a basilica.

He clenched his teeth. *It was his claustrophobia, nothing else,* he told himself grimly. *He'd come here on purpose, and he was damned if he would leave before he'd finished what he'd come to do.*

He cast the light around him, slowly and carefully, forcing himself to pay attention to what he was seeing. Yet there was nothing to be seen but how perfectly the stones had been set up to form this rounded, rather elegant space. There were no bones that he could see, no sign of fires, nothing. Just bare stone.

A gust of wind swept into the forecourt, and he heard his horse snort and move restlessly.

He turned to leave, first moving the light down the passage again. Something caught his attention, and he brought the beam back for a better look.

There, he thought, *just there.* An oddly shaped darkness. The question was, what was it?

He forced himself to walk slowly back down the chamber to that spot, and when he reached it, he raised the torch so that its beam spread into what he could now see was a narrow cavity. A polecat's cozy home?

Instead something black reflected the torch beam.

Rutledge hesitated, then with his gloved hand, slowly reached toward what he'd seen. As his fingers brushed it, he realized it was solid, and yet it moved slightly.

Intrigued, he closed his fingers over the thing and carefully lifted it out.

Black leather.

A woman's purse.

He stood there, staring at it. Good-quality leather, with two handles and a clasp. And far more modern than the stones that had hidden it. He felt the sides, and his excitement rose: there was something in it.

He looked once more into the cavity, but it was empty now.

Whatever had seemed to be there, following him, had vanished, but he could hardly breathe. Holding tightly to the purse, he moved forward, scanning the walls again as he went.

He was finally at the end of the chamber, almost into the forecourt. He took a deep breath, but the unease he'd felt inside didn't leave him. And he couldn't find the courage to turn and throw the torch beam back toward its rounded end. He was suddenly reminded of what Constable Henderson had said about the rising sun on the equinox that had sent that unexpected beam of light around the chamber walls.

He could understand now what the man had been saying—that there was something here that wasn't at Silbury Hill or at Avebury. Not a haunting. Just—something. The imprint of an ancient people—

Stepping out into the open, into what was now dusk, he was glad to see his horse was still there. Looking down, he switched off the torch, but kept it close.

The forecourt was shadowy. Rutledge debated looking into the purse there and then, or taking it back to the inn.

But his curiosity got the better of him. Opening the clasp, he peered inside.

A woman's things. Toward the end of the forecourt was a flat bit of ground, and kneeling, he turned on the torch again and then began to remove the contents, setting them out one by one in a tidy row.

A lady's comb. A linen handkerchief—no initials. A pretty compact holding face powder. Several hairpins. Three coins—two English pennies and a half-penny.

Surely a destitute man would have taken those?

He'd come to the bottom. There was nothing left as far as he could see.

No identification, no papers, nothing that would tell him who had owned it.

A surge of disappointment swept him.

The purse could have belonged to anyone. A woman in Cornwall or Northumberland. It could have been stolen a fortnight ago or weeks earlier. The stone chamber would have kept it safe and dry for a very long time.

He began to collect the items, but as he picked up the compact, he realized that it was silver, and just beginning to tarnish. There was a pretty design on the top, and he thought it must have been rather expensive. Or a gift, perhaps? He turned it over. On the bottom, near the rim, he could just make out the name of a French shop. *L'Oreille.* But such things could probably be bought in any large English town. Hardly proof of who had owned it. He was about to drop it back inside the purse when his hand brushed the torch, and it shifted a little. He was still looking at the compact, and as the light moved, he realized that what he'd thought was a mere design, intended to be pretty and nothing else, wasn't a design at all but three initials beautifully and intricately entwined. He turned the compact this way and that in the torch light, to see them better.

KLE. The *L* was slightly larger, as if it was her surname.

Katherine?

14

Rutledge knelt there on the cold ground, looking at the compact in the palm of his gloved hand.

He desperately wanted this to belong to the dead woman. The first thing of hers he'd found, save for that burnt bit of a hat.

Turning the purse upside down, he gently emptied it again, then felt around in the silk lining, his fingers urgently searching. Would she have been worried enough to hide something personal where prying eyes couldn't see it?

At first all he discovered was a small rip in the silk lining, and he pulled it out to have a better look.

Something fell by his knee with a delicate ring.

He looked down at it.

A small silver pin, shaped like a crescent moon. And caught in it was a long, fine black hair.

He didn't touch it at first. Almost afraid that it wasn't there, that it was only wishful thinking on his part.

Whoever had burned the gray hat couldn't bring themselves to burn the pretty pin as well. But it couldn't be kept, that was too dangerous. Too many awkward questions might be asked.

Instead, it had been slipped inside the lining. Out of sight. And even if someone did find it, it would have been meaningless to most people.

On the reverse, there was the same stamped name. *L'Oreille*.

Only a killer, a dead woman, and Rutledge knew about the crescent moon. And he'd known only because a sharp-eyed port official had noticed it. The woman wearing it was pretty and had caught his attention.

But who had put it here, in the purse lining?

Who, for that matter, had hidden the purse here, in a dark crevice behind a boulder that supported the stone chamber?

The dead Corporal? Or his killer?

By the time the weather warmed and walkers and visitors came to explore the Long Barrow, the forecourt and the chamber, even if one of them discovered the purse, who would connect it to an unknown woman found dead in Avebury over the winter? Even if it were reported to Constable Henderson by some conscientious visitor, this purse wouldn't shed any light on her past or her identity.

Hamish spoke, making him jump. "If it was hidden here by yon killer, it wasna' the cleverest idea to leave a dead man here as weil."

"Unless it was intended that he be blamed for the woman's death as well as the break-in at Stokesbury. A case could be made for that. He might have seen her walking along the road, and followed her to Avebury, killing her when she spurned his advances."

"It makes a verra' good story."

It did. One easily believed at an inquest. No one would think that a Chief Inspector at the Yard could possibly be involved.

But the question remained. *Why* was he involved? What did this woman have to do with him?

Rutledge knew he should take what he'd discovered to Chief Superintendent Markham. Yet if he did, the strange business of a murdered woman found in Avebury would surely become a closed file, he'd be ordered to look no further. This was the sort of tidy ending that Markham preferred. And he himself would be given the credit for solving a murder that even Chief Inspector Leslie had failed to unravel.

It would go a very long way toward mitigating the shame he'd endured in that last business about Alan Barrington. It could, in fact, resurrect his standing at the Yard.

Any man would be tempted.

But one person would know that none of it was true. That the evidence had been laid out for Rutledge by a clever killer who was experienced at covering his tracks.

And *he* would laugh.

"I can't believe the dead man was clever enough to have done all this," he said aloud. "And why hide the purse? If he'd kept it with him this long, why hide it now?"

"Aye," Hamish agreed. "But ye havena' found out *why*. And until ye do, who do you think yon Chief Superintendent will believe? You, with the shame of your past? Or the Chief Inspector, who has the respect of the Yard?"

That stung. But it was true.

Letting it go for the moment, Rutledge made certain he'd collected everything that had come from the black purse, then he got to his feet.

If the purse was here, if it had been left here to connect the dead Corporal to the murder of the woman in Avebury, what about the weapon? The knife?

That meant going back into the chamber.

He didn't think he could face it again. Not so soon.

He had no choice. It had to be done.

Picking up the torch and clenching his teeth, he ignored the thundering of his heart as he stepped back into the shadows.

It was an empty stone barrow, he told himself. There was nothing here, nothing to fear except his own imagination.

It took all the will he possessed to search every crevice he could find. There aren't that many of them, thank God, he told himself as he shone his torch in first one and then another, moving slowly deeper and deeper into the chamber.

But the feeling of not being alone, of sounds beyond his range of hearing, kept pace with him. When he reached the end, he could hear his own ragged breathing as he started down the other side. The opening was a black rectangle when he cast the light from his torch in that direction. And then the torchlight began to dim and flicker. He was barely a yard from the end, but forced himself to persevere, finally stumbling into the open forecourt and gulping in deep breaths of fresh, cold air.

If there was a knife hidden in the chamber, he had failed to find it. But he would have wagered his life that he had been careful and thorough enough to find it, if it had been there.

His face was bleak as he left the barrow and walked back to his patient horse.

Hamish was right. Who would believe a man everyone suspected of being shell-shocked? A moral coward, who might blacken a fellow officer's good name in an effort to win favor with his superiors, one of whom kept Rutledge's letter of resignation in a drawer of his desk?

I t was fully night by the time he reached Avebury. Overhead the stars were brilliant in the black dome of the sky, and he picked out constellations he remembered from the trenches of France. He'd let the horse have its head, giving himself whatever time he needed. And slowly but surely the odd sensations of the Long Barrow chamber faded until Rutledge wasn't sure he hadn't conjured them up out of the echoing darkness.

If he was right, if all his meticulous collection of bits and pieces of fact were right, he was nearly there.

If the dead Corporal had been the killer in Avebury, he'd have left the knife where he'd left the purse. Even hiding out in the barrow himself until it was safe to move on. He wouldn't have wanted either of them to be found on his person if he was stopped and questioned. But the knife wasn't there.

It could be hidden in a dozen of the mounds and barrows and standing stones that covered this plain. It would take an army of Constables days to cover them all.

But the sticking point was still this: what had driven one of the most experienced men at the Yard to commit murder? Not once. Twice.

Hamish said, "Aye, and so far ye've matched him, step by step, because ye're as clever as he is."

And that, Rutledge told himself, was something Leslie had *not* counted on.

Stopping by his motorcar, Rutledge opened the boot, unlocked his valise, and put the black leather purse inside. Then he put a fresh battery in his torch before locking the boot again.

That done, he quietly saw to the chestnut horse before going to the inn, where he was given his old room again.

Someone from the kitchen brought up the pitcher of hot water he'd requested, and he was busy washing his hands when there was a knock at the door.

"Come," he called, and Dr. Mason stepped into the room.

"You've been away all afternoon. Any luck?"

"I haven't been able to identify the dead man," he replied, reaching for a towel. "If that's what you're asking."

"And the Long Barrow. You found nothing of interest there?" the doctor asked, leaning his shoulders against the doorframe.

"I saw no indication that Corporal Radleigh, if that's actually his name, was living there." And if Radleigh had gone into that chamber and felt what Rutledge had felt, it wasn't surprising that he'd done his drinking in the forecourt!

"Still, the fact that he was lying in that open forecourt, not inside the chamber, seems odd to me. I expect that's because he'd have been better preserved if he'd been thoughtful enough to die out of the weather.

Why would a man sit and drink enough gin to kill himself where it's rained for days?"

"Possibly he had no choice." Rutledge hung up the towel again.

"That's saying either he was too drunk to know the difference or he didn't care."

"It could also mean that he didn't intend to die. Let's say he sat there, drinking, watching the sun set, fell into a drunken stupor, and when the temperature dropped, he couldn't wake up enough to protect himself."

Dr. Mason looked toward the window. "There was something else I found in the examination. After you and Henderson had left. It bothered me that there was enough gin in him to kill a hardened alcoholic, but there were no physical signs of habitual drinking. I took another look, and now I'm of the opinion that the dead man was forced to drink the gin. Usually there's bruising around the mouth and tongue, but given the state of his face, I couldn't corroborate that. Still there was too much gin in his lungs to account for simple choking on a mouthful. It's a wonder he didn't die from that. There's a cut on the temple as well. I can't be sure it was an animal bite. I can't tell you it was a blow, knocking him out."

Rutledge regarded him thoughtfully. "As I recall, you believed that this was Henderson's case?"

"Early on, yes, I did. But that bottle of gin—did you look at the label? It's expensive, not the cheapest he could buy. For that matter, he could have bought four bottles for what he paid for this one. And drunks aren't very particular about what they drink. Unless he'd lost all hope and decided to kill himself. When you put these facts together, my guess is that he was murdered."

"Is it indeed?"

"I haven't written a report for the inquest. I wanted to speak to you first. I had a feeling you might not want this to come to light. Not yet, at any rate."

"Why should I want to hold it up?"

"Because you think this death is somehow connected with that of the young woman. Some days ago, we heard that there had been a housebreaking on the same night she died. A Constable in Stokesbury was looking for an ex-soldier. Witnesses had seen him there, or so the man delivering beer to the inn claimed."

"Does Henderson know this?"

"I don't believe he does. He's just come back from Winterbourne, and unless the gossip has reached him already, he hasn't heard the news. Someone will tell him, now that the body has been found."

"If the soldier had killed her, why did he linger in the vicinity? Where he could be seen again. He couldn't be that stupid."

"Unless of course he was the sacrificial lamb." Mason's gaze was fixed on Rutledge's face. "That's why it's so urgent for you to identify him. Do they know his name in Stokesbury?"

"No."

"You haven't said, but it's clear you have some idea why that young woman had to die."

"That's what I don't know."

Mason crossed the room to take the only chair, and Rutledge went to stand by the window. "Is it one of us? Someone from Avebury?"

"No. At least if I'm right, Avebury is in the clear."

Mason sighed. "A relief, that. Does your killer live in Stokesbury? If he knew about the breaking in, he might have seen his chance to shift the blame."

Rutledge said, "No, he doesn't live in Stokesbury." It wasn't a lie. But it wasn't the whole truth.

"For the longest time," Mason said, running his fingers down the seam of his trousers, not facing Rutledge, "I've wondered about the man who'd killed her. I don't know why. I expect it was because she was so unusual. The sort of woman a man finds it hard to get out of his head. If he'd loved her, if he'd fathered her child, he might not be able to drive a knife into her. He'd have found some other way. I must rethink that, now that he's killed again."

Rutledge said, "What will you tell Constable Henderson? That you think this was murder?"

"I shall have to tell him. But as I said, I wanted to speak to you first. Do you know the name of the Constable in Stokesbury? He'll have to be told."

"His name is Benning."

"So you've been there? To Stokesbury?"

"I was looking for something else when I went there. One of a dozen villages I'd been to. It was only afterward that I stumbled over the story of the break-in."

Mason shook his head. "You kept it to yourself."

"No. Protective of information that might prove critical."

"You know you could have done this yourself. Kill that woman. The soldier too. You come and go. Who would ever guess?"

Rutledge laughed. Not at the absurdity of Mason's remark, but at the reality of it. It struck him then that, failing the dead soldier, Leslie might have tried to implicate him.

Mason got to his feet. "Will you tell me the dead man's name, if you learn who he is? His family might care to have his remains brought home. Or not. But we should at least ask."

"When I can. Yes. If we're right and he was murdered, he deserves to have his name cleared, for his family's sake."

"I'm going down to order my supper. There are two chairs at the table reserved for me. If you'd care to join me?"

Rutledge thanked him but refused the invitation. It was best, he thought, to put a little distance between himself and Dr. Mason.

Instead, he made entries in his notebook of the new information, and then walked out of the inn and went to stand where the tall stones were just visible in the darkness.

A cold wind swept across the open spaces and the sheep huddled near the bank behind the ditch, out of the worst of it. He could just see their shaggy white bodies, like mounds of snow waiting to melt.

What was he going to report to Chief Superintendent Markham? A progress report was long overdue. There was so much to tell—and so little he *could* tell. He rather thought that Markham had not summoned him before, hoping that the length of time it appeared to be taking Rutledge was an indication of a futile lack of progress.

As he walked on, Hamish reminded him of the dead woman in London. He would have to look into that too when next he was there. A third death at Leslie's door?

Without answering Hamish, he turned and walked back into the inn. Taking the stairs two at a time, he collected his valise, swept the room with a glance to be certain he hadn't left anything behind, and went out to his motorcar.

It was only half past seven, and if he hurried, he could reach London with time enough to sleep for a few hours.

R utledge was half expecting to find a message from Haldane waiting on his doorstep, but the mail that had been collected by his daily and set on the table by his chair was commonplace, a bill from his tailor, a prospectus for a new motorcar, an invitation to the christening of a friend's second child. He left them to be dealt with later and went to bed.

At nine he was up and dressed. But it was useless to call on Haldane, unless he'd been sent for. And Edwards had been promised another day in which to find the ex-soldier.

But there was the motorcar crash and the dead woman. He set out for Trafalgar Square and sat by the lions for what felt like an interminable morning. But his patience was rewarded when he saw the Constable he'd spoken to when the woman was struck. He was standing across the way, head bent to hear a little boy's chatter, a well-dressed father watching with a proud smile.

It took longer to cross the street than he'd anticipated, cabbies, motorcars, and omnibuses swirling past. By the time Rutledge had taken his life in his hands and made it to the opposite corner, Constable Fuller had moved on.

He caught him up, finally, and watched the man's face change as he recognized Rutledge.

"Any luck finding that motorcar?" he asked, falling into step with Fuller.

The Constable said, "We did. It had been abandoned on a quiet street behind the British Museum. There was damage to the left wing, and blood on the cowling of the left headlamp. Just where you'd expected it to be."

"Then you've found the driver? You have him in custody?"

"As to that," Fuller replied, clearing his throat, "Mr. Taverner is a prominent barrister and swears his motorcar was taken without his knowledge or consent. Since he was in court all day, there are more than enough witnesses to back up his claim that he couldn't have been behind the wheel."

"Taverner?" Rutledge repeated blankly.

"What's more, he has a man who collects him every morning during the week. The motorcar is for his personal use at the weekend. It's kept in the mews near his house. Lambert Square. According to Mr. Taverner, no one else in his family drives. We've questioned the staff, and they have supported that."

It was the mews near Lambert Square where Rutledge had gone after the accident to look for Leslie's vehicle. It hadn't been there. Nor, it seemed, had Taverner's, with its damaged wing.

"Then who was driving the Taverner motorcar?"

"We don't know, sir. There was nothing in it when it was found to help us locate the driver."

He had been so certain it was Leslie behind what had happened. He wanted to ask the Constable if he was satisfied with this outcome, even as he knew the police had done their work. The motorcar had been found. The owner questioned—

"Then what do the police suspect?" he asked instead. "That someone else was driving, without the owner's knowledge or consent?"

As if he sensed Rutledge's doubt, Fuller said grimly, "It's the Taverner motorcar right enough. There was a bit of fabric from her dress caught in the hinge of the bonnet, above the damage to the wing. Has to be another driver."

"No one saw him as he abandoned the motorcar?"

"We've questioned the households up and down the street, sir. We've accounted for all the fares picked up anywhere near the museum during the worst of the fog. I heard later it was thick well into Kent. My granddad swears they aren't as bad as they were in his day, but that's little comfort to Mrs. FitzPatrick's family."

"He must have walked well away from where he left it. Do the Fitz-Patricks and the Taverners know each other?"

"No, sir. That's to say, not until now."

"Thank you, Constable. I'd hoped for better news."

"I understand, sir. I've taken this personally myself. So has Mr. Taverner. He's offered a reward." He touched his helmet to Rutledge and continued on his rounds.

Rutledge stood looking after him for all of a minute. A reward. That might well stir the public's memory. But how had he himself been so wrong?

He had glimpsed Leslie behind the wheel of his motorcar not long before the woman was struck. And Leslie had stopped in briefly at the Yard close to the same time. But he couldn't have sworn under oath that it was also Leslie's motorcar that had seemed to swerve toward him as the headlamps were switched on—although Leslie's motor had the same large round lamps. Still, there were any number of motorcars of similar age and model on the streets of London. In the fog, colors faded, dark greens and dark blues appearing to be black.

Hamish said, "Ye had your mind set on yon Chief Inspector. And it's no' like him."

But Rutledge had felt since it happened that in switching on the massive headlamps and swerving in his direction, the driver had lost control, and as he fought to regain it, he'd come too close again to where Mrs. FitzPatrick had been walking.

"It wasna' his motorcar. Yon driver's. He didna' ken how to manage it."

Fuller's words came back to Rutledge. *Little comfort to Mrs. Fitz-Patrick's family.*

He walked on, in a dark mood. Not seeing the perfect winter day, clear and brisk, a hint of the spring to come in the blue sky over his head, until he found himself in front of Buckingham Palace. Instead of turning back, he crossed over toward Green Park and kept up his pace. When next he paid heed to his surroundings, he saw a hotel just ahead.

Was it too soon to put through a call to Edwards? To ask if he was making any progress? He was presuming on the man's kindness, but there had been other times when he'd helped Edwards with information. They were, for all the complaints on Edwards's part, useful to each other.

He needed answers.

Removing his hat, he walked through the elegant wooden doors into the crowded lobby, spotted the short passage beyond Reception that usually indicated a telephone, and headed in that direction. There was a dimly lit alcove halfway down the passage, and no one was before him.

He found that Edwards was in and at his desk.

"Any luck?" he asked, after identifying himself.

"You won't believe me, but it was easier than I'd imagined. In all likelihood I've found your man. I started with the Engineers, and they were very helpful."

"I was right then?"

"Close. It was *A,* all right, for Andrew. But the *L* and *J* were actually an *H*. For Henley. Andrew Henley Radleigh. Not a common last name, which helped."

"And where was he from?"

"Manchester. Well, just outside it." He gave Rutledge the address.

"Family?"

"You didn't ask for that. I did find a Sergeant at the Engineers who remembered him as a fine soldier and good at improvising."

"That's helpful. Thank you. I owe you a favor in return."

"I daresay you do. But will you remember that it's my turn, the next time you call? I'm sure I'm three favors ahead of you by now. I keep reminding you that this isn't an annex of the Yard."

Rutledge laughed. "Yes, and who found the police record of that Lieutenant in Surrey? You wouldn't have known about that otherwise. Consider this a good deed. Radleigh's family hasn't been told he's dead?"

"No. That's Yard business."

He rang off. Manchester was well north of Wiltshire. What had brought Radleigh there?

He was just crossing Reception when someone called his name.

He turned to look, and there was Kate Gordon, standing just inside the Foyer, smiling at him.

She was dressed very becomingly in a dark red coat with gold braid across the front buttons and on the shoulders, almost a military style. A matching hat was perched on her head.

He crossed to greet her, smiling in return. "Hallo, Kate. I'm surprised to see you here."

"I've been deserted by my luncheon partner. Well, hardly his fault. His mother has taken ill, and he had to leave quite early for St. Albans. He left a message for me, full of apologies. I've only just got it, however." She made a face. "I'd rather not go home to luncheon with my cousins. I only agreed to meet Josh to get away from them."

He'd decided to set out at once for Manchester. Abandoning that plan, he said, "I'd be delighted to step in for Josh."

"Would you? Thank you, Ian. I'd much rather dine with you anyway."

"Where had you expected to go? The hotel dining room? Somewhere else?"

"I'd really like to go to that new restaurant everyone is talking about. Not far from Simpson's. Baldwin's?"

He'd heard people at the Yard mention it but hadn't gone there himself.

"Baldwin's it is." He'd left his motorcar at the flat. Asking the doorman to find them a cab, he glanced at her. Why hadn't she married long ago? He was very aware that she was fond of him, but he didn't know quite how deep those feelings were. And he'd been very careful not to encourage them. For her sake.

They were settled in the cab, her red coat vivid in the dim interior.

"Do you remember my mother's cousins, Gwen and Meg? They are so set in their ways that it's very uncomfortable having them come for a visit. They complain about everything—the house is too cold or too hot, the tea is too strong or too weak, their breakfast isn't quite what they're used to. I'm not sure why they would ever wish to travel."

They had come to one of the parties held for Jean, after the engagement was announced. Two older women in matching lavender gowns who had sat together on a small sofa, lips pursed, eyes missing nothing. He'd made a valiant attempt to talk to them, and had been very grateful when Jean's mother had taken pity on him and rescued him. Jean had irreverently called them "the lady dragons."

"Oh, yes," he said, smiling. "I remember them."

"I ought to be ashamed of wanting to escape, but they ask prying questions and then comment on one's answers. There's no pleasing them. I don't think they've ever approved of me. Jean was always their favorite. But thank you for rescuing me today. It was very kind of you."

"Josh's loss was my gain."

"I didn't even think to ask if you had plans of your own—were you visiting someone at the hotel?"

"I'd come to use the telephone. I was given some information that means leaving London. But not today."

"Then I shan't feel too guilty."

The cabbie was drawing up in front of the door. Baldwin's had taken over a lovely old Georgian town house, renovated it, and turned it into a charming restaurant. The bones of the building remained in the interior, and there was a handsome gallery above the main dining room. Rutledge had been told that a harpist played there during the evening.

They were given a table for two near the fireplace, and as he helped Kate off with her coat, he caught a trace of her perfume, surprisingly exotic, sandalwood and lavender and something else he couldn't name.

The waiter took her coat from him, and then Rutledge handed the man his own. These were whisked away.

As they took their seats, Kate said, "The child's tea service that we chose. Was it successful?"

"Very. As it happened, when the tea service arrived, the little girl's brother had just come down with measles. If I'd known, I'd have sent him something as well." He didn't add that the children's mother had felt it was too expensive a gift.

"Poor little boy! I remember being thoroughly wretched and out of sorts."

"My sister had them first, and I followed. I'm sure we tried my mother's patience."

The waiter reappeared just then with their menus.

In ordinary circumstances Rutledge would have ordered for her. Instead, he shared the menu with her. "What do you like best?"

She chose a soup, followed by a fish dish, with vegetables, and he ordered the roast pork.

Kate was very easy to talk to, but he was still too aware of what had happened in Cornwall, when she had been at risk. He hoped she didn't think of that now, only of the art exhibit she was describing so amusingly. The last thing he wanted was her gratitude.

"And I wasn't quite certain why the woman was painted with two faces, one red and one an odd shade of blue, but I was told that this was how the artist saw his wife. It wasn't terribly flattering, good art or not. I shouldn't think she would care to have the world know what he thought of her."

The food was excellent, and he was enjoying her company. And then over their dessert, she looked at him for a moment, as if undecided about saying what was on her mind.

"What is it?" he asked, smiling. He thought for a moment that she was going to deny it, that he shouldn't have pressed.

"Do you still miss Jean?" She was careful not to meet his eyes, dipping her spoon into the flan instead.

"No. Not for a long time, now." He tried to be honest with her, but had to couch his reply in terms that didn't reflect poorly on her cousin. It was Jean, after all, who had broken off the engagement when she saw the shattered man who had come home from France two years ago. He had set her free, and she hadn't looked back, hadn't even asked how he'd survived. That had hurt, more than he'd been willing to admit to anyone, even himself. "We weren't suited, Kate. I think we both realized it finally. I'm glad she found happiness, brief though it was."

Jean had died in childbirth in Canada where she'd gone to live with her diplomat husband.

Kate nodded. "A good many of my friends rushed into marriage that summer before the war. Not all of them have been happy. Jean couldn't understand why you wanted to wait. It was wise, as it happened."

They hadn't talked about Jean before. Not like this. It was as if Kate wanted to make it clear that their friendship had little to do with the past.

"We expected the war to end by Christmas. Our lives might have been very different if it had. Four years is a very long time to wait for happiness."

Jean had been a bright flame, dazzling and beautiful, and he'd been drawn to it, blinded by it. Whether he'd have fallen out of love with her when the fascination with that flame faded he didn't know. She had demanded to be adored, while he had wanted what his parents had found, a loving partnership that had bound them together to the end. Jean, he thought, would have found any change in his adulation impossible to face, and he'd have spent a lifetime hiding it from her.

Kate said, "Unhappily, the war changed all our lives."

Rutledge was struck by the sadness in her voice, and he wondered if there had been someone she had cared about. Someone who hadn't come home.

He felt a sharp, unexpected stab of jealousy.

She looked up, offering him a smile. "How did we become so gloomy?"

He smiled for her, not trusting his voice.

"Are you leaving London for a new inquiry?" she asked, changing the subject.

"I'm trying to draw the present one to a close."

"Is it a difficult one?"

"It has been, yes."

"May I ask why you decided to return to the Yard after the war?"

He thought at first that she was referring obliquely to his shell shock. And then he realized her question was serious.

"It's what I did before the war. I seemed to be suited to it. There was no reason to look elsewhere." Yet it was more than that. He'd been grateful that the Yard welcomed him back. It had been his salvation, although Chief Superintendent Bowles had resented his university education. Still, the Yard needed to fill the vacancies left by those killed and maimed, and he was an experienced Inspector.

Nodding, she said, "I envy you. The volunteer work I did during the war was the most satisfying of my life. There are organizations. The Society of Friends is one. Although my father despises them for their opposition to the war and to conscription, I'm told their work with war refugees has saved thousands of lives. Not just in France but wherever there is a need. Russia. The Balkans. Armenia. The Red

Cross is another. My parents are against it. But I've wondered if one of these might not be the right place for me. It was Josh who put me in touch with the Friends. He hasn't served—so far I haven't been able to speak to anyone who has."

She was serious. He remembered something she'd said before, that she had learned that life was too precious to waste it worrying about small things.

"It's dangerous work, Kate." He felt uneasy, not certain that she fully understood the risks. "I'd be quite sure if I were you."

She grinned suddenly, looking very young. "I shall have to learn several new languages. Do you know anyone who speaks Russian?"

"I don't believe I do."

"Nor do I."

And they laughed together. But his uneasiness didn't leave him.

He saw her home, although she warned him that he might encounter the cousins.

At her door, she thanked him again for rescuing her, then said, "I'm rather glad it was you who took me to lunch, and not Josh."

"As glad as I am that he had to leave for St. Albans."

And he meant it.

Rutledge was in a cab, halfway back to his flat, when he glimpsed Chief Inspector Leslie walking along the street, head down.

They'd moved on soon enough, and Rutledge didn't think Leslie had seen him. He appeared to be deep in thought. But his face was grim, as if his thoughts weren't pleasant ones.

Was it absurd to believe that a colleague had committed murder? Surely it wasn't the first time in the history of the Yard, but he couldn't think of anyone else.

He'd known Leslie for years. That made it worse. He wasn't a new recruit, or someone whose career was checkered. He'd been seen as a good policeman by everyone who knew him. Steady and reliable.

But what about Radleigh? Had he been a good man at whatever he'd done before the war? Or had his past led inexorably to murder?

"Ye canna' be certain."

Hamish was right, he shouldn't judge Radleigh until he had gone to Manchester. Killer or victim, he deserved the benefit of the doubt. But what if he was also misjudging Leslie?

An hour later he was in his motorcar, driving out of the city.

M anchester was a gray town taken over by industry in the last century. Many of the workers lived in tenements put up for them, while others lived in lines of row houses, with almost no yard in front, street after street.

It took Rutledge half an hour or more to find the shabby back street where Radleigh had lived on the outskirts.

He went up the short walk and knocked at the door. Like its neighbors, 704 needed paint, but the brass knocker was well polished.

After a moment a woman came to the door. Her dark hair was put up in a kerchief, and she had a small child by the hand. A little boy of about three, he thought.

Her face changed as she looked him up and down. "You aren't here about the rates—" She stopped, her shoulders braced for the worst. Only she had no way of knowing what the worst was about to be.

"I'm sorry. No. I'm looking for the home of a Corporal Andrew H. Radleigh. I'm told he gave this address to the Army when he enlisted."

Hesitating still, she asked, "Who are you, then?"

"I'm a policeman from London. My name is Rutledge. May I come in? The street is not the best place to hold this conversation."

"He's not in any trouble, is he?" When Rutledge didn't answer immediately, she added, "His mother—she's upstairs resting. You'll keep your voice down?"

"Yes."

She opened the door wider, then pointed to an inner door just beside it.

He followed her in there. The room was cold, no fire on the hearth, but someone slept here, there was a comforter and pillows on the worn couch. She swept them away and asked him to sit, courtesy postponing the unavoidable.

"May I ask who you are?" He was afraid this might be Radleigh's wife and child. "I'm afraid I don't know who else lives here."

"I'm Andy's sister," she replied. "Patience Underwood. We live here. Andy, of course—our younger brother George—our mother. It was the only way to make ends meet." She took the chair by the cold hearth, her child at her knee, leaning toward her, staring at Rutledge from the safety of his mother's side.

Rutledge realized she was apologizing for his having seen a bed in the front room. As if crowding a family into one dwelling was something to be ashamed of. He wouldn't have been surprised to learn that half the houses on this street had more than one generation living together in the narrow three-story space.

She kept talking, her words tumbling out now. "My husband— Herbert—was killed in the war, and Andy's wife and our father died of the influenza."

"Your brother isn't here now?" He had to ask, to be sure, before giving her such news.

"He went south—to London. To look for work." Her gaze was riveted to his face, now, as if she'd read something there and was waiting for the bad news she was sure to come. "Why are you looking for him?"

"I should have thought there was work here. In Manchester."

"Nobody wanted to hire him. He's had seizures since the war. He was told that wasn't safe, around machinery. It was just an excuse. He's not well liked."

"Why not?"

"It was before the war, before he enlisted. But people have long memories. He went to the police about something he saw in the factory. Well, it was his future wife who told him, but she was afraid to go to the police herself. Some of the women workers were being asked for more than a day's work, if they wanted to keep their positions." Patience glanced down at the small child at her side. "If you take my meaning?"

He did.

"After that, they looked for a reason to be rid of him. It was the war that saved him, he enlisted straightaway. When he came home, there's only his pension and George's, and mine for Herbert. But they aren't enough to keep a roof over our heads. Ma talked to him about leaving to look for work, but he was worried about George. *He* was invalided out in the summer of 1918, he lost an arm and a leg in France, and he's taken it hard. Andy finally left just after the new year. For London. He was sure he'd find something there, promising to send us a little as soon as he could. But we've not heard from him, except the one message that he'd got there safely."

Rutledge remembered the thin body. No work, only enough food to get by, walking the roads looking for someone to hire him, and not finding anyone. He hadn't come home because he had nothing to offer a widowed sister, an aging mother, a disabled brother. And he was too proud to tell them he'd had no luck.

"Was Andy much of a drinker?" he asked.

"No. Ma doesn't hold with wasting money on drink or cigarettes. That was something else that made him unpopular. He never bought drinks for the lads." Smoothing the child's light brown hair, she said, "You never said why the police have come all the way from London."

"Do you have a photograph of him?"

She got up and went to the mantelpiece. "This is his photograph in his uniform. He looks so much older now." Taking down a framed photo, she brought it to him. "He was a Corporal at the end. I don't have a picture of him then."

He took the frame from her. It was hard to be sure, given the state of the dead man's face, but he was nearly certain that he'd found A. H.

Radleigh. The way his hair grew, the line of his eyebrows, the shape of the jaw, the placement of the ears—these matched the dead man's exactly.

"I'm afraid—" he began, but she shook her head vigorously.

"No. You're not telling me he's dead. I won't hear it. We're counting on him. He was going to find work and we'd be all right. *He promised Ma.*" She was staring at him, angry tears in her eyes, refusing to hear what he had to say.

"I think you knew, when you saw me standing at your door," he said gently.

"No, I'd hoped you'd come to hire him. And then I thought—I don't know what I thought. It's not true. I won't believe it's true."

"He was in Wiltshire. Why was he there, do you know?"

"He never wrote, I told you that. Maybe he went to Reading or Stroud, or—I don't know."

"He was wearing his uniform—"

"He was proud of it, he *wanted* people to know he'd served King and Country. He was wounded, a wounded soldier."

"—and an officer's greatcoat."

"He was given that. By the chapel. It was in a barrel of clothing collected for the missions. Only there was more need here at home. He didn't *steal* it. He wouldn't steal. Was that it? You took him up for theft? What did you do to him?"

The description fit. Too well.

"He wasn't taken into custody. He was found dead in a place called Avebury. Did he know someone there? In Wiltshire?"

"He never said so. He served with his friends, with a Manchester regiment. What was he doing in Wiltshire? I refuse to believe you. You've got it wrong somehow. He wasn't the only Corporal in the Army. There are Radleigh cousins in Shropshire. It's bound to be one of them."

Tears were running down her face, and her son, looking up at her, began to whimper, turning his back on Rutledge and burying his face in his mother's lap.

He thought about what she would see, if he took her south to identify the body.

But he had to say what he'd come to say. He'd never learned how to break such news. He didn't think there was a way to do it with kindness or even sympathy. And he felt like swearing. For the dead man, for this family depending on him. It was a senseless death.

"We can't bury him. There's no money. Why did you come here, with your lies?"

"Mrs. Underwood. I have to tell you. Andy—Andrew Radleigh was murdered."

She stood up, her face hard. "You can find your own way out. Don't ever come here again, do you hear me? Ever!"

"Is there someone I can bring—"

But she didn't answer him. She was out the door, on the point of slamming it behind her when she remembered that there was a woman resting upstairs.

By the time he'd reached the door, she had gone. The passage was empty.

Rutledge stood there for several minutes, thinking she would come to realize there was no escape. That the truth had to be faced sooner or later.

In the silence of the house, he could hear a child's whimpering. He couldn't tell where it was coming from, the sound was too soft to follow.

He finally turned on his heel and left, softly closing the outer door behind him.

15

It took time, but he finally found the chapel where the Radleigh family attended services, and he told the minister there that Andrew Radleigh had been murdered in Wiltshire.

The older man, white hair longer than it ought to be, his back stooped with age, shook his head. "He was a good son. He wanted to do what was right for his family. But are you sure? Are you certain that you've found our Andrew?"

It was an echo of Mrs. Underwood.

"Did Andrew drink?"

"I've never known him to take a drink. His mother is strongly opposed to it, and both she and her daughter have been active in the temperance movement."

Rutledge described the body, the uniform and greatcoat. The scars. But he didn't describe the manner of death.

Mr. Morgan bowed his head for a moment, then said, "I'll step around shortly. They will need the Lord's comfort. Will—how will the body be brought home?"

Before he could stop himself, Rutledge said, "I'll see to that. Still,

I'd not want them to open the coffin. Time—er—time has taken a toll that would be painful for his family to see."

"I understand. You said he was found in the open. Poor Andrew. He deserved better."

That was the epitaph that Rutledge carried with him on the long journey south.

And all it did was stoke his anger.

H e arrived in London late at night, went to his flat, and slept poorly, Hamish busy in the back of his mind, until close to dawn.

Rutledge had gone through his mail before going to bed, but there was nothing from Haldane. Disappointed, he'd had a small glass of whisky to help him sleep, then turned and tossed restlessly instead.

He had seen Chief Inspector Leslie. The man was back in London, the inquiry in Yorkshire clearly at an end.

If he wanted to speak to Leslie, it must be now, before he was sent God knows where on his next assignment.

But not at the Yard. That wouldn't do for many reasons. Leslie had friends there, but more to the point, it was not the best place for a confrontation, with an audience of policemen watching and judging.

He waited until close to the lunch hour, and went to stand outside the building and about fifty feet away, hoping to see Leslie come out.

He didn't.

But at four in the afternoon, some ten minutes after Rutledge was back in position, he recognized Leslie's walk, and moved forward to intersect him.

Leslie looked up, frowned in surprise when he saw Rutledge, and then said, "I must congratulate you."

"Indeed?" Rutledge said, falling in step beside him. They were almost of a height, although Rutledge was a little taller.

"You found the man who broke into my house in Stokesbury. I hear the Constable in Avebury—Henderson is his name, isn't it?—

also suspects the ex-soldier for that poor woman's murder. He sent word to the Yard, only this morning."

Had he?

"Early days," Rutledge said equably. "I haven't written my report yet."

"Chief Superintendent Markham is quite pleased, or so I understand. You should be as well."

"I was hoping for a confession," Rutledge answered.

Leslie glanced at him. "Were you, now?"

"It would be helpful to know what name to put on the woman's gravestone. And what connection there might have been between the two, victim and killer."

"As we both know, nothing ever turns out quite the way we'd hoped. Still. Case closed. I expect the poor man couldn't live with his guilt."

"As to that," Rutledge said as they reached the corner by the bridge, "I'm not completely convinced that Katherine ever met the dead man."

Leslie almost broke stride, then pointed to the bridge, and they turned together to start across it. "Well done. You've identified her, then?"

Rutledge smiled, but there was a grimness to it. He didn't answer.

They were halfway across the bridge, walking in silence, when Leslie stopped, and Rutledge followed suit. They stood together, looking over the stone parapet into the dark, tumbling waters below. There had been heavy winter rains to the west, and the Thames was in spate.

He found himself thinking that a body, tossed into the river, would disappear for days. If it was ever found. Boats plying up and down were just as likely to slice it to shreds. He moved slightly, away from his companion.

"Who is she?"

"It will be in my report."

Leslie couldn't ask again, and he knew it.

Instead, he said, "There won't be a trial, of course. But when the inquest is over, I should like to have the items he stole from my wife returned to us. I don't know that these will make her feel any safer in that house, still, I think she would be pleased to have them."

"I've already returned the lapis beads."

"Yes. Unfortunate, that, isn't it?"

"It doesn't matter. I have the witness who found them. And where. I know the owner reclaimed them."

"I doubt that will matter to the inquest. In my experience, the coroner's jury will wish to see them. If they can't be produced, they won't be deemed important evidence."

"Ah well, I expect I shall have to rely on my powers of persuasion."

Leslie laughed briefly. "Be grateful for the dead soldier. Otherwise, who knows? The evidence might point in any number of directions. I've heard that those who suffer from shell shock have been known to run mad or hear voices in their heads that drive them to murder."

He couldn't know . . . There was no way he could have learned about Hamish!

In almost the same breath, he heard Hamish speak as clearly as if he too stood on the bridge with them.

"Yet canna' let him rattle ye."

Rallying his wits with an effort of will that left him gripping the stone parapet in front of him, Rutledge said dryly, "I'll keep that in mind, while I'm looking for this particular killer. But if you want my personal opinion, the man I'm after is probably as sane as you are."

Leslie turned to look at him. But the light was fading, and Rutledge's face was hard to read, shadowed as it was by his hat.

Leslie said thoughtfully, "We should be grateful for our blessings. The inquiry is closed." He was about to turn and walk back across the bridge.

Rutledge said, "I should still like to know why she had to die. And if the child she bore and lost belonged to you."

He thought for an instant that he'd gone too far. Leslie stopped.

I've hit a nerve too, Rutledge realized, and braced himself for the blow that he knew would surely come.

Instead he watched Leslie fighting for control. And then the man said softly, black menace in his voice, "Be careful. She wasn't a whore."

And he was gone, striding for the end of the bridge with fists clenched.

Rutledge stayed where he was, watching him out of sight.

When he was certain that Leslie had gone, that he wasn't lurking in the shadows at the far end of the bridge, Rutledge walked back the way they'd come.

It wouldn't do for two Scotland Yard Inspectors to go at it almost on its doorstep. Wigs on the green. He was fairly sure he could take Leslie in a fair fight. They were of a height, but he was younger and he thought his reach was a little longer. But this wasn't the time to bring down the condemnation of the Yard on both of them. It would only serve to make any arrest he made look like a petty revenge.

And the woman's killer had used a knife, silent and swift and deadly. He wondered if Leslie still had it. Or if it was lying somewhere on the plain close by Avebury, waiting to be found, any traces of blood long since lost to the weather.

He rather thought the latter. Leslie was married. He wouldn't want his wife to find something he'd hidden, and ask questions.

She wasn't a whore.

The dead woman meant something to Leslie, then.

If that was true, why did she have to die?

Because he was married and back in England now? He'd been married well before the war broke out.

When he left France to return to England at war's end, had Leslie believed that she was dead?

There was another answer. But Rutledge didn't like it.

What if Leslie had thought she was dead because he was sure he'd killed her? Or left her for dead in France. It would have been a terrible shock to learn she'd come to England.

Reaching the riverbank, he went back to his motorcar, and late as it was, he set out to speak to Haldane.

He might have doubted his own conclusions before. But not any longer. Leslie had known the dead woman. Had known her in France during the war? And he'd hidden that knowledge from the start.

H e'd fully expected to find that Haldane had gone out for the evening.

Instead he was told that Haldane was dressing for the evening, and he would be down shortly. Rutledge was shown into the man's study, offered a drink, and when he refused, was left alone.

Twenty minutes later, Haldane came striding into the room. He was quite striking in his dress clothes as he nodded to Rutledge.

"My apologies. I'm expected at a party in half an hour. You've come about the woman?"

"Yes. Have you found anything that might shed light on who she is?"

"I have. She was a refugee from Armenia who made it to France in late 1915. There is a record of that, although how she escaped from Turkey is sketchy. One version says she somehow reached Egypt and got to Europe from there, another says she made it to Hungary, Vienna, and then Switzerland. Her family had connections, money. I expect a combination of bribes and friends got her out, and she was trying to protect them. In Paris she was very ill—she nearly died of grief and exhaustion. This was early spring of '16 before the Somme offensive. She disappeared for a time, and then when the Paris peace talks began in early 1919, she was one of a group of people who were advocating for the Young Turks to be punished for what they'd done."

Rutledge knew what he was talking about. The Armenians were a Christian minority in Anatolia, a part of the Ottoman Empire, and there had been some talk about bringing them to power if the Allies defeated the Turks during the war. Whether it was true or not, it became the excuse the increasingly militant Muslim faction had been looking for. And in the spring of 1915, the Armenians were forcibly removed from where they lived. Some were deported, others starved or killed in what was little short of a massacre. He had heard stories about thousands being driven out of their homes, men, women, and children, on forced marches. Anyone who couldn't keep up was savagely beaten or killed. A world at war could do little, but the account of atrocities began to spread to Europe. She was damned lucky to make it to France.

"What was her name?"

"Karina. I don't know if that was her true given name or not. No one did. She was afraid that the people who had helped her escape might be hunted down and killed. Some of them were Turks who knew her family and did their best to protect her."

Karina. The port official had remembered her name as Katherine. Close enough? Or had she deliberately used Katherine when she applied for her papers?

"Does the Government know she came to England?"

Haldane fiddled with his cuffs. "I can't answer that, you see."

Which meant that they did. "Do they know why?"

"It was purely personal. Nothing to do with the cause she'd espoused."

"'Personal' may have got her killed."

"So it would appear. But we don't know."

"And you're telling me she wasn't followed, once she landed?"

"Apparently not. Her papers were in order, she arrived quite openly. She reached London and made no effort to contact any known organization. Surveillance was discontinued."

But it might have saved her life, Rutledge thought.

He phrased his next question very carefully. "While she was in Paris, was there someone in England she worked with? Someone she might have come here to see?"

"There is a woman on the Armenian Refugee Committee. She volunteers with them. A number of small groups have taken up the cause.

They believe matters in Turkey will be worse before they are better. But she hasn't seen Karina."

"Do you believe her?"

"I do. She's quite straightforward about what she does. And there's no reason to lie."

"Do you have a name?"

"A Mrs. Brooke-Davies." He gave an address.

"Was Karina troublesome? In Paris, during the conference?"

"She was—effective. I'm told her firsthand accounts of the massacre were moving. It was nearly too much for her. As for troublesome, the answer is no. Unless of course you were one of the new breed of hotheads calling themselves the Young Turks. Do I believe she was deliberately assassinated? No. Of course not. If they'd intended to get rid of her, it would have been in 1919."

The little French ormolu clock on the mantelpiece delicately chimed the hour, and Haldane pointedly glanced at it.

"That reminds me," Rutledge said. "L'Oreille. A French maker of fine things. Do you know it?"

"Yes. A small but elegant shop in Paris. Quite fashionable. Why?"

"She carried a compact from there. And wore a silver pin from the same firm."

He frowned. "Rather out of her range, I should think. Unless someone bought them for her."

She was not a whore.

The words of a man who cared. Who might have given a very attractive woman fine things. Then why had he killed her? What had she wanted from him that he couldn't give her? A wedding ring? Had she known he was married? If she hadn't, it might have come as a shock. And like it or not, he'd had to decide what to do about her.

"Thank you," Rutledge said. "You've been very helpful." He couldn't keep what he was thinking out of his voice. *Would Haldane have told him anything about Karina, if he hadn't come in person to inquire?*

Haldane's gaze came back to Rutledge's face, suddenly intent.

But Rutledge was already on his way to the door, wishing him a good evening.

Haldane stopped him. "Is there something more I ought to know?"

"I don't believe so." Rutledge nodded. "Good night." And he was walking down the passage from the study to the outer door, not waiting to be shown out.

Haldane didn't follow him.

Mrs. Brooke-Davies lived in Kensington, in a house not far from the palace.

She answered the door herself when Rutledge knocked. A stout woman with iron-gray hair and gray eyes.

He gave her his name but didn't mention the Yard.

"Actually I've come to see if you might help me find a friend. She sent word she was coming to England, but I've heard nothing more. I believe you worked with Karina in Paris?"

She stared at him for several seconds, then invited him inside. The parlor was filled with small treasures, many of them from Europe. They held pride of place in what was otherwise an ordinary room. Horsehair sofa and chairs, a tilt-top tea table against the front wall, and a thriving green plant in the window. Very English, he thought.

"I haven't seen her," she said, frowning in worry. "I should have thought she might get in touch with *me,* if she was coming."

"You don't correspond?"

"Alas, no. We're quite a small group, as you probably know, but we've done what we could to help the cause. I met Karina quite by accident, did she tell you? She was visiting a hospital where a friend was convalescing, and I was there to speak to someone who had taken ill in Egypt, a scorpion bite or some such. Rather nasty, at any rate. She was sitting alone outside the ward, and we exchanged a few words. I listened to her accent, and then I asked if she was Armenian. She was. We talked for over an hour."

"When was this?"

"The summer of '16, I believe. Yes, that's right."

"Did she give you her surname?"

"No. There were people at risk. They could be killed for helping her, she said. Some of them were Turks, still living in the country. They'd known her family. Sadly, they were faceless, that multitude of displaced people. No one helped most of them. Karina's own family had been killed straightaway, because her father was an important man. She'd been in Izmir, visiting friends when the massacre began. She stayed with them as long as she dared, then was passed on to others willing to shelter her. Finally, she was given a false passport, and with that she managed to get passage on a ship." She considered him again. "There was a young British officer in Paris, he found her lying in the street, ill with exhaustion and too little food. That was in March, before the Somme. He got her to hospital, and visited her as often as he could before he was cleared for duty and returned to his regiment." Her head on one side, she smiled hopefully. "But perhaps you know all this. Was that officer you?"

"She didn't tell you his name?" he parried, returning the smile.

"She didn't want to cause him any trouble, you see."

"That was kind of her."

"I'm concerned. If you haven't heard—and I have heard nothing—what has become of her? Do you know where she is, if she is safe?"

Rutledge knew he ought to tell her the truth. That Karina was dead. Instead he asked, "Do you have a photograph of her?"

"No, she never gave me one."

He reached into his pocket and took out the photograph the Rector's wife had given him. Without a word, he passed it to Mrs. Brooke-Davies.

She took it, smiling, and the smile faded as the significance of what she was seeing reached her.

Her face crumpled. "Where did you get this? Did *they* do this to her?"

"She died in England, and is buried in Wiltshire. No one in the village knew who she was."

Tears rolling unheeded down her face, she said, anger in her voice, *"Who are you?"*

"My name is Rutledge. I'm with Scotland Yard. I've been tasked to find out who she was."

"How did you find me?" The words were sharp, abrupt.

He couldn't give her Haldane's name. "I was trying to find someone who might have known her. Someone who worked with the Armenian community."

Looking back at the photograph again, she said forlornly, "She's suffered so much. Had seen so much. Why couldn't she have found a little happiness?" After a moment, she asked, without raising her head, "How did she die?"

Rutledge took a deep breath. "She was murdered. We didn't know who she was, we don't know who might have killed her. Or why." Then he added, "The doctor who examined—he told me that she died at once. No time for fear or pain."

The woman across from him in the cold room nodded slowly. "I always feared she was living on borrowed time. And yet I told myself she had earned happiness. That one day she'd find it." Finally looking up from the face in the photograph, she said, "That officer. Do you know who he is?"

"No. That's the trouble, you see. We know so little."

"Yet you pretended to be him."

Rutledge considered his answer. "If you hadn't known her, I could leave and ask someone else, no harm done. It was better not to start rumors."

"Yes, I see that." Reluctantly she handed the photograph back to Rutledge. "I can't believe—" She searched the pocket of her brown jumper and found a handkerchief. "Are you sure she didn't suffer?"

"The doctor assured me that she hadn't."

"Who took the photograph? Was it you?"

"No. The Rector's wife took it, in the event someone came looking for her. A photograph makes identification so much easier. They cleaned her clothes, dressed her in them, and buried her in the churchyard. It was done well."

"Who killed her? Why was she killed? I don't understand."

"We don't know. Not yet. That's why I'm here."

"She was so lovely. I don't mean her features, I mean the person she was. In spite of all she'd witnessed, she wanted to help others. There were some who just wanted to forget. How could I blame them? And the world was tired of war, I don't think anyone had the stomach for more, and most of the Armenians were already dead. In Paris, at the talks, we tried to make a difference. But it is never enough, is it?"

"Can you tell me anything about the officer who took her to hospital?"

"You don't think—no, I can't believe he would harm her. Most people would have hurried on by, leaving her there in the street, but he stopped to see what was wrong."

"Do you think she confided in him? That he knew more than you learned about her? Was it possible he fell in love with her?"

"I have no way of knowing. She mentioned him a time or two, that's all."

And yet she had come to England.

"She had no husband, no children?"

"Sadly, I don't know. She said her family was killed, she had no one to turn to. I didn't ask—I should have, I should have asked her—but it wasn't something she found it easy to talk about, and I never pressed her."

"You said she wanted to help others."

"She did speak about what she'd seen. Bodies in the streets, people forced to march whether they were ill or not, the abuse by the soldiers. No food for the children." She shuddered. "Safe here in my home, I think about that sometimes. How very lucky we are."

Rutledge left soon after. Mrs. Brooke-Davies had confirmed what Haldane had told him. She had added little more, except to identify the woman in the photograph.

He went back to the hotel where he'd used the telephone before, and he called Edwards at the War Office again.

"I need a little more information," he began, when they were connected.

He could hear Edwards groan. "I thought I'd given you what you asked for."

"This is about a serving officer. I need to know if he was on leave in Paris in the spring of 1916. On leave or convalescing." He'd asked Haldane, but there hadn't been an answer.

"Is he dead?" Edwards asked.

"No."

"Why can't you simply ask him?"

"He's a person of interest in an inquiry. I'd rather not."

"Oh, very well. Who is he?"

Rutledge told him.

There was a long silence at the other end of the line. He was beginning to think they had been disconnected, when Edwards spoke again.

"Ian. I know him. We served together for six months. Before I was invalided out and sent to fight at a desk."

Rutledge swore.

"You can't tell him about my query. You do understand that?"

"Yes, but—Ian, I can't think why you couldn't ask him? For God's sake, he's an officer at the Yard. I don't feel right, doing this behind his back."

Rutledge hesitated, then said, "Here's the problem. If I go to him, I place him in a worse situation than yours. The thing is, he'll know what it is I'm after, and he'll know why. And it won't be at one remove."

"If it's someone he served with, I can find that out for you. And leave Leslie out of it."

"It isn't that simple, Edwards."

There was another long silence. Finally, Edwards said, "Look. I'll do this. But you must keep me out of it. Do you hear? I don't want to be involved."

"Yes. I understand that."

"Call me back tomorrow morning. But not before nine o'clock."

"Thank you."

But Edwards had already broken the connection.

There was more rain in the night, and fog was drifting up from the river as the temperature warmed slightly.

He hadn't slept well. Hamish had been at him from midnight to almost dawn. And beneath the soft Scottish voice, his own thoughts kept him awake. Why had Leslie told him that he knew Karina?

Soon after dawn, he'd come awake with a start from dreaming about the Long Barrow, being shut in there with whatever it was that he'd felt, no torch, and no way out.

It was too much like coming to in the trenches after the shell had dropped on his position, and his company had died around him. The still-warm body of Hamish MacLeod above him, and the pocket of air between them dwindling. He'd known he was about to die, and it wasn't the way he'd expected to go. Not a soldier's death.

And yet he had also been ready, for in the blackness all around him, he could see nothing but Hamish's eyes as he lay dying, waiting stoically for the coup de grâce, unable to speak, then finally whispering one word just before the revolver fired. *Fiona* . . .

He was still shaken later, as he left his motorcar on a side street and walked on to the hotel, mists swirling around him, dampening the sounds, making it impossible to see more than an arm's length away.

He found the hotel's doors, stepped into the sudden brightness of Reception, voices everywhere, people moving past him to the doors he'd just come through.

He strode through the guests toward the telephone, and found a woman in a dark blue walking dress already there before him. She looked up, glared at him, and turned away.

Trying to conceal his impatience, he moved back in the passage, to give her a little privacy.

The minutes ticked by. He'd arrived just after ten, but it was well after eleven before the woman put up the receiver, and as she walked past him, he saw angry tears glistening in her eyes.

Putting through the call to the War Office, he waited again before he was connected to Edwards.

The man's first words were, "You're late."

"I can't use the telephone at the Yard."

"No, I see that." He paused, the sound of rustling papers filling the silence. "It took me until midnight to find what you wanted to know. Leslie was wounded in the side, it healed, or so they believed, and then he ran a high fever, and the surgeons operated. He was sent to Paris to recover in the spring of '16."

"Spring? *When* in that spring?"

Edwards replied reluctantly, "March. Does it matter?"

"Yes. It damned well does."

"All right, you have what you need now."

"When in March?"

Silence. "Seventh March, to tenth April. The wound healed, but his return to service was delayed until he'd regained his full strength. Look, Rutledge, he was recuperating, and I don't know how this could possibly be of interest now."

"It's possible he met someone during that stay in Paris. I need to know who it was."

"Well, why didn't you say so in the first place?" The relief in Edwards's voice was palpable.

"It's Yard business. I'm not at liberty to tell you anything more. You should know that. I shouldn't have told you as much as I have. Consider yourself sworn to secrecy."

"You can be a bastard sometimes, Ian."

"I can't conduct an inquiry on the front pages of the *Times*."

"I'm not the *Times*." The connection was broken.

Rutledge put up the receiver. He hated the words *circumstantial evidence*. But that was still all he had.

He considered going back to Mrs. Brooke-Davies, but he knew she'd told him everything she could. The only other person who knew the truth was Leslie himself.

Karina was dead and couldn't give evidence.

Mrs. Brooke-Davies. Edwards. Haldane. Even Radleigh's sister. Pieces of the puzzle from all of them. But no one had the key to the whole.

He left the hotel and walked in the fog for more than an hour, trying to decide how to move forward. But by the time he'd circled back to his motorcar, he was no closer to an answer than he had been when he stepped from the bright lights of Reception into the gray world outside.

Hamish said, "Yon Constable in Avebury had no trouble declaring the deid soldier the murderer."

As he turned the crank, Rutledge could see the face of Mrs. Underwood, Radleigh's sister, refusing to believe Andy had died and left them with no hope.

He couldn't leave that family thinking their son and brother had turned to murder.

Nor could he walk the passages of the Yard every day, meeting Leslie and knowing that the man was most probably a killer, and that he'd let him go free. He couldn't face the quizzical look in Leslie's eyes every time they met, wondering why he'd backed off from the truth.

He might as well tell Chief Superintendent Markham to take his letter of resignation out of his desk drawer and mark it *Accepted*.

And then—then, what would he do with his life?

16

Rutledge arrived at his flat to find a police Sergeant from the Metropolitan Police standing on his doorstep, just reaching for the brass knocker.

He left the motorcar, and as he started up the short walk, the Sergeant turned, considered him a moment, and then said, "You're a hard man to find, sir."

"I'm in the middle of an inquiry," Rutledge answered, and left it at that.

"You didn't mention to Constable Fuller that you were with the Yard." It was an accusation, couched politely.

"I didn't think it was important at the time. I was concerned for the woman. She died as we watched."

"All the same, it would have helped us find you for your statement."

"Yes, I apologize, Sergeant. But Constable Fuller failed to remind me when I encountered him some days later. Not that that's my excuse. Have you found the driver?"

"No, sir, we have not. Just the motorcar. And the owner can prove he wasn't driving it at the time of the accident. He doesn't know who could have taken it from the mews, then abandoned it later. We have only the time that Mrs. FitzPatrick was struck."

"The mews. Did you speak to the other owners who keep their motorcars there?"

"We have, and they swear they never touched the vehicle we know to be involved. We were wondering, sir, if you've remembered anything at all about the driver. Anything would be useful."

"I'm sorry, the motorcar was moving fast when it suddenly appeared out of the mist."

"A pity. Thank you, sir. And you'll come down to the station at your earliest convenience to provide us with a formal statement."

"I will. Thank you, Sergeant."

He touched his helmet in salute and was just walking away when Rutledge called him back.

"Tell me, how many of the motorcars in that mews are alike?"

"Odd that you should ask, sir. There are three that are very similar. Small differences of course, but not at first glance. Well, it was a popular model, wasn't it, just before the war? There's no doubt we have the right vehicle. You need only look at the damage, sir."

"I take your point, Sergeant. Just a thought."

"Thank you, sir." He nodded and walked on to where a bicycle stood against one of the plane trees.

But it was more than a thought. The mews was not watched, and if he himself had planned to do some mischief with a motorcar, he'd not use his own. It required nothing more than a familiarity with the crank.

Rutledge waited until the Sergeant had pedaled out of sight, and went back to his own motorcar.

The Metropolitan Police were pleased that he'd stopped in to give his statement in the death of Mrs. FitzPatrick. It took no more than half an hour. But Rutledge made it clear that the motorcar was traveling at a high rate of speed in poor visibility.

He reread what he'd written and then signed and dated it. The young Constable who had sat in the little room with him, observing him write out his statement, took it from him, then thanked him for doing his duty.

"Where is the motorcar now?"

"We have it still, sir. The owner's asking for it to be returned, and I expect he'll have his way sooner rather than later."

"Could I see the motorcar? It might jog my memory." It was what had brought him here.

The Constable hesitated, then said, "You're at the Yard, sir. I wouldn't let anyone else see it."

And he took Rutledge to where the motorcar was being held. The wind had come up, shredding the mist as it brought in colder air.

Buttoning up his coat, he walked around the vehicle.

He could see why he'd thought it was Leslie's. There was a dark green rug on the rear seat, matching the dark green paint of the exterior, and a slightly paler wood had been used in the interior paneling. Otherwise it could have been Leslie's black chassis—or his own dark red motor. He examined the damaged wing, then shook his head. "Sorry. It doesn't help."

Leaving the station, he could smell the river as the wind shifted again.

He sat in his motorcar for several minutes, staring out at the pedestrians hurrying along, heads down, gloved hands holding on to hats.

He'd done what he could to track Karina's movements in London. Looked at the left luggage at Victoria, and shown her photograph at Paddington. Visited the more likely small hotels for women traveling alone. Spoken to the stationmaster in Marlborough.

He was beginning to think he had run out of leads. And that would leave him unable to prove what he suspected.

Hamish said, "There's yon valise."

But he hadn't been able to show that she had taken the train to Marlborough. And so he hadn't questioned whether or not she had her valise with her. Or if she had left it there.

He would have to go back there and find out. If only to satisfy himself. And Markham's eagle eye for any lapse.

I t was late when he left his motorcar just by the station. The older stationmaster was again on duty. There were no trains expected for the next half hour, and he was sitting in the tiny office, finishing his dinner.

Rutledge tapped on the door when he had failed to find the man on the platform or in the waiting room.

After a moment he opened it, napkin in hand, a bit of food at the corner of his mouth. "Can I help you, sir?"

He began with the unidentified woman. "Do you have a room for left luggage?"

"Hardly a room, sir. A closet. What is it you care to leave?"

"I'd like to examine the other pieces of luggage, if you please."

He took out his identification and handed it to the stationmaster. The man peered at it, frowned, and said, "If I'm not mistaken, you were here before. I can't say that I remember why. I don't know that I should let you look at what's there. It's rather irregular."

"I'm searching for a valise that might have belonged to a woman who was murdered in Avebury."

The stationmaster's eyebrows rose. "Murdered, you say?"

"I'm afraid so."

But the man didn't move. "The left luggage?" Rutledge reminded him, and the stationmaster went back to his desk, took out a key from the top drawer, and said, "This way, then."

The room was indeed no more than an overly large closet, occupied at the moment with a broom, a pail, and a feather duster.

And one valise. Brown leather, well cared for, of a size that a woman might carry for herself, rather than ask for a porter.

There was a torn piece of stationery wrapped around the handle.

Rutledge unwound it and read the words printed there.

Left luggage. Katherine Smith. To be called for.

Below that, a date had been hastily scribbled. He couldn't make it out at first, but after holding the scrap of paper under a lamp, he deciphered it.

It was the night of the murder.

Who else could it be but Karina? he thought. But aloud Rutledge said, "This appears to be what I'm after. I'll take it with me."

The stationmaster said, "I'm not sure—you must sign a receipt for it."

"Yes, all right." He followed the man back to the tiny office, waited while he searched in a drawer for paper, and then pulled the inkwell and a pen past the tray with his dinner, and offered them to Rutledge.

He signed the piece of paper, noting the name on the torn bit of stationery, the date left, and the present date and time. "No one called for this valise?"

"No, sir. As you see."

Finally satisfied, the stationmaster peered at the sheet, nodding in satisfaction, and was already back in his chair, tucking his napkin under his chin as Rutledge shut the door.

Valise in hand, he walked back to his motorcar and set it in the boot. Then he went to the hotel nearest the station. It was small, but popular with travelers coming in on the train.

The man behind the desk at Reception was not busy. Rutledge showed him his identification, gave him the date he was after, and the name, Katherine Smith.

"Let me see." Flipping pages in the ledger kept under the desk, he ran his finger down several of them before he found what he was looking for. "No one by that name, I'm afraid."

Rutledge tried to think. "Apparently Katherine used her friend's name instead. Karina—I'm sorry, I don't have her last name."

"Ah, yes. Yes, here we are. A room booked by a telegram from London. Late arrival on the London train. Karina Leslie."

He found it nearly impossible to hide his surprise. "So she kept the booking?"

"Yes, indeed. Paid in full, and transportation from the station. It's all here. Including the relevant telegram."

Rutledge said, "Does it indicate when she arrived?"

"It says 'Hold for late arrival.' It would have been waiting for her at any time after six in the evening."

And the London train was several hours later than six. It fit.

"You're quite sure she arrived?"

"Yes, certainly. I do see she didn't have breakfast here. It was included, of course."

"Please be sure. She did arrive to take that room that night."

"It was paid for, sir. She had only to sign the register and take her key." He pulled out the register, opened it to the date in question, and ran his finger down the names there. After a moment, he looked up, concern in his gaze. "There must be some mistake, sir. I don't—see for yourself. She appears not to have signed in."

Leaving Marlborough behind, he drove on to Avebury. The night was quiet, the pub had closed, and there was no one about when he took the stairs to his room, his own valise in hand.

Five minutes later, he went down again and brought back Katherine Smith's.

Shutting the door, he lit the lamp, put it on the table by the bed, and looked at the note again. It had been scribbled in haste. That was all it could tell him.

Why had Karina decided to leave her valise at the railway station? Assuming he was right, and this was her valise. Had she brought it, expecting to go to the hotel, and there had been a last-minute change of plans?

She must have done it quickly and quietly, shoving it inside the station waiting room while the hysterical woman from the train was being dealt with. After that, she'd disappeared.

Hamish said, "It's no' wise to leap to conclusions. Ye canna' be sure it's no' Katherine Smith's."

"Then she shouldn't have left it there in the closet for all this time," he replied, already examining the case.

He tried the locks. First one and then the other opened, and after the briefest hesitation, he lifted the lid of the valise.

Her clothing was scented by a very feminine perfume, the small vial wrapped in a handkerchief to prevent it from breaking and spilling.

Spreading each item out carefully on his bed, Rutledge lifted out three changes of clothing, undergarments, a pair of shoes, a nightgown and robe, stockings, hand lotion and face powder, three more handkerchiefs, and a small silk purse for jewelry.

There were earrings, a bracelet, and a locket. He opened the locket. A small child's face looked back at him from the photograph inside. A boy, smiling shyly. It was hard to judge his age when this was taken. Two? Three? The edges of the photograph were yellowing slightly, as if it had been cut from a larger one, to fit into the locket. Dark haired, like his mother, and the face oval, like hers.

Rutledge stared at it, trying to see if the child favored Leslie at all. But if he were honest, there was nothing to indicate who the father was.

He had no doubt now. This was Karina's valise. He put the jewelry back in the little silk purse, and lifted out the last item, in the very bottom, under everything else.

Wrapped in another handkerchief, it was a packet of letters.

Rutledge whistled under his breath.

There were eight of them, and they were addressed to Karina Larchian, with a street address in Rouen.

KL. The initials he'd seen on the compact in her purse.

He felt like a voyeur, but he took one of them out and stared at it.

The handwriting was familiar. He recognized it. Hell, how many times had he gone over the handwritten report that Chief Inspector Leslie had turned in about the Avebury inquiry? And the return address was his as well.

Rutledge had chosen one at random, and now he opened it and began to read. It was dated from August of last year.

My darling Karina,

I have been traveling across England, as you can imagine, and so I've had very little time to write. But I am well, and hope there will be a letter from you waiting for me on my return.

There is very little news, I'm afraid. Work occupies much of my time. And I'm grateful for that. It helps me forget. It has rained heavily here. My wife and I took a holiday to Cornwall, and we were kept indoors for most of it. She has friends in Truro, and she stayed three days with them, leaving me to fend for myself. I didn't mind. The cottage had a small library, and there was a Kipling and a Conan Doyle to keep me company. Of course I had with me my little volume of French verse, the one you gave me. It's a constant reminder of you, and it goes wherever I go.

Are you safe, there in Rouen? Is there anything you need? My darling, I'd do anything for you, anything to keep you safe, as you must surely know.

I was walking in the garden last evening, thinking of you, and the nightingale that sings from the pear tree was awake and addressing the moon. I stood there and listened to him for quite some time, then went in and got ready for bed. But I couldn't sleep, remembering Paris. Have you been back there to visit? A few of your friends must be there. Still, it must be very lonely for you now. I wish I could do something to make you happier. I'd come to you if I could, you know that. But leave is impossible, and how would I explain myself? It would break her heart, and so I must break my own instead. I don't know how our lives

turned out this way. I never expected to love you. I try to be a good
husband, I try to forget.

   With all my love,

   Brian

Rutledge sat there, looking at the letter in his hand. This was a side
of Leslie he'd never seen.

The war had changed all of them, he thought, in ways that none of
them had anticipated. Leslie had been quieter since France, but then
so had he. The burden of memory, for one thing, four years of one's life
spent in a place it was impossible to describe to someone who hadn't
been there. It was as if time had stood still for those who hadn't gone
to war, and speeded up for those who had. And the gap between was
nearly impossible to bridge.

He himself seemed to have spent every waking hour struggling to
conceal his shell shock from the world, and that battle had consumed
him since June of 1919.

Had Leslie been haunted by a love affair that had had no future?
Who could he speak to about Karina, who would understand how a man
might find comfort on the brink of battle, or a few hours of forgetting
after it, and been torn between the wife he'd left safely in England, and the
woman who had given him a little peace when he desperately needed it?

How much had Leslie's wife guessed? More to the point, why had
Karina decided to come to England?

The next letter was dated in November 1919. The earliest letter, he
realized, looking at the postmark.

   My dearest Karina,

   It has been nearly a year since I left France. It feels more like
   an eternity. Dear God, I swore I wouldn't write, and then your
   letter came, and all my resolve failed me.

I'm so sorry you had to leave Paris, I know the memories it holds for both of us. But you'll be happier in Rouen. I hope you'll be safe there. The town has changed with the war. But Peter is buried there, and that will bring some comfort.

I must leave straightaway for Hereford and an inquiry there. Write to me if there is anything you need, anything that I can do. You have only to ask.

I am well, and so relieved to know that all is well with you. I've had nightmares of worry for you. Thank you for the new direction. I will keep it safe.

I don't need to tell you how very much I've missed you. How much I've wanted to come back to you. But my place is here now, I mustn't look back.

Always, always,

Brian.

This letter was different in tone from the first one he'd read. The ache of longing was tender, moving. As if he had meant what he said about still loving Karina.

The rest of the letters were very like the one he'd read first, from August 1920. And a slightly false note had crept in. As if Leslie was tiring of her letters, yet feeling he must answer. But then he had been back in England longer by 1920, back with his wife, back at the Yard, his life following the path it would have followed if the war had never happened. As if he'd found contentment in that and the intensity, the passion of his love for Karina, slowly fading into a past love. Almost as if he was already regretting replying to that first letter, yet didn't quite know how to end the correspondence—or the relationship itself. And at the same time feeling some responsibility for this woman who had shared moments of his life that his wife would never understand.

It happened—wartime affairs were not uncommon. They were passionate and real at the time, and then a man came home to the sanity

of peace, and the excitement faded, the feelings that had burned so
desperately when death seemed to be waiting in the next dawn attack
felt more like madness than love.

And yet the final letter, far from proving that point, was a cry of
despair.

It was dated in January of this year.

> *My darling,*
>
> *I am not well. I've tried to keep it from you, but that's no
> longer possible. My doctor tells me there's not much hope, and I
> don't have a great deal of time left. I can't bear to die, without
> seeing you a last time. I'm not well enough to travel to you.
> You must come to me. I'll see that she doesn't know. I'll make it
> possible somehow. Trust me not to hurt her or you.*
>
> *I am trying to work as long as I can. There isn't much pain,
> thank God, and I have been able to keep my illness from the Yard.*
>
> *Will you come? Oh, my love, will you come to me one last time?*
>
> *Brian*

And she had come.

Rutledge dropped the letter onto the bed with the others.

Was Brian Leslie ill—dying? Tired, yes, Rutledge had noticed that.
But he had seen too many men who were dying. He found it hard to
believe. Leslie hadn't lost weight, or gained excessively. His color was
good, his stride hadn't changed, his conversations at the Yard had
never given the impression that he was worried or brooding or even in
pain. He'd spoken of the future with enthusiasm on several occasions,
and it hadn't been feigned. But then he'd successfully hidden a love
affair too, hadn't he?

Be careful. She wasn't a whore.

And yet he'd killed her.

Had he lied, to lure Karina here? Not with false promises, but with a lie that he must have known would bring her to him.

Rutledge spread the letters out and read each one again. Nine in all, from November 1919, to seven throughout last year, the final one this year.

Why had she kept replying? She must have done, judging by his responses.

He tried to see the letters through her eyes. All alone in Rouen, with only memories and the grave of someone called Peter. She had kept replying because she had loved him so deeply that she'd read what she'd wanted to hear in his letters. And the last one had brought her to England, because she needed to say goodbye.

Could Peter be the child she'd had earlier? That could explain why she'd come to England alone, without him. But who was the father? Leslie? Was a dead child the powerful tie between them?

And what if, in her replies, she'd been pressing him to come back to her? Threatening to come to England and expose him?

Was this what had changed his love? She could have destroyed everything he'd come home to. A divorce would have stopped his gradual rise through the ranks at the Yard. Chief Inspector . . .

Into the silence, Hamish spoke. "Ye ken, there's Meredith Channing. She chose her ain husband, as Leslie chose his ain wife."

"It's not the same," Rutledge answered him.

"Is it no'? Don't be blinded too."

Outside, a cold rain pelted the windows, and not long afterward, the sharp pinpoints of sleet danced against the panes for a time before turning back to rain.

In a way, hadn't Markham been right? Wasn't this a similar situation to the one he'd dealt with in Tern Bridge? Stripped of its names, looking only at the letters he'd just read, here was a married man who'd had a relationship of some sort with another woman, and in the end, he'd been forced to choose. And in both instances, the other woman had had to die.

The difference was, Dr. Allen and Miss Palmer had been strangers, he hadn't known her for years. He had viewed the circumstances objectively, and in the end, found the guilty party. He knew the Leslies. He'd worked with and respected the abilities of a colleague. And that had clouded the inquiry from the start. Along with Leslie's cleverness.

Brian Leslie had been reluctant to take the Avebury inquiry. He'd done his best to shift it to someone else. And in the end, he'd been the policeman investigating his own crime, and he'd managed the inquest with all the skill born of long experience.

Like Miss Palmer, perhaps Karina had cared more for her killer than he had for her.

Rutledge considered the letters before him. He needed to see the replies that Karina had written to Leslie. He needed to compare what he had seen in these with what she had said, how she had said it. He needed to ask for a search warrant to find Karina's letters.

But would Markham agree to that? Very likely he'd be furious that a finger was pointing at the Yard.

His hands were tied.

Rutledge began to collect the letters and put them back as he'd found them. "I can build a case," he said aloud to Hamish. "There are holes in the fabric of it, but it works. And Leslie had killed Radleigh in cold blood, a man who hadn't done anything to deserve that death. It bars him for any consideration on my part. He should have left well enough alone, let Constable Benning think Mrs. Shelby was a busybody, seeing shadows where there were none."

Did that mean Leslie believed Rutledge was coming too close?

Hamish said, "Ye ken, he had to outwit ye. There was the hangman."

17

The rain was still coming down in the morning, but not as heavily as it had done in the night.

Rutledge had one stop to make after leaving Wiltshire. It was more than a little out of his way, but he knew he could make up the time, driving.

And it was urgent.

That done, he set out for Haldane's house, where he was told the man had just finished his breakfast and was in his study.

Rutledge was taken there, and as Haldane looked up, his expression changed slightly.

"What's happened?" he asked. Then, "You don't need the name of Leslie's enemy, do you?"

"The enemy of my enemy? No. I found letters instead. They confirmed that Leslie knew the dead woman."

After a moment Haldane said, "I'm sorry."

"I have only one half of the correspondence. I don't have her letters to him. I may be reading too much into what he wrote to her."

"But you don't think so."

"He's an officer of the Yard."

"It doesn't matter what he does for a living. He's a man. Is he capable of murder, do you think?"

Rutledge took a deep breath. "I don't care to think it. But I do."

Haldane opened a drawer in his desk, pulled out a sheet of paper, scanned what was written on it, then handed it to Rutledge.

Taking it, Rutledge began to read it.

A Sergeant Tiller had served with Major Leslie for the better part of two campaigns, and he had been questioned in 1916 by the police in Paris about an incident that he had witnessed while he was convalescing there.

I recognized him, of course I did. But that was afterward. He was walking down a side street near the Madeleine, and there was a spot of trouble ahead of him. I didn't know who he was, I was hanging back, me with my knee only half healed. But he went for them when he saw what they was doing, and he damned near killed both of them. They couldn't have been more than lads, but they was throwing stones at something lying in the street. When I saw the police coming, I was out of there quick. The two lads were down by then, I heard one of them screaming his arm was broke, but he paid no attention. He picked up whatever it was lying there, and walked on. I thought it was only some old rags. I didn't know until later it was a person. A refugee, nearly dead of hunger. I'd have done the same, if I'd known. There's a lot of them about, begging on the streets when they can, I've seen them. Sorry sights, I grant you, but what can one body do?

Rutledge looked up. "This is when Leslie found Karina."

"The police never knew who it was, lying in the street. Leslie claimed he bought the man some food, it revived him enough that he was able to go on his way. But it wasn't a man, was it? He must have known she was afraid of being discovered. As Mrs. Brooke-Davies must have confirmed. The police apparently let the matter drop, once Tiller gave his evidence. If they interviewed Leslie, there's no record of it."

"How did the police discover that Tiller was a witness?"

"An anonymous tip."

"Leslie, do you think?"

"Yes. The lads—they were drunk, it seems—described their attacker, and the police put out a request for any witnesses. Tiller had been talking about what he'd seen. I don't know how Leslie found out, but during the fight, he might have seen someone else on the street, a British uniform, and kept an ear to the ground."

"How did you come by a copy of this?"

Haldane smiled. "I have my sources."

"It's odd that he saved her life, only to take it."

"Murder, as you yourself must surely know, depends on what one has to gain from it—one way or the other. There would be consequences if she reappeared in his life now. It was different during the war. Back in England, with a wife and the respect of his position at the Yard, he had more to gain from murder." Haldane took the paper that Rutledge held out to him, then said quizzically, "The question now is, what can you do about Chief Inspector Leslie?"

"Take him into custody as soon as I can," Rutledge replied grimly.

As he drove away from Haldane's house, his mind was on the next step to take, and he inadvertently turned the opposite way at the end of the street. Or was it, he wondered afterward, because it was so familiar, that turning?

Looking up, he saw the house where Meredith Channing had lived, slowing as memories came back to him.

Would she have lived, if she had decided not to go to Belgium to help the wreckage of her husband find some peace? But then it wouldn't have been Meredith, would it, to turn her back on the man she had married?

"She turned her back on you," Hamish said.

"She turned her back on happiness," Rutledge told him, driving on.

But would it have been happiness, if she'd remained in England? Would she have blamed *him,* in the end, when her husband died, alone and in pain?

Rutledge pushed those thoughts aside. He'd learned not to dwell on what might have been. Jean had taught him a hard lesson there.

He felt the stares as he walked into the Yard and down the passage to the Chief Superintendent's door.

Knocking, he waited for the grunted *"Come."*

Markham was in a foul mood. He would have to be very careful.

He opened the door and stepped inside.

Markham looked up, his frown turning to a scowl as he snapped, "Where the hell have *you* been?" Before Rutledge could frame an answer, he added, "Your case is closed. Where's your report? Or am I expected to take Constable Henderson's in place of it?"

"There have been loose ends," Rutledge said, choosing his words. "As a result, I'm afraid Constable Henderson's is premature."

"It appeared to be sound enough to me."

"*'Ware!*" Hamish said softly in warning.

Rutledge didn't need it. Keeping his tone of voice level and unchallenging, he said, "As far as it goes, yes."

Markham searched among the files on his desk, found what he was after, and said, "He and Constable Benning of Stokesbury conferred. This Corporal Raleigh—a Devon name, I'm told—is not only the man who broke into a house in Stokesbury, he encountered a woman between Stokesbury and Avebury, killed her, took her purse. He was later found in the Long Barrow—whatever that is, when it's at home— where he died of gin and exposure. Appears to be sound enough to me. What's more, Chief Inspector Leslie identified the gin bottle as one from his house."

"And when was Chief Inspector Leslie in Avebury?"

"He stopped in Stokesbury on his way back to London from Yorkshire, to see if there was any news. Constable Benning described the gin bottle. He has been to Avebury to view the body of Corporal Raleigh."

"It wasn't on the original list of missing items," Rutledge said. "And I've identified the dead man. His name is Radleigh, not Raleigh, and he lived with his mother and his sister outside Manchester." Then before Markham could object, he added, "I have seen his photograph. There's no doubt of the identification. He had come to London to look for work, found none. He was most likely on his way back to Manchester."

"Yes, I see. Henderson did say that the name in his pocket was hard to make out."

"What's more, Corporal Radleigh was not a man who drank. His family is Chapel, and his mother is in the temperance movement."

"That's enough to make a man take to drink," Markham retorted sourly.

"Dr. Mason believes he was forced to drink the gin. There was a wound at his temple."

"According to Constable Henderson, the man's face was already half missing. Hard to be certain of that."

"I trust the doctor's judgment."

"He's quite elderly, as I understand it," Markham said, stubbornly holding to his position. "And the dead man had Mrs. Leslie's earrings in his pocket. How did you explain *that*?"

"They were put there by the dead woman's killer. On purpose, so that suspicion would fall on the Corporal, when he was found. There must have been far more valuable possessions in that house. Why hadn't they been taken? I don't believe someone did break in. Despite the broken latch. I'm of the opinion it was a false alarm."

Markham smiled grimly. "That's all very well, Rutledge. Where's the proof?"

"Constable Henderson is a good man. But he neglected to backtrack Radleigh. I've just set that in motion. The Chief Constable has asked for reports of any sightings, with dates and locations. It's very likely that the Corporal was nowhere near Stokesbury when the break-in occurred. Or the murder of the woman in Avebury."

A gamble. He couldn't be sure of that. But Radleigh wouldn't have been killed if he'd been the culprit in either crime. He'd have been hauled before Benning and charged.

Markham considered him. "You're thinking that this is one of Dr. Allen's other victims. Is that it? It could make sense."

Rutledge shook his head. "Allen couldn't have killed the dead Corporal. He was in custody—"

Markham interrupted. "Do you or do you not know who killed the victim in Avebury?"

"I do. I'd like to finish what I started, and make an arrest as soon as possible."

Closing the file in front of him, Markham said, "See that you do that."

"Thank you, sir." He got out of the office and down the passage, finally breathing a sigh of relief.

There was Corporal Radleigh's body to deal with. He'd promised the family their brother and son would come home. He didn't think it would help them through the days ahead, but he intended to keep that promise.

He found an undertaker in Marlborough, gave them his instructions, and asked that the body be removed within two days. A Mr. Beech promised to see that all was carried out as he'd wish, and Rutledge left for Avebury.

Arriving in time for a sherry before dinner, he found that Dr. Mason wasn't at home. There had been an emergency in West Kennet, and he had been called away.

Rutledge drove on to the inn, went up to his usual room, and stowed his valise in the wardrobe before going down to his meal.

He was halfway through the parsnip soup when the doctor came through the door and crossed the room to Rutledge's table by the window.

"I saw your motorcar," Mason said, removing his coat and draping it over the nearest empty chair. "Mind if I join you?" he added, taking the other place at Rutledge's table. "I'm more than a little surprised to find you here. According to Constable Henderson, your inquiry is finished."

"So he's informed the Yard," Rutledge answered him. "Why the rush?"

Mason frowned. "Constable Benning came to see if the dead man was the same ex-soldier wanted for housebreaking in Stokesbury. They conferred—the two Constables—and they were of the opinion that the Corporal was the man Benning was looking for. It wasn't a giant leap to conclude that he must have met the dead woman on the road that same night and killed her for what was in her purse."

The woman who usually served them came to collect Rutledge's empty soup plate, and when she had gone away again, he said, "If that were true, why did Radleigh come back here? When he was well away, and no one could identify him?"

"It was Henderson's view that he was making his way back toward London, not having found any work to speak of west of here." The woman came back with a menu for the doctor, but he shook his head, ordering the mutton stew instead. When she was out of hearing, he went on. "He was careful not to show himself, traveling at night, and sleeping where he could. He must have remembered the Long Barrow from before, and he believed he'd be safe there. He may even have hidden there while the manhunt was going on. There are people who won't even go into the forecourt. They claim the barrow is haunted."

Rutledge said nothing.

"Henderson knew the date that the woman was killed, and Benning had the date of the housebreaking. It was too much of a coincidence. He knew Leslie hadn't solved the murder, and reckoned that was because the housebreaking hadn't been discovered and no one had seen the ex-soldier. You have to admit, he has a case. A wrong one, in my view, because I still believe the Corporal was forced to drink the gin in that bottle."

"He could have taken her purse without killing her. He was stronger than she was. Besides, what was she doing on the roads that late?"

"The supposition is that she started to scream. Look here, Rutledge, you'd gone elsewhere. It was tidy enough."

"I expect it was."

Mason was saying, "It didn't sit well with me, I can tell you that." He stopped as their main course was set before them, smiled for the woman serving them, then went on. "I won't be satisfied until we know who she was and why she was here. It's Henderson's opinion that we will never know. He believes she was simply in the wrong place, and whoever it was she intended to visit didn't know to expect her. And so he or she hasn't reported her missing."

"Finish your dinner. There are some things you need to know."

Mason stared hard at him. "I was going to send you a telegram, you know. If you hadn't come by now."

Half an hour later, they were walking in silence to the surgery, and once there, the fire on the hearth built up and a glass of whisky beside them, Mason said, "Go on. I'm listening."

And Rutledge told him.

I t was nearly midnight when he'd finished.

Mason sat in silence for a time, looking into the dark red heart of the fire. Then he said, "I thought you'd run mad, when you told me it was Leslie. That perhaps there was an old quarrel between you. But it isn't that, is it?"

"No."

"And you think he took those beads of his wife's, expecting to return them when the deed was done, a gift to make poor Karina believe that he had chosen her? Did she find out they were his wife's? Is that how the clasp got broken? That must have been the last straw, he had to kill her then. But what a cruel thing to do, Rutledge. I'd thought better of the man." He poured a little more whisky into their glasses.

"I've seen her, Rutledge. He must have loved her. Why didn't he just tell her it was finished? How could he use a knife on her, and leave her in a bloody *ditch*?"

"I wish I knew. I hope her letters to him will give us the answer to that."

"*Can* you prove this? I very much want to hear you can."

"Once I've spoken to Henderson."

"He's not a bad policeman. It's just that nothing like this murder ever came his way. And he wanted to solve it, he wanted to prove to two officers of the Yard that he could do what they couldn't."

"It disrupted the investigation. Markham—Chief Superintendent Markham accepted his report. It was straightforward and convincing. If incomplete."

Mason watched him for a moment. "Were you tempted? To let it go at that?"

"Once I might have been. God knows I didn't want to believe it. I've come to know Karina too well, now. She and Radleigh deserve justice."

"What will happen to you if you turn in the Chief Inspector? If he fights you—and wins?"

Rutledge shrugged. "It doesn't matter." But it did. He knew he was already on probation. Had been since the Barrington affair.

Mason raised his glass. "To you, then. And to justice for Karina."

R utledge waited until morning to call on Henderson. A visit late at night would put him on his guard. And that was not what Rutledge wanted.

He had tested his reasoning on Mason, and his conclusions had held up. That had been important before he spoke to Markham. He would have only one opportunity to make his case.

Henderson was in the tiny police station. When Rutledge walked in, he looked up, then rose warily.

"I saw your motorcar last night, sir, when I made my rounds at ten o'clock."

"Yes. I thought it might be too late to call. I've been tracing our late Corporal. I thought you might care to know what I learned."

"How did you find him? I had no luck sending word around."

"A friend in the War Office found him for me. I've been to Manchester to visit his family. The name is Radleigh, by the way. His photograph was framed and on the mantelpiece. His sister was in no state to travel to Wiltshire to make a positive identification, and a younger brother depends on her for care. But there was no doubt in my mind. The officer's greatcoat he was wearing was given to him from the missionary barrel at his chapel. He'd come to London to find work, but they hadn't heard from him for some time. His death came as a shock. The manner of it as well."

Henderson sat down, gesturing to the chair across from his desk. "Sir? The manner of it?"

"His family were Temperance. He didn't drink."

"There's always the first time, sir. A man in despair."

"Yes, that's what Chief Superintendent Markham suggested. I understand that Chief Inspector Leslie identified the maker of that bottle of gin."

"He believed it was the one taken from his house during the break-in."

"So I've been informed." Rutledge paused. "I've also discovered the woman's name."

Surprised, Henderson said, "Who was she, sir? Was she connected to Avebury after all?"

"I'm not at liberty to say," Rutledge answered. "I intend to make an arrest when I return to London. I'm sorry. It's essential to catch her killer off guard."

"I understand, sir," he said slowly. "It will come out at the inquest."

"Meanwhile, the Chief Constable is asking for reports of Radleigh's movements before he was found. They'll be coming in shortly. It's best if you wait for that information before holding the inquest."

"I thought—well, never mind what I thought." He looked away.

"See here, sir, I wasn't trying to step on toes. It seemed so clear to me that the Corporal was the man we were after. And I was afraid you were reluctant to do what had to be done. After all, the Chief Inspector outranks you. He might not have liked you finishing what he hadn't. I got to know him, a little, while he was here. He'd been an officer in the war—he's now an officer at the Yard. Nice enough, but I wouldn't care to be in his black books. To tell truth, I didn't always know what he was thinking, even when he was talking to me."

Rutledge said nothing.

Henderson hurriedly went on. "It's my patch, Inspector. I didn't like—damn it, she *deserved* justice. I had to lift her out of that ditch. All bloody, dead. I wanted her killer to *hang*." He broke off, realizing how far he'd gone. "I'm sorry."

Rutledge replied quietly, "What do you think has been driving me?"

Henderson drew a deep breath, his face flushed. "I couldn't be sure. Half the time you weren't even here."

"The truth wasn't here." Rutledge walked to the door. "I had to find it."

He hadn't taken half a dozen steps before he heard a fist slam down on the desk with such force that something fell off and rolled across the floor.

R utledge walked into his flat shortly after midnight. The rooms were cold, drafty, and he lit the fire, ready laid for him by his daily, and stood in front of it until it was drawing well, its warmth gradually displacing the chill.

Changing into more comfortable clothes, he sat down in the chair by the lamp and began his full report, his notebook on the table beside him.

It was well after five in the morning before he was satisfied with what he'd put down on paper. Karina's valise was in his motorcar, her purse in his own valise, and the letters were where he could see them, on the chair across the room. He'd referred to them several times, and they still jarred him. Leslie had always seemed to be a decent sort, a good policeman.

Putting down his pen, he looked across at the dying fire and thought that Karina herself had helped him find her killer. The port official had remembered her, recalled the valise and the pin in her hat. Mrs. Brooke-Davies had remembered her, as well as the British officer who had saved her life. And she had touched Dr. Mason, Constable Henderson, even Haldane. Why hadn't she touched her killer? He could have spared her. He could have stopped answering her letters.

What had she said to Leslie that sealed her death?

He got up, put the notebook and his report away, then slept for two hours.

Just before seven, he was standing at the door of the Leslie house. The sun was just brightening the morning, a golden haze spilling between the houses and along the street. It had a misty quality to it, as if he could put out his hand and touch it.

Instead he lifted the knocker on the door and let it fall twice.

After a moment Leslie himself opened the door, his coat over his arm, his hat in his hand, as if about to leave for the Yard.

"Yes—?" He stopped as he recognized Rutledge. Something in the other man's face must have warned him, because he glanced over his shoulder, stepped out, and shut the door behind him. "Not here," he said brusquely, and began to walk, pulling on his coat as he went.

Rutledge fell into step beside him.

"I found your correspondence with Karina."

Leslie turned to look at him. "Did you indeed. Where?"

"In her valise. I found that too."

"You had no business reading something that personal."

"I had no choice."

They had reached the corner, and Leslie turned to his right. It was almost as if he had done it by rote. Rutledge matched him, stride for stride.

"Why did you lure her to England? And then kill her?"

Leslie said, "I don't know. I expect—it was a wartime affair. You saw them while you were in France. I wasn't the only one. For all I know, you had one. It was different when I came home."

"She must have thought it was more than an affair. Was the child yours?"

Leslie swung around, facing Rutledge. "The child was hers. Not mine. Peter. He was frail, the escape from the Turks had been difficult for both of them, but he never recovered his strength. He died just after they reached the safety of France. She took him to the American Hospital in Rouen, but there was nothing they could do to save him. He's buried there, incidentally. In Rouen." There was anger in his voice, and sadness as well. "She had a photograph of the three of them. Her husband, her son, herself. It was all she had. Her husband was killed, but she was determined to save the boy. I met her in Paris, just a week after Peter died. She didn't want to live." He drew in a breath. "It would have been better for both of us if she hadn't."

Walking on, still setting the pace, he said, "You can't prove that I killed her."

"I think I can. There's enough evidence. Does your wife suspect anything?"

Leslie rounded on him. "Leave my wife out of this. She had no idea what I was doing. What I was about to do. She trusted me, and I used her. That's on my soul, not hers."

"Why Avebury?"

"The village had no connection with me. It was dark, lonely, those stones were almost ghostly in what little light there was. It seemed to be an ideal place to leave her."

"How did you persuade her to go there with you?"

"I told her I had a cottage there. That no one knew about it. No one knew *me*. We'd be safe there. It was so simple."

"But you went to the house first. The house in Stokesbury. Why? That was a grave risk." He didn't know for certain. But he put certainty in his voice.

"That was afterward. I had to clean up, get rid of evidence. I didn't know where else to go."

"How did you get there?"

"There was an old man who drove my wife when she came down alone. He was outside the station, waiting for a fare. I didn't know he was going to die soon after that. One less death on my conscience, that old man. I don't enjoy killing, whatever you may think of me."

"What did you do with the weapon?"

"Ah. You haven't found that, have you?"

Rutledge said lightly, "Yorkshire? Did you take it there?"

"That's possible, of course. By the way, your guess was quite good. It was the magician's assistant who did those killings. He used the magician to attract the young women, then sent them word that the magician wanted to meet them again." He glanced sideways at Rutledge. "You're a clever policeman, I have to hand you that. I had thought, given your suicide attempt, you might not be quite as good as rumor had it."

"Sorry to disappoint you—"

He'd been prepared for it, there was no other explanation for this roundabout walk Leslie had set out on. From the quiet square where he lived, he had come to a busier street where early morning traffic was feeding into one of the major thoroughfares, and now, as a lorry bore down on the slight curve in the road, Leslie turned and shoved Rutledge hard.

Prepared or not, he lost his footing on the uneven verge, and was falling toward the oncoming vehicle when he heard Leslie swear as he reached out and caught Rutledge's out-flung arm, planting his foot and using all his strength to swing him out of the path of the lorry. Rutledge crashed against the iron railing in front of the servants' entrance of the house beside them.

Grunting, he nearly overbalanced and fell into the stairwell, grasping at the railing with both hands as Leslie let him go. By the time he'd straightened up, Leslie was gone, dodging his way across the busy road to hail a passing cabbie on the far side.

Pressing his fingers against the aching ribs where he'd struck the railing, Rutledge watched the cab disappear, Leslie's white face peering out the rear window.

An hour later, when Rutledge had retrieved his motorcar and had driven to the Yard, he walked into Sergeant Gibson's office and said curtly, "Chief Inspector Leslie. Has he come in?"

Gibson looked up at Rutledge, frowned, and said, "What's happened to your hand?"

Rutledge looked down. There was a cut on the edge of his palm. He hadn't even noticed it in his anger. Taking out his handkerchief, he wrapped his hand. "Is he?"

"He was to leave this morning for Cornwall, sir. A new inquiry." Gibson coughed a little. "Chief Superintendent Markham was looking for you, sir. About the ex-soldier. He was in Hampshire on the date in question. I believe there was a message from the Chief Constable in Wiltshire. About your own inquiry. I'd avoid him at present, if I were you."

Rutledge thanked him and left.

He went back to the Leslie house, and this time it was the daily who answered the door.

"Chief Inspector Leslie has left, sir. If you're Mr. Rutledge, I was to give you this."

She reached in her apron pocket and pulled out a small, sealed envelope. "He said you would know what it means."

He took the envelope, thanked her, and walked back to his motorcar as she shut the door behind him.

He tore open the envelope and pulled out the single sheet inside.

There was no greeting and no signature. Just a few words in Leslie's handwriting.

I'm sorry. I seem to have lost my taste for killing.

18

Rutledge had a choice. To follow Leslie to Cornwall or to wait for his return.

Hamish said, "What if he's no' gone to Cornwall?"

If Leslie drove fast, if he knew the roads and could make up lost time quickly where necessary, he could go first to Avebury.

That was where the knife was . . .

He didn't hesitate. Leaving the square, he set out for Wiltshire himself, and as soon as he was clear of the outskirts of London, he pushed the motorcar hard. Even so, he had time to think.

If Karina's killer had come to Avebury by way of the West Kennet Avenue, where he might well have been seen by Mrs. Parrish, once the deed was done, he could leave by the most direct route. Cutting cross-country was faster, and there was less chance of being seen. It was how the purse had been hidden in the barrow, it was how the killer had known the forecourt and chamber were accessible.

But would Leslie have been clever enough to realize that leaving the knife and the purse in the same place was tempting fate?

If the purse had been found after Radleigh's body had been discovered, there was no connection to the dead woman. *She* couldn't have identified it, there was nothing in it to identify *her*. Radleigh could have taken it from anyone at any time. And if the crows and other scavengers had had a chance to finish their work, there would have been no way of telling how long he'd lain there. Weeks or even months, depending on when he was discovered. Possibly the killer that had got away—possibly not.

But the knife—that would be telltale.

Rutledge pushed harder on the empty stretches, almost colliding with a lorry turning into his path outside Marlborough. Swearing, he barely got clear, the horn on the lorry blasting the driver's anger at him.

He reached Avebury and went directly to Dr. Mason's, pausing only long enough to collect what he needed from the boot.

The doctor opened the door, took one look at Rutledge's expression, and said quickly, "What is it?"

"Have you seen Chief Inspector Leslie?"

"No, is he—?"

Rutledge cut across his question. "I need to borrow the chestnut gelding again, if I may. There's no time to explain."

"Yes, of course, I'll help you—"

But Rutledge was already striding toward the stable, and he had the blanket and saddle in place before Mason caught him up, his coat thrown on and his scarf trailing behind him.

"I'll give him the bit," he said. "What's happened?"

"The knife is still missing. And I think Leslie's going after it. I have to get there first."

The doctor swung the doors wider as Rutledge mounted. "Do you think he's armed?" he asked quickly, catching the bridle as Rutledge started out of the stable.

"God knows. Yes, if he's already found the knife."

"He's fast, Prince is. And he's not been ridden of late, he'll be ready to go."

But Rutledge was already headed around the house toward the

street, and the horse under him lengthened its stride as they cleared
the open front gate.

Where in hell's name had the knife been hidden? It hadn't been in the
chamber, there was nowhere in the forecourt that was as safe from the
curious, the summer visitor. And he himself had circled the barrow
without noticing anything unusual, any possible cranny.

He set off down the road, and as soon as he had passed through the
causeway, Rutledge swung left. The chestnut was used to that now,
and was eager for a run.

Soon the conical shape of Silbury Hill was in sight, and in the distance was the Long Barrow. Rutledge was pulling his mount in that
direction when he saw movement on the western end, away from the
entrance.

Urging Prince on, into a full gallop, Rutledge made for what he'd
seen, telling himself it hadn't been crows or even a stray ewe.

With his free hand, he reached inside his coat, pulled out his field
glasses, and gripping the horse with his knees, he scanned the barrow
ahead.

There!

He caught the movement again, and for a brief instant, there was
the figure of a man in the lens before he lost it. The horse was moving
too fast for him to hold the glasses steady, but he'd seen enough. He
shoved them back inside his coat, and concentrated on reaching the
barrow.

Leslie must have heard the hoofbeats. Suddenly he was climbing to
the top of the barrow, staring across the plain, a dark silhouette against
the fading light. He watched the oncoming horse for several minutes,
and then began to climb down on this side, preparing to meet Rutledge
at the foot of the barrow.

By his stance as he reached the bottom, he was braced for whatever
was to come.

Rutledge slowed the gelding as he got closer, trotting now, gauging
his adversary while letting him wonder what to expect.

By the time he was in hailing distance, Leslie said, "I thought I'd left you in London."

Rutledge didn't reply until he was within ten yards of Leslie, reining in his horse.

"Any luck, remembering where you left the knife?"

"It was dark. I couldn't very well mark the spot. You may have better luck." His shoulders were squared, his head up. "How do you expect to take me into custody, on horseback?"

"The horse can find his way back home. We'll use your motorcar."

Before he could stop himself, Leslie glanced toward the distant road. Rutledge looked in that direction, and he thought he could see the motorcar, off the road and behind some trees.

"Rather a long walk back, for you." He didn't dismount.

"Oh, very well, come inside the chamber over there, and I'll show you what I did with it. I was searching for a better choice when I heard you thundering toward me."

But Rutledge had searched the chamber. The knife wasn't there.

He smiled grimly. "I'll wait while you fetch it."

Leslie smiled in return. "Then I'd rather walk. The truth is, I don't particularly care for that damned chamber." He turned, moving toward the distant road, walking briskly. Rutledge turned the horse and followed at a little distance.

"I don't particularly care to hang, either," Leslie commented when they were halfway to the motorcar.

"You should have considered that before you killed the first time."

Leslie winced. "It wasn't my plan. The truth is, I don't like remembering it. And afterward, I had to watch Dr. Mason examine her body. It was all I could do to keep from screaming at him to stop."

Rutledge said nothing.

Before they'd reached the motorcar, Rutledge took out his handcuffs and tossed them to Leslie. "Put them on."

Leslie caught them and stared down at them for a moment. "How many times have I used my own cuffs?" he asked, almost to himself. Looking up at Rutledge, he said, "Are they necessary?"

"Do you think I'd trust you all the way to London, uncuffed?"

"To be honest? I wouldn't trust myself, in your shoes." And he flung the heavy cuffs straight at the horse, striking him in the white blaze on his nose.

The animal reared in pain and fright, nearly unseating Rutledge. He clamped his knees against the horse's sides, caught a handful of mane with one hand while the other held tight to the reins. And then the gelding took off, galloping down the line of trees, away from the man beside the motorcar. Rutledge's last glimpse of Leslie was of him racing for the bonnet to turn the crank.

And then he had to give his whole attention to the horse, who was close to sweeping him out of the saddle as it ran under low branches before clattering out to the road.

Leslie blew his horn as he started back the way he'd come, at speed.

It was a challenge.

By the time Rutledge had the horse under control, there was no way he could go after Leslie. Instead, he rode on, shouted for Mason as he came through the gate, dismounted, and called as the doctor opened his door, "Take care of him. Look at his nose. I don't have time."

And then he was turning the crank of his own motorcar, and tearing down the road after Chief Inspector Leslie, pausing only long enough to retrieve his handcuffs.

He was two miles from the outskirts of Stokesbury when he saw the brightening of the sky ahead and to his left.

"Damn the man," Rutledge exclaimed savagely, and pressed on into the village.

The house was fully engaged by the time he got there, and Leslie was out in front, standing a little apart from his helpless neighbors, watching it burn as they tried to save the houses on either side. The shed too was ablaze, but no one was paying it any heed.

Rutledge braked hard, got out, and strode toward Leslie. The man turned, gave him an odd look, then held out his hands.

Rutledge said, something in his voice that Leslie heard clearly, "If you try anything this time, I'll post you as a fugitive, armed, dangerous, and to be shot on sight."

"You've won, Rutledge. I've nowhere else to go."

And he stood there, waiting as his neighbors stared at the two tall men, while Rutledge clamped the handcuffs around both the Chief Inspector's wrists.

19

They drove in silence all the way to London. Leslie made no effort to escape, his hands in his lap, his eyes on the road ahead.

Counting the miles? Rutledge wondered, on his guard all the same.

They were threading through the dawn traffic of London, the sun rising and a stiff breeze coming up with the light.

"Why did you burn the house?" Rutledge asked then.

"Did I set it afire?" And then, "I did. But not the way you think. I'd gone in, expecting you to go directly to London, leaving me in the clear. There was some money there, I knew I'd need it. Constable Benning knocked at the door, and I thought it was you. I leaped up, and I knocked over the lamp in my haste to get out through the kitchen. When I saw who it was, I made some excuse and we went around to the front of the house. As I was about to turn the crank, we smelled smoke. It was too late. The carpet must have caught, or the drapes. I don't know. The heat was too fierce for either of us to try to salvage anything. There's no fire company in Stokesbury, did you know? Benning ran to ring the fire bell. Nothing anyone could do by that time."

"I don't believe you."

Leslie said, his voice suddenly drained of feeling, his face drawn with exhaustion, "I don't particularly care whether you do or not. I can't prove it, and I can't change what happened. Sara was fond of that house. That's my only regret."

But any evidence still there to find had gone up in the fire.

Hamish said, "Ye ken, he's preparing his defense. There's no knife, and whatever was in yon house is gone as well."

Rutledge suddenly remembered the photograph of Karina that had never been put in the case file. Had that been somewhere in the house too?

When they pulled up in front of the Yard, Leslie said, the mocking note gone from his voice, his eyes dark with something Rutledge couldn't define, "Whatever I've done, I've got a shred of pride left. Remove the handcuffs. Let me walk to Markham's lair without the speculation and stares."

Rutledge himself had walked that gauntlet. But he was about to shake his head when Leslie quickly added, "I swear to you on whatever honor left to me that I will do nothing, say nothing. I *swear*."

"If you break your word, I'll shoot you myself."

Leslie stared at him. Then held out his hands. Rutledge unlocked the cuffs and put them back in his pocket.

"Thank you." After a brief hesitation, Leslie got out of the motorcar, walked around it, and went directly into the Yard, climbing the stairs ahead of Rutledge and turning toward Markham's office.

It was Rutledge who knocked, after a quick look at Leslie. His face was expressionless, his eyes hard.

Markham called, "Come," and Rutledge opened the door.

It was an awkward and painful half hour.

Markham, glaring at Rutledge, had turned to Chief Inspector Leslie and asked, "Has he run mad?"

Leslie didn't glance at Rutledge. "Everything he has told you is true.

I'm responsible for the death of Karina Larchian and the ex-soldier whose remains were found in the Kennet Long Barrow."

"Do you have any idea how this is going to reflect on the Yard, if you are charged and tried?"

"I'm sorry, sir."

And that was all the apology that Markham got.

He fussed with the papers on his desk, glared again at Rutledge, as if he had personally planned this awkwardness, then said, "There will be an inquest, damn it. In Avebury. Until then you'll be remanded into custody. I will have your identification, Leslie."

The man winced at the use of his name without his title. He handed it over, and stood there stoically while Markham went through the necessary formalities, including a statement of guilt that the Chief Superintendent had insisted on having in Leslie's own hand.

Leslie signed his resignation from the Yard, held out his hands, and Rutledge put the cuffs on his wrists a second time.

Markham said to Rutledge, "I'll inform you when the inquest is held. Now get out of my office."

They walked together back through the Yard. Word must have run like wildfire before them, because the onlookers seemed to multiply with every step.

Rutledge met every eye, as he had done before, when he had been the one stared at. Leslie stared directly ahead. And finally, blessedly, they were on the stairs and almost at the door.

As they got into the motorcar, Rutledge said, "Why?"

Leslie answered after a moment, his defeat in every word. "I loved two women, you see. But I'd vowed to love and honor only one. I thought, in a sense, that death was less painful for Karina than my rejection."

Leslie had asked one more favor from Rutledge, just before they walked the short distance into the prison. "I don't want Sara to hear this from strangers. Will you tell her? She has friends, they'll stand by her. Her sister as well. Just don't tell her why. Or about France. I don't want anyone to know I loved her. It was an act of madness. That will do."

It wasn't a duty that Rutledge wanted to perform. But Leslie had been a fellow officer, and he'd known Mrs. Leslie.

"Very well. In exchange for an answer from you. The lapis beads?"

"They burned in the house. I thought it best."

Two hours later, he was knocking at the door of the Leslie house. The daily answered, and took him into the parlor, where Mrs. Leslie joined him shortly afterward.

He'd changed, rebandaged his hand, and she smiled at him. "Brian is in Cornwall. He left yesterday morning. But Lucy said you wished to see me?"

Rutledge said quietly, "I'm afraid he's not in Cornwall, Mrs. Leslie."

Her face changed, a growing horror filling her eyes. "He always drives too fast—did he suffer? Was it—was it too awful?" And then realizing, she added, "Was anyone else hurt?"

"It wasn't a motorcar crash, I'm afraid." There was no way to ease the blow. "He asked me to tell you himself. I've just arrested him for murder. He's confessed."

"Brian? No, I don't believe you. I refuse to listen to you."

She rose, intending to walk out of the room.

"It was a woman he knew. During the war." She would hear the rest, before it was over, he thought. She didn't need to know it now.

She broke down then, and after a while, he left her with the daily, who provided him with the direction of Mrs. Leslie's sister. He himself brought her to the house, and the two women disappeared up the stairs, both in tears. Twenty minutes later, he asked the daily, who was shocked and tiptoeing about the house as if a death had just occurred, to take tea up to them. He sat in the pretty drawing room for some time after that, but they never came down again.

Rutledge left finally, feeling that it was best to go, and went home. He felt no satisfaction. These were people he'd known.

The inquest was held ten days later. Leslie, drawn and looking as if he hadn't slept, was present. Rutledge gave his evidence clearly and concisely, ignoring the swell of shock and consternation among the people gathered in the inn's largest room.

He had told no one what he was going to say, except Dr. Mason. Not even Henderson knew. And the Yard had closed ranks around the problem in their midst. When he left out much of the truth about Karina, the former Chief Inspector cast him a grateful look. But Rutledge hadn't done that for the prisoner or his wife. It had been for the dead woman, who didn't deserve to have her story told.

The finding was what he'd expected. Leslie would now stand trial for two murders. The inquiry was closed.

Afterward, in Dr. Mason's surgery, well away from the inn, Rutledge drank some of the whisky he'd been offered and said, "The horse is all right?"

"I put some salve on his nose. It works for people, why not Prince? The cuffs broke the skin, but the cut didn't go deep or break the bone. He's doing well. I may even put up my shingle as a horse doctor now." He was making light of it, but Rutledge knew he'd been very angry at the time.

Changing the subject, Rutledge said, "I'll take the gin bottle back to London. I still don't have the murder weapon for Karina. Mrs. Larchian."

"Yes, I noticed it hadn't come up. I've been looking, you know. We've had a spell of dry weather, and I took Prince out to do some searching of my own. No luck so far. Is it essential to his conviction?"

"We have a statement from Leslie. Still, I'd be happier if I had it. It would be—tidier."

"I searched the barrow from one end to the other. Not inside, mind you. But the whole of the exterior. My guess is that he shoved it under one of those boulders around the forecourt."

"No. He'd have hidden it well away from there, I think. To confound us, if nothing else."

"That's an interesting possibility. I hadn't considered it. He's been that clever all along. Yes, of course, it makes sense."

When he'd finished his whisky, Rutledge took his leave, and thanked the doctor for all he'd done.

"It's you I must thank, for giving us a name to put on the gravestone. I'll see to it personally. A long way to come to die. I saw Mrs. Marshall demanding her photograph back, just before the inquest. I would have kept it myself, if she hadn't. You saw to it that the Corporal's family has been kept abreast of what happened to him? It must have been hard to bear."

"They declined to come to the inquest. Or attend the trial. I'm convinced they're waiting for him to come walking through the door one day."

"I pity them. And Karina had no family to notify?"

"None that we can discover." He'd asked Haldane to look.

"Well, Avebury will be her family, as long as I'm alive."

They shook hands soon afterward, and Rutledge left.

On his way out of Avebury, he stopped the motorcar and walked over to the shrouded figure where Karina Larchian had died. He stood there for a moment, thinking about her. Then he touched the stone lightly, and walked back the way he'd come.

It was three days later when the letter from Dr. Mason arrived in the post. Rutledge had just come in from the Yard, and it was lying on the salver where his daily put his letters.

He opened it and read the note.

There's a package on the way to Scotland Yard, directed to you.
In it you'll find both the murder weapon and a statement from
Constable Henderson and myself showing that I had found it

while out riding. Stuck to the hilt in the side of Silbury Hill. It fits the wounds, Rutledge. I remember them too well. The truth is, I searched that damned hill all one day, and I wasn't expecting to find anything. Next morning in the sunlight, there it was. Your evidence is now complete. And I feel better knowing that Karina can finally rest in peace.

He was still dressed for the cold wind coming down the Thames, and he turned, went out again to his motorcar. It was well after five, and the sun had already set. There had been no package before he'd left the Yard. If it had been brought upstairs afterward, it was best to see it put into evidence straightaway. Besides that, he wanted very much to see the knife.

There was activity on the river when he reached the Yard, twinkling lights marking the passage of small boats. Markham's vehicle had been brought around, and was waiting for him near the door. There was room for Rutledge's motorcar as well, and he expected to be at the Yard for only a matter of minutes. He took the space.

Stepping out, he shut his door and was about to walk toward the building.

" *'Ware!*"

Rutledge wheeled just as there was a flurry of movement from the shadows, and his first thought was that he'd disturbed roosting pigeons. Then someone in dark clothing was rushing toward him, and he threw up his left arm to protect his head and face, his back hard against the motorcar behind him as something slashed across his arm, through his outer coat, the one beneath it, his shirt, and then into his flesh. He felt the warmth of blood beginning to flow.

20

His attacker was gone before he could respond. A dark shape lost in the darkness of the night.

He pushed himself away from the motorcar, already lunging forward to follow just as the door to the Yard opened, a splash of light spilling out, a man in an overcoat and hat momentarily silhouetted against it.

Rutledge recognized Chief Superintendent Markham's voice, bidding good night to someone out of sight behind him. And then he was stepping out into the cold air. The door was still half open as Markham frowned uncertainly. "Is that you, Rutledge?" The door swung shut behind him, cutting off the light. "You're to have that report on my desk tomorrow," he called. "The earlier the better."

"Go back inside," Rutledge shouted, but Markham kept on walking in his direction.

"Get out of here, damn it. Go back inside!"

Markham froze, unaccustomed to be shouted at by one of his men. A shapeless figure darted forward, arm raised. The knife flashed as it swept downward across Markham's shoulders and back. The force of the blow threw him forward, and he fought to keep his feet.

Blood had filled Rutledge's glove, was spilling down his overcoat. But he ignored it, dashing forward just as Markham began to collapse with an odd cry.

Rutledge reached out, caught the attacker's sleeve, and pulled hard. The coat came away as the man wheeled, spinning out of it, leaving it in Rutledge's hands as he leaped over Markham's body and began to run. Rutledge tossed the coat aside and went after him.

He was gaining ground as a pair of men, talking quietly, came around the corner. His quarry slowed a fraction, uncertain how to avoid them, and Rutledge, paying no heed to them, saw his chance and launched himself. He brought his attacker down in a flurry of arms and legs, both of them falling hard. His prisoner, gasping for breath, cried out gruffly for help.

Shouting, the men were racing forward, catching Rutledge by the shoulders and roughly pulling him up and off what appeared to be his victim.

"Hold him—Scotland Yard," he managed to say before the tight grip on his wounded arm sent waves of dizziness over him. "Find the knife," he added thickly. "Markham—"

One of the men reached down and pulled the winded man to his feet. "I don't see a knife."

In the same moment, someone else had just come out of the Yard's door, stumbling across Markham as the light swept across his body. "Good God," the newcomer exclaimed. He looked up, saw Rutledge and a stranger in the grip of two men, and yelled, "What the hell—"

Another man came out on his heels, kept his head and called over his shoulder, "We need help here. You, there—bring those two inside. We'll sort this out."

Twisting his head to see who it was, Rutledge recognized Chief Inspector Murray.

Two men pushed Murray aside and were already kneeling by Markham, then trying to lift him to carry him into the lighted entry. Murray gestured angrily at Rutledge's captors. "You men—you heard me. Inside, damn it."

As they started forward, Rutledge's prisoner almost broke free, but one of the men holding Rutledge caught an arm, and all four moved toward the door. Others were coming out now, and they hurried forward to usher them inside. Everyone seemed to be talking at once.

Rutledge was shoved through the door, his prisoner just behind him. Gibson was there now, swearing at what he was seeing.

Afterward, when it was all over, Rutledge realized that the attack had taken no more than three minutes, start to finish. Now, he sat down on the stairs, his right hand clasped over his left arm, trying to stem the flow of blood. The cut was long, and part of it, where the knife first penetrated, was deep and hurting like the very devil.

Against the far wall, Inspector Harris was working with Markham, trying to remove his coat, and another man came to help him, exclaiming at the amount of blood pooling on the floor beneath him. "Get an ambulance. *Now*," Harris called over his shoulder, hands already wet and red.

Gibson noticed the blood on Rutledge's coat, and came forward, but Rutledge shook him off as his prisoner, ignored for one brief second, tried to slip out the door.

"Stop him!" he ordered Gibson, and in the struggle that followed, the attacker lost his cap. In the bright light of the entry, Rutledge could see he was wearing corduroy trousers and a heavy shirt. And then he watched in shock as the fair hair that had been pinned up under the assailant's cap slowly tumbled down around her shoulders.

There was stunned silence, even Inspector Harris turning to see what had happened. The fair hair, half obscuring the face, seemed to draw attention to clothes two or three sizes too large.

"Gentle God," Rutledge said softly.

Just then Chief Inspector Murray came in the door, a bloody knife with a broken blade lying across the palm of his hand. "I found this," he said unnecessarily. "Outside."

It was a kitchen knife, with a fine bone handle that boasted a silver tip with initials engraved in it.

Inspector Mitchell, now working on Markham with Harris, looked up from trying to stanch the blood and said, "The other half is still in his back. Where's that damned ambulance?"

But Rutledge barely heard them. He was staring into the flushed, angry face of Sara Leslie.

He said, "*Why?*"

Someone else had recognized her now, moving away, as if she'd suddenly come down with the plague. Others followed suit. No one seemed to know what to do or why she was there. Chief Inspector Murray moved to stand with his back to the door.

She looked harried, cornered.

"Gibson?" Rutledge said, still watching Mrs. Leslie. And the man stepped forward. "Was there a package for me today? It came through the post, I think."

Gibson nodded. "It can wait."

"Bring it to me, please?"

Murray was staring at Rutledge. "Is that the Chief Superintendent's blood? On your coat?"

"No. That package." It was the voice of command. "Bring it to me now."

Gibson took the stairs two at a time, fast for a man of his bulk. He was coming back down again just as they heard the *clang* of the ambulance pulling up. In Gibson's hands was a longish package wrapped in brown paper.

"What do we do about *her*?" Murray was asking now, preparing to let the ambulance attendants in. "I don't understand—"

Rutledge reached for the package, but his left hand was useless. "Open it," he commanded, and Gibson began to tear off the outer wrappings. He fumbled with the inner bit of paper, nearly dropping what lay inside, but then he had the contents clear.

Two St. John attendants came through the door, a stretcher with them. Murray guarded the entrance as Mrs. Leslie tried again to slip out. Harris was saying to the first attendant, "Careful. Back wound. There's a blade still in there."

The attendant was kneeling by Markham. His shirt was open, hanging about his waist, and the attendant's face was grave as he looked at the wound across Markham's shoulders.

Gibson was staring at what he held in his hands. It was another knife. It too had a fine bone handle with a silver tip. His lips were moving as he read the initials.

Mrs. Leslie's face went white as she saw what he held, and she slipped to the ground in what appeared to be a dead faint.

"It's the knife used in the Avebury murder," Rutledge said to Gibson as the other attendant knelt to hold smelling salts in front of Mrs. Leslie's nose, then got up to come across the foyer to Rutledge.

The two men who had pulled Rutledge off his prisoner had been standing to one side, trying to take in what was happening around them. They were frowning at Rutledge now, as if he had stabbed Markham.

The attendant helped Rutledge off with his outer coat, then took scissors from his pocket and cut away his tweed coat and the shirtsleeve beneath it. Clenching his teeth against the pain, Rutledge was trying to make himself clear to Gibson. "Dr. Mason found it. There are statements in there as well. For God's sake, don't lose them."

Gibson carried the knife to where Murray was standing, and the men compared the two.

The attendant was wrapping the wound on Rutledge's arm, saying something about a doctor and stitches.

With his good arm, Rutledge reached out to Gibson. "Keep that safe. Both of the knives. They're evidence. And don't let her leave."

"Trust me," Gibson said harshly. "Until we know what's happened here. Who cut *you*?"

"She did. Markham as well." The attendant was urging him to stand up. Rutledge did, and felt a wave of dizziness sweep over him. Markham was on the stretcher now, facedown, clearly unconscious, being carried toward the waiting ambulance. His back and shoulders had been roughly bandaged, to stop the bleeding, but the pristine white was already turning dark red in blotches, and the broken blade protruded obscenely.

"Mrs. Leslie?" Gibson asked, staring first at her as she sat up and then at Rutledge. "There's no blood on her."

Murray was speaking to the two men who had held on to Rutledge earlier, telling them they would need to give a statement. He sent them upstairs with a Sergeant who had appeared at some point, giving him instructions. They followed the man, carefully not looking in Mrs. Leslie's direction. No one seemed to know what to do with her.

The stretcher was in the ambulance, the motor already running. The second attendant came hurrying back inside. "We can't wait any longer. He needs surgery. And you're losing too much blood."

"I'm needed here," Rutledge protested. But Gibson was nodding to the attendant, who reached out for Rutledge's good arm to urge him toward the door.

"Not now, I tell you," Rutledge said harshly.

Harris, looking at Rutledge, said, "Go on. You're white as a bedsheet, man."

Stumbling over the threshold, Rutledge twisted around in the attendant's grip, turning toward Murray, the ranking officer. "Keep her in custody. *Do you hear me?* Those knives match. The initials. How could I have come by one of them?"

The last thing he saw as he stepped out into the night was Mrs. Leslie's flushed and angry face.

Rutledge's arm was painful the next morning, but he overrode Matron's protests, dressed, and went to look in on Chief Superintendent Markham. His room was filled with flowers, but the man himself looked gloomy, even in his sleep.

"He's sedated," the Ward Sister told Rutledge. She was an older woman, capable and gentle as she checked Markham's bandaging without disturbing him. "The wound required quite a number of stitches. It's best for him to stay quiet for a bit."

"The broken blade. Did they save it, when they removed it?"

"I'm told a Sergeant Gibson took charge of it. Evidence, he said."

"And the Chief Superintendent can expect a full recovery?"

"Unless infection sets in. But there will be an ugly scar at first." She looked keenly at him. "You shouldn't be up and about, much less dressed."

He gave her his best smile. "I must give a statement. It won't take long. I'll rest, then, I promise."

"See that you do," she told him firmly.

He left then. His motorcar was still at the Yard, but he took a cab home to change, looking ruefully at his torn, blood-soaked shirt and coat. The cabbie had stared at him as well, as if wondering if his passenger was going to be trouble. The bandaging was cumbersome, but Rutledge had also required stitches to close the wound, and the padding was thick. He managed to get a shirt and a coat over it, then found another cab to take him to the Yard. He felt a little light-headed still, but the Ward Sister had assured him that it would pass as he replaced the lost blood. But not, he thought wryly, in time to face the Yard.

Sergeant Gibson was surprised to see him. And wary. "They told me at the hospital that you'd be staying for a day or two."

"I've come to settle what happened last night."

"I sent Mrs. Leslie home with a police Matron to keep an eye on her. Her sister was frantic, she didn't know where Mrs. Leslie had gone. When she saw all the blood on the coat Chief Inspector Murray discovered outside, *she* nearly fainted. Matron had to assure her it wasn't Mrs. Leslie's." He took a deep breath. "What the hell was going on, sir? Did news of her husband's arrest turn her mind? She kept telling anyone who would listen that you'd killed a woman and attacked the Chief Superintendent. When I questioned her about how you were also wounded, she told me to ask you. But you were right, the two knives came from the same set. When Matron was relieved this morning, and came back to the Yard, she confirmed that. What's more, I found the statements in the wrapping paper. Dr. Mason's and Constable Henderson's. It suggests that *someone* in that house is guilty."

Rutledge pulled out the chair by Gibson's desk. "I had all night to think about it. I wouldn't let them give me anything for the pain, because I needed a clear head. I couldn't make sense of it, I thought she was trying to make Markham release her husband. But she never spoke to him, she just attacked. Right now, I'm not sure what to believe." He sat down, suddenly weak.

Gibson said, "Her sister has asked to have a doctor look at her. Matron told me she was still sitting there in those men's clothes, not speaking, not moving. Refusing to change or go to her bed."

Rutledge ran his good hand through his hair.

"The lapis beads were hers," he said.

"What lapis beads?"

"They were in the house that burned. Why hadn't he put them back where they belonged? It would have been easy enough. Had she found out that they were gone, that he'd given them to Karina, knowing he'd have them back? Was she that angry?" He put a hand on his arm, trying to dull the pain so that he could think. "But she wasn't at the inquest, was she? Did she visit him in prison, and did he tell her? No, I'd stake my life on it that he didn't. Although she probably was out for vengeance when she came here. I'd arrested Leslie, Markham had officially charged him. She hadn't counted on the fact that I'd be here. But she acted, as soon as she recognized me, getting out of the motorcar. In her eyes, we'd taken her husband from her."

Gibson was staring at him as if he too had run mad. "Sir. I think you ought to go home and rest. You shouldn't have left the hospital. I'll find a Constable to drive you."

Rutledge shook his head irritably. "No, I need to speak to Chief Inspector Murray."

"I don't know that he's in—"

Rutledge got to his feet, his gaze locking on Gibson's. "Do you think that I stabbed Markham?"

Gibson looked down at his desk. After a moment he said, "The thing is, two inspectors heard you shouting at him. You've had words before. And I can't quite see how she managed to cut you both. Two experienced men? She's not a big woman."

"She'd already stabbed me when Markham came out. I shouted to stop him, but he wasn't listening. And she got to him before I could. You saw his wound, damn it, with that blade in his back. How could he have been able to stab *me*? He never saw her, his back was to her all the time."

"There's this. He's not come to. They sedated him after the surgery." He sighed. "I wish he was here to sort this out. They're sending someone from the Home Office. Or they might have Jameson back. We'll have to take her up on charges, sir. Attempted murder. Himself will expect that. Very well, sir. I'll find Chief Inspector Murray."

He left Rutledge standing there. Ten minutes later, Murray came striding down the passage, frowning.

The Chief Inspector was older than Leslie, a quiet but steady man with years of experience.

He took Rutledge into a vacant office and said, "I haven't arrested her yet. She was in no state to be questioned last night. But it will have to be done. You know that and so do I."

"That isn't what I wanted to talk to you about. When you searched Leslie's house earlier, did you find letters to him from France? This is important."

"Letters? No. We weren't looking for letters, we were looking for anything that might be used at the trial. I have the list of what we found. It's short. Leslie had covered himself well."

"We need to find them. Trust me on this."

Murray was no fool. "Does this have to do with the woman Leslie killed?"

It took Rutledge a quarter of an hour to plead his case. It would have been simpler if he could have told Murray everything. But the letters to Karina hadn't come out at the inquest. Rutledge had seen to that. He didn't want them to come to light now.

Finally Murray nodded. "Very well. We'll both go. You to identify these letters, and I'll be there to take them in charge."

They didn't see Mrs. Leslie, when they called at the house. The Constable who answered the door told them that she had finally been persuaded by her sister to go up to one of the guest rooms. Matron was there with her.

"In her state of mind," the Constable was saying, "we thought it best."

When he'd gone back to guarding the door, Chief Inspector Murray said, "Where do we look? There's no need to duplicate the earlier search. These letters aren't likely to be in the kitchen, are they?"

"His bedroom."

They went quietly up the stairs and Murray opened the door to the master bedroom.

They searched it thoroughly, even lifting the mattress on the bed and looking on top of the wardrobe. But there was no sign of letters. On the table by the window was an old, well-used correspondence box, more decorative than useful, fashionable in the days when travelers carried a small, portable desk with them, something that could rest in their laps in a coach or on a table, when in use. This one was black lacquer with a hunting design in gold paint.

Rutledge went over to rummage through it. But the small square bottles of ink had long since dried up, the sealing wax crumbling in his fingers. The sheaf of paper was dry and stained with age. The place for the stamps was empty. Clearly decorative, not used since the days of coaches.

"Wild goose chase, Rutledge," Murray said. "I thought it was, from the start."

"Mrs. Leslie's room and dressing room. He knew we'd search in here. He would have had to put them somewhere."

They moved on and began their search all over again. Murray was clearly finding it distasteful, but Rutledge said, "They won't be anywhere that she could find them. Look for the most unlikely place." He began to take out drawers, looking behind them and under them, while Murray watched. Stretching out on the floor, he felt under the wardrobe. Still nothing.

Murray, standing in the middle of the room, said, "Give it up, Rutledge."

Rutledge, his arm aching enough to distract him, looked around the room, the wardrobe, the dressing table, the bedside table, the chair by the window, anyplace that might have been missed. He kept his expression neutral. "I want to go back to Leslie's room."

"What the hell for? We searched every inch of it." But he followed Rutledge back there and waited, arms crossed over his chest. "All right. Five minutes, and I'm calling this off."

Rutledge went to the desk, considered it carefully, and then opened the drawers, one by one.

"You've looked there."

They searched the wardrobe again, to no avail, and then Rutledge turned to the curio cabinet that held small treasures.

"Not likely to be there," Murray was saying. "I gave it a look."

"The writing box, then."

Rutledge opened it again, fitted the sloping top with its faded blotter into the slot made for it, and looked at the row of small cubicles for the ink, sand for blotting, nibs, sealing wax, and a tiny candle for melting it.

Murray, standing now at Rutledge's shoulder, said, "It probably belonged to his grandfather. He was an officer in the Guards, I think. All right, close it up."

But Melinda Crawford had had such a box, very like this desk, and Rutledge had remembered something. Hers had a secret compartment in which to keep correspondence. She had shown it to him when he was six or seven.

He bent forward, feeling along the sides. And there they were, two tiny rectangles of black ribbon. He grasped both of them, and gently lifted.

The entire section came up, revealing the lower level.

There were papers inside, filled with writing. He drew them out, and the two men spread them out on the bench at the foot of the bed.

"Leslie's handwriting," Murray said. "I've read enough of his reports."

Rutledge was shuffling through the pages. "Look here. Someone has been practicing. See—this sentence—that one—there are others here. Words repeated. Capital letters. Lowercase. I don't think this is Leslie's work. If I didn't know better, I'd say that someone was trying to copy his handwriting." He was beginning to recognize sentences too. Familiar phrases. Practiced over and over until perfect.

The letters that Leslie had written were still in Rutledge's possession, the ones that Karina had kept.

But there were no return letters in the compartment. Nothing from France to Chief Inspector Leslie.

He looked at Murray. "Dear God."

"What is it?"

Had Karina written only once? And Leslie answered only once? And someone else had kept up a correspondence in his name for a year or more. But Karina had never responded, until that last letter telling her that Leslie was dying. The letter that had finally lured Karina to England.

Running through some part of Rutledge's mind was a memory, and the thought, *From the time I held out those lapis beads, there in York-shire, Leslie must have known for certain who had killed Karina. If not before.*

He was a Chief Inspector at the Yard. Surely he'd have brought her in? Wife or not? After all, he was charged with the inquiry. And he had loved Karina.

In God's name, why had Leslie chosen to defend his wife, over justice for Karina?

He made an effort to collect his thoughts. "I think we've got this wrong. Dreadfully wrong."

Murray stared at him.

Rutledge closed his eyes against the horror of what he was realizing. Then, opening them, he said, "You need to listen to what I have to say."

And he sat down on the foot of the bed, and began to talk.

W hen it was finished, when it was all over, when Sara Leslie had been taken into custody and he could finally go back to his flat, his arm was throbbing. Putting up his hat and coat, Rutledge sat down in the chair by the lamp, but didn't light it.

After a while, he'd got up to pour himself a small whisky to help numb some of the pain—not all of it physical—when there was a knock at his door. In no mood for company, he stood there, ignoring it. But it was persistent, and his motorcar in the street was the best advertisement that he was at home.

Finally, setting down the decanter and the glass, he crossed the room and opened the door. A police Constable was just walking away, having at last given up on being admitted.

Not more questions. Not now.

Then he recognized the man. The young Constable who had been with him when Mrs. FitzPatrick was struck down.

He called, "Constable? Sorry. I didn't realize there was someone at the door."

Constable Fuller turned, relief in his face. "I'm sorry to bother you, sir. But it's about that accident where the woman was killed. I need your advice, sir, since you were a witness."

It was the last thing he wanted. But Rutledge put the best face on it that he could, and said, "Come in."

The Constable followed him inside, looking around with interest, then accepting the chair that Rutledge gestured to. Perching on it as if wishing now he'd never come here.

Rutledge was reminded of France and dealing with young Lieutenants just out from England. "What seems to be the problem?" he asked, in an effort to put Fuller at ease.

"I was wondering, sir. You said you didn't see the driver of the vehicle that struck Mrs. FitzPatrick. Is that still true, or have you remembered anything that might help in our inquiry?"

"That's still true. I didn't. Have you found the driver?"

"That's the problem, you see." Fuller cleared his throat. "We had a bit of luck. I've told you that the motorcar was found abandoned, and the owner was at a meeting with witnesses. We went around the neighborhood where it was left, asking if anyone had seen the driver. No one had. But it seems one of the residents had had surgery, and friends had come to call on the day in question, to see how he was faring. They came again four days ago, and he told them about a Constable calling. A bit of a fuss, as he put it. However, it seems that the two visitors, a man and his wife, *had* seen the person who was driving. They thought it was another friend coming to call on the patient, and then they noticed the crumpled wing as the driver got out and walked away. They contacted the Met and gave us a very good description. Both the man and his wife were interviewed separately, and their accounts agreed. We went back to the mews from which the motorcar had been taken, and made the rounds of all the households in the area. Several of the residents and their staffs told us that the description we'd given matched one of their neighbors, and they laughed at the absurdity, as they called it. We went to the house in question, but there was no one at home."

The report was clear and concise. Rutledge said quietly, "Go on." But Hamish was already hammering in the back of his mind and he braced himself for Fuller's answer. Leslie, after all?

"That's the trouble, sir. The description fit the wife of the owner of that house. And the owner is a Chief Inspector at the Yard. I've been holding off until I spoke to you. There's got to be some mistake. I can't report that, sir. And yet the neighbors we spoke with recognized the description, whatever they said about it being silly. They weren't aware that she drove, you see. I'm not sure myself that she does."

Rutledge said, "Are you certain of your evidence?" But even as he said it, he knew it was true. And that Mrs. FitzPatrick had died in his place.

"Yes, sir. If it weren't for who it is that we've found, I'd have no quarrel with it. I mean to say, *she* would've stopped, don't you think? A woman in her position?"

Rutledge drew a breath. "You must take this to your superiors at the Met, and ask them to inform the Yard. The husband's rank notwithstanding, the Yard will know what to do with such evidence." Better for it to come from this man. The Yard would listen to Fuller. They had heard enough from him today.

"How can you be sure?" Fuller asked anxiously. "What if I *am* wrong?"

Rutledge kept his voice level. "You've done your duty. It's not your fault that the answers are not what others might wish. Lay out your evidence clearly as you did just now, and they will listen. That's *their* duty." And he hoped to heaven he was right.

"Thank you, sir," Fuller answered, still doubtful, but grateful as well. "Shall I let you know what happens?"

"Yes. Please."

Rutledge saw him out, watched him walk down the street, then went inside, shutting the door. But it failed to shut out the thoughts racing through his mind. *She would've stopped, don't you think? A woman in her position?* The words echoed over and over in his mind.

He remembered seeing her on another afternoon with her sister and her friends, about to attend the theater. Smiling, laughing. He'd told himself she couldn't have been so carefree, if she'd had any inkling of what her husband had done.

But she hadn't been carefree—she'd been relaxed. And *relieved*.

He crossed the room to where the decanter was waiting.

They let the former Chief Inspector go a week later. Mrs. Leslie was in custody, the evidence that had been muddled by her husband's efforts laid out now in clean, clear detail. She had refused to speak, even to her sister.

The lies, the tandem, the murders. Neither Karina Larchian nor Corporal Radleigh had been afraid of her. They had believed her, and they'd died.

Rutledge sighed. There was no way of knowing now if Karina had taken that wild ride in the night to the stones. Both women were young enough and strong enough to attempt it. And how else would Sara have got to the Stokesbury house again? Or whether the old man from the station had driven the two women most of the way, waiting patiently for one of them to come back to him. But Karina must have believed she was going to where Leslie was being treated, and that his wife was willingly taking her there. She would have *walked*, to reach him. And all the while, Sara Leslie had brought a torch to guide them to the right stone, while hidden in her coat was the knife she intended to use. *His favorite— we have to pass it on the way to the surgery. He'd want you to see it.*

Nevertheless, it was the tandem that had led him to the Leslies. And those lapis beads.

Leslie would still face charges for meddling with evidence. That was made clear, even while he was vociferously protesting that he had confessed. Rutledge was sent to collect him from prison, and drive him to the Yard, where Chief Superintendent Markham, only just out of hospital and still in a wheeled chair, would deal with him.

A light rain was falling.

Leslie was a changed man. Rutledge hardly recognized him. He was badly in need of a barber, he was haggard as well, as if he hadn't slept very much. And his clothes were wrinkled and dirty. Rutledge could smell him as he stepped into the motorcar.

His first words were, "I can't walk into the Yard like this. A barber, please—and a change of clothing."

"You are expected at the Yard."

"Yes, I know. But dear God, not like this."

Once before he'd kept his word, and walked without cuffs into Markham's office.

Rutledge considered him. "I don't know of a barber who would allow you in the door of his establishment. Still."

He drove on, then decided that for a quietly passed sum, his own barber would probably shave Leslie and trim his hair.

It was done without trouble. Leslie spun a tale of being on assignment, and the barber commiserated with him, made him at least a little more presentable, and Rutledge paid him a little extra. Leslie had no money in his pockets.

"I owe you," Leslie said as they got back into the motorcar.

"There's something you need to know, before you walk into Markham's office and tell him he's got the wrong person. There's a box in the rear seat. Look at it, if you will."

Leslie gave Rutledge an intent glance, then leaned over to collect the box and bring it forward.

Too late, Rutledge remembered Hamish, and felt a cold shudder pass through him. But Leslie was intent on lifting the box lid.

He smothered something, as he read, whether it was a curse or a plea, Rutledge couldn't tell.

By the time they had drawn up in front of the Leslie house, looking oddly forlorn in the late afternoon light, as if the owners had gone away, Leslie's expression was grim.

"She wrote once. To tell me she'd left Paris. And I replied—" He held up the November letter that Rutledge had read. "This one. I never wrote again, nor did she. We'd agreed it was for the best, unless there was something the other needed to know." He spread out the remaining letters like a fan. "I didn't write these, Rutledge."

"They're in your handwriting."

"Yes, I know." He dropped them into the box. His voice was strained. "Sara was the only one who would have noticed—or cared—about the Rouen address. I remember I came home late that night—it was on my desk, it was the first thing I saw as I walked into the room. The French stamp. I burned Karina's letter the next day. After I'd memorized the name of the street, and the number. It's not far from the Cathedral. A safe place for her." There was a long silence. "Sara *lured* her here," he said in anguish. "On purpose. It's—it's beyond my ability to imagine it."

"She must have realized you'd changed. She finally learned why."

"I thought—after four years, none of us were the same. I expected her to put it down to the trenches."

"Sometimes women know."

"I did everything I could think of to let her feel how glad I was to be home."

"Perhaps you tried too hard."

He was looking out the window, so that Rutledge couldn't see his face. "I was staggered when I saw who this 'unidentified' dead woman was. If Mason and Henderson hadn't been looking at her body, they'd have seen. Why was she in England? What had brought her to *Avebury*? I didn't know, Rutledge. And then I saw the scarf she was wearing. And it suddenly made sense. She must have borrowed it, against the cold night. I knew that scarf, I'd bought it myself. But not for her. For *Sara*.

"I realized then that it was all my fault. I thought it was safe enough to leave the inquiry unsolved. I still didn't understand. But I felt I had to make it up to Sara if I could. Then you brought me the lapis neck-lace. Sara must have been wearing it that evening, and somehow the clasp broke as she—as she moved the body. And I knew it was only a matter of time. I told myself you wouldn't have any better luck than I did finding Karina's killer. I was wrong. I couldn't—I didn't want to believe it was Sara, Rutledge. Part of me still doesn't."

"Why didn't you turn her in? For Karina's sake?"

He shook his head. "I couldn't bring her back. I *could* make amends, the guilt was mine for having an affair. I owed Sara."

"Did you love Karina?"

"Oh, God, yes. With my whole heart and soul. I'd never felt anything like what I felt for her. And heaven knows why she loved me too. I'd have died for her, Ian. I was willing to hang for Sara. It was only fitting."

"I still don't know. How did she manage to kill that ex-soldier, Radleigh?" But Mason had told him—she must have stunned him before forcing him to drink the gin.

"Don't question it, Rutledge. I've had enough for one day. I don't even want to think about how she lured him to the Barrow. I've told myself it was the promise of work, for he must have been desperate." But he must have realized she'd promised more. The isolated barrow, the gin . . .

It didn't matter. For his sins, he wasn't finished with the Avebury inquiry. Markham had already given him the task of backtracking Mrs. Leslie, and documenting her movements from the time Karina had arrived in London until the ex-soldier had been discovered in the Long Barrow. Interviewing her household staff, her sister, and anyone else who might have helped her, wittingly or unwittingly. It was, Rutledge suspected, his punishment for bringing in Karina's murderer. But he said nothing to Leslie about that.

They got out and Leslie fumbled for his keys, letting them into the cold, silent house. He paused on the threshold, then squared his shoulders. "You can wait wherever you like. I just want to bathe a little, put on clean clothes, stuff these into the dustbin where I'll never have to look at them again. Twenty minutes?"

"No more than that. Or Markham will crucify both of us."

"Thank you, Ian." He swung open a door, and it was the small library-cum-study where he had a globe and a desk and books on the surrounding shelves. "This is more comfortable than the drawing room, as Sara called it. There's whisky on the shelf, there. I'd offer you tea, but I'm sure the cooker is out. I won't be long, I promise you. My word I won't try to slip out."

Rutledge let him go, leaning his head against the back of the chair, listening to the creaks of the house, the sounds of Leslie moving around upstairs.

He came down again some twenty minutes later, as promised, a clean shirt and suit, shoes polished. Looking better on the surface, but still haggard and too thin. He stuck his head around the door. "I'll just make sure the house is locked up before we leave. I don't think Sara or her sister would have been up to it. God knows when either of us will be back here again."

Rutledge half rose, starting toward him.

"I won't run. Where could I run to, for God's sake?"

He sat down again. Hamish was saying something, his voice pressing, but Rutledge ignored it. Leslie had given his word.

But when Leslie didn't return in five minutes, Rutledge stepped out of the study to see what was keeping him. And heard the shot, echoing from the back garden.

Markham took the news surprisingly philosophically. "He should have been made to face the consequences of what he did. Still, this has saved the Yard a good deal of trouble, and gossip. A Chief Inspector. His wife. What are we coming to?" His gaze lifted to Rutledge's face. "I wish you hadn't solved these murders. It would have been for the best. I don't care for officers who bring disrepute on the fine men who serve here."

"I was sent to do my duty," Rutledge said soberly. In his mind's eye, he could still see the crumpled body lying beneath the bare branches of the pear tree in the back garden. Leslie had been in the war. He'd made a good job of it.

"This is why delving too deeply into matters is unwise. A lesson you should take to heart, Rutledge."

He said nothing.

Markham, irritated, dismissed him.

Rutledge walked out of the Chief Superintendent's office and made his way down the passage to his own. He went in. The rain was running down the glass in rivulets, blurring the streetlamps below. Somewhere along the river, he heard a foghorn's mournful note.

Locking the door behind him, he crossed to his desk, and without turning on the lamp, sat down in his chair.

After a moment, he buried his head in his hands.

About the author

About the book

Read on

Insights,
Interviews
& More . . .

Meet Charles Todd

Michael Frost Photography

CHARLES TODD is the *New York Times* bestselling author of the Inspector Ian Rutledge mysteries, the Bess Crawford mysteries, and two stand-alone novels. Among the honors accorded to the Ian Rutledge mysteries are the Barry Award and nominations for the Independent Mystery Booksellers Association's Dilys Award, the Edgar and Anthony Awards in the U.S., and the John Creasey Award in the UK. A mother-and-son writing team, they live on the East Coast.

Behind the Book: Watching Characters Grow

One of the responsibilities of an author—or in this case, two—is to discover just how one's characters will grow as people. After all, if they're to seem "real," and interesting enough to hold the reader's attention, they must think and feel and know temptation, just as everyone outside the covers of a book has thought and felt and known hard choices.

Of course, you have to be judicious in how you choose to do this. It can get away from you, and your characters can grow right out of their story. That becomes a stand-alone, where the challenges and the individual growth end as the story itself ends, and the reader is satisfied that he or she knows those people well and therefore is satisfied with what happens to them—or, if not satisfied, at least understands why the book ends the way it does.

We've watched Rutledge grow in many different ways. He suffers from PTSD, and that's an ongoing wound that hasn't healed when the bandage comes off. People who have endured it will tell you that. And in one sense, it makes him more human, the way he struggles to deal with it and slowly learns to cope with the voice in his head. ▶

3

In *A Divided Loyalty*, there's a different exploration of what makes this man tick. Duty is by definition a moral or legal obligation, a responsibility. A matter of character. But it can also be defined in other ways, when the pressure becomes too much to bear: as just a job.

At this point we sat back and waited to see just how Rutledge would handle the corner he'd found himself in.

He can take the easy way out of a situation where he *knows* he's expected to fail. Best just to get it over with and go with the flow—go with the findings of an older, more experienced policeman, and let people believe that you are in agreement with his conclusions. Most won't fault you for that, right? And the hairier the situation becomes, the more pressure there is to conform. *Never make a superior look bad.*

To be fair, Rutledge isn't alone in facing this dilemma. We've talked to quite a few people in law enforcement who have dealt with cases where duty came at a heavy personal cost.

Rutledge still desperately needs the Yard; that hasn't changed. Will he risk everything, to find the truth about this unidentified woman's death? Does he owe her everything he's accomplished so far, everything he's worked so hard to salvage in the past two years? A divided loyalty indeed—to one's duty or to one's sanity?

It was a fascinating, challenging subject to explore. And the oddness of the setting—that strange and mysterious stone in Avebury—made it work. Added to that was the little-known Armenian Genocide, a part of history that got lost among all the other horrors of the Great War but ought not be forgotten. Put them all together, and it was a testing of one man's driving need to know the truth. To be faithful to what he believed in, what he stood for. ◝

Discussion Questions

1. It has been two years since the Armistice, but many of the characters in *A Divided Loyalty* cannot move past their experiences on the battlefield. How has this novel deepened your understanding of the long-lasting impacts of trauma, even once peace is restored?

2. How did the prologue change your assessment of Rutledge's investigation? What theories did you have, and how did they change?

3. Many of the soldiers who survived the Great War were driven to madness by the experiences they endured. What is the burden of being a survivor? Why might a survivor turn to suicide?

4. When Leigh muses that the dead woman did not look the sort to be involved in trouble, Rutledge replies, "But that's not proof that she wasn't." How does gender, appearance, and behavior factor into Rutledge's investigative methods?

5. It pains Rutledge that no one can identify the dead woman. Why might discovering her name be particularly important to him, beyond solving the case?

6. How did you respond to Meredith Channing's death? What did you make of Rutledge's reaction?

7. Kate Gordon and Rutledge share a comfortable, trusting dynamic. How do you think Kate truly feels about him? How would you like to see their relationship play out?

8. Hamish's voice guides Rutledge's attention to easily overlooked details or acts as a devil's advocate. Why do you think Hamish has taken on this role in Rutledge's mind?

9. Do you think Rutledge might have acted differently if the suspicious person had been anyone else? Do you think he conducted the investigation without bias? ▶

Discussion Questions *(continued)*

10. What do you make of Leslie and Rutledge's relationship at the end of the novel? Do you think there is hatred, or begrudging respect, or something else?

11. Markham warns Rutledge that "delving too deeply into matters is unwise." Do you think Rutledge also regrets what he discovered? Do you think he will take this advice to heart? ∽

Inspector Ian Rutledge:
A Complete Timeline of Major Events

JUNE 1914—*A FINE SUMMER'S DAY*

On a fine summer's day, the Great War is still only the distant crack of revolver shots at a motorcar in faraway Sarajevo. And Ian Rutledge, already an inspector at Scotland Yard, has decided to propose to the woman he's so deeply in love with—despite hints from friends and family that she may not be the wisest choice. But in another part of England, a man stands in the kitchen of his widowed mother's house, waiting for the undertaker to come for her body, and stares at the clock on the mantel. He doesn't know yet that he will become Rutledge's last case before Britain is drawn into war. In the weeks to come, as summer moves on toward the shadows of August, he will set out to right a wrong, and Rutledge will find himself having to choose between the Yard and his country, between the woman he loves and duty, and between truth and honor.

JUNE 1919—*A TEST OF WILLS*

Ian Rutledge, returning home from the trenches of the Great War, breaks off his engagement to Jean during his long months in hospital suffering what is now called post-traumatic stress ▶

disorder. Facing a bleak future, and fighting back from the edge of madness, he returns to his career at Scotland Yard. But Chief Superintendent Bowles is determined to break him. And so Rutledge finds himself in Warwickshire, where the only witness to the murder of Colonel Harris is a drunken ex-soldier suffering from shell shock. Rutledge is fighting his own battles with the voice of Corporal Hamish MacLeod in his head, survivor's guilt after the bloody 1916 Battle of the Somme. The question is, will he win this test of wills with Hamish—or is the shell-shocked witness a mirror of what he'll become if he fails to keep his madness at bay?

JULY 1919—*WINGS OF FIRE*

Rutledge is sent to Cornwall because the Home Office wants to be reassured that Nicholas Cheney wasn't murdered. But Nicholas committed suicide with his half sister, Olivia. And she's written a body of war poetry under the name of OA Manning. Rutledge, who had used her poetry in the trenches to keep his mind functioning, is shocked to discover she never saw France and may well be a cold-blooded killer. And yet even dead, she makes a lasting impression that he can't shake.

AUGUST 1919—*SEARCH THE DARK*

An out-of-work ex-soldier, sitting on a train in a Dorset station, suddenly sees his dead wife and two small children standing on the platform. He fights to get off the train, and soon thereafter the woman is found murdered and the children are missing. Rutledge is sent to coordinate a search and finds himself attracted to Aurore, a French war bride who will lie to protect her husband and may have killed because she was jealous of the murder victim's place in her husband's life.

SEPTEMBER 1919—*LEGACY OF THE DEAD*

Just as Rutledge thinks he has come to terms—of a sort—with the voice that haunts him, he's sent to northern England to find the missing daughter of a woman who once slept with a king.

Little does he know that his search will take him to Scotland, and to the woman Hamish would have married if he'd lived. But Fiona is certain to hang for murdering a mother to steal her child, and she doesn't know that Rutledge killed Hamish on the battlefield when she turns to him for help. He couldn't save Hamish—but Rutledge is honor bound to protect Fiona and the small child named for him.

OCTOBER 1919—*WATCHERS OF TIME*

Still recovering from the nearly fatal wound he received in Scotland, Rutledge is sent to East Anglia to discover who murdered a priest and what the priest's death had to do with a dying man who knew secrets about the family that owns the village. But there's more to the murder than hearing a deathbed confession. And the key might well be a young woman as haunted as Rutledge is, because she survived the sinking of the *Titanic* and carries her own guilt for failure to save a companion.

NOVEMBER 1919—*A FEARSOME DOUBT*

A case from 1912 comes back to haunt Rutledge. Did he send an innocent man to the gallows? Meanwhile, he's trying to discover who has poisoned three ex-soldiers, all of them amputees in a small village in Kent. Mercy killings or murder? And he sees a face across the Guy Fawkes Day bonfire that is a terrifying reminder of what happened to him at the end of the war . . . something he is ashamed of, even though he can't remember why. *What happened in the missing six months of his life?*

DECEMBER 1919—*A COLD TREACHERY*

Rutledge is already in the north and the closest man to Westmorland where, at the height of a blizzard, there has been a cold-blooded killing of an entire family—save one child, who is missing in the snow. But as the facts unfold, it's possible that the boy killed his own family. Where is he? Dead in the snow or hiding? And there are secrets in this isolated village of Urskdale that can lead to more deaths. ▶

Inspector Ian Rutledge: A Complete Timeline of Major Events
(continued)

JANUARY 1920—*A LONG SHADOW*

A party that begins innocently enough ends with Rutledge finding machine gun casings engraved with death's heads—a warning. But he's sent to Northamptonshire to learn why someone shot Constable Ward with an arrow in what the locals call a haunted wood. He discovers there are other deaths unaccounted for, and there's also a woman who knows too much about Rutledge for his own comfort. Then whoever has been stalking him comes north after him, and Rutledge knows if he doesn't find the man, he will die. Hamish, pushing him hard, is all too aware that Rutledge's death will mean his own.

MARCH 1920—*A FALSE MIRROR*

A man is nearly beaten to death, his wife is taken hostage by his assailant, and Rutledge is sent posthaste to Hampton Regis to find out who wanted Matthew Hamilton dead. The man who may be guilty is someone Rutledge knew in the war, a reminder that some were lucky enough to be saved while Hamish was left to die. But this is a story of love gone wrong, and the next two deaths reek of madness. Are these murders random, or were the women mistaken for the intended victim?

APRIL 1920—*A PALE HORSE*

In the ruins of Yorkshire's Fountains Abbey lies the body of a man wrapped in a cloak, the face covered by a gas mask. Next to him is a book on alchemy, which belongs to the schoolmaster, a conscientious objector in the Great War. Who is this man, and is the investigation into his death being manipulated by a thirst for revenge? Meanwhile, the British War Office is searching for a missing man of their own, someone whose war work was so secret that even Rutledge isn't told his real name or what he did. Here is a puzzle requiring all of Rutledge's daring and skill, for there are layers of lies and deception, while a ruthless killer is determined to hold on to freedom at any cost.

MAY 1920—*A MATTER OF JUSTICE*

At the turn of the century, in a war taking place far from England, two soldiers chance upon an opportunity that will change their lives forever. To take advantage of it, they will do the unthinkable and then put the past behind them. Twenty years later, a successful London businessman is found savagely and bizarrely murdered in a medieval tithe barn on his estate in Somerset. Called upon to investigate, Rutledge soon discovers that the victim was universally despised. Even the man's wife—who appears to be his wife in name only—and the town's police inspector are suspect. But who among the many hated enough to kill?

JUNE 1920—*THE RED DOOR*

In a house with a red door lies the body of a woman who has been bludgeoned to death. Rumor has it that two years earlier, she'd painted that door to welcome her husband back from the Front. Only he never came home. Meanwhile, in London, a man suffering from a mysterious illness goes missing and then just as suddenly reappears. Rutledge must solve two mysteries before he can bring a ruthless killer to justice: Who was the woman who lived and died behind the red door? Who was the man who never came home from the Great War, for the simple reason that he might never have gone? And what have they to do with a man who cannot break the seal of his own guilt without damning those he loves most?

JULY 1920—*A LONELY DEATH*

Three men have been murdered in a Sussex village, and Scotland Yard has been called in. The victims are soldiers, each surviving the nightmare of the Great War only to meet a ghastly end in the quiet English countryside. Each man has been garroted, with a small ID disk left in his mouth, yet no other clue suggests a motive or a killer. Rutledge understands all too well the ▶

darkness that resides within men's souls. His presence on the scene cannot deter a vicious and clever murderer, and a fourth dead soldier is discovered shortly after Rutledge's arrival. Now a horror that strikes painfully close to home threatens to engulf the investigator, and he will have to risk his career, his good name, even his shattered life itself, to bring an elusive killer to justice.

AUGUST 1920—*THE CONFESSION*

A man walks into Scotland Yard and confesses that he killed his cousin five years ago during the Great War. When Rutledge presses for details, the man evades his questions, revealing only that he hails from a village east of London. Less than two weeks later, the alleged killer's body is found floating in the Thames, a bullet in the back of his head. Rutledge discovers that the dead man was not who he claimed to be. The only clue is a gold locket, found around the victim's neck, that leads back to Essex and an insular village that will do anything to protect itself from notoriety.

SUMMER 1920—*PROOF OF GUILT*

An unidentified man appears to have been run down by a motorcar, and a clue leads Rutledge to a firm, built by two families, famous for producing and selling the world's best Madeira wine. There he discovers that the current head of the English enterprise is missing. Is he the dead man? And do either his fiancée or his jilted former lover have anything to do with his disappearance? With a growing list of suspects, Rutledge knows that suspicion and circumstantial evidence are nothing without proof of guilt. But his new acting chief superintendent doesn't agree and wants Rutledge to stop digging and settle on the easy answer. Rutledge must tread very carefully, for it seems that someone has decided that he, too, must die so that justice can take its course.

AUGUST 1920—*HUNTING SHADOWS*

A society wedding at Ely Cathedral becomes a crime scene when a guest is shot. After a fruitless search for clues, the local police call in Scotland Yard, but not before there is another shooting in a village close by. This second murder has a witness, but her description of the killer is so horrific it's unbelievable. Inspector Ian Rutledge can find no connection between the two deaths. One victim was an army officer, the other a solicitor standing for Parliament. Is there a link between these murders, or is it only in the mind of a clever killer? As the investigation presses on, Rutledge finds memories of the war beginning to surface. Struggling to contain the darkness that haunts him as he hunts for the missing link, he discovers the case turning in a most unexpected direction. Now he must put his trust in the devil in order to find the elusive and shocking answer.

AUTUMN 1920—*NO SHRED OF EVIDENCE*

On the north coast of Cornwall, an apparent act of mercy is repaid by an arrest for murder. Four young women have been accused of the crime. A shocked father calls in a favor at the Home Office. Scotland Yard is asked to review the case. However, Inspector Ian Rutledge is not the first inspector to reach the village. Following in the shoes of a dead man, he is told the case is all but closed. Even as it takes an unexpected personal turn, Rutledge will require all his skill to deal with the incensed families of the accused, the grieving parents of the victim, and local police eager to see these four women sent to the infamous Bodmin Gaol. Then why hasn't the killing stopped? With no shred of evidence to clear the accused, Rutledge must plunge deep into the darkest secrets of a wild, beautiful, and dangerous place if he is to find a killer who may—or may not—hold the key to the women's fate. ▶

Inspector Ian Rutledge: A Complete Timeline of Major Events
(continued)

NOVEMBER 1920—*RACING THE DEVIL*

On the eve of the Battle of the Somme, a group of officers have a last drink and make a promise to one another: if they survive the battle ahead, they will meet a year after the fighting ends and race motorcars from Paris to Nice. In November 1919, the officers all meet as planned, but two vehicles are nearly run off the road, and one man is badly injured. No one knows which driver was at the wheel of the rogue motorcar. Back in England one year later, a driver loses control on a twisting road and is killed in the crash. Is the crash connected in some way to the unfortunate events in the mountains above Nice the year before? Investigating this perplexing case, Scotland Yard inspector Ian Rutledge discovers that the truth is elusive. Determined to remain in the shadows, this faceless killer is willing to strike again to stop Rutledge from finding him. This time, the victim he chooses is a child, and it will take all of Rutledge's skill to stop him before an innocent young life is sacrificed.

DECEMBER 1920—*THE GATE KEEPER*

Hours after his sister's wedding, a restless Ian Rutledge drives aimlessly, haunted by the past, and narrowly misses a motorcar stopped in the middle of a desolate road. Standing beside the vehicle is a woman with blood on her hands and a dead man at her feet. She swears she didn't kill Stephen Wentworth. A stranger stepped out in front of their motorcar, and without warning, fired a single shot before vanishing into the night. But there is no trace of him. Rutledge persuades the Yard to give him the inquiry, since he's on the scene. But is he seeking justice—or fleeing painful memories in London? Wentworth was well-liked, yet his bitter family paint a malevolent portrait, calling him a murderer. But who did Wentworth kill? Is his death retribution? Or has his companion lied? When a second suspicious death occurs, the evidence suggests that a dangerous predator is on the loose, and that death is closer than Rutledge knows.

After saving an ex-convict's life, Ian Rutledge receives an astonishing tip about a legendary crime from the grateful man. If true, the tip could lead to capturing Alan Barrington—the suspect in an appalling murder during the Black Ascot, the famous 1910 royal horse races that honored the late King Edward VII. Barrington's disappearance before his trial had set off a manhunt that spanned the globe, baffling Scotland Yard and consuming all of Britain for nearly a decade. But why should Barrington return to England now? Scotland Yard orders Rutledge to quietly investigate. Meticulously retracing the original inquiry, Rutledge begins to know Barrington well, delving into his relationships and uncovering secrets that hadn't surfaced in 1910. As he draws closer to the man, the investigation is suddenly thrown into turmoil when Rutledge's life is changed by his darkest fear—the exposure of his shell shock. The Yard is already demanding his resignation, and Rutledge realizes that the only way to save his career, much less his honor, is to find Barrington. Against all odds, he must bring the Black Ascot killer to justice. But what if the tip was wrong? What if Barrington never returned to England at all . . . ? ∽